BOOK 2

THE WOLFDEN

LILLAH LAWSON

Midnight Tide
PUBLISHING

THE WOLFDEN

2nd edition

Copyright © 2024 by Lillah Lawson

Published by Midnight Tide Publishing.

www.midnighttidepublishing.com

Cover designed by

Shayne Leighton

Edited by

Jennia Herold d'Lima

Formatted by

Book Savvy Services

For "Marge,"
my sister from another mister.

PROLOGUE

It was early, barely dusk; the sky above the tall, dark pines a beautiful, eerie shade of lavender-blue—cold, not yet warmed by the peeking tendrils of early morning sun. The marsh was in its usual state of quiet-but-not-quiet, the sounds of cicadas and dawn-rising birds filling the air, but the silence underneath was heavy like wet velvet. As the beat-up, faded red Jeep rolled slowly, lights off, down the red-dirt road, dry and dusty from lack of rain, the tires making muted crunching noises, a lone heron lifted its majestic head and regarded it with one cold, dark eye. A figure emerged from the driver's seat, shrouded in a dark-black hoodie pulled down over their eyes. The heron slowly angled its neck around and took off silently and grace-fully beyond the trees as the mysterious figure unloaded some-thing heavy from the backseat.

The figure rummaged quietly in the back of the Jeep, only the marsh itself bearing witness, holding a black bundle. They crept over the soggy, uneven ground, blending into the muted darkness of the forest, the bundle heavy in their arms. They knelt by the water, placing the shrouded mass onto the soggy grass, and stared out at the marsh. The water was gray and murky, studded with stalks of faded-yellow grass that jutted straight up out of the algae-and-mud clogged marsh like soldiers standing at attention, a quiet salute to the incoming sun.

The fingers of light that had been mere traces ten minutes before were now creeping towards the tops of the trees. Another ten minutes and it would be daylight. The cicadas would cease their trilling, the birds would fly off in search of food, and cars would begin their groggy commute down the highway, dodging the darting does and fawns who made the foolhardy journey across the asphalt to greener pastures.

It was time.

With a quick, but not entirely effortless movement, the figure in black struggled to hold onto the heavy bundle, also cloaked in black, and with a clumsy nudge, slipped it silently into the murky water. It buoyed there for a moment, bobbing like a cork among the reeds, but then the black sheets that held it fast caught the weight of the water, and down it sunk, until nothing was visible but the face that emerged from the cloth— long eyelashes over shut eyes, pallid blue skin…and then the bundle was gone, gone, gone beneath the water, into the marsh that was now its final resting place.

Folks around here had long argued whether there were gators this far north; some claimed there were, and others said no, it was impossible. As they watched a dark, scaly figure rise from the depths and pull the bundle beneath the muck, they had no doubt as to the answer to that particular question.

The tall, gaunt figure stood, raised two fingers to the sky in a salute, then pressed those same fingers to their lips in a silent kiss goodbye. Then they turned and fled the marsh.

The Jeep crunched quietly backwards down the dirt road and turned onto the highway, not stopping until it was back in town. Only the spindly, parched pine trees knew it had ever been there at all.

As day broke over the marsh, the sound of cannon fire could be heard off in the distance, and the bundle at the bottom of the murky water settled in for a long sleep.

One

The sky was a damp, cold shade of gray, a hint of the storm to come. I peered at the fat clouds in the distance, just over the water's dark lip of dirty froth, and guessed we had maybe an hour before the storm rolled in and we would need to take cover. I leaned back against the bleached, gnarled corpse of an old tree perched on the beach. I held the green plastic water bottle I'd retrieved from my car to my lips, hoping it would slow the frenzy within, a storm of its own that threatened to burst forth at any moment.

"Day drunk," my best friend—well, *former* best friend—Sloan, who was perched to my left, teased, though she had her own canister and hers was twice as full as mine.

"I'm not the one who had the bright idea to bring sangria," I argued, relishing the sweet tartness on my tongue, trying to keep the irritation from my voice. I wasn't particularly feeling the camaraderie she was going for, but now wasn't the time to hash things out. "It's the middle of November; who drinks sangria in November?"

"Apparently you do, you lush." Sloan grinned, then her

face turned serious. "It was all he had in the kitchen, and I didn't want to linger, so..."

"It's fine." I pulled the scratchy black sweater tighter around myself, the goosebumps on my arms not abating. The morning was chilly and all-around gray, and our motley crew was assembled on Driftwood Beach, all of us freezing our balls off. We'd been assembled here with our quickly gathered blankets, pillows, and canisters of booze since three a.m., and now it was nearing on lunch time. My stomach rumbled painfully, but I couldn't fathom the thought of eating—not after the work I'd done just a few short hours ago. I did a quick scan of the beach, mentally counting to make sure everyone who had come here with me the night before was present and accounted for. I'd done the same mental scan a dozen times at least, and they were all still here on the beach.

All of us but one.

"Is he ever going to come out?" Sloan asked, mirroring my thoughts. Her lips were a cross between red and purple from the sangria; the bright stain lined her lips comically, making them look bigger than they actually were. She'd die if she knew how clownish she looked, as vain as she was. A week ago, I would have told her. Today, I just smiled. "Some of us live people are fucking freezing."

"Here he comes now," I said, my eyes moving back to the water.

The figure emerging from the gray-black water was tall, stooping slightly, bending down to take his cascade of dark, wet hair in his large hands. He turned his head to the side, stepping out onto the shore, wringing the hair in his hands, water pouring from it in a long stream. His hair was much shorter now, after an impromptu haircut, but it was still thick, and I could see the droplets flying off his jet-black strands from yards away. He was naked save for a pair of black cargo shorts, and his lean, muscular frame was peppered with tattoos, his broad chest pale in the milky light. He shook his head like a dog, droplets flying from his dark hair, and I could see the grin splayed across his fine features as he sauntered towards me. His legs and feet were coated with a blanket of dark mud, and his eyes met mine from across the beach, flashing and wild.

Phillip Deville, my favorite dead rock star, emerged from the gray sea after a cold November swim like Swamp Thing, some mysterious, dark sea monster, a goth Poseidon. He had sprung from the dirty water newly baptized and cleansed of his sins, despite being inches deep in muck. Despite the tumult inside me, I grinned back, unable to help myself, catching his eyes across the yards that separated us as he began to jog to me, sand flying up from the beach as he made his way across it. My body filled with heat as I watched him, a tether of warmth that was electric and raw and held us fast.

"You guys are gross," Sloan said, tipping back her drink.

"I know," I said, my smile reaching across my face. "Jealous?" I hoped she was. I hoped she was eating her heart *out*.

Much as I want it, this can't be my happily-ever-after, though. Phillip and I can't just ride off into the sunset and leave all this behind us. Not yet.

I still can't make heads or tails of what even *happened*, honestly. How so much went down so *fast*. I think of that night —Guthrie's sinister plan blowing up in his face and him biting the dust—or more accurately, biting a bullet and taking Phillip's bandmate Jason Langley with him—and I can't believe it's really real. The part that came after—me bringing Jason back, my third successful attempt at raising the dead— seems even less so.

And yet, it's true; it's all true. It's all real, no matter how much I might wish it wasn't.

The mess that's been left behind is so much bigger than I ever could have thought. And I'm the one who has to clean it up.

I don't like my new job, you see. If you can even call it a job. I'm what you call a reluctant heroine. It might be different if my story was only charming and cool, fun and exciting. But this isn't *Practical Magic* or one of those hot and hilarious Sookie books (though I'd give my eyeteeth to meet Eric Northman; don't judge me. I have a type). The truth is I have no idea what I'm doing, even after all this time, and I'm scared.

I'm lost.

I can't remember.

I'm heartbroken.

I have a mess to clean up.

And I don't know if I can find my way.

The trouble all started one drunken night when I was feeling particularly sorry for myself. I was lamenting my divorce from Tess, the brown-haired, puppy dog-eyed good ol' boy who had betrayed me, and wishing I could go back to a time when we'd been happy. I'd caught Tess knee-deep in both drugs and the woman he left me for, and even though the divorce was final, I wasn't quite done licking my wounds. To put it bluntly: I was turning into a day-drunk, probably about to lose my job, and trying to find some kind of meaning. Hell, screw meaning, I just needed to stay afloat.

I'm a librarian in small town southern Georgia, and it wasn't like I was gonna find much. That's how it felt, anyway. I already knew everyone in town and I still had like, two friends. There were no other jobs to be found, and it wasn't like I could just up and move to the mountains or the beach for a reboot. My life consisted of shelving books and letting people pay their fines in pennies, and then I'd go home to my singlewide in the woods. I'm snarky, I'm lonely, and for a poor, sad atheist like me, *finding meaning* meant throwing anything at the wall to see what might stick. You name it, I've blown money on it. For all my talk of not believing in the *hock and booey,* I'd sure fallen headfirst into it. Desperation is expensive. Tarot cards, sage smudging, crystals and incense, the whole nine, and for what? Jack shit.

On the night in question, I was using all my tools—i.e. coping mechanisms—and then some. You see, ever since I was a lusty, stupid teen, my favorite band has been the Bloomer Demons, a goth-metal foursome whose sludgy tunes guided me through the delicate years of my girlhood or whatever. The lead singer, one enigmatic, tall, black-haired drink of water named Phillip Deville, had passed away under mysterious circumstances in the mid-90s, leaving hordes of female fans bereft and hysterical, me most of all. True fangirl that I was, I had every album on vinyl, CD, *and* iTunes (probably only thirty-something dudes who share pictures of their vintage turntables with pristine vinyl jackets and matching IPAs on Instagram are impressed by stuff like that, but oh well). I'd recently acquired a rare vinyl copy of their album *God is Dead* that had some special artwork on the back, done by Phillip Deville himself. On reddit, where fans go to flail, a rumor had spread that the cryptic prose hidden in the liner notes was actually a real spell. The lyrics to one of the songs on the album, warbled in Phillip's strangely accented Italian, seemed to solidify this theory, since they roughly translated to *find the spell and bring me back.* Fans had tried—and failed—for years to cast that spell.

Until me, that is.

I'd spent years chuckling behind my screen about those conspiracy theorists. People like that were losers. It was all utter *hock-and-booey.* I lived in the real world, and while I might have spent the better part of twenty years collecting various versions of the same music I'd been listening to since I was a 13-year-old, saving Phillip Deville memes to my phone until I ran out of storage, dreaming about a dead guy in leather pants, casting spells from the album art was just a road too far. Or so I thought.

Turns out there's a fine line between a fan and a fanatic, between logic and lore, and that fine line is a bottle of cheap-ass pinot grigio you bought at a gas station, paying with quarters, wiping your snotty nose with your free hand while the cashier is averting his eyes, trying not to notice that you're sobbing in the Quikpik.

Glug-a-dub, and the rest is history.

God, I'm rambling. So, here's what happened. Sloan was on a blind date. I was jealous and lonely and sad about my divorce. I got drunk, I set up a makeshift shrine with my various new-agey knick-knacks. I did the spell, and the power went out.

And then my world turned upside down.

You might think you know how you'd act if your favorite rock star of all time, the guy you'd lusted after since you were barely old enough to lust, showed up on your doorstep after being dead for twenty-three years. You might imagine yourself leaning sexily against the door frame, taking a long drag of your cigarette—excuse me, your vape—and saying with a bemused, sultry smirk on your pouty lips, "Well, hello there, stranger." But what's probably closer to the truth is that you'd take one look at that not-dead, tall, lanky motherfucker and drop like a hundred and thirty pounds of potatoes onto the front stoop of your singlewide. Which is exactly what happened to me.

The rest is...well, it's a lot. Turns out Phillip Deville and I had someone on our tails from the jump, before I could even acclimate to my new normal, living with an undead rock god. One Lee Courtenay, who is the worst liar ever, pretending to be a detective looking for an escaped convict, along with his super-terrifying (and really dumb) henchman Shank, started sniffing around, being creepy and whatnot. Sloan—as I've formerly stated, my bestie, like my best, *best best* bestie—started acting all weird (even for her). Phillip and I fell in love (insert heart eye emojis here). That love, which was ignited in my teeny-tiny bathtub, the result of a salt-bath gone wonderfully awry, was finally consummated to the sound of a clunking, on-the-fritz air conditioner outside of a motel room in Boston. Romantic, huh? (It was.)

How did we get to Boston? Phillip and I decided to get away from my tin-box in Brunswick, Georgia and head to his old stomping grounds, in part to see what we could shake out in terms of money, but mainly to find Guthrie. Who is that, you ask? Occasionally known to those who loved and/or loathed him as "Guth," he was the guy who had given Phillip the spell all those years ago. We hoped to track him down and find out what on earth to do now. Once in Boston, we met up with Phillip's old bandmate Jason, who was living in Phillip's old house, and his other, stupid-hot bandmate Nate. We didn't find Guth, but we did find someone else. Guthrie's estranged—and very, very odd—wife, Lydia.

How best to describe Lydia? Well, cross Carol Kane's character in *The Princess Bride* with Kathy Bates's character in *Misery*, and you're on the right track. Short with frizzy gray hair, wearing housecoats and smoking cigarettes longer than your forearm, she's half waify-witch and half pure, unadulterated malice. She seems to have trouble deciding which. Which witch? Who knows.

For an hour, Lydia spoke to us in riddles, then cast a spell that rendered both Phillip and me immobile. She stood idly by while Lee Courtenay and Shank kidnapped me. Yeah, I'm still not quite over that.

I escaped with Lee's help, who, turns out, was fostering both a conscience and a small crush on yours truly. Shank came to our motel room to attack us and Phillip was shot (the wound healed immediately because apparently he's immune to everything but a visit to the salon—more on that in a second); after escaping from the hospital and the police, we went to see Lydia again, and found out that not only was Lee Courtenay her and Guth's son, but that he was like Phillip—someone who had been brought back from death—and that the only way to break the spell was to cut Phillip's hair, which he promptly did *without even consulting me first,* the jerk. I brought him back a second time, because as it happens, I'm a powerful fucking witch even if I don't know anything about my powers; Phillip was furious, but we talked it out, then made up, if you catch my drift (winky face emoji here). Lee dropped the bombshell that every move I'd made since doing the spell was carefully orchestrated by Guthrie, and that both Phillip and I were still in danger; I left Phillip behind for his own safety, dragging my heartbroken, weeping self back to Brunswick, where I discovered that my supposed-bestie, Sloan, had not only being seeing, but working for, Guthrie the entire time (and so had my ex-husband Tess, the bastard). It all ended with a showdown at Guth's house, where he wanted me to sign a contract binding myself and my powers to him in exchange for letting everyone else off his long, evil-ass hook. He didn't have to ask *me* twice. I was standing there, pen in hand, when Phillip burst through the door, furious and ready to kill Guthrie with his bare hands.

Then it all went awry. Guthrie fired his gun, I jumped in front of it, Phillip jumped in front of me, Lee fired off a round of his own, but...nobody was covering Jason, who took a bullet for Phillip and died. If you knew what a sweet baby cinnamon roll Jason Langley is, you'd cry over the sheer unfairness of it all.

I'd passed out cold from the shock, and when I awakened to Phillip's large hands cradling my face, I'd surveyed the room to find the bodies of both Jason Langley and Guthrie sprawled out on the floor in twin puddles of blood.

I wasn't having that. Nope, I couldn't live with Jason's death on my conscience. So, I'd cracked my knuckles and gotten to work. I'm quite good at raising dead rock stars, I've discovered.

Hours later, I hadn't really had time to process all that had happened. I'd rushed everyone out of Guthrie's house and to the beach, where the salty spray and cool, lapping tides made us feel somewhat cleaner. I was glad they were all safe; I was glad I was safe. But even now, with Guthrie dead, I had no idea what lay in store for them, or for me. Dread curled its way into my belly like a snake.

"It's over now," Sloan had muttered to me when we'd first scrambled out to the beach, the sky still full dark. She had helped me ease down onto the beach blanket she had laid out in the early twilight hours of the morning, because I'd been too exhausted and in shock to keep my balance. I'd barely glanced at her; the days of implicit trust between us were over, and I honestly didn't want her touching me. And how could she know if what she said was true, anyway? I couldn't shake the very real idea that it wasn't near over, not by a long shot.

Rather than closing the book, I feared I had opened a new chapter to something far darker.

Before Phillip reached me, droplets of water still falling from his dark, newly shorn hair, I scrambled up off the blanket and turned away from him towards the trail, feeling a sudden odd chill.

Off towards a cluster of trees near the trail was Phillip's bandmate Nate, known affectionately to his friends as "Ollie," crouched down low in a dry spot of sand, smoking a cigarette. I meandered over to him, biding my time, and smiled. "You shouldn't be smoking out here," I said, but my voice let him know I wasn't really angry. "It's against the rules."

"I don't see any blue shirts," Ollie said with a smile of his own, looking up at me through dark eyelashes. There were drops of dew in his closely cropped afro. "And it's been a stressful night, love."

"So it has." I sighed, then held out a hand. "Can I have one?"

He shook his head with a reproachful grin. "Not a chance, love. You don't smoke. Can't have you starting now."

"Oh, come on."

"Don't give her one."

I turned, though I knew it was Phillip. His voice, yes, but I also felt his presence, tugging on the imaginary string that seemed to tether us together. When he was nearby, my body vibrated in a feeling that I could only describe as *green*. I was beginning to wonder if it was his aura. I laughed inwardly at the thought, remembering how just a year ago I would have cackled at the mere suggestion of something so *woo*.

My heart thumped nervously; we hadn't been alone since everything happened and I wasn't ready to be just yet. If we were, he'd be able to read everything I was thinking and feeling without even trying. I shoved my hands in my pockets and ignored the searching look in his dark green eyes as they met mine.

"Hey, stranger," I said, going for a casual laugh. "Who are you to tell me I can't have a smoke if I want one?"

"Fine, have one, then," Phillip said, but he wasn't angry. His eyes glittered as they trailed over my face. "But you'll regret it later when the shock wears off and you've got sweaters on your tongue."

I sighed. "As always, you're right. And you're annoying."

He had a piece of seaweed clinging to his stomach, which I flicked off with a finger, pleasant shocks going through my skin as I touched him. "You look like something from the black lagoon. You're knee-deep in mud. And it's freezing out here."

"It felt great," he said. "I wish you'd joined me. Mud is good for the skin."

I made a face. "I think I'm good out here with the rest of the mortals."

Phillip's eyes flickered to the left and I immediately regretted my choice of words. I took his damp hand and pressed it against my own. "I'm glad you feel better," I said.

He smiled and placed a gentle kiss on my forehead. Then his cold lips trailed down to mine, where he bit me softly. "I'll shower," he said, his voice like gravel, "before I ravish you later."

Normally, my body would have erupted into flames at that. But instead, I shivered. Phillip's eyes flashed with concern and he placed his large hands on my shoulders, his eyes boring into mine.

"Are you okay?"

"Yes," I answered quickly. But from the corner of my eye I watched as Lee Courtney, cell phone up to his ear, muttering and cursing, made his way over to where Sloan sat, still upending sangria. He'd been trying to get a call out to his mother—Lydia—all morning, but there was no reception on Driftwood. He could have simply walked down the trail, crossed the street, and gone to his dad's—Guthrie's—house, but we all understood that he didn't want to be there any more than the rest of us did.

We'd all gathered up items and run out to the beach to get away from that house, that scene, as fast as our legs could carry us. We were coping in various ways—Phillip with his muddy, cold swim, Sloan with her booze, Lee with his pacing,

Nate with his chain smoking. I watched as Lee sat down beside Sloan, neither acknowledging the other, both of them silent, staring out at the churning, dark water.

"We need to go back," Phillip said quietly, his voice near my ear. His hands were still on my shoulders, but he seemed to sense not to pull me any closer, to give me some space. He looked slightly wounded and I felt guilty. I pulled back and pasted on my umpteenth fake smile of the day. "We can't stay on the beach all day. For one thing, there's a storm coming, and we need to call—"

"I know," I interrupted. "And we will. But Sloan and Lee…they needed some time. They need to figure out—"

"They aren't going to figure out anything," Phillip said gently but firmly. "It's going to fall on us, Stormy. You know it is. I know what happened was intense, but we can't ignore the problem and hope it goes away. We've got to call the police."

"I know," I said again, nerves twisting in my stomach like a knot. "And we will. But first, we should go over our story one more time, just to make sure everybody is on the same page."

Ollie stood up, crushing his cigarette butt into the sand. "Yeah, let's do that," he said. "Then we'll get the hell out of here. Phil's right; the cold is settling into my bones and I'm just about sick of the sight of this place."

Normally I would've argued, because Driftwood had always been my happy place, but today they were right. The cold, dreary atmosphere perfectly matched the way I felt, the way all of them must've felt. The three of us meandered over to where Lee and Sloan were perched on the beach blanket, and they both looked up at us, dull-eyed and in shock. Sloan's sangria was gone, and she was helping herself to the dregs in my bottle.

"Are we shipping out?" she asked in an odd voice.

"Yeah, but we want to go over the story one more time," I

said. "Before we call the police." The snake slithered around in my belly again, and I quivered.

"We'd better get *him* over here, then," Lee said, his eyes flat and listless, glancing over his shoulder. "He needs to know our story, too."

"He's still in shock," Ollie argued, but Phillip had already turned and started down the beach to the huddled form crouched against one of the bleached, dead trees.

He was wrapped in a soft blue beach towel, the biggest one Sloan had been able to find in Guthrie's closet, and his head was down, brown curly hair falling into his blue eyes. He'd been there for hours, staring at nothing, huddled into himself, quiet with the impact of everything that had happened. Every so often, I'd see him hold out a hand and study it, as though he couldn't believe he was real.

Jason.

We all watched Phillip jog on powerful legs through the sand to his best friend, who had only been alive again for a few hours. It seemed surreal; I almost couldn't believe I'd done it. And yet I had. Somehow.

"Do you think you did the right thing?" Sloan asked, so soft I could barely hear her.

"Yes," I said. "Without a doubt." I forced myself to meet her eyes, to let her see the steely glare in mine.

If she noticed, she gave no sign. Sloan stood up, throwing a sand-covered arm around me. "Well, fuck me sideways." She pulled my head down and roughly tousled my hair noogie-style, before I could pull away. "My best friend's a fucking necromancer, and she can't even do her own eyebrows."

Two

"Give me one of those cigarettes," I said to Lee as we crossed the deserted, dusty street and made our way to Guthrie's house. We weren't in a hurry, though we needed to be. When I'd told everyone that I'd accompany Lee to call the police, I'd expected one or all of them to insist on coming with us. As it happened, Phillip seemed to sense that I wanted to do this without him—I'd told him the less people involved, the better, especially him, with his recognizable face. The rest of them had no desire to go back to the scene of the crime.

Phillip had given me my space, but I knew him well enough to know he wouldn't leave me alone for long, not after I'd deserted him to come on my fool's errand alone, and not after all I'd been through since then. Despite my insistence that I could take care of myself, I knew he worried about me. I'd given him plenty of reasons to.

If Phillip knew what I was planning to do, he never would have let me leave the beach.

He trusted me. He assumed I'd do the right thing. My stomach twisted uncomfortably, and I felt my gorge rise. For the second time in as many days, I was going to betray him.

"You don't want one," Lee answered after a pause, looking over at me with a pained expression. His face was very pale, and the freckles stood out on his face like ink marks. His light eyes looked tired and a little glassy. "I've never seen you smoke."

"I don't," I answered dully as we approached the house. Guthrie's expanse of yard, cloaked with palm trees and large azalea bushes, all seasonably dead, gave a semblance of privacy. His car was still in the driveway, as was mine, though Phillip had already removed Jason's car and parked it down the street. "I hate smoking. I hate it when people smoke around me."

"Then why do you want one?"

"I dunno," I answered truthfully. It wasn't the cigarettes themselves—I still thought they smelled like tar-covered shit and hated what they did to people—but I felt like having one anyway. Like I needed to slum it a little, to lay down in the dirt and roll around. After all I'd done, the mistakes I'd made, the wrong choices, I just wanted to smoke a damn cigarette. "You gonna give me one or not?"

"Here," Lee held the pack of Camels out to me and I took one, tapping the filter against my hand the way I'd seen Tess do it.

"You can take my Lucky if you want," he said helpfully, a hint of a smile appearing like a ghost across his freckled cheeks.

"No, you keep that," I said, handing the box back to him. We had reached the yard, where we were standing just short of the porch stairs, unable to move forward. "You might need it. Anyway, I'm not going to smoke this now. I'm saving it for… after."

"Well, I guess it's now or never," Lee said, pulling his cell phone from his pocket and frowning at the screen. "Probably better if I place the call. They'll wonder who you are and what you're doing here."

"Wait." I put a hand on Lee's arm, which was cold in the winter air. He wasn't wearing a coat or even a light jacket, just a long-sleeved dark hoodie that had seen better days. He didn't seem to feel the cold; he was in shock. Lee Courtenay had been the source of much irritation and complication for both Phillip and me in the past few weeks, but I found myself feeling a great deal of pity for him. Having the parents he had could not be easy. I hoped that what I was about to say might take away some of his conflict and pain. "We can't call the police."

"What?" Lee frowned, still looking at his phone, as though he was trying to decipher a foreign language. "But we all agreed. We have to call them, Stormy. My dad is dead in the living room in a puddle of blood. Someone will find him. He needs to be buried. I need to tell my mom. We can't just *leave* him here."

"Lee."

"I know he doesn't deserve your concern, and I get it, but Stormy, he's my father. I can't just—"

"*Lee.*" I put my hands on his shoulders and forced him to look at me. "I'm not asking you to leave him." His eyes met mine reluctantly and I could see that he was holding back tears. His dad was a grade-A piece of shit, but we don't get to choose our family. "Lee, the reason I wanted to walk back with you—just the two of us—is because..." I found myself choking on the words a little; it left a rancid taste in my mouth just to say them. "We're going to bring Guthrie back."

THREE

"Does Phillip know about this?"

We'd managed to venture up onto the porch and were standing by the door. Lee's key was out and in his damp hand, but he hadn't opened the door. We were both hesitating, and for good reason. Neither of us wanted to see the carnage we'd fled from the night before: Guthrie's stiff body lying in a pool of congealed blood—but also, we were stalling on the inevitable task at hand. Lee had been surprisingly calm when I'd told him, but I could see the turmoil within him.

"No," I answered, looking him square in the eye.

"Look, far be it for me to give you advice on your relationship, and you know I don't even like the guy, but…" Lee licked his lips. "This is the kind of thing you probably want to run by him first."

"There's no way in hell he'd be on board with this," I said firmly.

"Yeah, I know. Which is exactly why he should probably know."

"Do you want to bring your father back or not?"

"Honestly?" Lee licked his lips again; they were pink from

the cold. "I'm not so sure, Stormy. I mean…he's my dad, and I love him, but…" He sighed. "I need more time to think."

"That's the one thing we don't have," I said softly.

"Why would you *want* to bring him back?" Lee asked, staring at me. "After all he did to you, to Phillip. And to Sloan. And to Tess. You don't even know…" He trailed off, then swallowed.

"I know," I said. "I don't want to bring him back. I don't. My personal feeling is he can rot in that living room until the end of time." Lee winced. "But there's a lot of reasons, Lee. For one, if we call the police and they come, they'll find all our fingerprints. They'll figure out you shot him. You'll go to jail. Sloan and Tess, too, and maybe even me. I wouldn't be able to protect Phillip and Jason—what if they're found out? I can't blow Phillip's cover, not now, not after everything we've been through." I swallowed. "And most importantly—I can't let you live with the knowledge that you shot your dad. And that you did it for me. It's not fair."

"Stormy," Lee said, turning the key over in his thin fingers. "What you're saying is admirable, and I appreciate it, but you can't make a decision like this lightly. I can't let you go in there and reverse this. He's not going to stop…if you bring him back, it isn't like he's going to thank you and give you a hug and then let you go on with your life. He'll never stop harassing you, chasing you." He bit his lip. "If anything, his obsession will only get worse."

"I'll make it very clear," I said firmly, "that he's to leave me alone."

"He'll ignore that."

"No, he won't," I said sharply.

"I know my dad, Stormy," Lee said. "You're being stupid."

"I can't have his death on my conscience," I argued stubbornly. "Or yours."

Lee sighed. "Stormy…this is bigger than you can understand. I'm begging you to reconsider."

"I know what I'm doing," I argued. "I've been thinking it over all morning."

"This could ruin your relationship," Lee said softly, playing his last card. "Phillip might not forgive you for this."

"I know that," I said, my heart thudding. "But I have to."

Lee stared at me for another moment, deliberating, and finally put the key in the lock. It clicked, and he turned the knob and opened the door. "Well," he said, pushing it wider with a creak, "I guess we'd better get it over with."

I followed him in wordlessly, wrapping my arms around myself for warmth as we entered the dark foyer. Someone had switched on the AC before we'd left, despite the freezing cold outside; I could only assume they'd had the foresight that the colder the house, the better Guthrie's body would be preserved. But as thoughtful as the idea was, it was the kind of thing a detective would notice. Everywhere I looked, I saw signs and clues the police would find to lead them to Sloan, Tess, Lee or even Phillip. As much as I didn't want to bring Guthrie back, I had no other choice.

When we'd first stumbled out to Driftwood Beach, all of us dazed and half-sick with shock, we'd huddled together and discussed how best to dispose of Guthrie's body. We'd talked of places we could bury him, how Phillip, Ollie, and Lee could wrap him in a tarp and take him to some remote location. We had decided against that; too risky, and with all the surrounding land being so close to the ocean, there was always the possibility of him coming unburied. We'd talked about going in and trying to sweep away any prints, removing any evidence of us from the home and splitting, leaving him to be discovered by someone else, in the hopes that the police would assume it was a drug deal gone bad, but that was too risky.

We'd decided somewhat reluctantly that Lee would have to call the police and tell them about his father's death.

We had concocted a believable story. Lee would tell them that he and his father had had a dinner party that evening with a few guests—me, Sloan, and Tess—and that he'd left to drive us all home, and when he'd returned, he'd found his father in a puddle of blood. We'd simply have to hope that they didn't pick up any prints belonging to Jason, Ollie, or Phillip, and if they did, that they wouldn't be able to track them down. Their prints were out there for sure…I thought back to an article I'd read years ago, back when I was a teenager. The band had been arrested after a show for some minor drug bust that had ended in Phillip trying to fight off a cop and a paparazzi photographer simultaneously—and those prints would be traceable, I assumed, even after all this time.

It was a lot of 'if's,' though, and even as I agreed to the plan, I knew it wouldn't work. I'd always be looking over my shoulder, waiting for Phillip and his friends to be discovered. I'd nodded and agreed along with everyone else, but in my heart, I'd known that I had to do this. I had to bring Guthrie back.

There was no other way. I couldn't let anybody I loved end up on the line for murder. Not when I had the power to undo it.

If that meant Guthrie never left me alone, then so be it.

Lee was right about one thing, though: Phillip would never, ever forgive me.

Lee flipped on a switch, and the living room was flooded with light. I held a hand to my brow, temporarily dazed. After spending hours on the beach with its dull, overcast gloom, the light was blinding. I stared down at the floor, my mouth falling open, my breath coming out in a gasp.

Finally, I found my voice and said, "Lee?"

"Yeah?" He was behind me. "Is it bad? I don't want to look."

"Um," I said, slow blinking, my voice coming out chirpy and dumb. "Um. Lee?"

"What is it, Stormy?"

"What the *fuck*."

I was staring at the spot where Guthrie had lain, the pool of blood congealed and almost black against the light-colored carpet, a stain that could never, ever be removed. So much blood…it was as if every last drop had made its way out of Guthrie's veins, dark and accusing, the slick, slippery fluid almost seeming to hiss, to unfurl its tendrils to grab my leg and pull me under…

But there was no body.

Guthrie was *gone*.

"Ready to smoke that now? Need a light?"

I sat on the back stoop of Guthrie's house, which now felt vaguely infamous, like some evil entity that I'd known and feared my entire life. It was odd to think that I'd only stepped foot in this place for the first time yesterday. Lee had emerged from the house, smelling faintly of Dial soap and laundry detergent; he'd had a go at trying to clean up the carpet, and from the looks of it, he'd failed miserably.

I grimaced. "Yeah, gimme a light."

"You sure?"

"Stop babysitting me, dude."

"Fine, fine." Lee handed me a Zippo, a dull silver one that

looked pretty old. It was engraved, but I couldn't make out the words and didn't bother to try. My nerves were on edge. I didn't know how I was going to manage the walk back to the beach, with what felt like a physical weight resting on my shoulders. Not that I had much choice. What was done was done. Nobody could stop what had already been set in motion, and I would have to face the music. My fingers fumbled with the Zippo, unable to get the flint to light, and Lee took it gently from my hands, lighting the cigarette dangling unceremoniously from my lips, then his own.

After a moment, Lee spoke. "I don't...I don't understand."

I sighed. "Neither do I."

"I saw him take that bullet. I shot him. There's no way he got up and walked out after losing that much blood."

"No," I agreed, biting down on my lip. "It's not possible. He couldn't have survived."

"Which means..." Lee trailed off.

I looked at him, meeting his wide, clear eyes. "Which means either somebody dragged off his body, or somebody else brought him back before we had the chance."

Lee shuddered. "I don't know which is worse."

"Do you know anyone?" I asked. "Anyone else who could...who would..."

Lee shrugged, a gesture that was very out of place for the situation we were dealing with. "Yeah...no...maybe. Honestly, I have no fucking idea." He shook his head. "This is all so fucked. Just last night, my dad was lying there in a puddle of blood, and now we have no idea where the fuck he is."

I sighed, taking a small puff from the cigarette, immediately starting to cough. What the fuck were we going to do now?

"The good news is, it isn't your problem now," Lee said, seeming to read my thoughts, scooting closer to me on the stoop. It was only after he put an arm across my shoulders that I realized I was shivering. "I guess that's a silver lining."

"How exactly is this a silver lining?" I asked, turning to him. "Now he's just…god knows where…out there somewhere. We don't know if he's dead or alive. Could somebody have brought him back? Will he come after me again? Will he come after you? Or Phillip? Or someone else? If he's dead… then who took him and what do they want with his body? Somebody will report him missing eventually…your aunt… someone. And when the police come and they see that huge bloodstain and our fingerprints everywhere, and no body—"

"Leave it to me. I'll take care of all that," Lee said quietly, but he looked unsure.

"Yeah, I'll just leave the whole thing to you—"

"I'm the one who shot him," Lee said, taking hold of my shoulder and giving me a firm shake. "And I'll be the one to clean up the mess."

I looked him squarely in the eye, opening my mouth to protest, but before I could say anything, he leaned forward and kissed me.

It was just for a second—his soft, pink lips pressed to mine, his warm breath mingling with my own smoky breath— and then I pulled away, my eyes wide, and pushed him, gently but insistently saying *no*. "What are you doing?"

"I'm sorry," Lee said quickly, pulling back and shifting away from me. His freckled cheeks filled with color. I glanced down at his lips, which had been surprisingly soft, and wrenched my eyes back to his. "I don't know why I did that. I'm sorry, Stormy. Forgive me. That was inappropriate."

"Yes, it was," I said, but the fire had already left me. I felt utterly defeated. My shoulders sagged and I stared down at my feet. It was all too much.

"It's going to be okay, Stormy." Lee said softly, but there

was something else in his voice; whether it was shame from kissing me, fear, or both, I couldn't tell.

"I guess we should get back," I said finally, "since there's nothing else for us here." But neither of us immediately moved.

"What do you see in the guy?" Lee asked after a pause.

"Who?" I asked, though I knew who he meant.

"Phillip Deville." He said his name like an accusation.

I shrugged. "I love him. He's…he's everything."

I felt Lee's shoulder stiffen beside mine. "You've only known him a couple weeks," he said. "How can you know that already?"

"I've known you the same amount of time. Anyway, it doesn't take long to fall in love with someone," I said thoughtfully. "I feel like I've known him my entire life. And in a way, I have."

"You mean because he was a rock star or whatever. And you were his biggest fan." Lee's voice had a tinge of mockery to it, and beneath that, envy.

"Sort of." I puffed on the cigarette, which had whittled down to almost nothing, and managed to hold in the unladylike cough that threatened to burst forth from my chest. "I've read a lot about him. So, I felt familiar with him when we met, and then I think the magic had something to do with it, too. It sort of bonded us to each other. And it didn't hurt that we're physically attracted to each other and we get on so well…" I shrugged, not meeting Lee's eyes. I didn't want to make him feel bad, but I couldn't lie, either. "But all of that is secondary to what's between us. It's like…it's like, bigger than both of us. Like its own entity or something. It's just…right." I felt tears spring to my eyes. "I love him. I really, really love him. And he loves me, too, god knows why."

"I know why." Beneath his smile, Lee's face was unbearably sad.

"It'll happen for you one day," I said blithely, trying to cheer him up, aware that I was being patronizing. But then, so was he. "Falling in love like that."

"What makes you think I haven't been in love?" Lee's eyes met mine, pale blue against the overcast sky.

I laughed. "You just think you love me," I said, suddenly flirtatious. I bit it off immediately; I wasn't being fair. "You'll get over me, I promise. You can do so much better."

"So arrogant…assuming I was talking about you," Lee chuckled, running the faded, engraved Zippo around and around his fingers. "Vain much?" His face turned serious. "I just think…Phillip's caused you an awful lot of trouble."

"He hasn't done any such thing," I retorted, taking another puff. The cigarette had wasted down to the filter and tasted like ass on fire. "It's your father—and to a lesser extent, your mother and you—who have caused me the awful lot of trouble."

"And yet you were going to—"

"Let's not talk about it," I said. "Let's have a moment's peace before we start worrying." I'd have enough to answer for once I saw Phillip.

"I told you, let me handle it."

"Don't be stupid, Lee," I said crossly.

"We should probably go meet them," Lee said as if he hadn't heard me, blowing smoke out in a steady stream. "They've been waiting for us for a while. And I don't want to be here, hanging out on the back porch, if somebody…comes back."

"Let's go, then." I grabbed the porch railing and pulled myself up, feeling a wave of nausea wash over me. The cloud of cigarette smoke wafted around my face, and I snuffed out the butt on Guthrie's porch, cursing. "I never should have smoked that."

"We never should have done a lot of things."

I frowned. I didn't like his use of "we." It seemed to imply things I didn't care for. I ignored it, though, and stepped off the porch, walking towards the road. Lee followed. It was time to go tell Phillip and the rest of them what we were dealing with, to figure out what our next steps were, if any. It was an awfully tempting thought to just leave it all alone and carry on as though nothing had happened. To get on with life.

I pulled out my phone as we exited the yard. I had two missed calls from Phillip and four texts from Sloan. *"Fuck, it's been almost an hour. Where TF are you guys? Are you fucking or something? Call Phillip back, he's frantic. Jeez, did you fall in while taking a dump?"* I smiled grimly. Sloan could be counted on to make light—and vulgarity—of any situation, despite whatever was going on. I put my phone to my ear and dialed.

Phillip picked up on the first ring. "It's about time. I was worried. Where are you guys?"

"Just left his house," I said quietly. "Heading back across to the trail."

"No, don't do that," Phillip answered quickly. "We left the beach already. I'll come pick you up in the truck. Does Lee have room for a couple of passengers in his car? That is, if he's able to get away?"

I asked Lee quietly and he nodded. "Yeah," I told Phillip. "He can run somebody home if he needs to."

"Be there in five."

Bless Lee Courtenay—whatever feelings of ill will he had towards Phillip, he'd known that I needed time alone with him to talk, and he'd taken Sloan, Ollie, and Jason with him in his car. He was dropping them off at my house, where we were meeting them, but I had a few minutes with Phillip. Minutes that would have otherwise been blissful, because we hadn't been alone since he'd followed me from Boston, and I was aching to get my hands on him. But there were things I had to tell him, and after I did, he might not want me to touch him ever again.

Phillip was driving my truck, an action he was familiar with after driving it for a week in Boston. It suited him. I allowed myself a few moments to just watch him shift gears, staring straight ahead out the windshield, watching the way his newly cut hair fell down over his ears, noting how sexy and dangerous his five o-clock shadow made him look. I sat back and sighed.

"We need to talk."

He glanced at me, then his eyes were back on the road. "Do you want me to pull over?"

"Maybe. No. I don't know." I bit the inside of my cheek. *How do I tell the man I love that I almost brought back the guy who tried to kill us, who stalked and harassed us, who has done nothing but cause us misery, back to life? And that the only reason I didn't is because somebody may have beat me to the punch?*

Phillip glanced over at me again, veering into the right lane to pass a slow car. "Stop biting your face to ribbons, darlin'."

I momentarily smiled at the southern term of endearment and how quickly Boston-born Phillip had taken to "country" talk, but kept biting anyway. "What I have to tell you…it could be dealbreaker. I don't know if you'll want to see me after."

"There's nothing you could do that would make me not love you," Phillip said, and his face softened for a moment. But he didn't look at me.

The realization dawned on me like a glass of cold water to the face. "You already know, don't you?"

Phillip pulled back into the right lane, a muscle near his

mouth ticking. "I might. You brought Guthrie back, didn't you?"

"No," I said quickly, then added, "But only because…" I faltered, looking at him, his eyes darting from the road to me with weary concern. "Only because he wasn't there."

"What do you mean, he wasn't there?"

"When Lee and I got there," I said, looking down at my hands, "Guthrie was gone."

"Gone?" His face turned thunderous in an instant. "Gone where?"

"I don't know," I said desperately. "All I know is that there was a bunch of blood on the carpet and no Guthrie. I don't know if somebody just took the body, or if—"

"If somebody did your job for you," Phillip finished for me, his face angry. I winced.

"So you *are* mad," I said, biting my lip again. "At me."

"I'm not mad," Phillip said, his eyes back on the road. "But I am disappointed. I was hoping you'd prove me wrong."

"What do you mean?"

"I'm not stupid, Stormy. I know you. I could tell you were struggling with his death. You brought Jason back…why wouldn't you bring Guthrie back too?" He shrugged. "And when you insisted on going with Lee when he went back to the house, I knew for sure."

"I can't believe you didn't try to stop me."

"I thought about it." He sighed. "But I can't control you… and I don't want to. Plus, as much trouble as he's caused, Guthrie still needs to answer for some shit. And honestly? I don't want his death on my head. Or yours."

"That's just how I feel," I said. I felt suddenly stupid. I could have confided in Phillip the night before and he would have supported my decision. Instead, I'd kept it from him, after running from him and heading directly into danger alone the day before. I'd really sold Phillip short, more than once. Hot tears filled my eyes. I deserved a lot more of his anger than I was getting. "Though how he can answer for anything, now that he's god knows where…"

"Does Lee have any idea who took him?"

"No," I answered, my voice wavering. "Or if he did, he wasn't saying." I felt a tear slide down my cheek. Would this ever stop?

"Don't think you're off the hook," Phillip said softly, reaching over to brush the tear from my face. "But I know your heart was in the right place. And if you had brought him back, I would have forgiven you." He sighed. "But you're right, we've got to talk. About us. And what we're doing here."

It felt like my belly was filled with hot, molten lead. His voice was so grim, so serious, and he wouldn't look at me for more than a second at a time. I knew with absolute certainty that I'd done irrevocable damage to our relationship. And it hadn't been this one action, but rather all of them—my keeping things from Phillip, not communicating with him, running from him, not letting him support me, that had ruined everything.

"I'm sorry," I said helplessly, feeling another tear roll down my cheek. "Please don't break up with me, Phillip. I love you."

I half expected reassurances, but he gave me none. He just kept staring ahead at the road. "Don't get yourself all upset," he said with a sigh. "Let's just get you home for now."

He was being so calm, so reasonable. Phillip was normally hotheaded, fiery, and loud, so it was eerie, him sitting there, cool as a cucumber. Whatever was going on in his head, I wasn't certain of, but I knew one thing: whatever it was, it wasn't good. And I had nobody to blame but myself.

Four

"What in the actual fuck were you *thinking*?"

"Can I get in my own house?" I asked, pushing past Sloan, who was blocking the doorway. I took off my dirty, damp coat and threw it over the couch and turned to face her. She had her hands on her hips and her face was the picture of fury.

"Thanks for telling me, and the rest of us, I might add, that after all Guthrie put us through, you just decided on your own to bring him back," she said, her tone bordering on snotty.

I sighed. Phillip had come in behind me, and the two of us stood in the doorway, surveying the scene in my tiny trailer. Sloan was staring at me expectantly, and Jason and Ollie were on the couch. They appeared to be sharing a blunt, and I looked at Jason in surprise. It wasn't the time to get into his former addictions, though, or to ask why they were smoking a fattie in my living room, given all he'd been through in the past few hours. Perched in my threadbare easy chair to the side of the room was Lee, who was twiddling his fingers nervously. "Sorry," he said to me without looking up. "I had to tell them. They'd practically guessed anyway."

"I hope you told them what we found," I said, and he nodded.

"So, he's gone, then," Phillip said to Lee. "Just up and disappeared like he never existed."

"I'm going to do some digging around," Lee said, his face a little green. "Maybe I can figure out what happened. I'm going to have to call my mother and tell her. She's going to freak."

Just the thought of getting Lydia involved made my stomach lurch.

"The fact that you were going to bring Guth back without even *thinking* of talking to me first—" Sloan continued, and I whirled to face her.

"Just who exactly do you think you are?" I thundered. "I discussed it with *Lee*. His son, remember? You are the *last* person in the world who gets to make demands of me, after the way you betrayed me, after all you put me through. And you are the last person on the planet I'd *ever* trust with any plans. Do you understand me?"

"But he was *my* boyfriend, Stormy. And you can't blame me for what Guthrie did; that's not fair..." she began. Phillip cut her off before I had the chance.

"Stop this," he said calmly, holding up his hands. "Sloan, why don't you go take a walk? Get a burger or something. Let cooler heads prevail."

"Thank you," I retorted, furious. "I don't know why she's even here in the first place."

"Excuse me for wanting to be kept in the loop," Sloan said in a small, whining voice. Her eyes had gone wide; she was looking at Phillip as though butter wouldn't melt in her mouth. I felt disgusted. She looked at him with wide, innocent eyes. "I mean, I'd like to know that I'm safe from him. From all of you."

"Sloan. Enough." Lee spoke up from the corner. He still looked uneasy. "Nobody here knows any more than you do. And you know good and well you're safe here. Harassing Stormy isn't going to fix anything." Her face clouded over; she'd been overruled. Her eyes met mine and I saw her barely disguised fury. Sloan was used to being the natural leader, the one in charge; for years, I'd deferred to her, and I knew my sudden refusal to do so was galling her. And while she'd done her best to convince me that she'd only been with him under duress, I could see that Sloan had been drawn to Guthrie, at least in the beginning. Part of me suspected she was worried about him, wanted to know where he was so she could follow him. Now that I'd met him, I could sort of see why, as gross as it was to admit. There was something about him that *drew* you, and I knew Sloan wasn't immune.

I swallowed. Sloan aside, I felt like I'd betrayed everyone in the room. The way their eyes all fell on me, waiting for some reasonable explanation as to why I'd been willing to render all their efforts from the night before useless, why I'd unleash a dangerous person they'd helped me to stop, made me queasy.

At least I hadn't done it myself. I hadn't had the chance. But that didn't seem to make any real difference, especially since Guthrie was gone.

I was flustered and lightheaded. "I'm sorry, you guys. I really am. Maybe I…maybe I wouldn't have gone through with it." The lie sounded ridiculous even to my own ears. "I swear, I'll explain later. I just need to…" I wandered into the hall towards my bedroom. I just wanted to be alone for a while, away from their searching eyes. "Rest for a minute." I didn't wait for a response. I reached my room in three big steps, flicked on the light, and breathed a sigh of relief at the familiar sight of my old bed. I hovered in the doorway, waiting a beat or two for Phillip to join me as I assumed he would. But he didn't come. I let a minute pass, then sighed and gently closed the bedroom door, sinking down on the bed, pulling a pillow over my eyes.

Through the thin walls, I could hear them all talking quietly, furtively. Phillip's voice rose and fell in my ears, and I felt tears start in the corner of my eyes. He hadn't followed me. He didn't want to be around me. I'd shown him twice that I didn't trust him, that we weren't a team. It was no wonder he couldn't stand the sight of me. It wouldn't do any good to explain to him that I'd tried to protect him, to keep him safe while I risked my own neck to make things right. He wouldn't understand, and didn't he have a point? Hadn't my actions been a little selfish, controlling? Wasn't part of the reason I hadn't filled Phillip in on my plans because I didn't want him to try to talk me out of them, didn't want him to have a say? I was no better than Sloan.

I was manipulative, selfish.

During our short-lived, emotionally fraught marriage, Tess had accused me more than once of being a "fuckin' control freak." It was something he'd hurl at me during fights. He claimed I was always trying to rule over him, that my regimented routines, my specific way of doing things, and the way I guided him into playing along, had made him feel like he was never good enough. "You make it feel like school," he'd sneered at me once, and though he'd been high as a kite, his words had stung. "I don't need a teacher or another mama. If I'd known you were gonna try to rule over me every goddamn day, I'd never have gotten married."

Tess had unleashed enough revenge to last me my days, considering all the drugs, the cheating, and the unceremonious way he'd left me. But he had a point. I'd done that to him a lot over the years, hadn't I? Gently pressured him into doing things my way, making plans without consulting him, just assuming he'd go along. Silently but obviously judging his decisions. Unable to let go of the tiniest shred of control because I was scared—scared everything would come tumbling down if I didn't keep holding it together.

And now I was doing it to Phillip, too.

A wave of fatigue washed over me. The past twenty-four hours had all but exhausted me. I felt dizzy and nauseated, my heart beating too fast, making me feel simultaneously wired and depleted. *I'll just take a tiny catnap,* I told myself, sinking further into the bed. My body was buzzing, and I willed it to settle. *Ten minutes, then I'll go out there and answer to everybody, apologize, and do whatever else it takes. I'll fix things with Phillip. I'll swear to him that I'll never keep him in the dark again. I've learned my lesson. I'll make it right. I have to.*

I drifted off into a fitful sleep.

I was at my parents' old house, the little trailer where we'd last been a family of three. I was riding my bike around and around the dirt and gravel lined driveway. It made a small figure eight from years of beat-up cars driving in, then out, and in again. My parents had a never-ending stream of visitors, friends who liked to come over for a quick beer or a not-so-quick one, friends who showed up to borrow ten bucks for gas or who came to buy dime-bags of weed from my dad. We were just one family out of dozens who had lived in this trailer, living lives of poverty and hopelessness, and we for sure wouldn't be the last. When we moved on after my parents' inevitable divorce (Mom and I would only stay here for six months after Dad split), another family would take our place, and on and on it would go.

For now, I was circling my dingy purple bike, riding in my bare feet, secretly enjoying the way the jagged points of the hard, plastic pedals dug into the tender soles of my feet. When I came inside, Mama would yell at me to get my "nasty ass into the tub," the way she always did—if she was still coherent enough to, that was.

I knew I was dreaming, but I was powerless to wake up; I was forced to ride the bike round and round, over and over. From inside the trailer, I could hear the Georgia game blaring on the TV, the satisfying pop of a beer-tab being opened, the crumple of a potato chip bag.

"Hey, Storm," I heard from behind me, and I skidded the bike to a stop, turning around wearily.

A boy with light, almost platinum blond hair, who looked to be a couple of years older than me, was standing there, holding a can of Mountain Dew. "What?" I asked. I didn't like being interrupted from my riding, and especially not by some older boy stranger. Mama had warned me about those. They all want the same thing, she'd said. I wasn't sure what that was yet, but I thought I might have some idea.

"They took him," the boy said, taking a sip of his Mountain Dew, his head cocking towards me as though I were a trusted confidant. His mannerisms suggested that he knew me—knew me well, in fact—but I was certain I'd never seen him before.

"Who?" I asked. My world was small. The only "him" I really knew was my dad, and I could hear him inside yelling at the game. From the sounds of it, he was already half past lit.

"They took him, and you'll never find him unless you wake up, sis," the blond boy said, his face suddenly very, very sad, as though he were moments away from tears.

"Hey, Nicky, we gotta go!" A voice sounded from the other side of the yard, and I turned to see another boy emerging from the back of the trailer park towards my house. He must have been another neighbor, and my brow furrowed. I didn't recog-

nize him. He was shorter, with a freckled face that erupted into a nice smile, and shaggy brown hair. He was pushing a scooter, a motorized one, and I felt jealousy bloom in my belly. My rusted bike needed air; I was riding around on deflated tires. "You shouldn't be talking to her," he said to the blond boy, his smile fading momentarily. His eyes flitted past me as though he were afraid to look at me directly. "We need to get gone."

"I was just trying to warn her real quick," the blond boy said, his blue eyes looking at me curiously, as if he was waiting for something to happen.

"No point," the brown-haired boy said. "It won't work. You know that." He pushed his scooter towards the entrance of the trailer park, the blond boy shrugging and moving to follow him towards the other side of the neighborhood, away from me. He looked back once, but then scampered away.

A door slammed, and a man emerged from the trailer off to our right, the one farthest away by the woods, and I shrank back instinctively. Elvin—my parents' friend (and my dad's dealer, I'd recently figured out) was walking down the steps of his porch, and from the looks of it, was making his way towards our trailer, no doubt to see my folks. Sometimes I had to go along when Dad would visit Elvin—"Uncle El," as he wanted me to call him, though I tried to get out of it as much as I could. I didn't like calling him "uncle." I didn't like Elvin at all. Something in my small body railed against him every time he was near, like a cornered dog stuck in a trap, snarling and biting at his captor. As far as my young mind knew, he'd never done a thing to hurt me, but I didn't trust him all the same.

His house was filled to the brim with dreamcatchers and snow globes, the snow globes catching the light and making me feel blinded. The dreamcatchers seemed to come down from the ceiling and tickle my face. I hated them. I hated Uncle El.

My shoulders tensed subconsciously as I watched Elvin move towards us, his long gait like that of some old warrior on a battlefield. He always carried himself like royalty, and he always wore brown Jesus sandals with his ripped jeans, like some sort of modern-day hippie god. The dust billowed around his sandaled feet as he approached, and that's when I saw the little dark-haired girl standing on his porch, leaning up against a railing, biting at her lip nervously. Who the hell was she? Who were all these kids in my neighborhood? How had I never met them before, noticed them before? I felt my face settle into a pout. I'd been so lonely; I would have liked to have friends...

My head started to hurt, a sudden sharp pang near my temple, as though something buried there was trying to bust its way out. I grabbed at my bike handles, dizzy.

Elvin had reached our yard. To my surprise, he did not walk up our steps onto the stoop and inside to find Dad and his never-ending supply of Natty Lights. Instead, he walked over to me. I turned toward the direction the boys had gone, suddenly fearful, not wanting to be alone, but they had disappeared, as though they were never there.

Then Elvin was right up in my face, and with a gentle, dark hand, he tilted my chin up so my eyes met his. "Stormy," he said, his face somehow kind and malevolent at the same time. "And how are you feeling today?"

"My daddy's inside," I said, but Elvin put the index finger of his other hand to his lips, tilting my chin up further so my eyes met his. They were very dark blue, so dark they almost appeared black. They seemed to swallow me, the wrinkles in his tanned face seeming to swim, to move along his skin. Time seemed to stop, the very air seemed to stand still, all sounds disappearing, all sight fading away except for the large, luminous near blackness of his eyes. "Let me just make sure, my dear."

"Make sure of what?" I asked, or perhaps I only thought it in my head. I had an abrupt sensation of falling, falling, like Alice down the rabbit hole.

"You will not remember this," Elvin said in a soft, gentle voice, the hand that held my chin feather-light and softer than his skin should have been. I had seen his hands; they were like sandpaper, callused and rough. "You'll not remember a thing, from this time or the other time, will you, my dear?"

"Remember what, Uncle El?" I said in a whisper, swimming in his eyes—

I awoke with a start, my eyes popping open as if some invisible tether had stretched and then broken, my skin covered in a light, cold sweat. I'd been dreaming, and I had the faint impression it had been a nightmare. If the cold, damp sweat on my skin and the rapid beating of my heart were any indication, it had been a doozy. I blinked rapidly, searching my still-sleepy brain, but I couldn't remember the dream at all. I stretched and ran my hands over my skin, wiping the light sheen of sweat away, noting that the sun was going down outside my window. My ten-minute catnap had turned into sleeping half the day. I'd never been one to nap, so no wonder I'd woken up feeling strange and discombobulated. I sat up and yawned, craning my neck to hear if anyone else was home, but the trailer was eerily silent.

I got up and went to the door, almost afraid to leave my room, because I had a lot to answer for and I'd left everyone waiting for hours. They had so many reasons to be mad at me. I sighed and turned the knob. Might as well get it over with.

As I swung the door open, a hand appeared in front of me, pulling it open the rest of the way. Phillip was standing there, holding out a cup of tea, the mug hot and steaming. "Good morning. Or should I say, good evening."

"How do you always know to be at the door at just the right moment?" I asked.

"I felt you stirring," Phillip answered, as though it was the most natural thing in the world. "I've been waiting for you to wake up."

"Is anybody else out there?" I asked.

"No, they've scattered. Lee went home to check on things" —he paused and grimaced—"I guess. Sloan went for a burger, and Ollie and Nate decided to tag along, though I think it was more to keep an eye on her than anything. They'll be gone a while."

"Sloan doesn't eat burgers," I said dumbly, sipping the hot tea. It was ruby chai, and if I hadn't been so queasy with nerves, it would have been delicious. "She's vegan."

"I think she went because I told her to. She got the hint that you didn't want her around." He gestured towards the bed. "We need to talk. Wanna sit?"

So, it was going to happen now. "Okay," I said, and dutifully sat, even though I'd just gotten up. "Let's talk."

"Don't be nervous," Phillip said, mirroring his words from before, following me over to the bed and sitting down. I curled back into the covers, a layer of protection from whatever this ominous feeling was swirling around the room. I held the tea in both hands, close to my face, letting the warm steam waft over my skin. "It's just me."

"Don't try to reassure me," I said, closing my eyes. "I can feel you too, you know. I may not be able to read your mind, or hear your thoughts, but I can feel you."

He didn't answer.

"Look," I said, staring down at the tea. "I know I fucked up. I shouldn't have kept things from you, went off on my own. We're a team—I'm the one who insisted on that, and then

I go and leave you out of things. Again and again. I'm sorry." I gulped. "If you can…find a way to forgive me somehow… well, I won't make that mistake again."

Phillip was silent for a moment, then smiled with closed lips. With his new short hair, he looked so young, so innocent. What a novel concept.

"Stormy." Phillip's voice was quiet and somber, like the rest of the house. "I already forgave you. I understand. I can read you. I can feel you. I suppose on some level, I knew that you were going to try and bring Guthrie back. I wasn't blind-sided like I was back in Boston when you ran out on me."

"I didn't run out—"

He held up a hand. "You did, though. You didn't trust me. You didn't take the time to talk to me, to work out a plan. You just left. And yes"—he held up his hand again, knowing on instinct that I was about to protest—"I know that you did it for me, thinking that you were protecting me, that taking care of it on your own was the right thing to do. I get that, I do."

"It was the same with Guthrie," I said. "I knew I couldn't be responsible for taking his life—and I couldn't let you be responsible for it, either. I just couldn't." I rubbed at my temple; the headache I'd gone to sleep with was coming back. "That's the kind of thing you don't just bounce back from, you know? Here you are, with this new start and you're going to have a murder on your conscience? But at the same time, I couldn't ask you to be part of it. I thought if I did it without you, and told you later, then maybe—"

Phillip shook his head. "I think it was a mistake, Stormy. But like I said, I forgive that, too."

"Okay, then," I said a little helplessly. I'd drained the tea, but I hadn't tasted it. I put the cup down on the nightstand and ignored the nervous rumbling in my belly. "You forgive me, so why do I get the feeling you're about to say something else and I'm not going to like it?"

Phillip sighed and put his head in his hands. That's when I knew it was really bad.

"I do forgive you," he said, then paused. "But I need some time to think about all of this. It's just...a lot." Phillip's face was grave. "This is a whole mess, Stormy. And I thought that you and I would figure it all out, face it together. But in barely a week, we've managed to double the number of people involved, we know even less than we did when we started, Guthrie has gone missing, and as if that wasn't bad enough, you abandoned me—not once but twice—to go off on your own. And both times, you did the exact wrong thing."

"Phillip, I—"

"I get that you feel responsible, but you won't let anyone help, you're stubborn as hell, and you're cocking things up, Stormy."

"I didn't—"

"You're going to get somebody—somebody *else*—killed," he said simply, and I gasped, hurt.

"I'm trying to *help*!" I shouted.

"Are you, though?" Phillip argued, irritatingly calm. "Nothing—and nobody—can be helped until you stop lying to yourself, and me and everybody else," he said. There were two red spots on his cheeks. "Can you just—for once—stop *meddling and just leave it alone!*"

I glared at him. "I know it seems like I'm meddling, but I have my reasons."

"Yeah, I know—you were going to bring Guthrie back because you don't want his death on our heads," Phillip said. "But I don't think that's really why." His face clouded over as he turned to look at me. "I think you did it for Lee."

"Lee? Why would I do it for him?"

Phillip smiled sadly. His long fingers curled over his cheek, his nails impeccably clean and short. His cheek was stubbly; he hadn't shaved in a while. "Stormy. Come on."

I sighed, my shoulders slumping. Maybe Phillip was right. I had thought of Lee. But only because I felt oddly responsible for Lee, indebted to him in some way. He'd put me through all sorts of shit, but he was in the same boat as Phillip and me. And he had nobody. Did Phillip really think it was more than that? "Okay, fine. I do feel a…a kinship with him. I feel sorry for him. Can't you understand that?"

"Maybe I can," he answered. "But there's something more between the two of you. Something bigger than you're letting on."

"Phillip, I've barely known him two weeks."

"So?" he said calmly. "You've known me even less time than that."

"Lee's done nothing but cause me trouble," I argued.

"I could say the same for you," Phillip said, smiling grimly.

Hot tears were prickling at my eyelids. What Phillip said made sense, but he had it all wrong. I didn't have feelings for Lee. I wanted to help the guy, but I loved Phillip and only Phillip. "You're crazy," I said, reaching out to take his hand. He didn't pull it away, but he didn't clasp mine in return, either. "You're the one I love. Everything I've done the past couple of days—the bad and the good—it was all for you, Phillip. For us."

"Stormy, don't do this," Phillip said. "I don't want to hear your mea culpas. I'm just saying that I have some doubts and I need time to think about it all."

"What does that mean, though?" I asked. "Don't tap dance around it. Put it to me plain." If he was going to break my heart, he could at least be frank about it.

"I'm going back to Boston with the guys," Phillip said after a pause. "I came down because I thought you needed me, but now that Guthrie's gone and you're safe…I'm going back home."

"What? Why?" I exclaimed, my heart crashing to my feet.

Phillip bit the inside of his cheek. "Well, for starters, Jason needs me; all this has taken a huge toll on him. Don't get me wrong, he's very grateful to you for bringing him back. But like I said, it's just…a lot. I can help ease him into things, understand what's happening to him. I think it'll be good for me, too, to reconnect with him and everyone." He looked away from me then, an awkward expression on his face. "Which brings me to…the other thing."

"What other thing?" I whispered, suddenly filled with dread.

"Barb…my ex…she knows…about me. That I'm, uh, back," Phillip said quietly.

For a moment, all I could do was stare at him. His green eyes met mine for a split second, but it was as if he couldn't bear to look at me; he wrenched his gaze away, choosing to stare at a spot on my wall rather than my face. I swallowed hard, then managed to squeak out, "You're going back for Barb, then? Is that it?"

"Not for her specifically," he answered, his voice still low. "But I do feel…a sense of obligation…I mean, she was my wife, Stormy. It must be a shock for her, finding out that after twenty years…she's asking to see me. I feel like I owe her that, and an explanation."

"How did she find out?" My voice came out accusing, but I couldn't help it. On top of everything else, now his ex was back in the mix? His ex, who I knew he had loved very much. "Did you call her?"

"No," Phillip answered. "When you left me in Boston, the guys—Jason and Ollie—they were worried about me. I was very upset. I'm pretty sure one of them called her. Neither one of them will cop to it, but I imagine they thought it'd make me feel better to see her. They meant well…"

"So, you're saying it's my fault, then," I said angrily. "Because I left."

"I didn't say that at all," Phillip said, finally looking at me. "Please don't make this into more than it is."

"That's easy for you to say," I said, blinking my eyes furiously against the tears starting to form. "I'm not the one leaving you to go back to my ex."

"I'm not leaving you for anyone. I'm just going to talk to Barb, to explain," Phillip said quietly. His calm tone was only making me more upset. "There's nothing more to it, Stormy, I promise you." He put a warm hand on mine briefly, giving it a squeeze. "But I *do* think it'll be good for me, to have some time and distance to think and make sense of all that's happened to me. And I think it'll do you good, to have distance and space to do the same. Just think of all we've been through together, in what, a little over a week? It's enough to make anybody insane. Neither of us have had time to think straight, much less figure out…" He sighed, giving me an apologetic smile, "The question of 'us,' whatever that is. You know?" I looked at him sadly. What we'd been through? I thought we'd put that question to bed, thought we'd already agreed that we loved each other, that this was real. Apparently, Phillip had not.

"And that's it? You're back in Boston for good?"

"I don't know," Phillip answered. "I can barely visualize tomorrow, much less the future. Let's just play it by ear, what do you say?"

But the problem was, I couldn't seem to find anything to say. Part of me understood, and even agreed that what he was saying was sound. It made sense. It was completely understandable. But it was hard to ignore the part of me that was so much larger: my completely broken heart.

Phillip nudged me with an elbow, a brotherly gesture that made my chest ache. "You need time, too." He smiled hopefully. "We've spent every moment together since you brought me back—you deserve space to deal with all you've been through and to think about how to move forward."

He was right, but I gave no sign of agreement. My heart was too busy breaking. "So that's it, then. You're leaving me to go back to Boston and who knows when I'll see you again."

"Stormy, you left me first."

"Just to take care of business."

"Well, if you want to put it like that—I'm taking care of business, too," Phillip said. "I need to do this. I need to think. Can you understand that?"

"You're breaking up with me."

"I don't want to use terms like that," Phillip said. "What we had…have…it's deeper than that. It's not like you'll never hear from me again. I want you in my life. I love you."

Something about his words rang hollow, though. Fear snaked into my spine; was he just trying to let me down gently? Could it be that Phillip Deville was about to break up with me? I swallowed the volleyball sized lump in my throat, wishing I was dead. All I wanted was to grab him and pull him to me, take him in my arms and smother him with kisses all over his cruel mouth, remind him of what we meant to each other. If I just had a moment to touch his skin, smell him, feel his soft hair in my hands, he'd be all mine again. He wouldn't need time to think—he'd just be mine, all mine, and I his. And he would stay.

But I was stuck to the spot, unable to even look at him, unwilling to lose what last shred of dignity I still possessed. Not even the late, great Phillip Deville would make me beg.

Slowly, I moved to take my hand away from under his, and he put it back in his lap, looking at me sadly. I could feel the intensity of his gaze, his pity, knowing that he could read my every devastated thought—and I hated it.

"If you're going," I said, trying to keep the tears from my voice, "you should do it sooner rather than later."

Phillip whipped his head back as if he'd been struck. "Do you mean that?"

"Yes," I said. "Why prolong the inevitable? She's waiting."

I could feel his eyes on me, could feel that he was hurt without having to look at him. Then, surprisingly, he tilted my head towards his with his hands, leaned forward, and kissed me. His kiss was rough and frenzied as he pried my lips open with his own, tasting me, his teeth biting at the tender flesh of my lip. Despite myself, I kissed him back, unable to resist the heat that coursed through me. As his mouth moved against mine, my hands went up into his hair, and his arms went instinctively around my waist, the two of us fitting together perfectly, the way we always had.

Then he pulled away suddenly, as roughly as his kiss had been, and looked at me, breathing hard. "I'd planned to stay the night here tonight and head out tomorrow," he said, "but I suppose I understand if you want me gone."

"Yes." My voice was choked, partly from how upset I was, and partly from his surprising—and incredibly hot—kiss. God, he was being so unfair. "If you mean to leave, what good would staying another night do?" I shook my head. "What were you expecting, break-up sex?"

"Stormy, that's not fair—"

"Nope, it's not," I agreed. "Not fair at all."

"The guys are still out," Phillip said, after staring at me for a moment, his eyes full of sad regret, "but as soon as they get back, we'll head out. If you're sure that's what you want."

"Of course it's not what I want," I said miserably. "But we've determined that my decisions can't be trusted."

Phillip stood there, staring down at me, his face still impossibly sad. It made me angry. How could he stand there looking devastated when he was the one who had brought the world down on us? What did he want me to do, bust him in the kneecaps and stop him?

"Go on," I said, anger and sadness in my voice. "Just get out."

I didn't have to tell him twice. Phillip spun on his heel and left my room without another word. I waited until I heard the front door shut before I dissolved into tears.

FIVE

I climbed out of my truck and shut the door, smoothing my dark-gray skirt over my thighs. On the drive to work I'd managed to spill coffee on it twice. I pushed my hair behind my ears and trudged up the steps to the library, pulling my keys out of my bag. Normally, I grumbled that my boss Jean made me open every day, because it meant powering on the ancient copiers, brewing coffee in the musty old break room, and re-shelving all the overnight turn-ins. But today—my first day back since my impromptu 'vacation'—I was glad to be the first one here so I could have a few minutes to think and compose myself. I knew she'd have questions. After all, I'd disappeared for over a week without any notice, and I knew that it was only my good standing and reliable work record (not to mention the twelve days of leave I'd accumulated over the years) that afforded me such off-kilter behavior. I had no idea how I'd come up with a convincing lie, when every time I thought of Phillip, I felt a boulder in my throat.

Phillip hadn't contacted me. Not so much as a text or an email, and it had been three days. There had been many times when I'd drafted out something, sat with my thumb hovering over the "send" button, and then chickened out. I wanted to talk to him so bad, it was an ache. Just to hear his voice, to know he was okay, that Jason was okay. But Phillip had said he needed space, and I didn't have the right to ask, anyway, especially after the way I'd reacted, throwing him out of my house. Everything they'd been through—it was my fault. The least I could do was give them some time.

But it didn't stop the ache in my heart, the desperation to see him, touch him. I'd thought back to that moment on the beach so many times, when I'd seen Phillip rising out of the black water of Jekyll Island, legs streaked with mud, black hair flying, running to me, in a hurry to get to me, to see me, touch me. He had been smiling, his eyes wild and vibrant, sand flying around his legs. I was his touchstone, the thing that made him happy, and I'd turned away. It had been nerves—my worry that he'd see through me like a sheet of paper, and judge me, that had caused me to jump up and move away, but the reason didn't matter. I was certain that the moment on Drift-wood Beach had been the moment Phillip had decided it was over.

I loved him more than anything else in the world and I'd turned away from him.

How could I blame him for turning away from me now?

Once Phillip and his friends left, I'd sent Sloan away, too. It seemed like light years ago that she and I had enjoyed an easy friendship full of quick-witted barbs, iced coffees, and sex stories. We'd been hanging out almost every day since we were young teens. For years, she'd been my go-to, my ride or die. Now, just the sight of her gave me anxiety. She'd tried to smooth things over, offering to crash on my couch and look after me. "Break ups fucking suck," she'd said to me, bringing me a glass of wine the night Phillip had left. "I remember how it was when Tess left you. You were a fucking mess. And I know you love Phillip even more. Let me stay and take care of you."

It was a nice gesture, but everything had changed between us. I no longer wanted her comfort. I no longer trusted that she wanted to help me. Now, her every action seemed coated in ulterior motives. It broke my heart, but I could no longer think of Sloan as my best friend. "No," I'd said, shaking my head. "You have your own stuff to sort out. Honestly, I just want to be alone. I'll be fine."

Sloan tried to argue with me, but I had insisted. Something in my eyes must have convinced her, because she finally left. She hadn't called or texted me in the past two days, which was a relief. Nobody else had either—not even Lee, who I assumed was at Guthrie's trying to sort out one hell of a mess.

I didn't let myself worry much about him. I was curious, but only mildly. I figured I didn't owe them anything more. After all, Lee and his family had put me and Phillip through hell, so there was only so much he could expect from me. Because of his family, I had lost everything and everyone who had ever meant anything to me. Tess. Sloan. Phillip.

The truth was, I just wanted to be alone.

Even if the loneliness was a cavern of blackness that I felt like I'd never get out of.

It was what I deserved.

But I had to go back to work. I needed money to live, after all, and if I didn't go back eventually, I'd lose my job. So here I was on Monday morning, looking worse for wear and wishing I was back at home under the covers, sleeping away my life. I unlocked the library door and pulled it open, muttering under my breath to the gods of magic that there had better not be one single thing out of place, especially no stinking tarot cards. I was not in the mood.

The library was still and quiet, the only sound the

humming of the fridge in the breakroom. It was cool and still. I breathed in the silence, enjoying it, saying a mental hello to the books. It was a thing I did. Books felt alive to me, like living entities, and they comforted me. It felt safe to be among so many books. Silent, unmoving, but full of untold worlds, waiting for you to take a whim and pick one up. They were always there for you.

I turned on the copiers, re-shelved the books from the drop-off, and set about brewing some coffee, easing into the familiar routine. As I settled behind the main desk, flicking on the computer, I remembered the last time I'd sat here. Phillip had called me from his burner phone, unable to figure out the touch screen, asking for paper so he could write down the lyrics to a song. That had been when we'd first started falling for each other, when things were brand-new, flirty, and dangerous. The next day, we'd taken off for the great unknown. It felt like a lifetime ago; so much had happened between then and now. In actuality, it had only been a couple of weeks. And I'd already managed to lose him. Hot tears stung my eyelids and I put my head in my hands. I was so upset that I didn't hear the tinkle of the bell at the front desk.

"Uh…ma'am?"

My head snapped up. There was a woman standing at the desk, her hand hovering over the little bell; a beautiful, dark haired and dark eyed woman, who was peering at me curiously. "I'm sorry," I said, trying to covertly wipe the tears from my cheeks, hoping she hadn't seen me full-on crying. "I don't think anyone's ever used that," I said sheepishly, staring at the bell. "Sorry. I'm still half-asleep. How can I help?"

"Are you Stormy?" the woman asked.

I looked at her warily. "Yes, I am." I took stock of her. She was tall, thin but curvy, and gorgeous, done up impeccably despite it being barely eight in the morning. Her hair was long and wavy, curled slightly at the ends, and she was wearing a gorgeous shade of lipstick. "Are you looking for something in particular?"

"Yes. Well, sort of," she said with a laugh, running a nervous hand through her dark curls. "But not a book."

I took a sip of my coffee, waiting for her to elaborate. The grief in my belly had given way to butterflies, and they weren't the good kind. I was beginning to get used to these odd feelings, even though they were less than welcome. There was something about this woman…

"I was hoping we could talk," she said after a pause, leaning forward even though there was nobody else in the library. "In private." I stared at her.

"It doesn't have to be right now," she went on, seeming a little frantic. The way she kept running her hand through her hair gave away her mental state. "Maybe I could buy you lunch? Could you meet me at the coffee shop around the block at, say, noon?"

"I don't know, maybe," I said, surprised. "But why? Who are you?"

Her dark-red lips curved into a slightly surprised smile. "Oh." Her olive cheeks had gone slightly pink. "I'm sorry, I thought…maybe…you'd recognize me. I'm Roberta."

The rest of the morning had been uneventful, so my inward mental freak-out had gone on unabated. There weren't any activities planned for the day, so I'd busied myself checking out books for patrons and keeping the printers stocked with paper, trying to ignore the nervous shaking in my hands and the way my heart was thumping through my chest with anticipation. Soon, it would be lunch time, and I'd have to decide if I was going to meet Roberta at the coffee shop or not. I couldn't fathom going, but I couldn't fathom *not* going, either.

I'd almost fallen off my chair when she'd told me who she was, though if I hadn't been out of my mind with grief over Phillip, I would have recognized her right off. I'd never met Roberta in person, but I'd seen pictures of her, and I'd met her brother when he had come to pick Tess up from jail after he'd been arrested for possession. I didn't remember much about him, other than his dark hair and eyes, which were the same almond shape as Roberta's. Sloan and I had hate-stalked Roberta's Instagram after Tess had left me, looking for clues about their life together, trying to figure out why he would have left me for her, and what she had that I didn't.

Turns out, it was everything. Roberta was charming and beautiful and seemed to have the carefree, open smile of someone who wasn't weighed down by much of anything. Her glossy, rosy-filtered Instagram photos showed a woman who was attractive but irritatingly approachable, active, fun-loving, and unruffled; like a Latina Jennifer Aniston or something. Easy, laid-back beauty, the kind most of us mere hags will never achieve because we're too petty and haven't yet found a night cream with retinol for under twenty-five bucks. Roberta seemed like a literal girl-next door: someone who laughed loudly at bars while holding fruity drinks, did yoga on St. Simons Island at daybreak, and who seemed equally comfortable and effortless at riding on the back of motorcycles as she did holding rare copies of *Dante* at the used bookstore in Savannah (that picture had driven me crazy with nerdy jealousy). Her dark, curly hair and dark, almond-shaped eyes were the only thing vixen-like about her—the rest of her was natural and effortlessly beautiful as her personality seemed to be. Her olive complexion meant she never had to deal with a tanning bed, and she rocked red lipstick like nobody's business, even when paired with a flannel shirt and chucks; I'd never found a shade that didn't make me look yellow. Roberta, it seemed, was everything I wasn't, everything I wished I could be. Gillian Flynn had inspired a generation of young women to cast off the shackles of the "cool girl" trope, but when I'd peeked at Roberta's Instagram, seeing just how easily cool and gorgeous she was without even *trying,* damn her, I'd wanted nothing more than to be "cool" like her. Not even imagining her as a secret psycho serial killer could deter my deep-green jealousy.

Why on earth would this "cool" girl want to meet me? And why *now*? I could only assume it had to do with the recent unpleasantness. I hadn't talked to Tess since he'd run like a chickenshit from Guthrie's, leaving the rest of us to deal with the fallout. Had he gone straight to Roberta to tell her what had happened? Was she planning to confront me about it? She had some nerve, coming to my work and demanding a lunch together, considering she'd stolen my husband right out from under me and had been Tess' co-conspirator in following me all the way to Boston. I'd never come face to face with her, but she'd been there; I knew that much. How dare she bother me now?

Well, maybe it was a good thing that she was seeking me out. She'd been all smiles when she'd crept up on me in a vulnerable moment, but she was kidding herself if she didn't think I'd knock her into next week. Maybe confronting her about her philandering, looking her in the eye and telling her to go to hell, would do me some good. She'd still be getting off light; in my view, I owed her a good old-fashioned Georgia ass-whooping for the part she'd played in breaking up my marriage.

Still, if everything with Phillip had taught me anything, it was that acting on impulse had caused me more than my share of problems lately. Best to avoid any further conflict to save my own sanity.

So back and forth I went. To go or not to go?

At 11:57, I decided I'd meet her. Who was I kidding? If I didn't go, I'd just wonder about it, drive myself nuts. Might as well get it over with. And anyway, it was better than sitting in the breakroom, picking at a Little Debbie coffee cake and crying over Phillip for the eleventh consecutive hour. In the library bathroom, I tried to smooth out my flyaway hair, slicked on some burgundy lipstick, and powdered my face. I was nowhere near as gorgeous as the effervescent Roberta—not with my puffy, sleep-deprived eyes and the perpetual sad face I couldn't seem to shake—but it was better than nothing.

When I walked into the coffeeshop, the manager, Kevin, waved a hello and called out that he'd have my usual vegan donut and a mint-mocha sent over before I'd even had a chance to sit down. That made me feel a little better as I noticed Roberta in a corner booth, her eyebrows lifted in surprise. I shouldn't care, but it was nice for her to see that I was well-liked here, that this was *my* home, my turf. I had to stop forgetting that I had people who cared about me. "Hey, gal," Kevin said to me from behind the counter, wiping at the laminate with a damp cloth. "Your other half meeting you here?"

"No Sloan today," I said as cheerily as I could muster. "Meeting someone else."

"Well, it's nice to see you," he said. "Been a while."

I smiled in agreement and sidled into the booth across from Roberta, feeling a little buoyed, though her smile, which seemed genuine, irritated me a little. "I'm glad you came. I worried you wouldn't."

"I figured I wouldn't, either," I admitted, nodding a thank you to the waitress as she sat down my donut and coffee. "But here I am."

Roberta ordered a hot tea and water, and the waitress scurried off, leaving us alone. "I'm sure you're wondering why on earth I asked you here," she said, immediately grabbing her water as the waitress sat it down in front of her and taking a long sip.

I shrugged. "It's about Tess, I assume." I dipped my straw in the iced coffee. "Though I have to be honest, I've moved on and I'm not sure I want to dredge up a bunch of old crap. He and I aren't on the best terms." That was the understatement of the century.

Roberta looked at me strangely. "Some time, when you're comfortable, I'd like to ask you for your side of that story," she said.

"My *story*?" I asked in surprise, more acid creeping into my voice than I intended. "The story where he cheated on me and ran drugs behind my back, then left me for you? Or the part where he got himself put in jail and then came sniffing back around just as I was getting my life in order? Or the part where he started working for a crazy hitman warlock and y'all followed me halfway across the country then bailed when shit got dangerous?"

Roberta put her hands up in a gesture of surrender and continued as though I hadn't spoken. "But I'm not here to talk about Tess today."

"Why are you here, then?" I was puzzled.

"We need to talk about my aunt."

Now *my* eyebrows were raising to the ceiling. "Your aunt? I don't know any aunt of yours."

"Yeah, you do," Roberta said, then leaned towards me, lowering her voice. "My aunt Lydia."

I stared at her for a beat, then began to laugh. The look of confusion on Roberta's face made me laugh even harder. I clutched at my belly, unable to stop myself, the peals of laughter flowing out of me like running water.

"Why are you laughing?" Roberta asked, sounding unsure.

"Just the…the sheer…" I searched my brain for the words,

still giggling uncontrollably. "The sheer…*ludicrousness* of all of this…" I wiped at my eyes. People were starting to look over at our booth. "I think the most surprising thing in all this magic stuff, most of which I can barely wrap my head around…is just how *inbred* it has turned out to be. There's really just no escaping it." Roberta stared at me silently—was that a ghost of a smile on her lips, or was I only imagining it? "Only slightly more surprising than the fact that Tess actually told me the truth. About one thing, anyway."

"What thing was that?" Roberta asked.

"When Phillip and I ran into him, just outside of Boston… he followed me to our motel room. He came in acting as though it was all a coincidence. When I accused him of following me, he insisted that he wasn't, that he was in town to visit your aunt. I figured he was full of shit." I wiped at my eyes again, the laughter finally dying down. "But I guess he meant Lydia. He wasn't lying after all."

"Oh," Roberta said with a cool look. "He was and he wasn't."

"What does that mean?"

"Lydia *is* my aunt," Roberta said, "but we weren't there to visit her. We were sent to trail you. Because Guthrie knew you'd end up at her house." She shrugged. "You called it."

"So if Lydia is your aunt…" I pieced all of this together. "That means Guthrie is your uncle, and Lee is your cousin?"

"Yes," Roberta said with a look of distaste. "Guthrie… well, he's blood, but he's not *family.*"

"And yet, you work for him," I accused.

"No." Roberta shook her head. "I don't. Tess worked for him. I just got myself dragged into the mess."

"You poor thing," I said drily.

"Look, there's a lot that you don't know—" Roberta cut herself off as the waitress approached, putting our check down on the table. "Anything else for you two ladies?"

"I'd love to grab a cappuccino to go, for Jean," I said with a bright smile, and the waitress nodded.

"Of course! Let me go get that right now," she said. I couldn't hide my smile of satisfaction. It was petty, but I wanted to assert to Roberta one final time that this was *my* turf, and these were my people. And that I was getting ready to leave. This wouldn't be a long visit. I wanted shut of her.

"I thought you were Latina," I said suddenly.

Roberta's eyebrows raised again. "I am." She chuckled. "Why?"

I shrugged. "Tess mentioned it a few times," I said bitterly. "But Guthrie's the most pasty-white motherfucker I've ever seen."

Roberta laughed at that. Then her face turned a little sad. "My mother. She was Guatemalan."

I gathered from her expression that her mother must be dead, but I bit off any empathy I felt with a tight smile. "But we're not here to talk about that side of your family."

"No," Roberta agreed. "Like I said, there's stuff you don't know…" She was fidgeting with her napkin.

I didn't give her a chance to finish her sentence. "Yeah, yeah, I'm sure there's a lot I don't know. Every day, it seems like I'm uncovering more and more layers of shit. How one family—who I didn't even know two weeks ago—could cause me so much pain, I'll never know. But I'm done playing along. I want all of you—Guthrie, Lydia, Lee, you—to leave me the hell alone. Forever."

"I'm not here to try and mend fences or make excuses," Roberta said defiantly. "I'm not asking your forgiveness."

"Good," I said. "Because I don't forgive any of you."

"Of course you don't," Roberta said, still irritatingly calm. "But you should know. Because you're at risk just as much as she is."

I sat in silence as the waitress brought my to-go cappuccino. My donut sat untouched on the plate; my appetite gone out the window. When the waitress ventured away, I leveled my gaze at Roberta. "I don't follow. In as much danger as who is?"

"Lydia," Roberta answered slowly, as if talking to a child, taking a long draw of her coffee. She squared her shoulders. "That's why I asked you to meet me here. Lydia's missing."

Six

I slow-blinked and stared at Roberta for a moment, digesting this news. Then I shrugged and took a long sip of my water. "And I'm supposed to care?"

"I get why you wouldn't," Roberta said calmly, unruffled by my attitude. "And I don't blame you. But…as much as I hate to say it, you do bear some responsibility here."

"How exactly is that?" I demanded angrily.

"We think Lydia's disappearance has to do with Guthrie going missing." She looked at me pointedly.

So Roberta knew about Guthrie's body pulling a Houdini. I wondered how. "Seems likely. I still don't know what Lydia going missing has to do with me, though."

"You visited Lydia of your own accord, twice," Roberta said, and I bristled. "You may have been the last person to see her. And then you went to Guthrie's to make a deal with him. Then, later, you went back to…to bring him back." How did she know *that*? "You're tied into all of this, whether you like it or not—and you might say that you just want them all to leave you alone, or whatever, but Stormy—you're the one who went back."

I stared at her angrily. I had no retort, because she was right. Hadn't Phillip basically said the same thing? "Only because I was trying to keep the people I care about safe," I spat, knowing how silly it sounded.

"And the people I care about?" Roberta asked.

"No longer my problem. I've learned my lesson, finally," I said, but the venom was leaving me. "It was Lee, wasn't it? Did he tell you? About all of this? Me visiting Lydia, and going to Guthrie's?"

Roberta nodded. "Lee called me after he realized his mom was missing and told me everything. He's beside himself. He can't do this alone, so he called me in. And now I'm calling you in. He didn't want me to, but…we need your help."

Fat chance I'm helping either of you, I thought to myself, taking another sip of water. I was heartened to hear that Lee had told her to leave me alone, even if she'd ignored it. *I've done enough.* But still, I asked, "How did he find out Lydia was missing?"

"I think he called to warn her after Guthrie disappeared. He figured she should know. She was frantic right off the bat, super worried and concerned that whoever had Guthrie—or maybe Guthrie himself—was going to come after her," Roberta answered. "She and Lee called back and forth several times that night. He tried to talk her down, to reassure her that she was safe. But she had a bad feeling. He said she sounded scared out of her wits."

"There's no love lost between her and her husband," I mused, remembering the way Lydia had talked about Guthrie, how dodgy and defensive she had been when Phillip and I visited.

"No, there isn't," Roberta agreed. "Anyway, the last time they talked, Lydia told Lee she was going to lock up, make sure everything was secure, and she'd call him back to say goodnight. She said to give her about twenty minutes. After thirty minutes passed, Lee got antsy and called her. No answer." Her eyes flashed. "He tried again after forty-five minutes, and again after an hour and half. Lydia never answered the phone."

"Maybe she fell asleep?" I offered. "I know it's hard for her to get up and down with her health problems and that oxygen tank." I remembered how difficult Lydia had found it to move around, how she'd tried to hide how much she struggled.

Roberta shook her head. "Lee tried her again a few more times, and finally around midnight, he broke down and called the woman who lives across the street from her. She helps Lydia sometimes, brings in her mail, takes her on Fridays to get an egg cream, stuff like that. He asked her if she'd be willing to go over and check."

"And?"

"And when Ms. Pendleton went to the house, she found the front door ajar, all the lights on, and Lydia nowhere to be found," Roberta said, her face full of worry. "And her oxygen tank was still there."

"So she definitely didn't leave of her own accord," I said, a chill creeping up my back.

"I don't see how she could've," Roberta said grimly. "It was hard for her to get around, and she certainly wouldn't go anywhere without her tank, or her cigarettes for that matter, bad as it sounds. Those were on the night table. Her slippers were on the floor. Her coat was still hanging on the peg. Not to mention Aunt Lydia is agoraphobic. She only leaves the house on Friday nights to go to the diner and she never goes anywhere else, ever. I'm really worried someone dragged her from that house."

I rubbed at my temple. From what I'd seen, Lydia wasn't able to function without her tank. And I could definitely believe she was agoraphobic; both times I'd seen Lydia on her front porch, she'd practically raced inside, shutting the door behind her as if she were being chased by monsters. I was beginning to understand why Roberta looked so frightened, and despite myself, I began to feel a cold trickle of fear at the nape of my neck.

"What does Lee think happened?" I asked reluctantly.

"Well, he obviously thinks Guthrie took her," Roberta answered. The waitress appeared with more coffee, and Roberta accepted it gratefully. "But he doesn't know why. Or where they are. He's frantic."

"But Guthrie is dead," I said stupidly, but even as the words came out of my mouth, I wondered if they were true.

Roberta spoke my thoughts aloud. "Is he? Lee said his body was just *gone.*" She took a sip of coffee. "Even if it wasn't Guthrie who took Lydia…" She trailed off.

"It could be someone associated with him," I whispered, then added, "What if…whoever took Lydia is hoping she can bring Guthrie back?"

Roberta stared at me with wide eyes. "Fuck," she said in a low voice. She opened her mouth as if to say something else, then shut it.

"Lydia doesn't have the strength, though, not anymore," I said. "She told me so herself."

"Fuck," Roberta said again, putting her head in her hands.

"Well…whatever," I said, uncomfortable. "I still don't see what this has to do with me. I haven't talked to Lydia since I was in Boston, and we weren't exactly the best of friends. She stood by while I got kidnapped, for god's sake. And I was on even shittier terms with Guthrie, so I'm really not in a position to help."

"It's not about whether or not you like them," Roberta said. "It's about your magic."

"What about it?"

"There's a"—she searched for the word—"magical tether that joins you."

I sighed heavily, pushing the straw in and out of my rapidly-melting drink. The damned tether. It always came back to that…the tether that bound Phillip and me; when I'd brought him back, he'd known how to find me by following it. I didn't know anything about it, couldn't explain it, but it was there. At one point, I'd thought it was the spell binding us. But now, I knew different. Because I seemed to have a similar connection to Lee, though fainter, weaker. Did that mean I was connected to Lydia, too? To Guthrie? "This tether…doesn't that just mean that someone can find me? I don't think it works the other way, does it?" I asked, confused.

"I don't know," Roberta admitted, gulping more coffee. "I never had the powers my aunt has. I can't say I understand it all. I know a little bit, but…well, for the most part, I'm just a muggle." I had to smile at the *Harry Potter* reference. "I think Lee is hoping that…you'll at least try. To help us find her."

"But you said he told you not to ask me."

"He did," Roberta answered, pushing her coffee cup away. "But deep down, I know he was hoping I would."

I sighed and pushed my own cup away. "I need to think about this. Not that I'd know how to start, even if I *did* want to help."

"I understand," Roberta said. "It's just that—"

"I know," I interrupted. "Time is of the essence, and all that." I moved to stand. "Look, I have to finish my shift at the library; I can't shake that off. Just…I don't know…get in touch with me when I get off work. Lee has my number. Tell him to call."

Roberta didn't look altogether pleased, but she nodded and stood, running her hand through her curls. "So you'll help us?"

"I'll consider it," I said firmly, putting money on the table for my part of the bill. "But I'm not making any promises."

I'd left Roberta in the café without a goodbye, my head in a whirl, and had spent the next several hours at work quietly going insane. I couldn't take the rest of the day off, not after I'd just taken a vacation, so I was forced to suck it up and spend the rest of the afternoon shelving books and throwing away old magazines from the donation bin—years-old copies of *Good Housekeeping*, back issues of *Cosmo*, *Highlights* with snot sticking to the pages. Most folks didn't even think to rip their address labels off the front cover. *People are so careless,* I thought to myself, taking the third stack of publications out to the dumpster and heaving them in. *Nobody stops to think anymore, to consider the consequences of their actions, even for their own protection.*

My phone vibrated in my pocket, but I'd wait until I clocked out to check it. I didn't like to use my phone in front of Jean too often. She wasn't the type to say anything, but her judging look was more than I could deal with right now. Not to mention, I was hardly looking forward to the inevitable drama that was waiting on the other end of the screen.

I knew who it was without looking—Lee. It made me uncomfortable, the weird connection he and I had to each other. I could sense him sometimes, and I knew he could sense me, too—a duller version of what I had with Phillip, but still very real. It was as if we were all tied to each other in an invisible network somehow…occasionally I'd feel a ping, just a haze, of Lee. It was a connection I didn't want, and didn't encourage…but still, it was there. I knew, thanks to this invisible tie, that Lee was calling me.

I tried to ignore the buzzing of the phone next to my leg, not wanting to answer while I was at work, gritting my teeth and walking back into the library, wondering if Lee had changed his mind about not wanting to involve me, or if something else had happened. As for Lydia, she didn't deserve my concern, but I was worried about her anyway. How could I not be, knowing she might be in Guthrie's clutches? I'd seen what kind of person he was firsthand. I was worried about Lee, too. I knew he'd try to go after his father, to protect his mother, and I wasn't sure he was powerful enough to combat Guthrie on his own. I thought of that word, *tether*…Roberta had used it, and it kept coming back to me. I could understand the deep, tangible connection between Phillip and me. But why was I also tethered to Lee? And why would I be tethered to Lydia, as Roberta thought I was? All of this was magic I didn't understand.

Phillip had been certain there was something between Lee and me, and I'd denied it vehemently. Could Phillip, who was able to feel my every emotion, and pick up on the silent cues nobody else could, see something between Lee and me that I could not? I had to be honest with myself—Lee was slowly becoming my friend against all the odds. He had gone from an enemy to someone I cared about, worried over. He'd been through an awful lot these past few weeks, and everyone had their breaking point. Phillip might worry there was something between us, and maybe he had good reason to. There was no reason I should care about Lee Courtenay, but…I did.

Phillip…my heart hurt. I wondered if I should call him to update him on these recent developments. A week ago, he would have been right by my side, helping me solve this, but now…

I shook my head, resolute to give him the space he had asked for, and not wrap him up in more drama and danger. He deserved that much, even if he'd broken my heart. Besides, I had my pride. I wasn't going to run to him to save me when he'd walked out my door. He'd lectured me about not keeping him in the loop, but the way I figured it, when he dumped me, all of that had gone out the window. No, I'd take care of myself.

By the time 5:00 p.m. hit, my phone had gone off in my pocket two more times. I grabbed my things, told Jean goodbye for the evening, and headed out to my car, willing calm into my chest. Whatever was going on, I was outside of it. If I decided to help, it would be on my own terms. I wouldn't allow Guthrie or Lydia, or Roberta or Lee for that matter, to drag me back into danger. I would stay in control… in control…

I pulled my phone out of my pocket once I was safely ensconced in my car and was surprised to see that the missed calls weren't from Lee after all. That was strange; I'd felt him so strongly, or thought I had. It was a local number, one that I didn't recognize. They'd called three times. Roberta, I assumed. I decided I'd wait to call back. Whoever it was, they could wait until I made it home, where I could pace around my living room and reach for a beer if needed.

By the time I reached my house after the ten-minute drive, though, I was worried. It was starting to get to me, thoughts of Lydia somewhere without her oxygen tank, being held hostage and possibly hurt. Who was I kidding? Of course I was going to help them. I had no other choice; my conscience wouldn't let me sit it out.

I parked the car and jostled myself out, heading towards my peeling front porch. At some point, I was going to have to find the time—and the money—to paint. The person we'd bought the trailer from had painted the small wooden porch with a burgundy paint that probably looked nice when it was new, but was now a peeling, gross mess that left paint flecks all over my lawn and made it look like the site of a grisly murder. I pulled a chunk of loose paint off the railing and moved to go up the stairs, then stopped in my tracks. Out of the corner of my eye, I could see a black SUV coming down my tree-lined driveway, going fast enough to kick up red dirt. Had I been followed? I started to bolt into the house, but then a fit of anger seized me. I was so sick of this shit. I was done running. I stood there, hands on hips, and gave my best death glare to whoever it was that was parking behind my car, boxing me in. I wasn't scared anymore. I was pissed.

To my surprise, it was Roberta who got out, shielding her eyes from the sun. I felt my anger abate as she slammed her door closed and approached me. "Hey," she said, as if it was the most normal thing in the world for her to be at my house, as though we'd been friends for years and years.

"How do you know where I live?" I demanded.

She shrugged. "Tess."

I blanched. Did that mean that she and he had... My anger was suddenly back. White-hot rage flared up inside me, and I felt my hands curl into fists by my sides. The electric rage coursed through my veins as though my blood was alive, pumping into my arms, the power building as I raised my forearms in front of me, a movement that almost seemed independent of me, out of my control. All I had to do was splay my fingers outwards, and...

"Whoa!" Roberta exclaimed, putting her arms out in front of her as if she were dodging a blow. "Don't zap me, Stormy! I'm sorry! I didn't think...I shouldn't have..."

I gripped the porch railing so hard, I could feel splinters digging into my skin, my heart pounding. Had I really been about to harm her, to *zap* her, as she'd said? Was I even able to do that? I supposed I was; I'd done it before. I rubbed at my temple, noticing flecks of burgundy paint sticking to my arms where the skin was indented from gripping the railing so hard. I had to get ahold of myself.

"For future reference, probably best not to bring up your affair with my husband," I said, trying to keep the seething rage from my voice and failing. "Or the fact that you've been in my house."

"I'm sorry," Roberta said again, her voice small. "I shouldn't have said that. And I shouldn't have come here unannounced. It's just that you weren't answering your phone."

"I was at work; you knew that," I said irritably. "I told you to have Lee call me this evening after I got off."

"That's just it," Roberta said, moving towards me, her face full of worry. She tugged at her curly hair anxiously. "I couldn't wait."

I thought about the weird feeling I'd had that afternoon, how I'd been certain it was Lee calling me because I'd felt him. Perhaps what I'd felt had been something else. "What do you mean?" I asked, feeling a stone of dread in my stomach. "Has something happened to Lee?"

"I don't know," Roberta said. "I called him right after you left the coffee shop. But he didn't answer. I tried calling him all afternoon, I texted him, messaged him on Facebook, and… nothing. He was waiting to hear from me, Stormy. He should have picked up."

"Maybe his phone is just off or he's busy," I said dumbly, though I knew it was no good.

"No." Roberta shook her head. "I drove over to the house just before I came here." She bit her lip. "Lee's car is there, and the door was unlocked, TV still on…but nobody home." Her eyes were wild and scared. "The blood stain in the living room is all cleaned up, and Lee is nowhere to be found. Stormy—I think something has happened to him."

Shit. I groaned. "Do you think it's the same person who…"

Roberta shrugged. "I don't know. But likely. I don't know what to do. My aunt is missing. And now it looks like my cousin is, too."

I sighed. I was still angry, but that emotion wasn't going to serve anybody right now. Besides, it was warm under the glare of the sun, and I was thirsty. I shrugged my shoulders and gestured towards the door. "You might as well come on in and get something to drink. We won't solve anything out here on the porch where décor goes to die."

"We need to make a list," I said, filling a pot with water to boil on the stove. I was in the mood for tea. Roberta was sipping from the wine glass I'd dutifully filled with red, but I didn't want any myself. I was too nervous. "Of people who could be involved."

Roberta dug into her purse and pulled out a small leather-bound notebook and a pen. "I already started." She flipped through the pages. "Guthrie is numero uno of course. Guthrie's sister Renee…" She grimaced. "She's my aunt by marriage. She's not my fave, but I doubt she's capable of hurting anybody."

"Tess," I interjected. "Put him on the list."

She looked at me in surprise. "I really don't think Tess is involved in this. Do you?"

I shrugged. "I thought I knew him pretty well, but I was pretty damn wrong, wouldn't you say?"

Roberta winced. "Be that as it may…I don't think Tess is smart enough to pull off a kidnapping on his own. And I don't think he'd have a motive anyway. He hated Guthrie as much as everyone else did—it was just a job, you know? A way to score drugs."

"Nice way to talk about your boyfriend," I said with more vitriol than I intended. "Didn't you introduce the two of them?"

Roberta looked at me in surprise. "Tess isn't my boyfriend.

He hasn't been for a long time, if he ever was." She looked back down at her list, avoiding my eyes. "And no...he knew Guthrie before. I really don't think he's involved, Stormy."

"Maybe he's being blackmailed or threatened," I argued. "Or Guthrie could've made him an offer he couldn't refuse. He might not be able to pull it off himself, but he could be helping."

Roberta hesitated, then wrote "Tess" at the bottom of her list, biting her lip.

"Are you in love with him?" I asked on impulse. The sad look in her eyes when I'd brought him up made me wonder.

Roberta looked surprised, then chuckled. "In love with Tess? Lord, no."

I dropped a sachet of Irish Breakfast into my cup and brooded. "Nice to know he left me for someone who didn't even love him." I swirled the teabag in my cup. "I'm not sure if that's infuriating or hilarious." I knew I was being difficult; no matter how she had answered, it would have made me angry. I'd get over my bitterness about my marriage eventually, but having the woman Tess had left me for sitting at my table was not easy, and I was feeling petty.

Roberta sighed. "Look, if we're going to work together, you're going to have to let the Tess shit go."

I turned and fixed her with a stony look. "I don't *want* to work with you. I don't want to be involved in this at all. I'm trying to put my life back together after your family destroyed it. I've lost everything dear to me and everyone I love, and it all comes back to Guthrie and Lydia and fucking Tess." I slammed my mug down on the counter. "I figure the very least you could do is not sit at my kitchen table all high and mighty and tell me what I have to let go of."

Roberta sat her wine glass down and looked at me with a chagrined expression. "Okay, point taken. The thing with Tess was just...well, it was a mistake. And I hate to get into all that again. But that doesn't give me the right to be flippant about it. I'm sorry. I guess I'm just anxious…I'm worried time is running out."

"I said I'd help you," I said, mollified. "But you don't get to censor my feelings. Especially where my ex-husband is concerned. You *were* his mistress, after all."

Roberta snorted. "You're what, thirty? When you say *mistress* it makes you—and me—sound about a thousand years old. Like I'm some polyester-clad old biddy trying to whiz in and out of doorways with my cane, stealing Tess away to bingo night behind your back."

I glared at her. "You just do not stop." She was still smiling, and I could feel my own face beginning to twitch despite itself. "Okay, fine, you were Tess's *side piece,* then, is that better?"

That got her goat. Roberta's face fell. "I get it, Stormy," she said, her smile fading a little. "Okay? I do."

"Thank you." I turned back to my tea, my hands shaking.

"Have you called your people?" Roberta asked, changing the subject. "Sloan, and the guy you're seeing? Phillip? Lee told me about him. Maybe they could help?"

"No," I said, leaning against the counter. "I haven't called either of them. Things…are estranged between us."

"Between you and Sloan or you and Phillip?"

"Both," I said painfully. "I haven't talked to Sloan in days, and that's how I'd like to keep it. A lot has happened." I blinked, trying to beat back the incoming tears. The last thing I wanted to get into with Roberta was the mess with Sloan; I still didn't know quite what had happened with her ,and it was humiliating. "And Phillip…he broke up with me. Because of all this. Because of your family."

"Oh." Roberta's voice was small and full of sympathy. "I'm sorry, Stormy. I didn't know."

"How could you have?"

"What happened?" Roberta asked.

She was the last person I wanted to confide in—this woman who had carried on an affair with my husband, who was tied by blood to the family who had caused me so much misery—but I found myself filling her in anyway. It had been a long time since I'd had female company to just *talk to*. And, somehow, telling her about my disaster of a love life was decidedly *less* embarrassing than talking about my friendship with Sloan and how I'd stupidly trusted her. I had to admit, it felt good just to talk. So I quickly gave Roberta a recap on Phillip and our adventures in Boston, how we'd fallen in love, and how when I'd heard from Lee that fateful day I'd struck out on my own, leaving Phillip behind. And how I'd left him out in the cold for a second time, even after he'd come to my rescue, because I'd thought it was the right thing to do.

"I messed things up," I admitted, staring down at my feet. A tear threatened to fall. "I fucked it all up."

"I'm sure he'll come around," Roberta said. "I mean, it was a hard situation. Of course you didn't know how to handle it."

"I don't think it's just about that, though," I admitted. It was something I'd come to realize over the past few days. "I don't know what it is...maybe he decided he just wanted to be free, or he realized we aren't compatible...or the spell broke..." I sighed. "Whatever it is, something is off. I don't think he wants to be with me anymore."

"I'm sure that's not true," Roberta reassured me, her voice warm and kind.

"How would you know?" I snapped.

"Well, alright then," Roberta said, eyebrows raised, picking up her wine glass. She actually looked hurt. I took a moment to look at her—really look at her—from something other than jealous, envious eyes. Beneath her pretty features, there was something else. Something fragile, something damaged. Maybe we weren't as different as I had originally thought.

There was an eagerness there, too…it seemed that Roberta wanted me to like her. Considering she'd carried on a relationship with my husband made that somewhat strange, but there it was.

I wondered if she'd gotten in touch with me because she'd truly needed my help, or if she had other reasons—reasons of her own—to make things right.

"I'm sorry," I said finally, taking a sip of scalding tea. "I'm on edge. I thought all of this was over, and now I find out it's only just beginning. It was hard before, but now without Phillip here…how could he think there's anything between Lee and me? He knows I love him. He *knows* I do!"

"Well…" Roberta shifted uncomfortably in her chair.

"What?" I looked at her.

"I mean…Lee *is* nuts about you," Roberta said with a shrug. "In case you didn't know."

"You've never even seen us in the same room together," I argued, wrapping my fingers around the mug, relishing its warmth. "You only just met me today. How would you know that?"

"He told me, of course," Roberta answered with a coy smile. "He tells me everything. Lee and I are really close." She fixed me with a look. "Are you seriously suggesting you didn't know that he likes you?"

"I mean, I had some idea," I said, remembering the first time I'd met Lee. He'd bumped into me at the farmers' market, a bouquet of flowers in his arms. The blooms had gone everywhere, and his cheeks had flushed bright red, illuminating the freckles that dotted his pale cheeks. Since then, I'd run into him a dozen more times, each more worrisome than the last. It was only after things had come to a head with Guthrie that I'd truly begun to understand who Lee was, and his motivations. He'd been trying to keep me safe without blowing his cover and hadn't succeeded. But deep down, I knew that even though his loyalties were divided, and he was torn between two manipulative parents, he was a good guy who cared about me. Cared about trying to make things right. "But I've tried to discourage it. We're barely even friends. I know he means well, but he didn't exactly endear himself to me. He kidnapped me, for the love of Christ."

"That was actually Shank," Roberta began, but seemed to think better of it and resumed drinking her wine. She knew a whole lot about everything that had gone on for someone who supposedly didn't work for Guthrie. I eyed her suspiciously. Her glass was almost empty, but I made no move to refill it. We weren't two girlfriends hanging out, after all. I'd keep reminding myself that this woman stole my husband and conspired with people to do me harm as many times as I needed to. She might seem sweet and like she wanted to mend fences, but that didn't mean I had to reciprocate. I was vulnerable and lonely, but I wasn't stupid. "I was happy when I realized Lee liked you," she said. "Even if he can't have you. He needed to move on, realize there's other fish in the sea."

My curiosity was piqued. So Lee had been involved in some type of heartbreak. I wanted to ask, but bit my tongue, admonishing myself for being interested. Whatever life Lee had outside of this drama was none of my business, and anyway, the point was moot since the feelings were decidedly not mutual. At least not in any way that mattered. "So, what's our game plan?" I said, deciding not to take the bait and changing the subject to the matter at hand. "I want an early night tonight. I'll help you if I can, but I'd like to shower and get in my pajamas sometime soon. I haven't been sleeping well."

"Well, I figured tomorrow morning I'd go see Renee," Roberta said. "Like I said, she's not my favorite, but she's obviously the next point of contact for both Lee and Guthrie. I'd go tonight, but Renee is old and goes to bed super early.

She's usually in bed by seven p.m." She smirked at me, drawing a clear parallel between my just saying I wanted to go to bed and Renee's old-lady habits.

"But wait…I thought she lived with Guthrie?" I said, dread forming in my stomach. That was the last house I wanted to go to, for a variety of reasons, the biggest being that I could see that sticky, disgusting puddle of blood on his living room floor every time I closed my eyes. I was still wrapping my head around the fact that the old lady who sold sage bundles and goat's milk soap at the farmers' market, who dressed in burlap and Jesus sandals, could be related to Guthrie, who seemed to be pure evil.

"No," Roberta said, placing her empty glass on the table. "She lives on Tybee Island."

"What?" I was confused. "Sloan and Lydia both told me—I remember distinctly—that Guthrie's sister Renee lived with him. And it makes sense, because she has a booth at the farmers market here in Brunswick. Tybee is an hour away from here."

Roberta shrugged. "Nah, she has a house on Tybee. She lives just a block from the beach. She's got one of those vacation rentals up on stilts. Ugly as hell, painted pastel like an Easter egg." She laughed. "She sublets it sometimes during the busy season, and then she'll come stay with Guthrie. That's when she got into the farmers' market thing. But the rest of the time, she just drives up on the weekends."

"That's a pretty big commute for an older lady," I mused. Renee seemed spry enough, but also very off kilter. "Surely she doesn't make enough money selling crystals and sage to justify driving all that way."

"I'm sure she likes seeing Guthrie, too," Roberta admitted. "And keeping an eye on him. Since Aunt Lydia got rid of him and he stopped talking to…" She trailed off, her face turning a little pale, then continued. "It's fallen on Renee to keep him out of trouble. Not that she's done a very good job."

"No," I agreed. "I guess not."

It nagged at me that Sloan hadn't told me that Renee lived on Tybee. It was a tiny detail, more of an omission than an outright lie, but why hadn't she told me everything? It seemed that no matter how much truth I uncovered, there were always more half-truths and outright lies buried beneath. I wondered if I'd ever get the whole truth from anyone I loved ever again.

"You're sure you don't want to call Sloan or Phillip?" Roberta asked, seeming to read my thoughts. "It might help to have someone else on our team, and to keep tabs on everybody. In case this turns into…well, a mess."

I sighed. I was really hoping it wouldn't come to that. "No," I said. "I don't want to call them. At least not yet."

"Will you at least go with me to see Renee?" she asked.

"I guess," I said, though I didn't want to. "But I have to work tomorrow, which means we either get up at dawn and drive all the way to Tybee and back before I clock in at nine, or you'll have to wait until I get off work at five." Roberta made a face, and I immediately went on the defense. "Look, you should be flattered that I'm agreeing to this at all, after what I've been put through."

"Don't be upset, Stormy. I am grateful," Roberta said. "But like I said, Renee goes to bed early. If we wait until after five, she'll be in bed by the time we get there, and no matter how loud we knock, she's not going to answer. But if we leave first thing in the morning, I don't think I could get you there and back by nine." She bit her lip. "I know you said you wanted an early night, but…"

I groaned, knowing what she was about to say. "You want to go now, stay the night, and see her first thing in the morning."

"It's just that the longer we wait…"

"Fine," I said. "I'll go pack a bag. But you're driving. And we're getting separate rooms, and you're paying."

Roberta luckily had the good sense not to argue, and I stalked off to my room to pack for my second road trip in two weeks, with one of the last people on earth I wanted to have an overnight trip with—my ex-husband's mistress—excuse me, *side piece*.

SEVEN

Roberta's SUV was a lot nicer than my beat-up old truck, and I was enjoying the cushy leather seats and pleasant smell coming from the air freshener. I didn't even mind the hair metal she was blasting, since she'd already played both Scorpions and Skid Row, two of my guilty pleasures. The morning sun was shining through the windows, and I was coasting on a pretty decent night's sleep—the hotel bed had been comfortable and inviting, and I felt more rested than I had in weeks—and I caught myself bopping my head to the music. Had I been with anybody else, I'd consider it a fun girls' trip. I'd almost be having fun.

We were nearing the bridge to Tybee, and from there it would only be about ten minutes until we were on the island proper. I assumed Renee's place would be close, since Tybee was a relatively small island and Roberta had said she rented her place to tourists. Despite my protests, I was a little excited to see Tybee Beach in the middle of a weekday; it'd be a nice palate cleanser from the gray, dreary sight of Jekyll from a few days before. I might never be the type to slap a *Salt Life* sticker on my truck, but I would always be a bonafide beach girl.

Roberta had tried to get us rooms right on Tybee, but the rates for a last-minute room had been astronomical, so we'd ended up staying in Savannah for the night. Our hotel, while cheap, was an artsy, hip little building just past the historic district, and I was secretly hoping we'd get back in time for me to check out the digs. I wanted to soak up every minute of the luxury, since I hadn't wanted to come on the trip in the first place. I knew it was futile—I had to be at work by nine, and god knew how we'd manage it, even without a trip to the hotel gym. It was already after six.

The sky was full of interesting pastels in the early morning light—cotton candy pink, robin's egg blue, gray-lavender. The pink-orange sun was just peeking out over the horizon as we started over the first bridge, spilling a few golden rays through the windows of the car. I stared out over the marshy grass, looking at the docked fishing boats and makeshift shacks, and sighed, feeling a little of the tension leaving my shoulders.

"If you want breakfast, I can stop at the Mickey D's," Roberta said. "Once you pass the last bridge, there's nowhere to stop other than the touristy breakfast spots, and they aren't going to be open this early, especially in the off season. Food's not great, anyway."

"And Mickey D's is great?" I asked with a chuckle.

She grinned. "Well, no, but at least we won't pay fifteen dollars for a greasy egg sandwich with limp bacon."

"I think I'm good either way," I said with a grimace. "I'm vegan, so it's not likely any of those places are going to cater to me."

"Oh," she said. "I didn't know." Out of the corner of my eye, I saw her bite her lip. Between that and the way her hands gripped the steering wheel, I could tell she was nervous. Whether it was being in a car with me, or going to visit Renee, I wasn't sure, but a small part of me felt smug. The fact that

Roberta so obviously wanted me to like her gave me some petty satisfaction.

"It's fine. I can just grab a coffee," I said, feeling slightly guilty for my unkind thoughts.

"There's a gas station up here, too," Roberta offered. "Not ideal, but you could probably grab a banana and a granola bar, or some chips or something."

"It's fine," I insisted. "Just go to McDonald's and I'll get a coffee. They have soymilk now."

As it turned out, the McDonald's on Tybee did not have soymilk.

I stared at my black coffee and pile of sugars and tried not to let my irritation show. It wasn't Roberta's fault. She folded up her bag, containing hash browns and a McGriddle, whatever that was, and placed it by her feet. "I'll eat later."

"Don't be silly, go ahead and eat," I said.

"Are you sure?"

"Seriously, it's fine." I tried for a smile. "What was it you said, we'll just have to let stuff go?"

Roberta looked relieved and tore into her food as we drove back onto the main road. "It's just that I'm starving," she said in explanation. "I didn't eat at all yesterday; I was too nervous. I'm just so worried." I remembered how she hadn't ordered anything but coffee at our lunch. "I'm beginning to feel a little lightheaded, and I don't need to pass out behind the wheel. I'm liable to drive us right off the road into the sea."

I thought that that wouldn't be the worst thing with the way I'd been feeling lately, but I stayed silent, concentrating on stirring packet after packet of sugar into my tar-black coffee. And the truth was, since I'd been with Roberta on our little excursion, I'd been feeling a lot better. Maybe having something to focus on was the ticket.

Roberta inhaled her sandwich, barely taking the time to

chew. "We're here," she said, swallowing. "Renee lives on the road just past the chapel."

"That's funny," I said, noting the chapel, its door painted seafoam green, with a hand-painted sign hanging near the balustrade. "Pick a destination, and there's always a dinky little chapel, ready for the next set of drunk idiots to come in and get married."

"My dad and I lived on Tybee for a while when I was a kid," Roberta said, making a right turn. "He was a maintenance man at one of the hotels. I went to church there a few times. It isn't just for drunk college kids getting married."

I wondered if I had offended her, but she didn't look angry. "Here." She pointed as we pulled into a rock-lined driveway in front of a coral-colored cottage up on stilts. It loomed as tall as it was wide, and had a distressed, white front door that looked to be made from an old boat. A dinghy hung beside it, above a sign that said *"Salt Life"* in generic script. I rolled my eyes, inwardly laughing. I'd just been thinking I'd never be one of "those people." I remembered all too well what a woo-woo hippie Renee was. She smelled like patchouli and sold gemstones and herbs. This place, the epitome of rich—yuppie beach kitsch, didn't seem like her at all.

"For the tourists," Roberta said, turning off the car, again appearing to read my thoughts. "If she had a giant pentacle on the door, nobody would want to rent it."

"I beg to differ," I said as we exited the car and walked towards the steps. I knew of at least a handful of people, myself included, who would die for a goth beach house.

"Yeah, well, the type of renter who pays the super big bucks wants a certain kind of...aesthetic." She smiled. "Shall we?"

"No time like the present." I squared my shoulders and followed her up the white stairs, which looked freshly painted. I could hear waves crashing on the beach, which was just across the street. Other than the sound of the waves, and the screech of the odd hungry seagull, it was quiet. No shouts of frolicking children or revving engines; it was the off season, and with it barely six a.m. Everyone must've still been home tucked in bed. I thought back to a few days before, standing on the frigid beach at Jekyll with my ragtag group of shell-shocked companions, and shuddered. I pulled my jacket around myself and tried to swallow the nerves that were threatening to spring forth. The chill I felt was not just from the cold sea air; the sense of foreboding was thick and urgent.

I wondered if Roberta felt it, too, but decided not to ask. Maybe it was a witch thing. I watched her step past a tied-up garbage bag on the welcome mat, which was navy blue and shaped like an anchor, and ring the doorbell. After a few seconds, when nobody answered, she rang again.

"Surely, she's up by now," Roberta said to the air. She peered in the window. "I can't see past the curtains. But I know she gets up before sunrise every day to do yoga. And there are lights on inside." After a few more seconds, she knocked, calling out, "Renee? It's me, Roberta. Are you here?"

There was nothing but silence from inside the house. "Did she maybe get up and walk to the beach?" I asked helpfully. "You said she's an early riser. Does she have a dog she takes out for walks or anything?"

"No, no dog," Roberta answered. "She does have a cat. But he stays at Guthrie's most of the time." I thought back to the mangy looking cat I'd seen on Guthrie's front porch what seemed a lifetime ago. "I doubt she'd be down at the beach this early, especially in winter. It's so cold…" She frowned and knocked again. "Renee! Renee, are you home?"

"She's clearly not here, Roberta," I said after another minute. "Why didn't we think to call first?"

"I didn't call because Renee doesn't do phones," Roberta explained. "She has one because Guthrie made her buy it, but she keeps it turned off, like, all the time. Especially if she's at home or at his place. She only uses it in emergencies because she's convinced if she leaves it on it'll use up all her minutes. It doesn't matter how many times you explain it to her." She rolled her eyes.

"So we can't call her, and she's clearly not here," I said, exasperated. "Maybe we should just head back."

"What the hell," Roberta said, kicking at the garbage bag. "I know she's not at Guthrie's. I went by there again last night after I left you to pack, just to make sure. So if she isn't on Jekyll, and she's not on Tybee, where the fuck is she?"

I looked down at the bag she'd kicked. "She clearly brought her trash out, though…so maybe that's a good sign? That she was here very recently?"

Roberta didn't seem to share my optimism. Her face was grim. "But she didn't even take it to the curb, though. Like I said, she rents this place out a lot. She's meticulous about keeping it neat and tidy. This is careless, even for someone as flaky as her." She bit her lip. "It's like…like she left in a hurry."

Wordlessly, I followed Roberta as she stepped off the porch and trudged back into the car. She put the key in the ignition and turned to me with a frustrated expression. "Here's the thing, Stormy: Renee doesn't just flit around town. If she's not here, she's renting the place, and she stays at Guthrie's. If she's not there, she's at the farmers' market. That's not open except on weekends. She doesn't go anywhere else. So if she's not there, and she's not here, where is she?"

I shrugged. "With other family, maybe?"

"She doesn't have much family. Just Guthrie, Lee, Lydia…" Roberta said, her voice trailing off. I wondered if she'd been about to say someone else. "All three of whom are currently MIA." She bit her lip. "Which means Renee is, too."

"Why don't we check out the beach, just really quick," I

offered, trying to be helpful, though the sinking feeling in my gut no doubt matched her own. "Just to rule out she isn't there."

"Okay," Roberta said, backing the car out of the drive. Her voice was low as she looked into the rearview mirror. "But I think…I think this is bad."

The waves on Tybee Beach were rough and choppy. I could see them as I crossed the public parking lot and headed towards the pier, past the marine museum with the huge ceramic frog out front that I remembered from my childhood. Somewhere, there was a picture of a snaggle toothed, pigtailed version of me sitting on that frog, from one of the few times my parents and I had gone on vacation. The salt smell in the air was strong, and I could feel drops of spray on my face even though I was many yards away from the water. There was probably a storm coming later in the day. The sun hadn't fully risen yet, but I could still see the ominous gray of the horizon.

Roberta and I were going to walk down the pier and scope the beach for Renee, just in case she might be there, though we both knew she wasn't. The truth—that she'd gone missing, too —lay thick between us. The air was frigidly cold, colder than November in South Georgia usually was, but also clammy and full of moisture. It felt gross on my skin, so I pushed my jacket sleeves down and crossed my arms as we walked up the ramp and out to the sea.

There were a couple of hardened fishermen out enjoying the solitude, but the pier was largely empty. The big, open, octagon-shaped pavilion where locals sold pizza, sno-cones, and fishing bait to hundreds of tourists were all shut-up and silent. There was no music piping from the ceilings, no lifeguards patrolling the beach. Other than a few early rising year-rounders stumbling around in the sand, Tybee was deserted. Roberta and I passed through the pavilion and down to the wharf, where we walked quietly, both of us lost in thought. A large black crow was perched on the railing, regarding me silently, his head cocking back and forth, one large black eye peering at me quizzically as I walked by. I held eye contact with the beautiful, inky-black bird until he was behind me.

"The place is a ghost town," Roberta said to me as we neared the end of the wharf, which opened into a rectangular area where people fished; it was where the all-day fishers congregated, the ones who were serious. There were only a couple of guys out, lines cast, sitting on benches with their hats down over their eyes. Not much biting today, apparently.

I meandered over to the railing and leaned over it, my arms resting on the splintered wood. The sea at Tybee was always the most interesting shade of murky gray-brown, due to the water from the Savannah River that mixed with the sea. Jekyll Island also boasted murky gray seas, but they were less warm, more desolate and subdued. It was a difference almost imperceptible to anyone who hadn't grown up in the area, but I could tell. I watched the waves gently licking at the sand, the seagulls swaying on heavy wind gusts, and smiled. It had to be in the mid-forties, and the sun, coming up over the horizon, deep orange and moody, wasn't providing a lick of warmth. One lone surfer crested a big wave before succumbing to the icy water and exited with his surfboard under his arm. How on earth anyone felt like surfing at six a.m. in frigid, winter seas was beyond me, but I envied him his passion and energy. An older woman and a man I assumed was her husband, both white-headed under their straw hats, hobbled along the beach, the surf occasionally coming up to their ankles, stopping here and there to pick up shells. A teenage girl leaned against the abandoned lifeguard stand with a pad in hand; it looked like she was sketching. I wondered if she was skipping school, and what she was drawing—the dark, dreary waves, the freight ship off in the distance, hulking and red, the swaying seagulls, or—

My mouth dropped open as my eyes came to rest on the figure the girl was drawing: It was a man, emerging from the water after a swim, droplets of white flying off his shoulders and his jet-black, shaggy hair as he shook himself off. His legs were long and muscular, and as he exited the water, he almost appeared to be dancing, his movements in tune with the waves crashing behind him. Letting his ankles stay submerged, he ran his hands back through his hair, squeezing it to get rid of the water. He wiped at his face, and looked up towards the pier, his dark eyes seeming to flash with glimmers of the morning sun.

"Holy crap," I yelped, jumping back from the ledge, a bolt of lightning shooting through my heart. "It's him!"

"Who?" I heard Roberta exclaim behind me, but I didn't take the time to answer.

I bounded back down the pier, heading for the stairs, which were yards away. When I finally reached them, I took them two at a time, almost tripping over my own feet and plummeting into the cool sand. I ripped off my Vans, knowing they'd only slow me down, and bounded through the sand towards the stretch of beach where I'd seen him emerge. The girl was still leaning against the stand, drawing. I ran towards her, and as I crested the small hill, my heart began to pound. It was him. He was here. I had no idea how, but he was here.

By the time I reached the water, I was out of breath. I scanned all around me, my hand over my brow, looking. There was nobody there. The elderly couple had disappeared down the beach, heading towards the dunes. Everyone was gone. But I knew I'd seen him.

"Stormy, what the hell?" I turned to Roberta, who was clumsily traipsing through the sand, holding my shoes. She held them out to me. "What on earth had you running like a madwoman without shoes in the middle of winter? Did you see Renee?"

"No, not Renee. I thought I saw…no, I *know* I saw him," I said, taking the shoes, my heart sinking in my chest. "I know I did. He was right here, swimming. And then he came out of the water, and I know it was him because he shook himself off and dried his hair exactly like he did at Jekyll—"

"Stormy, what are you talking about? Who did you see?"

"Phillip," I said miserably. "I saw Phillip."

She looked confused. "Your boyfriend? I thought he lived in Boston."

"He did, or does, or does again… I don't know." I threw up my hands. I felt like I might cry. I *had* seen him. I was certain of it.

"It was probably a trick of the light. I saw a guy, too, but it was a surfer. That was probably who you saw."

"No, it wasn't the surfer. I saw him too, but Phillip was closer to the wharf."

"I didn't see anybody else, Stormy," Roberta said.

"I know I saw him." Desperate, I ran over to the girl at the lifeguard stand, who was still drawing. She had earbuds in her ears and didn't notice me. I had to wave my hand in front of her to get her attention. Reluctantly, she pulled her jacket hood down and took the buds out of her ears.

"I'm sorry to bother you," I said, feeling ridiculous. "I just saw a man out there, swimming. But when I got to the beach, he was gone. I was wondering if you saw him? That's who you're drawing, right?"

The girl's brow furrowed, and she turned her drawing pad around to show me. My heart sank. She'd been drawing the huge freight liner off in the distance, and above it, the gray horizon. "I'm sorry. I didn't see any guy. Unless you mean the surfer?"

"No, not him," I said. "A guy with black hair, green eyes. I think he was wearing black swimming trunks. Really handsome."

She shook her head. "Locals wouldn't swim in this weather. Only the surfers are stupid enough to get in. Sorry." She put her earbuds back in and resumed drawing.

My shoulders sank and Roberta cuffed me on the arm. "Look, you're distraught. And tired, and stressed, and we just hit a dead end. I'm sure you just…thought you saw him. It's totally understandable."

"I guess so," I said reluctantly, but she was wrong. I hadn't imagined it. I hadn't imagined Phillip.

"Let's head back to Savannah," Roberta said in a kind voice. "There's nothing left to see here. We'll check out, pack up the car, and I'll treat you to a coffee on River Street before I take you to work. If that doesn't fix you up, nothing will."

Nothing will, I thought glumly, but I pasted on a fake smile and followed her, shuffling through the cold sand, barefoot and freezing, toward the parking lot. Phillip had been here; I'd seen him, felt him. But there was nothing to do but go home after such a fruitless trip.

I turned to look at the stretch of cold, gray beach one more time, scanning desperately in the hopes of seeing a streak of black hair or pale skin—but the beach was as desolate and empty as my heart. I suddenly no longer felt like hitting up the gym; instead, I wished I could crawl into bed and sleep forever.

Eight

I was in the process of bouncing a check to Walmart.

I didn't get paid until Friday, but it was Wednesday and there wasn't a crumb of food in the house. I'd spent the last five dollars to my name paying for a fancy coffee on River Street with Roberta two days before. She'd offered to treat, but I'd refused, not wanting to be indebted to her. I'd been rattled, after seeing what must've been a ghostly apparition, or figment of my imagination on the beach—it couldn't have been Phillip; I knew it was impossible—but the feeling of unease hadn't gone away.

Adding to my frayed nerves, I'd run smack into someone when we were checking out of the hotel. I'd been staring down at my phone, hoping for texts from Phillip, not paying attention, and had walked headfirst into someone standing there—a man with piercing, cold eyes who had been none too pleased when I accidentally knocked over his briefcase. Papers had spilled out and he'd scrambled to pick them up, rudely shaking off my arm when I'd moved to help, ignoring me as I apologized profusely. The chilling glare he'd given me had sent chills up my back and left me in a funk that had been hard to shake. Buying overpriced coffee and candies on River Street with Roberta was my attempt to salvage the morning, but it hadn't really helped. I'd just ended up with a bunch of leftover fruit slice candies that I'd given to my boss, Jean, and a bad case of heartburn. To say nothing of the vague sense that I was losing my mind, and my now-empty bank account.

Savannah sure was expensive to be so cheap, to quote everyone's favorite southern heroine, Dolly Parton.

I'd known my finances were in dire straits ever since Boston, when I'd been with Phillip, but I'd stubbornly refused his help then. I thought back to the bag of cash he had unearthed from his old house and admonished myself. I didn't have to take any extra, but he had been trying to pay me back. Add being totally broke and starving to the list of things my stubborn pride had caused. Why did I push people away so much? Why did I insist on being so stubbornly independent, knowing how it messed up my life?

I adjusted the basket on my arm and stared into it, frowning. I didn't even like to shop at Walmart—I was morally against the big box store—but my champagne tastes were a no-go until I could build my bank account back up. So there I was, buying tofu, rice and beans, tortillas, apples, and an ill-advised family sized package of Oreos at Walmart with a check I knew I didn't have the funds to back up. Memories from my childhood swirled behind my eyes as I remembered standing in the Winn Dixie with Mama more than once, watching her write checks for SpaghettiOs and beer with money she definitely didn't have.

I had officially hit rock bottom.

My phone buzzed in my pocket as I signed the check and slid it towards the cashier, hoping she couldn't glean from my expression that the check was bad. I pushed the phone further into my pocket, holding my breath as she fed the check through the little machine. I hoped it wasn't one of those newfangled machines that automatically deducted the check amount from my bank account like a debit card. The stodgy old Brunswick Walmart hadn't been remodeled—or cleaned, from the looks of it—in decades, so it was probable that they'd still be using outdated technology and depositing their checks at the bank every few days like it was still the 1990s. Still, I held my breath. The check printer was loud and slow, and my heart raced as I waited, clutching my ID so hard I could feel it cutting into my skin. I had every intention of depositing my check in the bank Friday to cover the overdraft, so it wasn't technically stealing, right? My heart pounded.

Finally, the cashier presented me with the check and a receipt, smiling brightly, and I exhaled, grabbing my bag of sort-of-stolen loot and scrambling out the door as if someone might follow me and demand I give it all back.

Once I was back at the truck, I grabbed my phone, hoping for a message from Phillip, whose absence was becoming unbearable. A small part of me had assumed I'd hear from him after a day or two, that his missing me would be too great, but there had been nothing but silence. It was beginning to creep into my head. I wished I would hear from Lee, that he'd crop up and say everything was fine, that it had all been a misunderstanding. Hell, at this point I'd even welcome a message from Sloan.

But the text wasn't from Phillip, Sloan, or Lee. It was Roberta again. I frowned.

"*Still no news,*" the text read. I scrolled down to the next message. "*I'm guessing you haven't heard from Lee, either.*"

"*No,*" I tapped out with my thumb. "*I'll let you know if I do.*"

I got into the truck and put the keys in the ignition with a deep sigh. I wasn't looking forward to going home for yet another night alone. It was wild to think I'd felt so lonely before everything had happened, before Phillip, Lee, and the rest of them had come into my life. Truth be told, I really hadn't been. I'd hung out with Sloan most nights, had other friends on stand-by, had gone on a date every now and again. The loneliness I'd thought I felt then paled in comparison to what I felt now.

I plugged my phone into the auxiliary and hit "shuffle" on Spotify, simultaneously hoping and not hoping that the Bloomer Demons would come up on my playlist. Hearing Phillip's beautiful, razor-sharp baritone would be painful, but it was the kind of pain I craved. I kept seeing him emerging from the water on Tybee, the droplets clinging to his newly shorn black hair, his eyes flashing in the early morning sun. I hadn't imagined him; I couldn't have.

Right?

I sighed with relief and disappointment as the first few bars of Queens of the Stone Age came on. It was entirely possible that I was losing my damn mind. So much had happened in such a short time; it was putting me under an insane amount of stress. I didn't want to admit that Roberta might be right, that I'd hallucinated him out of thin air. But it was the only logical explanation, wasn't it? Why would Phillip, who had gone back to Boston, suddenly turn up on Tybee, swimming at six a.m. in the middle of winter? It made no sense.

Josh Homme was singing in his sultry, booze-soaked voice about sitting by the ocean and drinking a potion to forget his lover.

If only I had such a potion. Well, I was a witch, wasn't I? Maybe I should learn how to make one. One that would make me forget all of this so I could go back to the life I had before. One that could make me forget my heartbreak.

Fastening my seatbelt, I decided to try and put Phillip Deville out of my mind, potion or not. There was no way to explain it in a way that made sense. Roberta was right. I'd just imagined Phillip on Tybee. He was back in Boston with his friends, rekindling his old life, and I was here, and that was that. No sense dwelling on things that were impossible. Especially when there were more pressing matters to attend to.

I put the truck in drive and rolled slowly out of the parking lot, mentally compiling ingredients in my kitchen with the meager items I'd just bought, trying to put together a menu for dinner. I knew I needed to keep up my energy. The past two nights, I'd gone to bed having only had tea.

I pulled up at home, sighing at the sight of my weather-beaten trailer, ramshackle and vulnerable to the elements, the overcast evening sky as dreary as my mood. The place needed so much work; the roof needed to be patched after the last storm—the storm that had brought me Phillip—and I could see one of the shutters beside my bedroom window had started to crumble and rot, in addition to the peeling paint on the porch that was starting to drive me crazy. How had I not noticed so much was going wrong? How had I let everything go to shit like this?

I grabbed my bags and exited the truck, unlocking the door and grimacing as the smell of cat pee greeted me from the doorway.

"Blinken, I was less than an hour late! Did you seriously pee on the carpet?" I exclaimed angrily, but the damn little ball of fur was nowhere to be found, no doubt hiding to avoid my wrath. "Go outside! Now!" I demanded, but he didn't emerge, and I had no energy to fight with him. He'd been acting weird ever since my trip with Phillip, where he'd been abandoned with no food, thanks to Sloan. I trudged into the kitchen, depositing my bags on the counter and grabbing a bottle of carpet cleaner and a towel from under the kitchen sink with a heavy sigh. Could nothing just be easy?

I paced around the living room, looking for a wet spot, still grumbling. It had been a long time since Blinken had peed in the house; he was old and well-trained. But it was odd—the carpet looked fine. I flicked on the overhead light and kicked off my shoes, padding around in my bare feet, certain I'd find the damnable spot, but the carpet was dry as a bone. "Blinken, where are you? Where did you pee?" I could smell it, strong and cloying, full of pheromones and ammonia, almost like that of a tomcat marking his territory, though Blinken had been fixed for years.

My eyes fixed on the doorway, where there was a small puddle by the door. It was sheer luck that I hadn't stepped right in it when I'd walked into the house. "Blinken, you jerk…" I muttered, but as I leaned down to clean the puddle, I got a weird feeling. It was cat pee alright, but…something was off. Rather than one puddle, it was a trickle, a series of dots leading right up to the door and presumably out of it. I opened my front door and peered out at the porch. Sure enough, there were more dots trailing the flaking porch and down the steps.

I threw down the towel and cleaner and ran through the house, opening cabinets and peering under tables and chairs. I searched the closet, under the bed, and ransacked the living room. I checked the windows, making sure they were all shut. I felt a cold snake of fear unfurl in my belly as I went back to the living room and again surveyed the trickle by the door. There was no doubt in my mind what had happened.

I grabbed my phone from the kitchen with shaking hands. Roberta answered on the first ring.

"Someone stole my cat," I said, my voice giving way to tears. "They broke into my house and carried him right out the front door. And he was so scared he pissed himself."

"Right," Roberta grabbed a toasted tortilla and dug into my hastily-thrown-together beans and rice. She'd raced over after I had called her. "So whoever did this obviously has access to your house, since nothing was disturbed or broken and there's no sign of forced entry."

I stared down at my bowl, which I'd drenched in sriracha and topped with mustard greens I'd found in the back of the crisper. I'd been starving at the grocery store, but now my appetite was all but gone. I was too worried about Blinken. He was old, not used to being outside for long, and wary of strangers. He was likely terrified, if he was even still alive. Who could do such a thing, and why?

Roberta waited for me to respond, but I was too distraught. She gently prodded, "Stormy, who has a key to your house?"

"Nobody," I said glumly, digging a fork absently into my food. "Tess used to, but I changed the locks after I threw him out." I frowned. "Sloan doesn't, either—she was always so bad at keeping up with things that I never bothered. But they both know where I keep the spare."

"What about Phillip?" Roberta asked, and my heart burst in fresh pain at the mention of his name. If only he were here right now.

"No," I said, shaking my head. "He was only here for a couple of days before we left for Boston, so I never had the chance." I sighed. "And anyway, he's nowhere near here now." Or was he?

"Where is this secret hiding place of yours?" she asked, eating with gusto. I was glad she was enjoying the food; at least I hadn't bounced that check for nothing. "Is it a place that someone could easily guess?"

"Under the porch, there's this old, cut off milk jug we found when we first moved here," I told her, figuring there was no harm in disclosing the location since I'd never use that hiding spot again. "You know, like a redneck water bowl for a dog? I keep a spare key wrapped up in saran wrap under that jug." I shrugged. "I guess that's a stupid spot, but it isn't visible unless you go looking for it; it just looks like old trash under the porch."

"Do you think it could have been either of them? Tess or Sloan?"

I shrugged again. "I told you I have my suspicions about Tess, but honestly, now I'm not sure. He could have found the key and let himself in, but Blinken knew him and loved him. He wouldn't have pissed himself in fear, not unless he was hurt. And Tess wouldn't hurt him." My ex-husband might be a jerk and a bit dim besides, but he wasn't a monster. He'd loved that cat. "And honestly, Blinken knew Sloan really well, too. I mean, he wasn't the type to sidle up to her and make biscuits on her lap, but he wasn't afraid of her. She always takes care of him when I'm away." *Well, except for last time, because she was too busy betraying me.*

"But is she capable of it, do you think?" Roberta asked me, sensing my feelings.

I frowned. I wasn't sure if my friendship with Sloan would make it through the storm, honestly. And I wasn't sure if I cared. I could barely think about her without my anger boiling over, without rehashing everything she'd pulled. I couldn't trust her anymore. She'd shown she was capable of not only startling disloyalty and outright lying, but also total apathy about her own role in all of it. I remembered how we'd sat on the beach after the incident at Guthrie's, her upending sangria, acting as though butter wouldn't melt in her mouth. Either she lacked the comprehension of just how serious all of this was, how badly she'd hurt me, or—and I wasn't sure which was worse—she just didn't care.

I'd always known Sloan was self-centered and self-absorbed. It had always been the Sloan Show and I was usually happy to be a guest star. I was used to being her part-time therapist, her wing man, and her go-to. I'd simply made the mistake of assuming that had afforded me some loyalty, some gratitude. I'd been wrong.

For the life of me, though, even with everything that had happened, I couldn't think why on earth Sloan would break into my house and take my cat. Someone who hadn't even bothered to feed him while I was away wasn't likely to catnap him. I shook my head. "I can't say for sure, but I really don't think it was her."

"Well, whoever did meant it as a warning to you," Roberta said, pushing her now-empty plate away and taking a sip of Tropicalia. I was so glad she'd brought beer.

"A warning about what, though?" I asked, forcing a bite into my mouth. I chewed thoughtfully. I hadn't done anything recently to warrant someone taking my cat.

"A warning to stop sniffing around, I guess."

"But other than going with you to Tybee, I haven't done anything," I argued, forcing another bite. It was spicy and salty and delicious; I was beginning to feel my appetite stir. I ripped into a tortilla.

"Maybe they intend to stop us before we start," Roberta said, still sipping her beer. "Then maybe we should lay off," I said, popping the tab on my own beer. "It's not worth the trouble. I can't go through this again."

"That's easy for you to say," she said, her face glum. "This is my family we're talking about. I can't just leave it alone."

"I guess I don't understand," I said with a sigh. "They're your relatives, and yet it's me that's being harassed and threatened."

"No, it isn't just you," Roberta said quietly. She pulled her phone out of her pocket, scrolled for a second, and pushed the phone over to me with a deep sigh. "Look at that."

I put down my fork and picked up the phone, scrolling through the series of pictures. It was what looked to be a bedroom, but it was totally ransacked. The mattress had been nearly pulled off the bed, the sheets ripped, trash piled all over the floor, and there was a huge hole in the wall that had unmistakably come from a fist. "Is that glass?"

"Yes." She sounded angry. "I collect vintage snow globes. I'd had some of them since I was little. Whoever it was dropped them on the floor and smashed them all."

"When did this happen?" I asked.

"Yesterday," Roberta said, looking down at her plate. "I didn't tell you because I was afraid you'd spook and then you wouldn't help me anymore. I thought if I just stayed quiet about it…"

"And now they've taken my cat," I said, standing up from the table, angry. "And next time, when they come looking for *me*—"

"Look, I'm sorry, Stormy!" she exclaimed, her eyes bright with tears. "I'm just so worried about them. Lydia can't survive without her oxygen! She could be dead, for all I know!"

"Roberta, it's not fair of you to guilt me, especially considering how Lee and Lydia have treated me," I began, but the words died in my throat as I heard a loud *thunk* from the direction of the living room.

"What the fuck was that?" Roberta whispered, immediately on her feet.

"It sounded like it came from outside," I whispered back, and made my way towards the living room, terrified of what I would find. Just as I reached the front door, I heard what sounded like a screeching, rusted bolt being pushed into place, followed by a slight *thud*. I knew what it was before I saw it— the window. Someone was trying to open my window!

I ran into the living room, holding only my phone, Roberta fast on my heels. I stopped in my tracks.

Blinken sat in the living room, licking at a paw, nonplussed.

I ran to him, scooping him up and snuggling my face into his fur. He smelled terrible, like an old barn, a combination of turpentine or some other chemical, and his own pee.

Roberta said behind me, "Any chance that cat was just hiding all this time?"

"No," I said, my voice quiet with anger. "He reeks. He's been held somewhere."

"I saw a barn just outside," she said. "Any chance he was hiding in there?"

"Blinken hates the barn," I said. "Tess used to keep him in there when he was a kitten and he'd meow and meow to be let out. He'd never go in there now unless someone forced him." I inspected him all over. "Didn't you hear that thump? Somebody came up on my fucking porch, opened the window, and just tossed him inside." I pointed. "See? Look at the glass. There's fingerprints."

"We should probably call the police, then," Roberta said, though she didn't sound so sure. "And now we know that window has a broken lock. You should get that fixed. But at least we know they didn't use your spare key."

"It wouldn't have mattered," I said bitterly.

I continued pressing my face into Blinken's fur, despite his meows of protest. I had been so afraid that whoever had taken him would hurt him, maybe even kill him. I didn't even care that he smelled awful, or that he was scratching my arms, trying to get down. I looked up with resolve. "But first, I'm going out there to see if I can't catch whoever it was."

"Stormy, that's a bad idea. It's not safe—"

But I was already out the door, bounding down the steps and into the woods.

It was growing dark already, and the tall pine trees cast shadows on the needle-covered ground as I ran. I could tell by the disturbed forest floor that someone had been here very recently, and I followed the haphazard tracks until I was far into the woods. I turned and looked back; my trailer was barely visible in the distance. I'd been back here before, with Tess; we'd occasionally go on walks, or what he jokingly called "pre-school hunting." Having been raised in a family of boys in South Georgia, Tess had grown up with a rifle in his hand, and he loved deer hunting. To his credit, when he'd married me, the vegan, he'd stopped—we didn't even own a rifle in our entire time together. But he still enjoyed the sport of it— tracking and scavenging the woods for signs of a buck. He'd teased me relentlessly, but I knew he'd enjoyed those times we'd spent together, foraging through the thick, dense woods, him teaching me the ins and outs of hunting without ever firing a gun. Together, we'd spotted many a majestic stag, beautiful does, and my favorite, the gangly, spotted fawns. I smiled at the memory, stepping further through the trees. We'd been in this exact spot many times before, but I'd never gone further than this, and definitely not alone. The prickles on my arms didn't do much for my confidence.

I was fairly certain I was alone, and whoever it was had long since run off into the night, but the sense of foreboding was still very much present. I crept forward, following the disturbed patches of earth, taking note that it was getting darker, and made my way through the trees. The last time I'd been deep in a forest like this, back near Boston, Phillip had thrown me over his shoulder and carried me, running like lightning, to safety. I'd protested hotly, insisting I could take care of myself, and I still could, but damn if I didn't miss the feel of his arms around me, feeling him close to me, hearing the beating of his heart.

Another quarter mile into the forest, the trail went cold.

Spiky, waxen pine needles covered the ground in every direction, in an undisturbed and thick layer. Gossamer spider webs trailed from the spiky branches, and I walked straight into one, blinking rapidly and tearing the feathery, sticky strands from my face. Whoever had taken Blinken was long gone, disappeared into the thick of the woods. There was no way I'd find them now, and there wasn't a single clue to go on.

As I picked the wispy strands of web from my face, I noticed a beautiful, huge orb-weaver perched on an intricate web just above my eyeline. She was black with bright yellow markings, suspended perfectly still in her elaborate home. "I'm sorry I disturbed your home," I said stupidly, peering at her markings, captivated. "Aren't you just a *beauty.*"

I'd never seen an orb-weaver this large before. I stared at her, willing her to move, to flex those spindly, inky-black legs and meander up her intricate web, wishing I'd brought my phone to take a picture. But she was suspended in dusk, seemingly in a meditative calm I wished I could feel.

I stared at her for another moment, marveling in her beauty, then turned to go. It would be full dark soon. I'd never ventured this far out into the woods before (in fact, I'd passed the property line long ago; this had to be someone else's property, and I had no idea whose), and clearly I wasn't going to find whoever had trespassed on my land. With a sigh, I turned around and headed back towards the house, but as I did, a flash of color caught my eye.

On the ground several yards away, tucked deep into a bush of wild blackberries, was a black ball cap.

I ran over, ignoring the brambles and thorns that pricked my hand, immediately erupting in stinging, itchy madness, and grabbed the cap. It was a black cap emblazoned with the Georgia "G" in white, lined with red, the opposite of the usual logo, which was black. It was an odd cap, not one that you normally saw, and I recognized it immediately. Lee Courtenay had been wearing this cap the day I bumped into him at the farmers' market, and I had seen him wearing it many times since. I turned the cap over in my hands, imagining it still felt warm, though that couldn't be possible. The cap was pristine, no dirt or webs stuck to it, not even a streak of red Georgia clay marring it. As I held it in my hands, I knew without a doubt that Lee had been here, and recently. I held the hat up to my nose, recognizing the scent, a smell that had become ingrained somehow. The scent was of clean hair, cologne, and his own unique cocktail of pheromones. This was no doubt Lee's.

Cradling the cap in my hands, I walked back towards the house, carefully following my own tracks so I wouldn't get lost. It was fully dark now, and I could hear the sounds of the night ramping up—the crickets and cicadas, the crunch of pine needles far off in the distance, warning me of some critter—a fox or coyote, perhaps—out in the birthing dusk to find their nightly prey.

By the time I got back to my porch, the stars were out, shining coldly down on me in silent observation. Roberta was waiting on the porch, holding an irritated-looking Blinken in one hand, and biting her nails on the other. "Fuck! I thought you'd never come back!" she exclaimed as I came up the steps. "Did you find anything?" Then she saw the hat in my hands, her eyes wide. She sat Blinken onto the porch, and he darted into the house. "Um, Stormy. I know that hat. Is that—"

"Yes," I said, holding it out to her. "It's Lee's."

Roberta didn't say another word, just turned on her heel and ran back into the trailer, clutching the hat to her chest.

As I trailed behind her, I said, "I just can't see how—or why—Lee would take Blinken, and then bring him back." I talked to Roberta's back, leaning against the kitchen counter as she peered at the hat under my stove light. "I know he's done some shady shit in the past, but I felt like we reached an understanding. And this isn't like him, anyway. I don't think—"

"Stormy, shut up." I looked at Roberta in surprise. "Come see this."

I walked over to the stove where she held the hat under the bright light of the vent hood. "Look."

I hadn't been able to see it in the darkened woods, but on the inside of the hat, written in what appeared to be Sharpie, barely visible against the matte black of the cloth, was a message.

"He's got us. He's going to make her do it again. Time is running out. Go to The Wolfden." Below the message, scrawled in a messy, quick script, was simply, "Lee."

"What—and where—in the hell is the Wolfden?" I exclaimed in frustration, staring at the hat. "How are we supposed to find it?"

"Don't worry," Roberta said with a strange, grim smile. "I know where it is."

Nine

In the end, I broke first.

I had to keep Phillip updated, after all. I couldn't just *not* tell him everything that was happening, right?

That's how I justified it, anyway. In truth, I really just wanted to hear his voice.

My hand shook only a little as I listened to ring after ring, my ear pressed against the phone, sweaty and slick. Could ears sweat? Evidently, they could.

The phone rang three more times, and I was getting ready to hit "end" when finally, a voice on the other line answered, sounding breathless and gruff. "Hello?"

"Phillip," I said his name like an accusation, and immediately winced. I cleared my throat and tried again. "Phillip…it's Stormy. Are you busy?" I winced again. I sounded like a fool and he'd only just picked up. Why was I finding this so hard? It felt like years since we'd last spoken.

"Uh…no." Phillip's voice sounded far away, and yet close at the same time, as though he had climbed into my ear and taken up residence there. Just hearing him made my entire body erupt in warmth, even if I was coming off like a total goon. God, I missed him. "I'm not busy. Are you okay?"

His concern made me smile. So, he still cared. "Yes, I'm okay," I said, taking a beat to breathe in deeply, to collect my bearings. "But there is something."

"So, it wasn't just to hear my voice?" Phillip teased. There was something of our old chemistry there. My heart began to beat faster.

"Well, there's that," I said, trying for subtly flirty. But unfortunately, there was no time for more. "Something…something's going on here. I just…I just wanted to let you know about it." I swallowed. "I know that was a problem…before. Me not keeping you in the loop, taking your feelings into consideration. I'm not sure if you care at this point, but…I thought…just in case."

"What's happened?" Phillip's voice had turned cool with an edge of worry.

"A couple of days ago, Roberta came to see me. Remember her?" I quickly filled him in on Roberta's initial visit and how she'd enlisted me to help with Lydia and Lee's (and presumably Renee's) disappearance. Then I told him about Blinken, finding Lee's hat in the woods, and Roberta's ransacked apartment. Phillip was quiet as I recounted everything, and when he finally spoke, his voice sounded odd.

"I suppose you and Roberta are planning on visiting this place, this Wolfden," he said, his voice low. I could hear noises in the background; it almost sounded like children laughing, and…was that seagulls? I felt the skin on my arms prickle.

"She wants to, obviously," I said, biting my lip. "I told her to leave me out of it…at first. But now…"

"You're worried about Lee," Phillip said simply. "And you want to go."

"Well, not only Lee. Whoever it is, they stole my fucking

cat, Phillip," I said. "They've been in my house. They're obviously sending me a warning."

"Don't you think you ought to heed it?"

"Would *you* heed it?" I asked.

He paused. "Probably not. I'd be fucking pissed."

"Exactly."

Phillip groaned. I had to smile at that.

"I'm not asking you to help me," I said quickly. "I know you have your own stuff going on. This isn't your fight, not anymore." Phillip didn't respond. I swallowed again, wishing he'd fill some of these silences. "Hey, where are you, anyway?"

"What do you mean?" he asked.

"It's a simple question, Phillip. You're not in Boston," I said. "I can hear seagulls in the background. You're at a beach." I thought back to Tybee, the figure I thought I'd seen emerging from the water. I'd finally managed to convince myself that I'd imagined it, but now…were there any beaches near Boston? My knowledge of geography was shockingly bad.

"Where are you?" I repeated.

The silence was becoming uncomfortable; Phillip was being so careful, cautiously editing himself before speaking. As though he needed to censor himself, keep himself aloft from the conversation. It hurt my feelings. All this talk of trust, and how I'd broken it, and now he was being cagey. I was beginning to think Phillip didn't really want to be talking to me after all. So why, then, had he answered my call? I dug my fingernails into my hand. If he wasn't going to talk, then I wouldn't, either. I'd be damned if I was the only one making a fool of myself.

"I took a few days on my own, to decompress," Phillip said finally in a strained voice, after a long pause that stretched out like taffy. He coughed. "Stormy, are you sure you want to be handling this on your own?"

"I don't want to be handling it at all," I admitted. "But I'm sure. And I'm not on my own. I've got Roberta. I don't want to drag you into anything else. I just wanted to…let somebody know. Let you know. Just in case something happens."

"I don't like the sound of this," Phillip said.

"I know," I agreed. "But I have to check it out. I can't just ignore it."

"I get it. Just…Stormy, please take care of yourself," he said. I could hear the wind whipping around him through the phone, and I yearned to be standing with him on some peaceful stretch of beach, just watching the wind move through his dark black hair, the tides flowing around his ankles. When we'd gone to Driftwood together, he'd been so captivated, so moved by it. He'd been so beautiful that day; it had been the start of my falling for him. We'd shared stories, shared our pain, then hugged standing there in the sand. I'd have given anything to go back to that day. That he'd go to the beach without me made me sick with envy and regret. Where was he? He obviously didn't want me to know and that hurt.

I wanted to let it all pour out of me, to tell him how I felt, how much I missed him, to beg him—*just let me come to you, let me be with you, please…I'll come to wherever you are, I'll do whatever I have to to earn your trust back…just let me be with you*—but instead, I swallowed again and said, "I will. I promise."

"Call me if you need me."

"Okay."

I hung up before he could hear the tears in my voice. I sat the phone on the coffee table and stared at it, willing him to call me back, to tell me he was coming, not because he had to, but because he wanted to. But the phone didn't ring.

It was silent in my living room. Roberta had left to go

pack, and Blinken, newly restored to his habitat, had sauntered back to my bedroom to sleep on my fleece blanket. He seemed remarkably recovered from his ordeal already, one life down and eight to go.

My nerves were shot. Who had Lee, and why had they come here, taken my cat, and risked being found out? Why had they brought Lee along? That part made the least amount of sense. Or was Lee behind the whole thing? He had kidnapped me, after all—it was true that I'd trusted him, had believed his story about Guthrie and Lydia and how they'd used him as a pawn, but was it possible he was still trying to manipulate me? Was he capable of doing me real harm? I had to entertain it as a possibility, even if I didn't really believe it.

God, I missed Phillip. Hearing his voice had momentarily restored me, but now that I'd hung up, the empty hole in my heart seemed three times as big as it was before. My chest actually ached with it. Knowing he was off somewhere, enjoying leisurely time at the beach, moving on with his life, while I was back home getting myself knee-deep in more shit, filled me with sadness.

The truth was, nobody was to blame. Phillip and I could go round and round with our guilt, blaming each other, blaming ourselves, but the reality of the situation was we had both been treated like pawns, dragged into some weird game of magic that neither of us knew the rules to. We'd acted in accordance with what we thought was right, what we thought would keep the other safe. We'd made a series of missteps, trusted the wrong people. Maybe we'd both been wrong every step of the way, who knew, but there was one thing I knew for sure:

I would hunt down every last person responsible for what we'd been through, and I would deal them some justice.

Roberta and I had been travelling for about forty-five minutes, and already my butt had gone numb. The isolated stretch of highway was lined with marshes, and I could still smell the sea, faint but detectable, even though we were many miles north of the ocean. Roberta had told me that the Wolfden was on the outskirts of Hinesville, heading towards Glennville, a dry, scorched wasteland of faded storefronts and dirty fast-food shacks that I'd only been to once. "You'll just have to see the place," she'd said when I'd asked about it. "There's really no way to explain it."

Her cryptic attitude annoyed me, but I didn't press her further. I had too much on my mind. My conversation with Phillip had left a weird feeling in my gut—he was keeping something from me, besides just his location. Which I supposed he had every right to do, since we were no longer together, and since I'd done the same to him just a few short days before. But it was an odd feeling for me, not knowing his mind. Maybe now I knew how he'd felt about me all along.

I had tried to get into Phillip's mindset to figure out why he was so conflicted. Whatever was eating at him, whatever had caused him to break things off and head out on his own, had nothing to do with controlling me or being a savior. I didn't think he was even mad at me, not really.

I did bear some guilt for Phillip's feelings towards Lee. I had kept him in the dark about Lee's motives, about the strange, unlikely friendship that had sprung up between us. There was no way to explain it to Phillip in a way he'd understand, that I had a fondness for the guy who had kidnapped me, whose parents had been using me in a magical tug of war, the guy who had trespassed at my house and lied to me and watched me get hurt. He'd indirectly landed both Phillip and me in the hospital. And yet, I still wanted to help him.

Phillip would not understand that. He'd think it was madness, brainwashing, complete and utter idiocy. Of course he felt betrayed, jealous, and suspicious—after all, how could I explain the weird tie I had to Lee without acknowledging that the guy clearly had a thing for me? I couldn't deny it.

I had kept my plans a secret, not once but twice, and ruined my own relationship. For Lee. Why the hell had I done that?

Phillip was worried about Lee and me, sure—part of it was probably good old-fashioned, red-blooded jealousy, and I had to admit that if the tables were turned, I'd likely feel the same. But deep down, Phillip had to know there was nothing there. He knew he could trust me. Whatever it was had nothing to do with Lee, or even Barb, or anyone in our circle. Something else was eating at Phillip, making him worry.

I shook my head, staring out the window. The land that whizzed by as we drove along the straight, cracked asphalt of the highway was flat and joyless. Faded, even. Tufts of dried out, yellowed grass covered the dusty red ground—it had been a long, long time since this town had seen rain—from my vantage point, I could see crumbling cabins and mobile homes with decaying front porches, busted out windows; dried-up ponds, slick with green algae; an abandoned pool hall, bars on the windows, the parking lot empty but for one lone Ford pickup with the tires removed, propped up on cinderblocks with the hood open to the elements. It was stark and invoked a feeling of loneliness, or despair, even. I hadn't seen a single soul on the drive, only the hollowed-out remnants of homes, the odd beat-up car, and the lingering gray smoke from a fire off in the distance. "What's with the smoke?" I asked, wrinkling my nose. I could smell the acrid stench even with the windows rolled up. "Is somebody around here stupid enough to actually burn trash in a drought?"

"No," Roberta answered. "They're controlled fires. From Fort Stewart."

"Why do they do that?"

She shrugged. "No idea. Training stuff, maybe? You grow up around here, you get used to it. It's always smoky as hell and the air stinks."

"Delightful," I grabbed my bottle of water and took a long sip. "So, you grew up around here?"

"In Hinesville, mainly," Roberta said. "And here and there and everywhere."

"I grew up in Hinesville, too," I said, and she smiled a little, her eyes still on the road.

"By the time I was fourteen, I was out of there, though. One of my dad's brothers was stationed at Fort Stewart for a long time, and he lived really near here. I stayed with him a lot as a kid. I always hated it."

"How come?" I asked, interested despite myself.

"Look at it." Roberta gestured, her hand hitting the glass of the window. "It never rains, everything is crumbling and falling apart, and everyone is poor as shit, drugged out, or a drunk, or both. It's a wasteland. I never hated my uncle, but I did hate this place."

"Those trees are pretty, though," I said as we passed a cluster of pine trees surrounding a marsh. "It's so nice and flat out here. I bet it's pretty at night, all the stars visible and everything."

"I guess." Roberta shrugged. "We never stayed till dark. All my uncle's dickwad drunk friends were usually at his house by then. They got handsy. They—he and my brother— tried to keep me from them as best they could." She looked at me from the corner of her eye. "Funny you like that patch of land, though. Just down that dirt road is Uncle Albert's land. He had a trailer back there, tucked off in the trees. I had a few happy times there."

"Did you want to stop and say hello?" I asked, realizing with surprise that I was actually interested in Roberta's family. There was something about her I found intriguing—intriguing and likeable.

"Nah," Roberta said, the SUV picking up speed. Her lips were pressed together tightly. "Albert died a few years back. Lung cancer. Trailer got sold and hauled off to Ludowici." I smiled at the way she said it, with even more drawl than I did —*Loo-dah-wissy*. "There's nothing back there now but pine trees and mosquitos and a crumbling shed or two. And a swamp that stinks like death."

I had met Roberta's brother once, when he'd come to bail out Tess from jail. It was curious that she'd not mentioned him until now. "Your brother...does he still live around here?"

She shook her head. "No." She paused for a moment, then sighed. "He's actually in jail. He gets out next year."

I wanted to press Roberta for more—I was curious if his incarceration was drug-related, considering the connection to Tess—but her tone stopped me. It was like brittle, broken glass —vulnerable and jagged at the same time. These were painful things for her, things that were hard to talk about. That, I could relate to.

"I'm sorry," I said, putting a hand on her arm. "I imagine it's hard being back in the area among all those memories." I could relate to that, too. In fact, I hadn't been "home" in years. I avoided both of my parents like the plague.

"Nah," she said again, shooting me a crooked smile. "Home sweet home."

The way Roberta's chin had jutted out when she'd mentioned the drugs in the area, the judgmental gleam in her eye, the sad, broken look that had passed over her face when she'd talked about her uncle...Those were tell-tale signs of a woman who had not quite reconciled her childhood, who was still trying to work through the trauma. I knew because I was that same woman.

Dammit, I liked her. Liked her a lot. I could relate to Roberta. I settled back against the seat and tried to make sense of her. Proud, strong but a little broken, loyal to her family, but still working through some major shit, doing all she could to put her past behind her…None of that seemed to jive with a woman who'd date someone like Tess. She seemed completely at odds with my ex-husband in almost every way. If anything, she was more like me. That might explain Tess's attraction to *her*, but…every time I'd brought him up, she'd almost blanch, as though she were ashamed of her history with him. She seemed to have no affectionate feelings towards him—I had more lingering love for him than she did. And yet, I knew that she'd been dating him as recently as two weeks ago. She'd been in Sloan's shop, trying to book a haircut. She'd gone with him to Boston to follow Phillip and me. But why? She'd said Tess's involvement was all business, and I could believe that, but what was Roberta's end goal?

So, I liked Roberta. But could I trust her? Why was I going on this fool's errand with a woman who had betrayed me, who I didn't really know? In fact, the more I got to know Roberta, the less any of it made sense. I had to find out more.

"So tell me…how—why—did you get mixed up with Tess?" I asked, unable to stop the words from tumbling out of my mouth.

"Let's get to where we're going," Roberta said, glancing over at me. She was gripping the steering wheel hard. "And I'll tell you everything. I promise."

"Stormy, I'd like you to meet Nikolai, and this here's Jamie." I stood awkwardly in the tiny, musty-smelling foyer, staring into the warm glow of the small room at two men who both rose to greet me. I took quick notice of the way the trailer was decorated—pagan tapestries in varying colors, a fuzzy black light poster that would've been at home in the early 90s, band posters—Thin Lizzy, Black Sabbath, Iron Maiden, AC/DC— and an elaborate piece of framed artwork that took up one entire wall. I was pretty sure it was an Alex Gray print, the artist who worked with Tool. So one of these dudes was a hippie metalhead, and the other more of an old school rock good ol' boy. A match made in heaven. I had to laugh, imagining just how much weed must get smoked in this place.

Extending my hand to shake each of theirs, it was pretty clear which guy was which. Nikolai was tall, almost as tall as Phillip; I guessed he had to be at least 6'4". His platinum blond hair was long, pulled back in a long braid, and perched atop his head was a ragged-out black beanie. He wore a flannel shirt over long johns with thumb holes cut out and had paint splatters on his hands. As I shook his hand, I felt a jolt of electricity course through me; his bright blue eyes bore into mine, as though he were trying to memorize me in a glance. He was intense, this one. "Hi, Stormy," he said in a quiet voice, a low croon that forced me to lean into him.

"You kind of remind me of that guy from *Game of Thrones,*" I said to him nervously. "Viserys."

"I'm pretty sure you just insulted me," he said, but smiled.

Jamie had warm, dark-brown eyes that sparkled as he extended his own calloused hand. He was shorter, clad in a simple white t-shirt and black leather biker jacket, cargo pants and scuffed black boots. He had a bandana tied around his dark, shaggy brown hair, though I could see in the dim light that his temples were threaded with gray. "I'm Jamie," he said, his full lips erupting into a sweet smile, illuminating the freckles on his cheeks. "Welcome to our humble abode."

I felt myself relax, an ease I hadn't felt in weeks. Standing in the small trailer, I felt a sense of kinship, of peace, as if I'd known these two forever. It was strange, but I really felt as though I knew them. It might be just a small singlewide in the middle of a trailer/RV park, but the place was warm and inviting, even scattered with liquor bottles and Natty Light cans, and with a bright purple bong on full display on the chipped glass coffee table. I had the sense that I was safe here, and always would be.

"That your Harley parked outside?" I asked the brown-eyed man, Jamie, trying to make conversation.

He beamed. "Hell yeah, it is. That's my baby. Wanna go for a spin?"

"I might take you up on that sometime," I said with a laugh. "When I get up the guts."

"Ain't nothin' to it, sugar," he said with a grin. I might've bristled at anyone else calling me that, but there was no hint of ownership or malice when he said it. He was just being friendly. "Just hop on the back, scoop up your legs, and let the wind take ya."

"You guys look tired," the tall, blond guy—Nikolai —said, his icy blue eyes still staring into mine. Something about the way he looked at me made me feel strange and almost dizzy. "Why don't you sit? Can I get you guys a drink?" His voice had a clipped quality to it, as though he carefully chose every word before saying it.

"I'd love a shot of something," Roberta said, gesturing towards the liquor bottles on the counter. "Whatever you've got."

"Just water for me," I said, settling onto the threadbare but comfortable couch. The room smelled of sandalwood and weed and some old-fashioned cologne. Halston, maybe? My grandfather had worn that. I didn't remember him, but my mother had kept a bottle that had belonged to him on a high shelf. Sometimes I had taken it down, inhaling the sweet, musky scent and trying to imagine what he had been like.

"They're both great guys, salt of the earth," Roberta said to me in a quiet voice as Nikolai and Jamie made their way into the small kitchen. "We'll be safe here."

"Are you sure?" I asked, even though I felt that she was right.

"I'm sure," she said firmly. "I've known them both my whole life. Lee has, too. Trust me, they're good guys."

I didn't really doubt her; they both seemed sweet enough, even if the blond guy made me feel a little odd. It wasn't a bad kind of odd, though. The shorter guy gave me an easy, friendly vibe. I couldn't help but have my dander up, though. After all I'd been through the past few weeks, I was finding it hard to trust anybody, including myself. If there was anything I'd proven, it was that I was incapable of adequately judging a person's character.

Nikolai came back into the room first, holding a cold bottle of water, which he handed to me as he sat down. "So, what brings you guys here?" he asked in that same low, clipped tone.

"Let's wait for Jamie and I'll tell you both at the same time," Roberta said. Nikolai's brow furrowed as he realized this wasn't a social call. He leaned back against the cushions and flipped on the stereo, and I felt the hairs on my arms stand up as the Bloomer Demons' debut album began to play through the speakers. I swallowed and pasted on a smile; Nikolai had no way of knowing anything about my involvement with Phillip, or that Phillip was alive. Surely not...but the goosebumps continued up my arms and back as I looked into his pale eyes and saw a ghost of a smile playing on his lips. I had the strangest sensation that he had something he wanted to tell me, but he wasn't going to until we were alone.

Jamie came back into the room cradling four shot glasses filled with an amber liquid. "Apologies, darlin'," he said as he handed each of us a glass. "All's we had was a dusty old bottle of amaretto."

"Fuck's sake, Jamie—" Roberta began.

"I really shouldn't," I broke in, trying to hand the shot glass back. "I'm fine with just water."

"It's barely Kool-Aid, darlin'," Jamie said with that same easy grin. "Gotta feeling we're gonna be talking about some heavy shit, so you go ahead and tip it on back, now."

I smiled, disarmed, and did as I was told. The second the liquid hit the back of my throat, I felt as if I'd swallowed fire, and I gasped.

"You liar!" Roberta sputtered, breaking into a raucous cough. Jamie began to laugh as he took a seat beside Nikolai, slapping the side of his leg. "You said it was amaretto! What the hell *was* that?"

"Just whiskey," Jamie said, still laughing. "You're getting soft on me. Can't handle honest liquor no more."

"That's no whiskey I've ever had," Roberta said, her face red. She was still coughing. I stayed silent, trying to swallow through the fiery pain that was coursing down my throat. Holy shit, that was some strong booze. "What brand is it?"

"I ain't got around to naming it yet."

"Fuck, that's home brew?" Roberta wiped her mouth, glaring at Jamie. "Seriously, dude. Not cool."

"It's good!" Jamie protested, his eyes still a-twinkle. "I thought it was a real good batch."

"Asshole," she said, but the fire had gone out of her. I was still having trouble swallowing, and my eyes watered miserably. I wiped at my face, trying not to meet Nikolai's piercing gaze, which was unwavering as his eyes worked over me. He was starting to freak me out.

As if sensing my discomfort, he wrenched his eyes away from me and said softly, "So what's going on, Roberta?"

"It's Lee," Roberta said, putting the shot glass on the table, her own voice going low, as though somebody might overhear. "And Lydia. And maybe Renee." She swallowed. "They're missing."

She recounted the story to them quickly, starting with Lee's disappearance, mentioning the break-in at her house, my cat being stolen, and my finding Lee's hat in the woods with his odd message. I was grateful that she hadn't mentioned Phillip or gone into too many details about why I was involved. Though I knew that if these guys were going to help us, they'd have to know more eventually. Maybe they already did. Whoever they were, they were obviously part of some familial unit that included Roberta and Lee. I felt the old loneliness creeping back in as I sat there, watching Roberta tell the story. I wasn't part of this group; I was an outsider.

Both men nodded as they listened, Jamie's soft face conveying no sense of urgency or danger, though his eyes flashed. Nikolai kept glancing over to me, as though he were searching my face for something. But for what, I wondered. Did he suspect me of wrongdoing? Did he think I was a liar? Did he know about Phillip? I stared back at him defiantly, willing him to say something, but he was silent. As Roberta finished getting them up to speed, he threw back his shot and swallowed it easily, putting the glass down on the coffee table with a *clink.*

"And Lee told you to come here," Nikolai said, his question coming out more like a statement. "That's…surprising."

"Oh, come on, that drama is so over," Roberta said, giving him a look. "Isn't it? I mean, seriously, after everything that's happened…"

"He can always count on us," Jamie said. "Always could. Lee knows that. But Nikolai's right. It is weird that he'd send you here. After everything with…"

"I think I'm missing something," I said.

All three of them turned to me. Jamie laughed affably. Roberta looked uncomfortable. "There's a lot to fill in on both sides," she said finally, seeming to hesitate.

I anxiously grabbed my bottle of water and took a long swig, my heart thumping in my chest. Phillip's voice was still coming out of the speakers, one of my favorite songs, "Blood and Silver"—a thumping, industrial tune. "Why don't we start with why you guys are being weird about Lee," I said. "And why he'd send us here."

"It's hard to explain," Roberta began, just as Jamie said:

"Well, it's complicated, darlin'…"

"Let's go outside," Nikolai said suddenly, sitting up straight on the couch. He was still looking only at me. "It'll make more sense if we can show you."

I looked at him warily, but Roberta and Jamie both jumped up, so I did too, sighing with reluctance and swaying a little on my feet. Surely Jamie's home brew wasn't *that* strong. Nikolai stood and walked over to open the trailer's front door, holding it open for us. I followed him across the yard and into the trees down a small path that wasn't unlike the trail at my own place, but off in the distance, I could see a bright, shining orange light. Roberta and Jamie both followed me wordlessly, Jamie stopping briefly to light a Newport. The air around me smelled heady and fragrant, like burning pine needles and sage. I breathed it in, enjoying the experience.

We came into a little clearing just off the road, and I stood there for a moment, staring. When Roberta had first pulled into the trailer park, I'd been scrolling on my phone, hoping for messages from Phillip, of which there were still none, and I hadn't been paying attention. Now that I was really looking, my breath caught in my throat. I wasn't sure why, but I felt almost overcome with emotion, and the weirdest feeling of déjà vu, as though I had been here before.

State Route 196 loomed in front of me, dark and straight and completely empty; not one single headlight showed in the dark. The entrance to the park was lined with smooth, tan-colored rocks, and just above was a large, handmade wooden archway, made with what looked to be little pickets, like something you'd see on a campground. The pickets spelled out the words *the wolfden* in all lowercase letters. On either side of the archway were mismatched cheap solar lights, illuminating the words and casting an eerie glow onto the stones beneath. A smaller metal sign was tacked to one side of the archway. *Mobile home park, RV lot, and community for wayward souls,* it read in painted black letters.

Just off to the right of the archway, a bonfire blazed; it was so large, I could feel the heat on my backside from yards away. It glowed bright and huge, casting shadows onto the highway. Gathered around the fire in various forms of seating—everything from plastic lawn chairs to upside-down paint cans to an actual easy chair, with huge tufts of stuffing coming out of each arm—were what could only be described as a motley crew, the various people warming their hands by the fire, drinking out of Solo cups, chatting and singing and dancing to the music that came out of a small portable radio that looked like a relic from the 80s. Lynyrd Skynyrd's "Ballad of Curtis Loew" was currently playing, and I began to feel like I'd stepped back in time. A woman was swaying to the music, clad in Daisy Dukes shorts and a bright purple halter, her hair an even brighter shade of purple. Beside her was a man wearing a trucker hat and light blue overalls. Beside him, an elderly gentleman that could have been anywhere from fifty to a hundred and fifty, was sipping a Natty Light that he held with both hands, cradling it like a prized jewel.

"Welcome to the Wolfden," Nikolai said in a low, proud voice. He stood to the right of me, his hands tucked into the pockets of his heavy black coat. His eyes seemed to glow in the dark as he stared at me.

"So, it's a mobile home park and an RV park," I said, staring into the fire, not sure what else to say. It was a strange scene, but so weirdly familiar. The hairs on the back of my neck were standing at attention.

"Hardly," Nikolai said with a smile. "I mean, it is a trailer park and an RV park, yes. But that's the least of what it is. This is a community. The people here, all of us—we're outsiders, stragglers, the ones who get looked down on in society because we're too poor or we're addicts, or we've made mistakes. The loners without families, folks who might otherwise be homeless, those of us who aren't quite right up here." He pointed at his temple. "We're family. We have each other's backs when nobody else does. And this circle here"—he gestured to the people gathered around the bonfire— "some of them have nothing in common except this place, but that's all it takes. Because we're family, for better or worse. There is always protection within this circle. Here, we stand together. Here, we all belong."

The woman in the purple halter top stopped swaying to the music long enough to glance at me and give a timid little wave. The song changed to Lou Reed's "Perfect Day," an odd segue anywhere but here, and she resumed her swaying, this time in a more ethereal, spiritual rhythm. Suddenly, she appeared less silly and cliché, and more beautiful, peaceful, serene. I smiled back at her.

"And I take it Lee Courtenay was, but for some reason is no longer, part of this group?" I asked.

"Yes, ma'am," Jamie said, pressing a Natty Light into my hand. I didn't bother to protest, even though I hated the stuff. When he turned away, Nikolai took it from me with a wink.

Out here in the darkness, he didn't seem half as menacing as he had inside.

"Lee and Roberta are both part of this family." he said. "We had a little bit of a falling out with Lee, but…well, he's still family."

"And Lydia?" I asked. "I can't imagine her traipsing all the way here from Boston."

"No, but she's an honorary family member," Jamie answered. "We feel like we know her. And because she's Lee's mama, she can count on us."

"How did you end up here?" I asked Roberta. The cool air had brought out two red blossoms on her high cheeks. She was leaning into Jamie in a way that made me think perhaps they had once been involved…or still were.

"I'll tell you that story, but…it's a long one, and we're short on time," she answered, taking a sip of beer. It was the second time she'd deflected me when I'd asked her those sorts of questions, and I was beginning to wonder why that was. "I gotta tell you guys, I'm really worried about Lee. He can take care of himself, and he's been in no shortage of clusterfucks, but this time, it feels different…like, I get the feeling he's really in danger."

A chill crept up my back and it wasn't just from being outside in the cold. I nodded. "As much as I hate to admit it, I get the same feeling." I let out a heavy sigh. "Ever since I found his hat in the bushes, I've felt it."

"Well, in that case," Jamie said, shrugging his broad shoulders and fixing us with a business-like smile, "We'd better get to fixing shit."

It turned out the woman with purple hair was named Clara. She had piercing green eyes, brought to life by all that purple, and I couldn't stop staring at her. Her arms and legs were full of roped muscle, and despite her girly clothing, her feet were clad in what looked to be steel-toed combat boots. She was one of the prettiest women I'd ever seen, but there was something lean and mean about her, like a string that was wound several degrees too tight. She could clearly kick my ass to hell and back. I decided I'd stay on her good side, no matter what.

She tipped back her bottle of Mountain Dew and fixed her eyes on Roberta and me. "What the devil have you gals gotten into?" she asked in a husky voice.

"Rather, what has *Lee* gotten us into," Roberta answered, and Clara broke into a smile. "It isn't the first time, as you recall."

"He is rather…uh…what you millennials call…what is it?" the man sitting down cradling his beer said with a grin. I noticed that his gray hair was in a neat, and very outdated, mullet. It curled at the ends, just at his shoulders. "Problematic? Yeah. Lee can be problematic."

"The meaning is different to how we use it, but yeah," Roberta answered with a laugh. "I'd say that's fair. He's always getting into trouble. And now he's gotten himself in real danger. I'm scared, y'all."

"Are we going to say his name?" the man across from Clara said in a tight voice. "Or are we still treating him like he's Voldemort?"

"Tyson loves Harry Potter," Jamie said to me affably, tipping back his beer with a grin. "He's forty-five years old and he doesn't have any kids, but he's obsessed. Don't ask me why, I couldn't tell ya."

"Are you talking about Guthrie?" I asked point-blank, and Clara made a little surprised noise, like a frightened mouse. It sounded strange coming out of someone so imposing and tough.

"You know Guthrie?"

"More than I care to." I wondered how they would react if I told them just how well I knew Guthrie. I looked to Roberta, who was staring into her beer can. Obviously, these folks didn't know what had gone down at Guthrie's a few days ago. They didn't know that he'd been shot and was presumably dead. Roberta hadn't gone back that far when she'd told Jamie and Nikolai what was going on, and I wondered why. Was she trying to protect me, or was there another reason? One thing was certain; if Roberta didn't want to tell them, I wasn't going to, either.

"If you know Guthrie, then you also must know—" Clara started, then suddenly bit off her words with another squeak. I noticed Roberta giving her an odd stare.

"If you know Guthrie, then you know," Nikolai cut in, gesturing towards an empty chair, which I took gratefully, "that we can't be too careful dealing with him. He's dangerous, and he'll fucking kill anybody as soon as look at them. Even Lee, if he's involved."

"He's not involved." A voice, clear and deep, sounded from behind us, and everyone turned around, craning their necks to see who had spoken.

I gasped. The man who belonged to the voice, standing just by the archway, had to be at least six foot five—almost Phillip's height and twice as stocky—and to say he was *imposing* was an understatement. Clad in a black leather jacket with a gray flannel shirt showing beneath, and ripped jean shorts that came just below the knee, he was wearing the same black steel-toed combat boots that I'd noticed on Clara, and what looked to be black knee braces. What little skin I could see was covered in tattoos. His hair was inky black and cut short, with an expanse of bangs sweeping over one eyebrow.

His ears were pierced, with little metal studs going from the lobes all the way up to the top, a ring in his nose and another in his eyebrow. As he stepped toward me, his hand outstretched to shake mine, I noticed a couple of light brown freckles across his broad nose, the only splash of muted color among all the black he wore. Dark eyeliner framed his beautiful almond shaped eyes. As I took his warm hand, I realized that one of his pupils was a snake-eye, and the other solid black; he was wearing contacts, obviously. The effect was striking and a little bit scary.

He smiled. "I don't believe we've met. I'm Benny."

That this imposing figure would have such impeccable manners and be called something mundane like *Benny* made me want to laugh, but I found myself frozen to the spot. Up close, I could see that Benny was literally covered head to toe in tattoos, and he was *huge.* Hard muscle rippled beneath his leather jacket, and his calves below where his cutoffs ended were enormous. I swallowed and dropped his hand, giving him a nervous smile. "Stormy Spooner," I said, my voice a little gruff. I cleared my throat and tried again. "Nice to meet you."

"So, what did you mean?" Roberta asked, appearing beside me. She seemed to know Benny well; he leaned forward and gave her a brotherly squeeze. Then he grabbed Clara with one huge arm, pulling her into his side and placing a kiss on her temple. She arched like a cat, clearly relishing his touch. "What did you mean when you said Guthrie's not involved? How do you know?"

Benny smiled, splaying out his large hands and his long, tapered fingers towards the fire to absorb its warmth. "Buddy of mine at the PD called me a minute ago. He wanted to give me a heads up," he said, grabbing a beer from the open cooler and cracking it open. He drank half its contents in one gulp. "Some guy and his son were out hiking, and they got lost. They saw something weird poking up out of the mud up ahead.

Turns out there was a body in there." He shook his head. "Normally, you sink a body in the marsh, it ain't coming back up. But the cloth he was wrapped in got snagged on a dead tree limb, so he was never fully submerged. Guy figured it was just a bag of trash somebody had dumped, so he pulled it up. Him and his kid got the shock of their life."

"What's that go to do with…" Jamie began, but his voice trailed off, two splotches of red appearing on his full cheeks.

"The body was Guthrie," Benny confirmed, turning his hands over and over in front of the fire. "Buddy recognized him right off. Ain't a cop for fifty miles that don't know what Guthrie Courtenay looks like. Turns out somebody murdered the son of a bitch. Shot him and threw him in the swamp." He looked at me with a strange smile. "Crazy, huh?"

I looked to Roberta for reassurance, but my fear only ramped up when I saw her face. She'd gone completely white.

TEN

A collective gasp rose up from those clustered around the bonfire. Roberta clung to me, her face still white. "Are you sure it was him?"

"Pretty damn sure," Benny replied. "My contact at the PD hasn't steered me wrong yet." His face was grave. "He couldn't wait to tell me. Guthrie had a lot of enemies."

"Us included," Clara said with a sniff.

"So he's really dead," Roberta said to me in a murmur. The unspoken word *still* hung between us in the air.

"Good riddance," a voice in the crowd called out, and I had to silently agree. Guthrie had done nothing but torture me. He'd ruined the lives of so many—Tess, Sloan, Lee, Phillip, and mine, too—and I'd be glad to see the back of him. I could only assume that some of the people here at the Wolfden had seen his ugly side, too, if their reactions to his death were any indication. At least now we knew that nobody had brought him back, that he was well and truly dead.

But looking at Roberta, whose face was still oddly pale, I figured she was thinking the same thing as me: How on earth had he ended up in a swamp, miles away from his house? Who had taken him and moved him, and why? And if Guthrie was dead, who had Lee?

I stared at the bonfire, wondering if I should tell these folks the whole truth—that it had been Lee who had killed Guthrie, and that I'd planned to bring him back, only he'd gone missing when I went back to do it. Didn't they deserve to know if they were going to help us find Lee? But the way Roberta had shaken her head at me, combined with Benny's odd little wink, made me think I should keep my mouth shut. I didn't know these people, and while they seemed to be no fans of Guthrie, I had no way of knowing if I could trust them.

Roberta looked really shaken, and it unnerved me. I hadn't seen her this rattled before. I went over and gave her a gentle squeeze to rally her. She put an arm around my waist and laid her head on my shoulder. "What does this mean for Lee and Lydia?" I asked, deciding to voice my concerns out loud. "They're missing, and their father and husband was just found dead in a marsh. Does that mean that whoever dumped Guthrie might have them?"

Roberta's eyes were scrunched shut. She shook her head, looking suddenly girlish.

"I hope not," Nikolai said, his eyes meeting mine again. My temple began to pound.

"Wait, back up. I'm missing something. Lee's missing?" Benny demanded, his eyes flashing with concern. His entire demeanor changed. "Since when?"

Roberta took a shaky breath and relayed the story for the third time, and as she spoke, Benny paced back in forth in a little circle, which looked ridiculous since he was so huge. His face was full of fury, his playful mood from before all but gone. When Roberta got to the part where I'd found the hat in the woods with Lee's instructions to come to the Wolfden, a brief smile flashed across his face, but it was short-lived.

"Good. I'm glad he led you guys here," Benny said,

stroking his chin thoughtfully. His goatee was every bit as black as the rest of his hair. "But I don't like this. I don't like it at all. We know what this means."

"Lee and Lydia are still in danger," Clara said, her face grave. "More so than they were before."

"You bet your ass," Benny agreed. "If Lee reached out to us—to me—he's in a fucking mess. He wouldn't do that otherwise, not after what went down." I was curious what that meant, but we had more important concerns, so I didn't ask.

Roberta was still holding onto me. "Stormy and I have been trying to find him, but we have no idea where else to look. We've already been to Renee's, and she's gone, too. He's not at Guthrie's and nobody is at Lydia's. So where are they?" I could feel wetness on my shoulder from where she'd rested her head—she'd been crying.

"Roberta," I said abruptly. "Can we talk alone for a second?"

"Okay," she said, sounding surprised, and followed me away from the bonfire to a picnic table in Jamie and Nikolai's front yard. The air was at least twenty degrees colder away from the fire, and I shivered and pulled my jacket tighter around my body.

"I just thought of something," I said, my teeth beginning to chatter. "I'm surprised I didn't think of it before."

"What is it?"

"When Phillip and I went to Boston—well, before we went, actually—when Guthrie sent Lee and Shank and Tess, and well, *you*"—Roberta had the decency to look chagrined, knowing where I was going with this—"after us, we were being followed right off the bat. But Lee kept showing up in these weird places, warning me ahead of time. Trying to get me to change our plans and go home. He betrayed Guthrie to try and help me. More than once."

Roberta smiled. "Sounds like him. It wouldn't be the first time he had to run interference between his parents."

"What if he's doing that again? What if he hasn't been kidnapped so much as roped into being party to something, and he's creeping around behind the scenes, warning us, like he did before?"

"That does sound possible," Roberta said after a pause. "I'm surprised we didn't think of that, too. I just assumed he'd been kidnapped at gunpoint or something."

"I bet he returned my cat," I said, more sure of my theory as I thought about it. "Because he knew I'd be freaking out. And he left his hat, telling us to come here, on his way out."

"He's playing the long game," Roberta said thoughtfully.

"Evidently," I answered. "Too bad we don't know what game it is we're playing."

"Even if this is all true, though," Roberta said, "we have no idea what we're supposed to be doing *here.*"

I looked at her. "You know who has him, don't you?" I said. "All of you do."

She scrunched her eyes shut again.

"Roberta."

"I might," she said. "But I hope to hell I'm wrong."

"Can we trust these guys?" I asked her again. "*All* of them?"

"They're family," Roberta said firmly.

"That's great for you," I said. "But after everything I've been through, I can't just go along with you guys, hoping you're true to your word. I need more than *they're family.* I need to know that I'm safe here, and that these folks can be trusted—you know, with certain information, should it come to light." I pushed further. "They don't know who shot Guthrie, or that I was there, and I figure there's got to be some reason you're not in a hurry to tell them."

"You're right," Roberta said. "It's hard to explain, but

there's like a…a hierarchy here. I wanted to get the right information to the right people *first,* before everybody knows, if that makes any sense."

"Sounds like a mafia setup," I said, half-joking. "You've got to check in with the boss."

But Roberta didn't laugh. "You can trust these guys far more than you know," she said firmly. I stared at her, and she put a reassuring hand on my shoulder. "I swear," she said. "I'd stake my life on it. And yours." She lowered her voice, her face suddenly sad. "Though I hope it doesn't come to that."

Eleven

Back inside Jamie and Nikolai's cozy trailer, I was perched on the sofa with a glass of water in my hand, unable to calm my jumpy nerves. Sitting around the tiny living space were Roberta, Jamie, Nikolai, Clara, and Benny. Everyone else was still outside. I'd come to understand that this 'hierarchy' Roberta had mentioned included these people, plus herself. I wondered how I fit into the equation. I couldn't sit back and relax, and instead sat forward on the cushions, my shoulders tense, ready to jump up at any moment.

Jamie had finally gotten the hint that I didn't want to drink myself into oblivion and offered me something other than moonshine and beer. He was still being friendly and kind, but his face was a lot more serious now. Evidently learning of Guthrie's death had really shaken him. Gone were his easy-going smile and tinkling laugh; his face was set in a hard line.

"Where do we start?" he asked Benny, lighting a cigarette. "I can hop on the bike and go case a few places, ask a few folks when they last saw Lee. Get a feel for who might know something."

"He's good at that," Roberta said to me quietly. "He's got such a sweet baby face; people love to talk to him."

"You better shut up, darlin'," he said, a smile finally creeping through. There had definitely been something between the two of them at some point. The way Roberta kept cutting her eyes at him was decidedly not innocent, and the sexual tension when he teased her was evident.

Benny was rolling a clove cigarette around and around his fingers, but not smoking it. "That's a good idea, Jamie. But why don't you take Clara with you? Safety in numbers, plus she can talk to some of the guys who might appreciate a pretty face."

Clara looked pleased with that. She had changed from her purple halter and skirt into a pair of athletic shorts, a black t-shirt and hoodie, but she still had on her boots. On anyone else, it would have looked like a ridiculous get up, but it worked on her. Her huge leg muscles were on full display in the shorts, and I couldn't help but wonder what she did for a living to get so ripped. She and Benny were both massive.

"I can try to trace his phone," Nikolai piped up from the corner where he'd been plucking at a black bass guitar that didn't look unlike Phillip's. "I assume nobody's done that yet?"

"Nobody has that skill but you," Roberta said. "Maybe that was what Lee was hoping."

"Probably." Nikolai stood and headed down the hall, calling as he went, "I'll let you know if I find anything."

"What, is he gonna trace a phone from his bedroom?" I asked incredulously.

"Yeah," Roberta said, looking at me like I was a fool. "He's done it for us a bunch of times."

"You guys are next level," I said with a nervous laugh. "Jamie's a part-time interrogator, Nikolai traces phones, and Benny's got the cops in his pocket."

"And I'm the assassin," Clara said with a giggle. I cracked a small smile, wondering if she was telling the truth.

"I was joking outside, but you guys really *are* like the mob," I said with a grin, but nobody else seemed to find it funny.

"We've been working together a long time," Jamie said, one eyebrow slightly raised, and Roberta gave him a look.

My phone vibrated in my pocket, and I pulled it out. My heart lifted when I saw it was Phillip texting me. I missed him so much that every crumb of contact was enough to fly me to the moon. I opened the message immediately, eager to hear from him, ignoring everyone's curious looks.

Found him? was all the message said, but I still smiled. Phillip hated Lee, so even asking showed that he cared. About me, if nothing else. About what I was doing.

I typed out a response. *No, but we're hoping we'll know something soon. Got some interesting news. Can I call?* I frowned down at my phone, my thumb hovering over the "send" button. Should I ask to call? We'd agreed not to contact each other too often, and the last time I'd called him, he'd sounded like he hadn't wanted to talk to me. Flirty at first, then he'd cooled down to the point where I'd felt frostbitten when I hung up. I wasn't sure I wanted to put myself through that again. I deleted the last sentence and sent the message, hoping he'd call me instead.

But he didn't. As I sat there for the next twenty minutes, quietly listening to Roberta, Jamie, Benny, and Clara devise a plan, I waited and waited, but not only did he not call, he didn't text me back, either. I checked my phone several times, willing it to vibrate with an incoming message, but there was nothing.

I couldn't help but feel Phillip *was* sending me a message. He'd *just* texted me; it wasn't illogical to think he'd write back right away. His phone likely would have been in his hand when I responded. The fact that he didn't told me that he was deliberately being distant, putting space between us. I'd made the right call, deleting that last line.

Why reach out at all, if he was only going to go cold again? This was the second time he'd done it, and I couldn't understand it. Nor did I deserve it. The more I thought about it, the more I was beginning to think that all of Phillip's reasons for abandoning me were pretty weak, and pretty unfair.

Not to mention pretty fake.

There was something else going on. If only I had time to get to the bottom of it. But finding Lee was more important right now.

The entire two-line exchange with Phillip had put me in a funk, but I tried not to let it show, putting on an eager face for my newfound friends. A haphazard plan was being made to try and pinpoint Lee's location and then, if necessary, to extract those being held and bring them back to the Wolfden. I needed to pay attention lest I become a liability. I wanted to pull my weight, wanted to fit in. Right from the moment I'd stepped foot in their doorway, I'd known I wanted to be a part of this group, wanted them to accept me.

But even as I tried to pay attention, I couldn't think of anything but Phillip. Phillip, who didn't love me anymore. I loved him every bit as much as I ever had, and even though I had a cool new group of friends, nobody's company compared to his. I could distract myself as much as I wanted during the day, but when I laid in bed at night, the moment I closed my eyes, I saw him. Wanted to feel his arms around me, to know he was mine. All of that was gone and I didn't know what to do. Tears threatened to spill from my eyes, and I beat them into submission.

"...special skills?"

"Huh?" I jerked up and met Benny's dark, disconcerting eyes, the one with the snake-iris contact almost seeming to wink at me. If he noticed the tears dotting my eyes, he didn't acknowledge them.

"I asked if you had any special skills we should know about, anything that would help us find Lee," he said patiently, lighting another cigarette with a long, thin lighter, the kind you'd normally use for a candle or fireworks. I felt my shoulders straighten; this was just the kind of question that would have once thrown me into a spiral of self-doubt and insecurity, but I wasn't the same person anymore. I did, in fact, have some very special skills.

"Oh. Well...yes," I said, reaching a decision. I decided to throw caution to the wind and just put it all out there. "As a matter of fact, I'm...I'm a witch."

Clara snorted, but a look from Roberta silenced her.

"She's serious," Roberta said, and I gave her a grateful smile. She seemed a little uncomfortable with my sudden revelation, but I was glad she'd decided to have my back. "She's the real deal."

"I'm also a librarian," I said, feeling my cheeks color, worried I'd come off as braggy. "So I can rock the fuck out of some research."

"We'll double back to that," Benny said, pulling his chair close to me, turning it around backwards and sitting on it with his arms resting along the back. "Let's talk about this witch thing. I want to know *everything*." His eyes—well, the one eye that I could see clearly—seemed to dance.

Jamie and Clara had been gone for about half an hour, and Nikolai was still in his room, presumably trying to run a trace on Lee's phone. Benny had disappeared to god knew where. Roberta and I were outside in the dark, cleaning out her car.

First thing in the morning, we'd head out to investigate a few spots where Benny thought Lee might be holed up. He was going to ride with us, and huge as he was, he'd need some room. Roberta's car looked like a nuclear fallout site—soda cans, candy wrappers, Styrofoam packaging, bent books, melted lip balms, a box of dog treats, and an entire dehumidifier missing its chamber were just a few of the things that had been living in the backseat.

"You might have to let him sit up front," she said to me, grabbing a scoop of wadded up receipts and dumping them into a trash bag. "Unless you want to drive, that is. Even with the backseat cleaned out, I think it's going to be too tight for Benny to sit comfortably."

"That's fine," I said. "How tall is he, anyway?"

"I think he's like 6'3 or 6'4," she said. "And built like a brick shithouse."

"I noticed," I said with a giggle. "Phillip's 6'5, and Benny's almost as tall as him."

"That's the first time I've heard you mention him—Phillip —since we left," Roberta said, looking at me. I worked on digging half-melted Skittles out of her carpet and said nothing; I didn't feel like talking about Phillip right now. He still hadn't called, and it hurt to even think about him. Why had I brought him up in the first place?

To divert her attention, I kept talking about Benny. "What's Benny's deal? Are he and Clara big time bodybuilders or something?"

Roberta laughed. "Nope. Well, sort of." She fished a McDonald's bag out from under the seat and made a face. "That's been in here at least three months. Benny and Clara are pro wrestlers. Well, he is. She used to be, but she retired last year."

"Retired already?" I asked. "She can't be much older than me!"

"It's a hard profession," Roberta answered. "A lot of head injuries, very physically demanding. She wants a family one day, so she decided it was too dangerous. Now she's like a Nitro girl. Or like Gorgeous George." She grinned at my expression and continued, "Like the girl who stands at the edge of the ropes in a ball gown or a bikini and screams words of encouragement to her wrestler. Sometimes they're dating or pretend dating. She'll occasionally take a folding chair and whack the opponent over the head. They give interviews and stuff, too. Basically, they're arm candy."

"I know what a ringside girl is, thanks," I said, sounding more affronted than I meant to. I snorted so she'd know I wasn't offended. "I just can't see someone as tough as Clara being content doing that. I mean, she *is* pretty, though." I paused, thoughtful. "I can see what Benny sees in her. Are they married or just dating?"

"Neither, anymore," Roberta said, unearthing a hairbrush. "Clara's still madly in love with Benny, and I guess they're still…whatever…I don't ask…but he officially ended things a few months back." She looked wistful. "He told her he couldn't give her the family, the picket fence, that whole life. Clara's not quite over it yet. She thought they were going to get married, you know, and he doesn't help by being so touchy-feely all the time. I'm always telling him he's a narcissist and a whore."

I laughed, though I could certainly understand being madly in love with someone who had ended things, who hadn't lived up to your hopes and dreams, and being unable to let go. "I'm surprised I've never heard of either of them. Tess was a huge wrestling fan."

"I know," Roberta said, tying up the trash bag and throwing it at her feet. I was surprised to realize I no longer felt a pang of anger when she talked about him. "He loves Benny, or did. Anytime I'd bring him around, he'd freak out. I can't believe you've never heard him mention Benny; he was one of his favorites."

"I definitely would have remembered him mentioning a wrestler named Benny," I said. Every time I heard the name, I'd think of "Benny and the Jets."

"He doesn't go by Benny in the ring," Roberta said, looking at me like I was stupid. "And he wears a mask, too."

"What's his stage name?" I asked.

"The Black Wolf," Roberta answered.

I stopped cleaning and stared at her. "Benny is the Black Wolf? You're shitting me!" The Black Wolf was a name I definitely knew, and Roberta was right—Tess had mentioned him a whole bunch. In fact, he'd made me watch dozens of his matches over the years. Every Monday night GNW, which stood for Georgia National Wrestling, aired their "Monday Cage Fury," two hours' worth of nothing but cage matches between bitter rivals. The "battles" were intense; the match wasn't over until both wrestlers were bleeding from multiple places. The Black Wolf was one of their biggest personalities, and if I remembered correctly, seven-time heavyweight champion. Thinking about Benny's tall, stocky frame, I could see it now: the jet-black hair, the black goatee that showed from the bottom of his tight wolf mask, the heavily tattooed arms, and legs thick as tree trunks, encased in shiny black shoes, laced up to just below the knee. The Black Wolf had been an imposing figure, a true "heel," and strong as an ox. He'd won nearly all the matches I'd ever seen him wrestle. And I had seen a lot. Tess had been obsessed with the guy; he'd gone to several matches, and I could still remember him making signs, trying to draw a realistic outline of a wolf in black Sharpie on poster board I'd bring home from the library. "No wonder Tess was in love with you," I said, "if you're such good friends with his idol."

Roberta's cheeks colored, and she looked down at her feet.

"It's fine," I said. "I mean it, Roberta. I've let it go. I think I've held onto it long enough."

"I feel bad," she said.

"You should," I laughed. "But don't tiptoe around me. Seriously. I'm over it…or getting there. And over *him* completely. I might still be angry about some of the stuff he did, but I don't love him anymore."

"Good," Roberta said with a smile. "Because he doesn't deserve you."

"I know."

An awkward silence fell.

"So, what was Clara's stage name?" I asked, eager to change the subject. "I wonder if I ever saw her."

"Gloriana Hole," Roberta replied, and I snorted again.

"You've got to be kidding me," I said. "Please, god, tell me that's a joke name."

"Nope."

"I'm trusting my life to a guy named The Black Wolf and a chick named Gloriana Hole." I shook my head, tears of laughter pooling in my eyes.

Roberta giggled, then shut the car door. "Well, this fucker is as clean as it's going to get. I give up." She brushed her hands off on her pants and stood. "You coming in? It's cold out here. I bet Jamie has some tea or cocoa. I could make us a cup, get some blankets on the couch." She winked at me. "Snuggle up, watch a chick flick?"

I laughed, but inwardly, I was thinking how amazing that sounded. For all my jokes, I really did feel safe here. And after the stress of the past few days, a movie and cocoa sounded like heaven. "Yeah, I'll be right in," I said. "I just have to send a quick text first." Roberta nodded and went back into the trailer, the screen door slamming behind her.

I grabbed my phone and typed out the message before I changed my mind. *"I just met a guy named Benny who also goes by The Black Wolf and get this—his girlfriend is almost as stacked as he is, and her name is Gloriana Hole. You can't make this up. I just had to tell you."*

I hit "send" and sent the message to Phillip. It was so funny, I just knew he'd write me back right away. If anything would get him talking, it would be that, with his twisted, dark sense of humor.

Two hours later, cocoa gone and movie over, Phillip hadn't responded, and I was regretting ever reaching out. When would I learn? I just kept putting myself out there and being ignored, rejected. It was humiliating, to say nothing of how painful it was to know he didn't care.

I stared at Roberta's face in profile, watching her, trying to decide if I wanted to bring it up. A deep, sad part of me really missed Sloan—backstabbing bitch or not—and being able to vent about boys and the ways they hurt us. I missed good old-fashioned bitch sessions. Maybe now that I'd told Roberta I no longer cared about Tess, we could have that sort of conversation without both freezing up like icicles. But I wasn't sure I could make the first move.

Roberta had put on a second movie, her eyes following young, long-haired Brad Pitt's every move (she had insisted we watch *A River Runs Through It,* though I hadn't exactly protested), but she wasn't really paying attention. I could tell by the way she was chewing on her thumbnail. The ends were frayed and jagged, and she kept chewing away absently, biting off little pieces and spitting them onto her lap. It was kind of gross, but I didn't say anything. She was faraway, lost in some deep thoughts, and whatever they were, they were decidedly unpleasant. She was scared. Or nervous. And my gut told me it was about more than Lee and Lydia.

Boy talk would have to wait, it seemed.

The sound of knuckles rapping against the metal trailer

door startled us both. Roberta almost jumped out of her skin and bit down on her thumb, hard. "Fuck!"

"Want me to get it? Do you think the guys would mind?" I asked, but she held out a hand to stop me.

"No, let me," Roberta said, her face a little gray. "I know who it is." She looked at me, her eyes, wild and bright, meeting mine for a second, then trudged to the door and yanked it open with more force than seemed necessary. As she wrenched it open, she looked back at me. "I told you I'd tell you everything in time. Well, Stormy Spooner, it's time." I looked past her shoulder to the doorway.

The woman who stood there was skinny as a rail, with dark blond hair—dishwater, like my own—and though I couldn't see her eyes, I knew from memory their exact shade of cornflower blue. The woman stood there for a moment, lingering uncertainly, and when she spoke, her voice was a wavering croak. "Hey, girl," she said, looking at Roberta, who was standing in the doorway, her posture tense. She pitched forward and gave her a short hug with a pat on the back, and an air-kiss on her cheek. "It's good to see you, hon. You look good."

Then her gaze fell over to the couch, where I'd stood up and then froze, unable to believe who I was seeing. She straightened her thin shoulders, brushed past Roberta, and came into the room, clutching her faux fur coat in her skinny arms. "Stormy Fiona? Is it really you?"

"Mama," I said, stepping from the couch to her in a single movement, the hairs on the back of my neck standing up. "What in the *hell* are you doing here?"

Twelve

"Somebody needs to start explaining," I said, pacing back and forth in Jamie and Nikolai's little kitchen, the acrid smell of microwave popcorn burning my nose. Roberta was, for some ungodly reason, popping popcorn and setting out a pitcher of neon-green Kool-Aid as though we were all children at a cheap-ass birthday party. My mother (my mother!!) was seated at the scratched-up kitchen table, staring at me the way only a mother who hasn't seen her kid in a long time can. Searching my face, trying to memorize it, a ghost of a smile on her lips, though there was something guarded—which wasn't unusual —about her eyes.

I stared back at her, trying to get my bearings. Mama was far too thin—her face was gaunt, making the wrinkles around her eyes and her mouth more prominent. But her eyes were not the usual bloodshot red I had become accustomed to in recent years; they sparkled blue and clear. Either Mama was sober, or she was making a good show of it. The ends of her hair were an interesting shade of bright orange, either a botched dye job or an ombre that had grown out, and she had acrylic nails on, a pretty French tip that was outdated but looked good on her. My brows furrowed. Mama had never been one for getting her hair done and never her nails. "I ain't got money to waste on that vanity shit," she'd said to me once at thirteen when I'd asked for a makeup palette. "You're either born pretty or you ain't. All that paint and slick is just lies."

So this was a side of her I didn't recognize, all made-up and manicured. Under her faux fur coat, Mama was wearing a familiar t-shirt—she'd gone to see The Who with my dad when I was just a kid and she'd worn that concert tee down to holes long before I'd ever moved out of the house—but her nice black skirt and leather boots were obviously new, and not cheap. And since when did she wear faux fur?

She looked like herself and she didn't. I had so many questions—where she'd been, why she hadn't called in so long, was she really sober, why she suddenly looked *like that*—but there was one very important question that needed answering before any of the others. The one that would determine whether I'd stay in this kitchen and listen to either of them— her or Roberta.

"Why…how…are you here, Mama?" I asked again, the word *Mama* rolling off my tongue as though I'd never stopped saying it, though of course I had. When forced to talk about my mother— which wasn't often—I usually just said "my mom" or "my mother." "Mama" felt too much like a term of endearment, a reminder of my childhood, and I'd stopped saying it completely when I'd moved out. "I'm so confused."

"Roberta called me," Mama said after a pause. She reached into the pocket of her coat and produced a cigarette—she was still smoking her usual brand, Marlboro Reds, so at least that was the same. She offered me one and I shook my head. She lit the cigarette and nodded towards Roberta, who was shaking popcorn into a bowl. "She called me, what…two days ago? Told me to meet you two down here, that things were starting to shake up." Mama regarded me, her eyes sad and hollow, but they were clear. "I knew this day would come," she went on, puffing on the cigarette. "But after a while, so much time passed…I guess I just stopped believing it would. Or maybe I just hoped, I don't know."

"What on earth are you talking about?" I demanded. "What day would come?"

Roberta sat the bowl of popcorn on the table and took a seat beside my mother. She gestured at the empty chair across from her. "Sit down and eat," she said, pointing at the bowl. "It's all the guys had in the cabinets. I checked—it's artificial butter. Totally vegan. You need something in your stomach."

"I'm not hungry," I said, my voice coming out defiant and childish. Being near my mother was making me regress, apparently. I might as well have crossed my arms across my chest.

"She hasn't eaten all day," Roberta said to my mother, and they both fixed me with a pointed stare. I would have laughed if it were any other situation. Instead, I glared back at them.

"I'm not a fucking child," I spat, despite the fact that I sounded like one. "Y'all tell me what's going on. Now."

"I will if you sit down," Roberta said calmly, though I noticed her hands on the popcorn bowl were shaking.

As I sat down with a deep sigh, I was filled with a sudden, all-encompassing yearning for Phillip. If I'd missed him before, the feeling was a chasm now. I'd give anything to have him with me, to help me navigate this, if only to have a solid presence by my side.

As I'd gotten to know him, I'd often thought that I'd like him to meet Mama—Phillip was the type, I knew instinctively, who wouldn't judge her and wouldn't judge me *for* her.

That was actually one of the things I'd always liked about Tess—how he had accepted my parents; accepted and loved them, without any judgement. Of course, he'd been more like them than I'd known at first. Still, he'd put in a real effort to be good to them and to let them know that he loved me, too. He'd treated them like family, even when they'd been raving and toxic and downright weird. It was one of his finer qualities. There had always been the sense, though, that he enjoyed spending time with them because he thought they were fun and entertaining, in spite of my discomfort. That had always hurt, even though I'd tried not to let it.

I knew instinctively that Phillip would accept my parents, would never judge them, but he'd keep them at arm's length— for *me*. He would let me draw the boundary, and he'd support me, understanding that I needed his support, his love, while dealing with them. That's just the kind of guy Phillip was.

I loved my parents. I did. But my memories of them were like an open wound that had never healed. Sitting across from Mama, having her show up so unexpectedly and catching me off-guard, only drove that point home.

"I don't know where to start," Roberta said by way of apology, reaching into the bowl and throwing a handful of salty popcorn into her mouth. "There's just…so much. Ugh."

"Start with how you two know each other," I said, leveling my gaze on both of them. "That's what's throwing me for a loop."

"I've known Laureen since I was a kid," Roberta said, and I stared at her, confused. She was on a first name basis with my mom? How was that possible? And if she'd known Mama, wouldn't she have also known me?

"Where did you meet?" I asked, incredulous.

"At the trailer park," Roberta answered, and my mother looked uncomfortable. "The one my dad and I lived in when I was a kid, before I moved in with my uncle. Remember I told you about that?"

"Is she talking about the trailer park where we lived?" I asked Mama, and she nodded. "But how? I would have met you if you did. And there wasn't a single other kid there, like, almost the entire time we lived there!" The only kids I remembered, other than myself, were the Harris Brats, as Mama had called them—the step-kids of Ginny Harris, the curler-clad woman who lived to the left of us, who spent most of her time bitching about the husband who had run off on her and watching daytime soaps in her pink fuzzy bathrobe. The step-kids came and went—whenever she could stand them, which wasn't often—all of them with snotty noses and tangled up hair. I didn't like a single one of them, from the bullying oldest girl, Katie, who had pushed me down in a mud puddle and stole my favorite Barbie, to little Ronnie, who was pulling shit out of his diaper and smearing it places long past the age when he should have. I'd steered clear of those kids, and there hadn't been any others, beyond the occasional move-in, move-right-back-out families who were plentiful in trailer parks, none of them staying long enough to make friends. I wouldn't have missed Roberta, a girl my own age, living there, especially if she knew my mother.

"I lived there, Stormy," Roberta was saying now, meeting my eyes with finality. "You just don't remember."

"That's pretty unlikely," I said with a laugh. "Ask Mama. I never let her forget a single thing from those days. I remind her of my shitty childhood every time I see her."

I looked at her for support, but Mama did not laugh back, only looked at her lap.

Roberta went on as if she hadn't heard me. "I met Laureen and Chad—your folks—when I was what…eight? I think that's right. That was around the time that my dad started hanging out with them, going over to their house a lot. And you guys would come to ours. By the time I was eleven, Dad was…well, he wasn't able to take care of me. So I started spending summers with Uncle Albert, and by the summer I was twelve, I had moved in with him permanently. But I still kept in touch with your parents—well, not your dad so much, but your mom. She'd call to check in or write to me occasionally."

I looked at them both in disbelief. Mama had spent the majority of my childhood and teenage years drunk as a skunk. She'd been in no position to write or call to check in on some random kid. She'd barely even kept watch over *me*.

"I stayed so messed up in part because I felt guilty," Mama spoke up, knowing what I was thinking, sensing I needed some kind of explanation. "I checked in on Roberta when I was able to, because I was just so eaten up with guilt. I felt like it was my fault—our fault—that she got sent away to her uncle."

"Really, it was the best thing for me," Roberta assured her, and my mom smiled, putting a hand on her elbow. A weird feeling crept through me, equal parts jealousy and befuddlement. "He was good to me."

Roberta turned back to me. "We've kept in touch over the years, but I tried to stay away as much as I could, so I wouldn't complicate things," Roberta said. "Especially after all the…the mess…with Tess."

"You knew she was sleeping with my husband?" I demanded, and Mama flushed again.

"She knew we were hanging out," Roberta answered for her. "I knew—somehow—that you'd eventually start to pull at the threads and figure it out and I didn't want your mom to be in the line of fire. I didn't want you to think she had anything to do with all of this."

"But I haven't pulled at any threads," I said, lost. "I don't have the first clue how any of this ties together. How my own mother could know you or how she could keep it secret that Tess was cheating. None of it makes any sense…"

I cut myself off suddenly. All the random bits of information I'd absorbed over the past few days, all the little things I'd noticed, *were* starting to weave together in my mind, forming something from the past, coming unburied. I gasped and peered at Roberta with narrowed eyes. "You were the girl," I said, my head starting to hurt.

"What girl?" she asked.

"In the dream I had," I said, remembering the odd nightmare during my nap after the morning on the beach. "You were the girl on his porch."

"On whose porch?" Roberta asked, her eyes wide. But she already knew what I was going to say; a grave look had come over her face.

"You were the little dark-haired girl on his porch in my dream. The one who was hanging off the wrought iron balustrades at his trailer." Was that right? I closed my eyes and thought back. Did singlewide trailers even have porch columns like that? I was certain that one did. With—

"With the dreamcatchers?" Roberta cut in quietly, and I nodded. "Whose house?" she asked again.

"Him…" I didn't have to search for the name. I knew it, but I suddenly felt strongly that I didn't want to say it. "Uncle…" I bit the term off with my teeth. I wouldn't call him that, not even now. The guy had always given me the creeps, and he still did. "Elvin."

"Yeah, that's him," Roberta said, swallowing. "Elvin. My daddy dearest."

I shook my head. I knew it was true as soon as she said it, but how could it be? Other than that dream, I had no memory of a little girl ever being around him. And I had the feeling I'd been around him a lot.

"He wasn't nice to Roberta, at least not there at the end—" Mom interjected, but I stopped her.

"Is that how you ended up with Tess?" I demanded, staring at Roberta. "You met him through my mom? Because you'd kept in touch?" I'd get back to why I couldn't remember her later. For now, I needed to know how she'd ended up in my current life. None of it made sense. I couldn't wrap my brain around how I could be connected to one person in so many ways, through so many different people, and have no memory of it.

Roberta shook her head. "No, not exactly. I've known Tess since…I met him when I was a kid. When I met your parents and…when I met you."

"So you've known my mama and my husband…ex-husband, I mean…since you were a little kid, and yet I don't remember you at all." I shook my head. "I didn't meet Tess until high school; you're saying you knew him first?"

She shook her head. "We met him at the same time. You just…"

"No," I said firmly. "I met Tess in high school. "He was working as a pool cleaner, and I met him one weekend at Sloan's."

Roberta shook her head again in the same maddening way. I was starting to get angry. "No, Stormy. We all met when we were kids." She sighed and looked at me with her dark brown eyes. "You just don't…"

"If you say 'don't remember' one more time…" I threatened. "I can't take it. None of this makes any sense," I said, looking at Mama, who was looking back at me with an odd expression, one of almost guilt. "Unless I had childhood amnesia, and nobody fucking told me."

Mama's eyes dropped to her lap again. Roberta bit her lip.

"What," I said, my heart thudding in my throat. "What is it? Just tell me. Right now."

"I've been trying to tell you…" Roberta said, her voice trailing to a whisper. She looked to my mother for guidance but got none. Mama was still staring into her lap as though something very interesting was occurring there. "Stormy, there's a lot you've forgotten. Well, forgotten isn't really the right word…I was hoping that maybe Laureen being here might jog your memory, might ease you back in, but I don't think it has."

"Why would this place jog my memory?" I was really getting mad now. "Are you going to randomly tell me that I actually grew up here and just don't remember it?"

"No." Roberta shook her head. "I just thought seeing Jamie and Nikolai might, I don't know, bring something back."

"What do they have to do with anything?" I said weakly, but my mind was wandering back again to that dream. The two boys standing near my yard, the one with the blond hair who had looked at me so sadly, and the freckled kid with the scooter who had ushered him away. Oh, *fuck*.

"I'm sorry about all this, Stormy," Mama said, as if she, too, could see my thoughts, her voice full of guilt. "Me and your daddy, we always felt so bad...we hoped you'd never remember. But it's got away from all of us now." She puffed on her cigarette hurriedly, as though it was giving her courage.

"So...you guys—all of you, including Jamie and Nikolai... and you and Tess...you're all connected. You were all part of...whatever it is that I don't remember?"

"Yes."

"Look," I said, freaked out. We were talking in circles, and I still knew nothing. "I had the one dream with you and...I guess it was Nikolai and Jamie, but I didn't realize it at the time. But that's all I remember. Everything else is a total blank."

"What happened in the dream, hon?" Mama asked me curiously.

"I was driving around our driveway; you know how it was a figure eight?" She nodded. "I was just riding my bike around and around it, in bare feet. Kicking up dust. And this kid comes out of nowhere and says he has to warn me. Light blond hair and blue eyes, older than me. I guess maybe it was Nikolai." Roberta nodded almost imperceptibly, and Mama's face had gone even paler. "And then this other kid came up on a scooter—Jamie, I'm guessing—and he was like 'we've got to get out of here,' and they split. I looked over to Elvin's old trailer, the one that always gave me the creeps, and there was a little girl on the porch, with dark hair and eyes, just staring at me, looking sad. And then Elvin came off the porch and walked over to me, and he cupped my chin in his hand and said something…I don't remember what." I shook my head, confused. "And then I woke up. I kinda made myself wake up;, I think. Because I was so frightened."

"That wasn't a dream, Stormy," Roberta said. "That was a memory."

"But of what?" I asked.

"Of the day," Roberta said with a deep sigh, "my dad wiped you clean."

"When I count to three, you'll wake up."

One, two…three. Snap. My eyes sprung open and I sat up, grasping the cracked plastic handle of the lounge chair, swinging my bruised and scabbed up legs over and placing my jelly-shoe clad feet on the ground. "I want to go home now." The words were out of my mouth before I'd even fully come to.

"Now, Stormy," Elvin said to me in a kind tone, though I could hear the sharp teeth beneath it. "You know the rules. You must wait five minutes before leaving."

"But why?" My lower lip fell into a pout. I hated it here. Hated the gross, cluttered trailer, hated the backyard with its makeshift privacy fence, which had been cobbled together from random pieces of pallets and rusted tin, hated the cracked lawn chairs that dug into the tender flesh on the backs of my thighs, hated the ugly dreamcatchers always dangling in front

of my face, and most of all, I hated "Uncle El," who I called plain old Elvin behind his back. He might make me call him uncle, but he wasn't my uncle. No way.

"I need to monitor you to make sure everything went fine, and that you're alright. Roberta, give me the boost," Elvin said in a calm voice, passing me a cup of lukewarm Kool-Aid. It would either be grape or orange; he never had any other flavors. I took a meager sip and made a face. Orange. The one I hated. And it needed more sugar; it was sour.

I shouldn't be ungrateful, I thought to myself, knowing even in my seven-year-old heart that Roberta was the one who always made the Kool-Aid, and if it wasn't for her, I wouldn't even have that. Elvin's talk of making sure I was fine was a load of crap. He didn't care if I was comfortable or even if I was safe. I might not know much, but I knew that.

Roberta was Elvin's daughter and she was my age, with dark, shining hair that I secretly envied, and big, sad brown eyes. When I was "in" (that's what Elvin liked to call it when us kids were here), she flitted around in the corners of their trailer, making herself helpful yet scarce. I was at her house almost every day, and yet we had never played together. In another life, we might have been friends, but in this life, I was the student and she was some kind of apprentice, and play was not allowed. Nor was friendship. In fact, I wondered sometimes if Roberta hated me. She lingered, pulling ugly faces at me whenever her dad and I were in a session. The too-sour Kool-Aid was probably on purpose. She didn't like me and didn't want to be my friend. She wanted me to stay away from her, them.

I'd be only too happy to, but unfortunately, I had no say in the matter.

I'd long ago figured out that the little baggies of green stuff my dad got from Elvin were part of a business transaction, and that my participation was some kind of payment in lieu of money, of which Daddy had none.

I'd complained about it once, working up the courage to say something to my friend Nicky, who was a couple of years older than me and one of the few kids in the trailer park who was always nice to me. He let me play with his metal Tonka trucks and never teased me or treated me mean because I was a girl. He had pretty blue eyes and was very smart. I told him lots of stuff I'd never tell anybody else, and he always listened to me, quiet and thoughtful.

"I don't like that my daddy trades me to Uncle El," I'd said to him one day by the sandbox, and his eyes had gone wide.

"What do you mean 'trade'?" Nicky had asked me, alarmed.

So I'd told him about the sessions, about the dream-catchers and the weird sleepy feeling I'd get. How Elvin would ask me to do this or that or ask me to remember weird lines that sounded like poetry but made me feel strange when I said them. How sometimes I really would fall asleep, and how there would be Kool-Aid after and Uncle El would watch me with his strange, cold eyes and then I'd go home, and my daddy would have another bag of green stuff to last him a few days. Nicky had sighed with what seemed like relief, and said, "Chin up, Storm. Could be a lot worse."

At the time, I didn't know what that meant.

All I knew was that it was bad enough. I hated the sessions, hated the way they made me sleepy and gave me a headache for hours afterward. More than that, I hated that I had no idea why I was doing the sessions or what they were for. For months we'd been at it, and I still had no idea why he put me to sleep or what he was doing, other than the vague answer he'd given me once, snapping my head off when I'd pressed him. "You'll thank me when you're an adult," he'd said, his face turning red with impatience. "When nobody can mess with you. You're going to be a powerful weaver. Till then, just shut up and do what I tell you."

I didn't know what that meant; I'd always thought weavers just made fabric. I had the sense it had to do with something spiritual, though I didn't really know what that meant, either. My parents didn't go to church and I had only the vaguest concept of "God." But something about the way Elvin would sway beneath the dreamcatchers and his sing-songy voice, sounding like he was reciting spells, made me think that he was invoking a power beyond himself. Something big and scary and outside of his control. I wondered if that was why he used me. If the power backfired, I'd be the one hurt, not him. The repercussions would all fall back to me.

Yes, I would find that out in the end. I certainly would.

"Elvin," I said, feeling woozy and nauseated. "Uncle El. Your dad. He's the one who has Lee, isn't he?"

"Yes," Roberta said, two spots of color appearing on her tanned cheeks. "I think so."

"How on earth did Elvin get involved in all this?" I asked.

"He's Guthrie's brother." I could hear the shame in Roberta's voice.

I swallowed hard. I could hardly believe what I was hearing, and yet every single bit of it rang true. I knew it, deep in my bones, in my blood. Roberta had said from the beginning that Guthrie was her uncle, that Lee was her cousin; I just hadn't tied it together. I closed my eyes and took a long, shuddering breath.

"Just tell it to me straight, all of it," I said, my voice sounding weird to my own ears. "Just tell me how it all happened, and I'll believe you."

"Okay." Roberta shot a quick glance in Mama's direction and sighed. "So, here's the deal. My dad—Elvin—has always been really interested in magic. Growing up, Harry Houdini was his hero. He and his siblings would do magic shows in the backyard, and they dreamed of growing up and being magicians." She traced the pattern on the bowl of popcorn. "Life had other plans, I guess. I never met my grandparents, but from what I've heard, they were not nice people. They beat their kids and did all sorts of other awful things. They starved them and…and other, worse stuff." She shuddered. "It got so bad that the department of family services got involved and took them all away when my dad was a teenager."

"That's awful," I said. My folks hadn't exactly been parents of the year—far from it—but thankfully, I couldn't claim any real abuse, other than a little neglect, and being exposed to their drinking. That had been bad enough.

Roberta nodded. "All of them—Daddy, his brothers and his little sister—were separated, and sent to different homes. The way he tells it, Dad bummed around from foster family to foster family, sometimes going to school, sometimes working odd jobs, until he was of age. Then he moved to South Georgia, got a job as a janitor at the local high school, and rented a trailer. He met my mom and they got married pretty young— he wasn't even twenty when they tied the knot and she was barely eighteen. and already a single mom—to my brother, Jorge—when they met." She smiled sadly. "I think she was desperate to find someone to take care of her. So they got hitched. Had me a year later. Then my mom died when I was six months old."

"I'm so sorry," I said, my hand reaching out to hers instinctively. "How did she pass?"

"Drug overdose," Roberta said, her face a little gray. Mama winced and went to light another cigarette. Roberta took a shaking breath and went on. "My dad raised me. The first few years were pretty okay. We never had any money and I had to grow up way too fast—he had me doing chores when I should have been out playing, stuff like that. But he wasn't ever *bad* to me. He was just…busy and broke."

"Ain't that the truth," Mama agreed, ashing her cigarette.

"And Jorge?" I asked, curious.

Roberta shook her head. "He went to live with his father the week after our mother died. I only ever got to see him in the summers…all the way up until we were adults." Her eyes were faraway. "And then…well, I told you where he is."

She shook her head again, and went on. "When I was about seven, Daddy's youngest brother called out of the blue, wanting to reconnect. Daddy was so excited. He packed us a bag and we went and stayed on Tybee. Remember I told you I was there for a while? It was just close enough to Jekyll that we were able to visit often, pretty much every weekend." Roberta smiled. "It's one of my favorite memories. I'll never forget it: meeting my aunt and uncles and my cousin, who was just a little younger than me. We swam in the ocean and grilled out every night. We camped under the stars. It was so much fun." Her smile faded and her face turned dark. "That was my last happy memory. After that…things changed." She began to pick at her fingernails.

"What happened?"

"Daddy was thrilled to reconnect with his brothers of course," Roberta said, her voice not much more than a whisper. "But he was even more thrilled when he met his sister-in-law."

"Why?" I asked. "What was so special about her?"

"Turns out my uncle's wife was a powerful witch," Roberta said. "I know how it sounds, but it's true. A real witch, not some playing-at-magic hipster white girl like you see at the farmers' market with store-bought tarot cards and thick Ikea candles. Like a real, possesses-actual-powers witch." She smiled grimly.

"You're talking about Lydia," I said, and she nodded.

"Uncle Guthrie didn't really care about that stuff anymore, so he just humored his wife. He'd long ago given up any interest in magic. But when Daddy met Aunt Lydia…it was like he was a kid again. He was immediately obsessed with her powers and with the idea of becoming a witch himself. He talked to me about it. He told me he could *feel* the power coming off her." Roberta's face was full of sad wonder at the memory. "He wouldn't let it go. He begged Lydia to teach him her ways. She said it didn't work that way, that you have to have a calling, a natural talent for it, and that often the teacher doesn't choose the student. But Daddy wouldn't give it up. He bugged her and bugged her until she finally relented. And Guthrie—well, he wasn't going to be left out. Even though he'd lost interest in all of that, barely even believed in it anymore, he wasn't going to stand by and let his brother hang out with his wife. So he went along, too. She ended up teaching them both."

"What did she teach them?" I asked.

"Mainly just little spells," Roberta answered. "Among other things. She said that every person has natural gifts, and magic is about how to weave your gifts—your talents—with the spirit world. That if you have a true calling, then intention is more than enough. For someone without the calling, well, you can try every spell in the world and you'll never have any real power." I felt a chill go down my neck. Roberta went on. "So yeah, Lydia taught them, but she only taught them small stuff. Neither of them had 'the gift,' as she called it, so she only showed them basic spells." Roberta smiled. "Easy stuff. Witchery for Beginners, if you will."

"Like how to bring someone back from the dead?" I asked with a snort. "I'd hardly call that 'basic.'"

"Oh god, no." Roberta gave me a look. "She never would have taught them that. Never in a million years. And anyway, that…that came later." She and Mama exchanged a glance, Mama's cigarette burned down to ash.

I grabbed a fistful of oily popcorn and shoved it into my mouth, barely tasting the salty, hot kernels, suddenly ravenous, like a starving wolf. I grabbed another handful and shoveled it in, thinking furiously. My hands were buzzing with electricity—was it nerves or was it magic? I had no idea. But I felt like I might jump out of my skin.

"You okay, Stormy?" Mama asked me, concerned. "You're not even chewing your food."

As if on cue, I felt something catch in my throat and began to cough. I grabbed the Kool-Aid and nodded, swallowing carefully. Mama was watching me with nervous eyes.

"I can't believe I didn't figure it out on my own," I said. Roberta was looking at me warily. "That Elvin was your dad, and that Guthrie and he were brothers. I mean, you even said that Guthrie was your uncle…but I just…didn't make the connection."

"There's a lot you don't remember," she said kindly. "And that was by design. Nobody expects you to have everything figured out."

I gathered that everyone at the Wolfden already knew about all of this…or most of it. And yet, I was left in the dark. The thought was both a comfort and an annoyance. I hated being in the dark. "Guthrie and Elvin," I said, shaking my head. "Brothers in evil."

"However evil you think Guthrie was, Stormy," Roberta said, her lip trembling, "Daddy is so much worse."

"Tell me, then," I said with a sigh, grabbing another fistful of popcorn. I was still starving and wondered if it had something to do with depleted energy—or depleted magic—that made me feel so weak with hunger.

Roberta was still tracing the popcorn bowl's design with her finger, and I could see her hands shaking from across the table. "Aunt Lydia taught Daddy and Guthrie just enough to make them happy, like I said, spells that didn't amount to much, that any intuitive person could do just by subconsciously reading body language and learning how to pick-up cues. Like how to make someone notice you, how to predict the future with the tarot, how to read minds...tricks that any medium in a back alley could do. But Daddy suspected she was holding out. Lydia always insisted that she just played at magic with no real talent and she'd taught him all she knew."

"That's definitely not true," I said, and Roberta nodded.

"Daddy knew she was lying," she agreed. "And one night, unfortunately, Lydia proved it." Roberta looked at Mama, and they both shuddered. "Laureen should tell this part."

Mama had already lit another cigarette, seemingly in preparation for this moment. She took a puff, and when she pulled the cigarette away, I could see a ring of her lipstick around the filter. I focused on this detail as she began to speak, a minute something to hold onto.

"Something happened...when you were little," Mama began, her voice shaky. "You don't remember it, because Elvin wiped it from you along with everything else. But you were there. God, I wish you hadn't been." Her voice broke, and Roberta put a gentle hand on Mama's arm. "You probably *do* remember some of what your daddy and I...we fought a lot back then." Her face was full of guilt. "We were so broke, always robbing Peter to pay Paul, and we had our vices. Most of the money went to my drinks and your daddy's pills. And whatever else we felt like doing at the time. To think we raised you in that house...well, I just have to live with that."

She took another puff, her fingers still trembling, and went on. "We fought a lot. About money. About drugs. About everything, and most of all about your daddy's women." Mama shook her head, her face flushing with embarrassment. "I guess I can't fully blame him for his wandering eye, because I was always drunk. I never paid him no attention. But what I do hold a grudge about is that he brought it so close to home, dangled his affairs right in my face, and in yours, Stormy."

"I don't remember," I said, my voice quiet. I believed her, though.

"I know you don't," Mama said with a grim smile. "And I'm glad of that." She took a deep breath. "The night it all began, we were fighting about a woman. Your daddy had what old timers used to call a 'fancy woman,' though she was far from fancy—real name Nancy, who he'd been seeing on and off for…oh, years. He'd dated her before we even met, then picked back up with her after we were married. He cheated on me with her for a long time." Mama snorted and snuffed out her cigarette. "What she saw in that man—not a pot to piss in, living in a beat-out trailer, with a wife and a kid to boot—I'll never know. But she sure did love him, and she was stuck on him like a barnacle. She'd call the house, taunt me…at one point, she even rented a trailer in the same damn trailer park as us." Mama's face flushed with anger. "Oh, she was something. She tried everything to get him to leave us for her. After I finally got fed up, I told him that he was gonna have to leave his fancy woman or I was leaving him. And he said, 'No, no, I broke it off, you're the only one for me, Lar.'" She tapped her cigarette pack on the table. "I was a dumb ass to believe him. He was still seeing her, alright, and I found out the two of them had been keeping secrets from me that were unforgivable. Right under my damn nose."

"It was the final straw, after years of putting up with his lies and his cheating and being broke…I was just done. I couldn't face it anymore…" Mama put her hands over her eyes, and I realized she was crying, something I'd rarely seen her do. "It was a cowardly thing, what I did. I wouldn't do the same now. But then, I just felt so helpless, so used up. I…I took a bottle of sleeping pills and downed them with a fifth of vodka. And that's all I remember."

I looked at Mama in horror. She brought her hands away from her eyes, which were bright with tears. "Your daddy found me a few hours later, but it was too late. I was already gone."

What? I looked at Mama, my eyes wide. "But...wait, you said..."

She held up a hand. "Just let me finish, hon." She pulled another cigarette from the pack then seemed to change her mind, sliding it back into the box. "Your daddy—when he found me—knew I was gone. I was already cold. There were drugs all over and he knew he was going to be in for it, because everyone in the trailer park had heard us fighting. He was afraid they'd accuse him of supplying the drugs, or worse, of murder. He was scared. So instead of calling 911, he called Elvin.

"Your daddy asked him to come over and help him sweep the house, to get things in order before the police came. But Elvin had a different idea."

I glanced over at Roberta, who was wringing her hands in her lap.

"Elvin called his sister-in-law—Lydia. Chad was skeptical, but Elvin insisted she could help. Said she was a witch and could do spells...said he'd always suspected she had powers far beyond what she claimed, and he thought maybe she could be persuaded to help. At first Lydia said no, told Elvin to do the right thing and call the law. But he begged her. He told her that I had a little girl that needed her mama. Finally, he got Lydia to agree.

"She and her husband—Guthrie—came to the house. According to Chad's story, Lydia ushered everybody out of the room and set to work. I don't know what she did in there, obviously—and neither does your daddy, because she banished him, too. At some point, though, you snuck into our room, Stormy. You stood there and watched as this witch-lady tried to work her magic on me, to bring me back. You watched, and after a while, you began to help."

What on earth was she saying? "What do you mean, 'help'?" I whispered.

"I don't know what exactly happened—nobody does but Lydia, and she's never talked of it to my knowledge. But your daddy told me what *they* saw. He said that he, Guthrie, and Elvin were sitting in the living room when they suddenly saw a flash of bright gold light from under the doorway of the bedroom. They all came running, threw open the door, and were shocked to find you there in the room with Lydia. They hadn't even known you were home."

I winced. That tracked. I'd been allowed to run free as a kid, not because my parents trusted me, but because most of the time, they didn't care.

"More shocking than the fact that you'd snuck in unnoticed, though, was what you were *doing*," Mama said, looking me straight in the eye. "What they saw shocked them all. You were standing there with Lydia, both of your hands outstretched over my body, and you were pooling that bright golden light together and sending it into my heart." Mama took a full deep breath, as if to illustrate how alive she was. "Your daddy told me that your light was every bit as shining and full as Lydia's."

"But I…" I shook my head. "That's not possible!"

"It is, honey. You saved me. The two of you," Mama said, her eyes brimming with tears. "And you were just a little wisp of a thing, too." Her voice was full of pride.

"Unfortunately, though, what you did opened a whole can of worms," Roberta cut in, her own eyes wet. "Once my father and Guthrie saw what Lydia could do—and saw what *you* could do—they were like sharks smelling blood. The power to bring someone back from the dead? They were obsessed and wanted it for themselves." Her eyes were faraway, lost in memories. "Lydia straight up refused to show them. She told them it was a power that only certain people had, that it couldn't be taught, and even if it could, it *shouldn't*. She said she'd die before she ever taught them." Roberta fixed her gaze on me, her face angry. "Which left them only one other person who had the ability…*you.*"

"But I was just a kid!" I exclaimed. "I didn't even know I could do it, obviously! How could they expect I'd teach them?"

"Exactly," Roberta said, nodding. "They knew you couldn't. But Daddy thought if he hypnotized you…that maybe he could tap into the power that way. Through your subconscious."

"That seems like a stretch," I said. "How could they know if it would work?"

"They couldn't," Roberta answered. "But I guess they figured there was no harm in trying."

No harm in trying. I could almost taste the anger burning on the back of my tongue like bitter bile. I thought back to all the weird sessions in Elvin's house that I couldn't quite remember, the sleepiness, how fearful I had felt, the loathing that would course through my little body every time Elvin was near. He'd been hypnotizing me and tapping into my brain, trying to force my mind to give up secrets I hadn't even known I'd possessed.

"So…was I…already this way, or did Lydia like…impart something into me?" I asked. "When I snuck into the room?"

Roberta shook her head. "I have no idea. We've wondered that, too. But she's so protective of you, Stormy. She won't talk about it. She never has."

I snorted. "Protective of me? Hardly. If anything, she hated me on sight. Phillip too…" But even as I said the words, I wondered. Hadn't I immediately felt a kinship, a tie, with the old, eccentric woman? Hadn't I detected a hint of pride in her voice as she'd talked to me about magic and spells, and the power of intention? Hadn't I heard an almost affectionate tone in her voice when she'd called me 'Fee'?

I felt woozy. I put my hands on the wooden table and tried to center myself, but I felt like I was going to fall through the floor at any moment. My head spun. "This…this is too much," I said, my voice tinny and small.

"There's more we need to talk about…" I heard Roberta say, but then a door slammed, and she abruptly went quiet.

From somewhere far away, I heard a loud burp and a laugh. "Oh, shit, sorry, I didn't know y'all had company—*hey!* It's Ms. S! Holy shit, Ms. S, I haven't seen you in years! Come here and give me a hug!" Jamie had come inside and was hugging my mom. I clutched at the table and forced my eyes to open, to survey the scene in front of me. He was hugging my mother tightly, his boyish face full of genuine glee. "Gosh, aren't you a sight for sore eyes! I ain't seen you since I was a little kid!"

I swallowed, trying to get my bearings. Roberta wordlessly pushed the glass of Kool-Aid towards me, and I knew instinctively—and now from memory—to take it. I drank the glass empty, noting absently that it finally had enough sugar. I tried giving her a grateful smile, but my insides were whirling.

On top of all, I'd just learned about myself and my powers, I now knew that my mother was friends with all these people. These people whom I didn't even remember but was already desperate to belong to. Mama had tried to take her own life when I was just a little kid. And she'd been brought back.

By me.

My mama was like Lee.

Like Phillip.

I stood up suddenly, furiously. There was so much more I

needed to know, and I didn't care if Jamie—or any of the rest of them—were here or not to hear them. No more secrets. Mama and Roberta were going to tell me *everything,* and they were going to tell me now. I pushed the chair back from the table and took a step forward.

But before I had a chance to open my mouth, my vision went black and I hit the floor.

I came to on the lumpy couch, Roberta, Jamie, and Mama hovering over me, their faces etched with concern.

"You passed out," Mama said, putting a cool hand to my cheek. I closed my eyes; it had been a long time since she'd been motherly. "Are you alright, honey?"

"I think so," I said, blinking a few times and moving to sit up. Mama took her hand away and I felt a pang of regret. "I don't know what happened. I just felt woozy all of a sudden."

The truth was, I knew well and well what had happened. I remembered now. I'd always felt that same wooziness when I'd finished with Elvin. The Kool-Aid had always helped for some reason, had quelled the nausea and grounded me back to reality. Roberta knew it too, it seemed.

But why had I suddenly felt the same way at the table? Was learning distressing news enough to send me into a spell? What was going on?

"Are you sure you're okay?" Mama pressed as I sat up against the pillows. "Maybe you shouldn't try to get up just yet."

"I'm fine, Mama."

"Maybe we should—" Mama began, but then Nikolai came through the front door, and she fell silent.

"What's going on here?" he asked, noting the three of them

hovering over me, his face filling with concern. "Stormy, you look pale. What happened?"

"I just passed out," I answered with a sheepish smile. The worry on his face was embarrassing. It made me feel weak and silly. "Everyone's fussing over me like I'm a baby, but I'm fine."

"You don't look fine…" But Nikolai's words trailed off as Mama stood up and gathered her faux fur coat, throwing it around her small shoulders. "Oh…hi," he said, an odd expression his face.

"Hi," Mama replied, then turned back to me, her face a little flushed. "Stormy, honey, I hate it, but I've got to go."

"What, right now?" I asked, confused.

"Yes." She nodded. "Call me if you need me, okay?" She turned to Roberta and said, "Bring her to the house in a few days, okay?"

"I will." I watched as Mama gave Roberta a quick hug, grabbed her cigarettes from the kitchen table, and left.

"Well, that was weird," I said, feeling abandoned and even more embarrassed. Oh god, was I about to cry? I blinked a few times, willing the tears to dissipate. "But then again, it's my mama, so that's downright wholesome behavior for her."

"Oh, come on, Stormy, she's okay," Roberta said, turning to me with a hopeful smile. "Are you, though? I mean, do you feel alright now? That was some spill you took."

After many more assurances and forcing down a few bites of a peanut butter and jelly sandwich that Jamie had insisted on making me, they all finally let me alone, cuddled up with a soft, worn comforter and a few lumpy pillows to bed down with for the night. I could hear their whispered voices in the next room, but I was so tired…so very tired. Despite everything I'd learned and the sheer horribleness of it all, I couldn't fight my own brain and I fell into another fitful sleep.

When I awoke the next morning, feeling stronger but with

a hint of a headache in my temple, there was a text waiting for me.

From Phillip.

Hey. I just wanted to check and see if you're okay. I had a weird feeling earlier tonight. Stupid, huh?

I tapped out a response with shaking hands. He'd felt me, had felt I was in distress. The tether between us was still there.

Not stupid, I responded. *I had a bit of a shock tonight. Too much to type out in a text. But I'm physically fine. I promise.*

I hoped my somewhat cryptic response would mean that he'd call me immediately, wanting all the details. But once again, Phillip didn't text me back.

Did he hate me or not? Was he still with Barb? Was it truly over? I couldn't gather shit from the way he was acting, and I was too afraid to just ask him directly. He was throwing me little scraps here and there, but no real communication. It was driving me nuts.

I was surrounded by people here at the Wolfden—more people than I needed, so many people I couldn't get more than a moment to myself—and yet the one person I really, truly wanted, seemed light years away.

"Ready to go?" Benny threw a black duffel bag over his shoulder and headed towards Roberta's car without waiting for an answer.

It was way too early for me. I was so tired. Jamie and Nikolai's couch was lumpy and hard, with a spring that had stuck right into the small of my back. And Roberta snored. But none of that had been as annoying as the nagging thoughts that I couldn't silence ever since Phillip's text, which had only succeeded in making me feel more unsure.

Plus, I was still spooked from the short-but-strange interaction I'd just had with Nikolai.

As I'd grabbed my purse from the couch and moved towards the door to leave, he'd emerged from the shadowy hall, clad in a ratty Black Sabbath t-shirt and blue plaid pajama pants. "Hey, Stormy. Wait a minute," he'd whispered, beckoning to me with a pale finger.

I'd walked over to him reluctantly, briefly wondering if he was going to try something with me. I had never gotten that vibe off him, but after a lifetime of being a woman, one thing I was certain of was you can never be certain. But when I'd come to stand beside him in the shadows, he'd surprised me by handing me a small, yet very heavy, cloth bundle. As I took it from his hands, I heard the jangle of metal.

"What's this?" I'd asked, and he'd put a finger to his mouth, gesturing for me to be quiet.

"Take that with you," he'd said in a whisper. "For your protection. But don't tell the others you have it."

"What is it?" I asked, but I was already unravelling the cloth. Nestled in the fabric was a long, elaborate, and very old-looking knife. Gingerly, I slid it out of its sheath and touched a finger to the blade, wincing. It was very sharp. "Why are you giving me this?"

"Take good care of it," Nikolai had said as though I hadn't spoken. "It's very old, and worth a lot. The guys would be pissed if they knew I was giving it to you. It technically isn't mine alone to give."

"Nikolai, I'm not sure I want this—" I began, but he cut me off.

"Never mind that. You need it. You need something for your own protection, to keep you safe. I already blessed it for you. Just see that you only use it when it's necessary. And then, one day, when things are calmer, you can give it back to me."

I wanted to ask him the story behind the knife, but I knew Roberta and Benny were waiting. Nikolai had smiled then, and said, "I'll tell you all about it later. I promise."

He'd read my thoughts. I found myself smiling, rather than being annoyed as usual. I was starting to find it endearing, though I wasn't sure if I'd ever fully get used to it.

"Well, thank you," I'd whispered back, touching him on the arm. "I'll take good care of it."

"And take care of yourself as well," he'd said, his intense eyes meeting mine. Then he'd disappeared down the hallway and back into his room. I'd slid the knife uneasily in my coat pocket, glad to find that it fit, and had gone back outside, my mind whirling. He'd *already blessed it* for me?

It seemed there were still many things I did not know.

"Are you ready?" Benny called again from beside the car, jolting me from my thoughts of Nikolai and our weird exchange. He and Roberta were staring at me expectantly.

"As ready as I'll ever be," I groaned, shaking off my morbid thoughts. I hoisted my bag over my shoulder, trudged over to the SUV, and slid into the backseat. "But if we happen to pass a Dunkin' Donuts or a Starbucks, I'm going to be needing a very large mocha. With an extra shot."

"There's a gas station on the way out of town, a RaceTrac," Benny said, sliding into the passenger seat and turning to look at me. "They have one of those cappuccino machines with the different flavors and fancy creamers and stuff. That's probably as close as you'll get."

"I'll make do," I said. "As long as it's caffeine, I don't care." When I'd peeled myself off Jamie and Nikolai's couch and into the kitchen earlier, I'd noticed their coffee pot was broken and given an audible groan of despair. I didn't function without coffee in the morning. Even Phillip's fascination with tea hadn't broken me of that. "Think they have oat milk?"

"For someone who was born and raised in a trailer park in

South Georgia, you sure have some champagne tastes," Benny joked, and I shot him a look.

"So, where to first?" Roberta asked, putting the key into the ignition and starting the car.

"I've got a list of addresses here," Benny said, pulling a piece of paper from his pocket. "Places that Nikolai traced through Lee's phone and email."

"Benny, before we go, there's…something you should know," Roberta said, and Benny looked up, wary. "Something about Lee."

"What is it?" he asked in a weary voice.

"Lee…he's the one who shot Guthrie," Roberta said, after a moment's hesitation. We both looked at him, waiting for his reaction. "I just…thought you should know that. Before we resume the search."

"Oh?" he said, staring straight ahead.

"He had no choice," Roberta rushed to explain. "It was basically self-defense—"

"I'm not surprised," Benny cut in. He exhaled deeply, then said, "Good for him."

"That's seriously all you have to say?" Roberta's eyes were wide, a hint of a smile working at the corner of her mouth.

"What do you want me to say?" Benny smiled. "The guy was a bastard. He abused Lee as a kid. Lee did the world a favor."

"But it complicates things," Roberta said slowly. "And after all you two have butted heads on, I thought—"

Benny shrugged. "Everything is complicated as fuck as it is. He's made a lot of dumb decisions, but I can't fault Lee for putting the kibosh on that bastard."

"So I take it this means we can trust you," Roberta said, "not to say anything. Not to tell anyone." I'd gathered from various conversations that Benny had friends in the police department. I assumed that was who she was referring to. A chill went through me, imagining the authorities getting involved in all of this.

"I'm kind of offended that you even have to ask, Roberta." Benny unfolded the paper he was holding and looked down at it. "So, should we go?"

"Okay, sure. What are the addresses?" Roberta asked, her face an expression of surprised bemusement.

"Um…345 Redbud Way, Jekyll Island, and…" Benny peered at the paper. "I don't have my contacts in yet. This one is…257 Pine Branch Road, Brunswick."

"That's my address," I said, feeling a weird creep up my back, even though I'd known that Lee had been there several times. How else could he have left the hat? It shouldn't have been a surprise that he'd written my address down. "So, no need to go there." There was something really familiar about the other address, too. It niggled at me, but I didn't want to say anything unless I knew for sure.

"Maybe we should run back to your place," Roberta said, seeming to sense my uncertainty. "Check on your cat, and make sure Lee didn't come back. It's worth a shot."

"Time is of the essence, Burt," Benny said, and I cracked a smile at that. *Burt.* I liked that. "If we can avoid wasting time, we should."

"I know, but I think it's worth checking," Roberta said as Benny scrolled through his phone.

"I think we should try this other address, the Ludowici one. Maybe try some of the other local places Nik wrote down, and then if we have no luck, and it's not too late, we'll run over to your house, Stormy. Feed your cat and check the place out. Cool?" Benny asked.

"God, I hope we find him today," Roberta said, her hands gripping the wheel. "I'm going out of my mind."

"He's okay, Burt," Benny said, putting a large hand on her shoulder. Roberta smiled and leaned into him slightly, and I wondered if Benny's flirty nature extended naturally to everyone. Even I'd looked at him with an appreciative glance more than once.

After last night, memories were starting to come back, memories of Friday and Saturday nights spent at the G&G Flea Market and Entertainment Center, going with both of my parents to watch the wrestling matches, which were held in an outdoor arena at the weekends, coated with peeling paint and mismatched ring posts. We'd sit on cold bleachers and munch stale corn chips with bright orange cheese, hot dogs, and Dr. Pepper so thick with carbonation, it burned the throat as we watched wrestlers go toe to tie. I remembered screaming for a young, dark-haired athlete, who wasn't much older than me, handsome and strong. He was barely a teenager, no more than fourteen at the oldest, but he'd captivated the audience and shown up wrestlers twice his size and three times his age. I remembered, now, screaming along with all the girls as this boy—known even then as The Black Wolf—would inflict suplexes, clotheslines, and DDTs onto his opponents.

I still had no clear recollection of ever being there with Roberta or any of the other kids from the trailer park—I still didn't remember most of them at all—but I knew it would come back to me eventually, and I could see why we'd all been so enamored with him. It was the same reason everyone was enamored with him now. He'd been amazingly strong—and very goth—even back then, and the man he'd grown into was a sight to behold. Charismatic, strong, a little menacing—a natural leader. Some people are just destined for greatness.

I could see why Clara was impossibly hung up on the super —buff, handsome wrestler. I felt sorry for her; I knew what it felt like to lose someone you thought you'd be with forever, to say nothing of Benny's physical attributes.

"Clara's a tough chick," Roberta said from the front seat.

"Not just on the outside, either. She's tough where it counts. She'll bounce back."

I stared at the back of Roberta's head, my mouth wide open. She'd heard my thoughts. Heard them and responded. I'd long suspected that she—and if I was being honest, a few of the others—had an odd intuition that allowed them to be especially in tune with how I was feeling. But Roberta had outright *heard* my thoughts.

The only other person who could do that with me was Phillip. And I'd been hanging out with her for days and she'd never let on that she could…

Roberta turned to me, a smile beginning on her lips. "You're not the only one with a special power or two," she said, breaking into a full-on grin. "Like I said before you kissed the floor with your face, there's more to the story, more I have to tell you."

I stared at her, wondering just how much of me she had read, if I'd given anything away that I didn't want Roberta, or anyone else, to know. But as I wracked my brain, my phone began to vibrate, pulling me away from my thoughts.

I pulled it from my pocket, my heart starting to pound when I saw it was Phillip.

I'm glad you're okay. Oh, and Gloriana Hole? Sounds like something I'd name one of my albums.

It was weird; Phillip hadn't initially responded to my text joking about Clara's stage name, but suddenly decided to when Roberta and I had just been talking about her? Were we all in some kind of brain wave sync?

I smiled despite myself. It was good just to hear from him, forget the other weirdness. Before I could reply, another text pinged through.

Where are you?

I began to type out a response, though if I had any pride, I'd ignore the text a while, make him wait like he'd made me wait. But who was I kidding, I had no willpower around Phillip.

In a car with Roberta and The Black Wolf himself. On a bit of a rescue mission. Where are you?

His reply: *Looking for the person you told me about before?* I didn't fail to notice how he'd ignored *my* question.

Yes. No luck yet

Keep me posted, he typed. *Let me know.*

I frowned at the phone. Well, if he wanted to be cagey, that was fine, but I wasn't playing the game. I fired off a response.

*Where are *you*? You don't seem to want to tell me.*

His reply made my heart sink.

Think it's best not to tell anybody for the moment. I hope you're being safe, though, Stormy. Being careful.

I put my phone back in my pocket without replying. There was a lump in my throat, and I tried to swallow it down, but my feelings were very hurt. That was twice now that I'd asked him where he was, and twice that he'd refused to tell me. Obviously, Phillip Deville didn't want me coming to find him. No amount of half-assed concern or flippant, silly, flirty remarks would change that. I wiped a wayward tear from my eye before it fell and stared out the window, hoping that Burt —I'd already come to call her that in my head—wasn't trying to pry into my thoughts right now. If she was, she'd be crying in short order, too, such was the heartbreak I felt.

I fished my house key out of my pocket and exited the SUV, utterly exhausted. I was half tempted to suggest we stay the night at my place. I didn't much fancy the idea of a drive all the way back to the Wolfden tonight. We'd been driving across half of Georgia for most of the day, had visited multiple houses and hangouts of Lee's, and hadn't seen sign of him or anyone else we were searching for. I was looking forward to seeing Blinken, and the thought of vegging out on my couch with a glass of merlot was very appealing. Benny was still in the SUV, making more phone calls. I had to respect his tenacity—he really was like a wolf following a scent—but he was wearing me slap out.

"I'd be okay with it, but I don't know that Benny would," Roberta said behind me as I approached my front stoop. I turned around and fixed her with a glare.

"Okay, *Burt*," I said. "I'm not quite used to this power of yours, since you just told me about it a few hours ago. Try to put the kibosh on prying into my noggin, okay?" I grimaced. "I barely got used to Phillip doing that."

"Sorry," Roberta said, and managed to look chagrined.

"Anyway, what's Benny got against staying at my house?" I demanded.

"It's not that," she explained. "I doubt he's gonna stop and rest up for the night anywhere. Not with Lee still missing." Then, as she looked past me up the stairs, her face clouded over. She lowered her voice to a whisper. "Stormy."

"What?" I started up the stairs, still irritated.

"Stormy. *Stop*." Roberta put her hand out, stopping me. "Wait. We need to get Benny to go in first."

"Why?" I asked, but as I looked up the stairs, my eyes narrowed into slits.

My front door was standing ever so slightly ajar.

"*Goddamit*," I seethed, stomping up the steps. "Somebody has broken into my house *again*? If they hurt my cat, I swear to god, I'll break their arms—"

"Stormy, for fuck's sake, stop!" Roberta begged. "It's not safe! You don't know who's in there. Let Benny go first."

"Stay here," Benny said as he bounded onto the stoop. He brushed past me and pushed the door open. "You both stay out here. Don't come in until I say." He didn't wait for either of us to answer, and hurried into the house, his stance tense and aggressive.

For a moment, all we heard was silence, and I began to think nobody was there. Then there was a loud crash and a yell, and I froze in terror. Roberta and I stared at each other, wide-eyed.

"Who the fuck are you?" we heard Benny yell. "And why the hell are you in Stormy's house?" I tensed and moved to push inside, but Roberta stopped me, holding me fast to her. She was breathing hard; she was scared. There was another crash and a great booming shout; this time, the voice was unmistakably not Benny's.

"Stormy, no!" she whispered furiously, her breath hot in my ear. "It's not safe!"

I wrestled away from Roberta's grasp. I knew that voice.

Roberta grasped my shirt, but I wrenched myself free and ran up the steps and into the house, stopping short in the living room with a gasp. The sight before me was one I could barely comprehend and would commit to memory forever.

My coffee table had been overturned, a vase of flowers was leaking onto the floor, the vase itself shattered into pieces, and my sweet Blinken sat in the corner, bathing himself as though nothing was amiss, his flicking tail the only indication that he might be mildly annoyed.

In the middle of the room, next to my overturned coffee table, Benny was locked in what could only be described as a mutual, struggling headlock.

I heard Roberta run up behind me and let out a choked sound.

Benny's broad shoulders were tense as he pushed against a dark-haired man who was only slightly taller than him, and the man was pushing right back with his arms around Benny's head. Both men's broad shoulders rippled with exertion, each man trying to overpower the other. The dark-haired man was breathing hard as he pushed back against Benny, his own arms white and huge in the darkened room. I felt goosebumps erupt on my arms as I watched them, unable to move, transfixed at the sight.

"Holy shit," Roberta breathed next to me. "That guy is strong as hell. Who *is* that?"

"Oh, that's just Phillip," I said, my heart thumping wildly in my chest, my lips curling up in a grin despite myself. "Phillip Deville. The one and only."

Thirteen

"That's Phillip Deville?" Roberta asked in a whisper. I nodded.

"Holy shit," she whispered again hotly, blinking. "Well done, you."

I smiled, unable to tear my eyes away from the scene in front of me. The two men were straining against each other in a battle of strength, and neither seemed to be losing—or winning, for that matter. Phillip was strong—I knew that for sure—but Benny was a literal professional wrestler. The fact that he hadn't immediately toppled Phillip without breaking a sweat spoke to just *how* strong Phillip was.

Whoever the victor, it was certainly nice to watch.

Phillip shoved his full weight against Benny, almost throwing him over but not quite succeeding. Benny pushed back, unable to get purchase over him, the muscles in his shoulders rippling with effort, and he gave a frustrated cry of rage. "You…fucker…" he spat out. "Why…the…fuck…are… you…in…Stormy's…house…?"

"Stop…trying…to…fight…me…and…I'll…tell…you…" Phillip sputtered right back. Both of them were out of breath, but neither one was letting up. They were at an impasse.

neither could best the other, it seemed. I noticed, out of the corner of my eye, a lit cigarette in an ashtray on the side table beside a piece of paper, half-filled with Phillip's familiar scrawl. Propped against the pillows on my couch was my old black bass. Evidently, Phillip had been hanging out here, just chilling on my couch, playing music. But *why?*

And why hadn't he told me?

Benny was still pushing against Phillip. "Did…you… take…Lee…"

Phillip made a noise that could only be described as a half-chuckle, half-grunt, and shoved Benny with all his might, pitching his entire bulk forward. Finally, he managed to shove him off. Benny went flying, falling against the wall, collecting himself at the last moment, panting heavily as he charged towards Phillip. I ran over to the wall to inspect it; as huge as Benny was, he'd probably gone right through the cheap drywall.

"Guys! Just stop! Please!" I exclaimed. At the sound of my voice, Phillip started, wrenching his eyes from Benny and over to me. Benny took advantage of his momentary distraction to throw himself at Phillip. Phillip threw up one arm, casually blocking Benny's advances as though he was swatting a fly. His eyes were still on me, the struggle from a moment before totally forgotten as we locked eyes.

"Storm?" he said in a curious voice, as though it was unusual for me to be in my own house.

"What are you doing here, Phillip?" I demanded.

Benny was still panting, his chest heaving, and he stared at Phillip like he wanted to rip him limb from limb. "Do you have Lee?" he asked again. "If you hurt him, I swear to fuck, I'll—"

"I've got nothing to do with that dude," Phillip said, a flicker of annoyance crossing his face. He turned back to me. "Stormy, will you call this meathead off, please?"

"Benny, this is Phillip," I said, my voice wavering. I was

finding it hard to look anywhere but into Phillip's deep green eyes. I'd missed him so much. It was so good to see him. But seeing him standing in my home after days of deflecting me made me angry. "My...my ex. He doesn't have Lee. He wouldn't do anything to him, I swear."

"Are you sure about that?" Benny's eyes were wild and scared.

"As much as I am about any of you, or Lee himself, for that matter," I answered after a pause, and Benny looked at me thoughtfully, then nodded. He took a step back and squared his shoulders.

"Sorry I punched you," he said to Phillip reluctantly, and I was surprised to see Phillip nod and rub absently at a spot on his cheek. Benny had punched Phillip in the face. He must have brass balls to do something like that.

"Forget it. Sorry I punched you back."

Benny had the beginnings of a shiner himself. I had to stifle a laugh. I was glad things had broken up when they had. I didn't relish the thought of the damage these two could have inflicted on each other.

Benny looked at Phillip. "When I heard Stormy say someone had broken in, I freaked. We've been looking for Lee all day and I just...I just feared the worst." He walked over to my couch and slumped down onto it, his face more dejected and fearful than I'd seen it before. It was as if the fight had all of a sudden completely gone out of him, and I realized just how worried he was, how frantic. We'd searched all day and hadn't had so much as a lead. I watched as Benny put his head in his large hands, his huge shoulders slumping into a posture of defeat.

I turned from Benny to Phillip and back again, not knowing what to do, who to talk to, who to comfort. Luckily, Roberta elbowed me in the side. "I'll talk to Benny," she said in a low voice, her eyes flashing. "You find out what mister rock star here is doing in your house."

"Thanks," I said.

I shot her a grateful look and gestured to Phillip to follow me outside. He did, wordlessly, his heavy footsteps sounding on the cheap flooring of my trailer behind me. So much for enjoying a quiet night of de-stressing in my place with a glass of merlot, as I'd been hoping to talk Benny and Roberta into doing.

We walked together to the corner of my front yard, where there was a picnic table set up that I rarely used. I couldn't remember the last time I'd sat here—maybe grilling with Sloan last summer, or maybe even before that, before Tess had left. As much as I loved this quiet spot under the trees, I was usually eaten up with ticks and mosquitoes any time I ventured out here, so I mostly avoided it. I wondered, stupidly, if I could formulate some kind of spell to repel the little critters. If we ever found Lydia, I would ask her.

Thoughts like that were creeping in more often now, despite how busy and chaotic everything had been. I was beginning to think like a witch, to embrace this new normal, whatever it was. Whatever it meant I was.

Phillip and I both sat down quietly, neither of us seeming to have any words, the ability to communicate with each other momentarily suspended. Oh, who was I kidding—it had been ever since the day I'd told him to get out of my room and out of my house. The day he'd broken my heart. I watched as Phillip lit a cigarette, his mouth fixing around the filter and taking a long drag, the cherry shining bright at the tip. I hated that he smoked; it reminded me of Mama and the way she always lit one off the other. His hair was scruffy and wild, and already starting to grow back out, but it was as black as ever, shining under the muggy, hot Georgia sun. His green eyes were deep and curious and a little sad as he regarded me silently, puffing away. I knew he was giving me space to collect my thoughts. He was empathetic like that, intuitive and kind.

But he still had a lot of explaining to do.

I swallowed, then fixed him with a cold stare.

"You've got a lot of nerve, dodging my calls and texts, refusing to tell me where you are, only for me to find you crashing at my fucking house," I leveled at him, my face stony.

"I'm not crashing. I just came to check it out," Phillip said, blowing out smoke in a long stream. "When you said you'd gone off with Roberta, I thought it might be a good idea to come back and see if anything was amiss. Just in case anybody showed up here looking to make trouble."

"I didn't ask you to do that."

"I'm sorry," Phillip said. "I was trying to help."

"So you just got here?" I asked, disbelieving. "You really haven't been here the whole time?"

"I promise. I came this morning. After we talked," Phillip said.

"You said you were going back to Boston," I said accusingly. "When we…when you left me. You were going back to see Barb and…what did you say? Do some thinking? I'm assuming that was a lie?"

Phillip shook his head, looking momentarily guilty. "I never went back. I'm sorry, Stormy—I did originally plan to. I wasn't just lying to you. Something…came up at the last minute, and I decided to stick around. I didn't tell you because…well, I figured it'd just complicate things, make things harder."

"How so?"

"Oh, come on, Stormy. After that fight we had? If you knew I'd stuck around after all that, you would've been furious. And it would have been harder for us to stay apart. One of us would have wanted to talk things out some more, to see each other, you know? I meant what I said about us both needing time. To think, to figure things out. I promised to give you space, so I didn't want to go back on that. It wouldn't have been fair."

"What I'm hearing is that you thought if I knew you were in town, that I'd harass you, hang around, and cramp your style," I said, angry. "Do you really think so little of me? You think I'm some clingy stalker fan-girl?"

"That's not what I mean at all," Phillip said, looking pained. "I meant it the other way around. If I told you I was here, then *I'd* want to see *you*. I wouldn't be able to stay away." His eyes burned. "Plus…I thought it might be easier to keep an eye on things, keep you safe, if I was a little removed from the situation."

"Um, I'm pretty sure *you* broke up with *me.*" I said angrily. "How's looking after me still your job?"

"I'll always look after you," Phillip said plainly, his green eyes staring into mine. My heart lurched. "I owe you that much. And I didn't break up with you. I don't remember saying those words."

"You didn't have to say them," I replied meanly, feeling hurt. His eyes flashed, but he didn't look away. "It doesn't matter anyway. You don't owe me anything anymore. I released you, remember? Anyway, we're even."

"This isn't some game of tit for tat," Phillip said, puffing on his cigarette. "Saying I owe you…I shouldn't have put it like that. I *care* about you, Stormy. I want to make sure you're safe, I need to. Especially now that you're neck-deep in all of this…" He trailed off, his eyes flickering over to the woods. He seemed to be considering something. Then he smiled. "That guy—Benny, is that his name? The one you called the Black Wolf? He's a fucking meathead, but I'm glad you're with him. He'll keep you safe. He'll look out for you."

"He's not a meathead," I said. "And I don't need looking

after. I can take care of my fucking self, or have I not proved that already?"

"Yes, you've proved it and then some," Phillip said, tossing his butt on the ground and crushing it under his heavy black boot. He picked it up and pushed the butt into the pocket of his black jeans. "Don't wanna litter up your yard," he said with a grin, then, in a softer voice, "I like the way you're wearing your hair. Up in a bun like that, with all the little tendrils falling down. Messy. It's cute."

"Don't try and distract me," I said, not ready to be disarmed. He was so good at that. "And I'm not impressed. You want me to be impressed, *quit* smoking. It's a gross, nasty, outdated habit. Seriously, nobody smokes anymore. It's so over."

"Noted," Phillip said, still smiling at me. The way his eyes flashed, the bemused smirk on his face…it was impossibly sexy, and it was all I could do not to touch him. Which only made me angrier.

"So where *have* you been, then? Where were you before I left my house?" I demanded. If Phillip had decided not to go back to Boston…that likely meant he hadn't seen Barb after all. Maybe he'd changed his mind about reconnecting with her. My heart lifted.

Phillip hesitated, so I answered for him. "You were on Tybee, weren't you?"

He looked at me in surprise. "How did you know?"

"Because I saw you." His brow furrowed in confusion, and I explained. "Roberta and I visited the wharf one morning and I saw you out in the water, swimming. It was right after dawn, and the way the sun lit on your hair…I *knew* it was you…I tried to convince myself it wasn't, but…anyway, I heard waves crashing behind you that time we talked on the phone, too. I knew you were at a beach. I grew up on the freaking ocean, or did you forget?"

Phillip looked at me curiously, then smiled a long, slow smile. "You were stalking me, Stormy Spooner?"

"Ha. No. It was pure coincidence."

"I find that hard to believe," he said, his eyes fixed on mine. "You just happened to be on the same beach as me on some random morning?"

"I don't care what you believe," I spat, and he grinned. "I grew up around here, these are *my* places. It's just as believable as you coming here to check on things for no apparent reason. For someone trying to stay away from me, you sure do flock to places where I'm bound to be." Phillip was silent, still smiling at me like I was some precocious child. It was pissing me off and turning me on at the same time. "So why Tybee? What were you doing there?"

"I've been staying at a hotel in Savannah," he said. "One morning, I was missing the ocean—missing you, if I'm being honest—and thinking about the time we'd spent on Driftwood Beach. So I decided to rent a car and drive to Tybee for a swim." He smiled at me hopefully. "It wasn't the same though. Not without you."

I wondered if we'd been staying at the same hotel that night. The thought of being in the same building as him, that close, close enough to sneak off to his room and quench the thirst I'd had for him…but no, it couldn't be. Rather than speak these thoughts aloud, I said, "Why were you in Savannah?"

Phillip looked uncomfortable. "Stormy, you're already so deep in all this…"

"Tell me, Phillip," I demanded, and put my hand on his, giving it a firm squeeze that meant business. A shock went through my skin as I touched him; so that still happened, too. "Or does the whole 'honesty and trust' thing only go one way?"

Phillip sighed. His hand flipped around, and his fingers

found mine, curling them up in his own. His hand was warm and heavy, and it felt good to be touching him. "Fine. I'll tell you. Someone called me and asked me to stick around."

"Who?"

"Lee Courtenay," he said, looking me in the eye.

"What on earth?" I exclaimed. "Why on earth would he have called you?" Lee and Phillip hated each other, or so they'd led me to believe.

Phillip shrugged. "He was worried, what else? After you and I had that big fight"—I winced at the memory—"and I left your house, he called me shortly after. I was already in an Uber halfway to the bus station, ready to buy a ticket."

"And what did he say?" I asked.

"He said he had an uneasy feeling that none of this was over, and that Guthrie—or someone close to him—would come back to finish what he'd started. He wanted my help." Phillip's face was uneasy. "I was angry. I told him none of that was my problem anymore, and that I was leaving." He swallowed. "That upset Lee. He begged me to stay. He said that he needed—that *you* needed—as much protection as you could get."

"I'm so tired of men telling me I need protecting," I said vehemently, rolling my eyes. "Usually right before they need their own asses saved."

Phillip chuckled, his face lighting up for a moment. Then it went dark again. "I know, and I said as much to Lee. But man, he did sound terrified, if I'm being quite honest. Before he called, I was ready to get on the first bus to Hartsfield Airport. After his call, I told my Uber driver to take me straight to Savannah. I figured it was close enough that I could come back at a moment's notice, but far enough away that you'd never know I was there." He smiled at me slyly. "I guess I underestimated you, though, because you found me."

"You can't hide from me," I said, trying for a joking tone and failing. I felt lousy.

"Imagine being at a whole other beach at six a.m. on a random weekday and your girlfriend *still* tracks you down," he said with a smirk. "You've got quite the powerful witch noggin in that pretty head of yours, Stormy Spooner."

"Very funny."

"There's one more thing I should tell you," Phillip said, looking at me seriously. "Lee told me…he told me that there was someone else behind all of this. Other than just Guthrie." He looked at me gauging my reaction. "Does the name Elvin ring a bell?"

"Of course it does," I said bitterly, looking him in the eye. "Dear old Uncle El, staple of my childhood."

He gaped at me. "What? What do you mean?"

I answered his question with a question. "So Lee told you about Elvin—which means you knew there was someone else out there, planning to do us harm—you knew it several days ago, and you didn't think to pick up your phone and call?"

He didn't immediately answer. I looked into Phillip's face, hoping for chagrin, or at the very least, vague guilt, but instead, he just looked shocked. Like someone who had been had. Lee had told him about Elvin, likely before *I* had even known about his involvement, before I'd ever even remembered the man! Lee and Phillip had both known, and yet neither had thought to warn me, to give me a heads up. Instead, I'd had to find out from Roberta, who I barely knew.

Phillip's green eyes worked me over; his mouth thankfully silent; never mind him sensing my anger. He could likely see it splayed all over my face. He knew about Elvin. He'd known for days, and even though he knew, he'd ignored my texts and calls and lied to me when I'd asked him where he was.

Phillip, my love, who had lectured me on trust and honesty,

had deceived me and kept secrets. We always came back to this.

"You knew," I accused him, unable to control the seething anger in my voice. "You kept me in the dark!"

"Stormy." Phillip's voice was pained, but defiant, too. "If you know about Elvin now, then it doesn't matter…"

"It matters," I said, standing up and moving away from the table. "It matters because you raked me over the coals for not being honest with you, for not telling you everything I was thinking and feeling every second of the day. You went on and on about me not trusting you, not letting you in. You *left me* for not being honest, Phillip! And then you sat there on something so big, something so important. This is my *life,* Phillip!"

"Like I said, Lee and I thought that, to keep you safe…" he began, but I cut him off.

"No, you were getting revenge! Keeping things from me as payback for me keeping things from you. Sitting on your laurels at the beach while I was trying to find all these folks, learning about all these terrible things from my childhood, finding out a literal boogeyman is trying to hurt me! All the while freaking out! All these awful fucking memories. And wanting you by my side the whole time. Missing you so much the whole time."

Phillip looked down at his feet, his face full of regret.

"You avoided me, Phillip, right when I needed you the most. And all the while, I thought it was my fault, that you didn't want to talk to me because I'd fucked things up so bad. You *asshole.*"

Phillip stood up and walked around the table, extending his arms out to me. "Stormy, please. It wasn't like that. I only knew about Elvin for a couple of days. I had no details, no leads, for the love of Christ. I wanted to get more information for you, to figure things out, while still keeping you—"

"If you say, 'keep me safe' one more time, I swear to god, I'll knock your dead ass into the dirt."

Phillip stared at me, his mouth dropping open, one eyebrow raised slightly. "Just how do you propose to do that?"

I glared at him. "Don't try to play the tough guy with me, Phillip Deville, and don't you dare underestimate me. I'm not some 'meathead' wrestler with more muscles than sense. I'm a certified fucking witch and you know good and well I can knock you into next week with my fingers if I feel like it."

"Jesus Christ, what's happened to you?" Phillip asked in an awestruck voice—looking positively thrilled.

"You can stop grinning like a Cheshire cat, too," I commanded. "I'm serious. I can't believe you, Phillip. You should have called me the very second you met her."

"I'm sorry, Stormy," Phillip said. "I did consider it. I swear. But I was afraid of what would happen if you knew. The day after he called me, Lee just disappeared. He was supposed to come into Savannah, to meet for coffee. He never showed. I called him and called him, and he never picked up." He swallowed. "I started to get scared, and then when you told me he weas missing…I was so freaked. I almost told you then, but then I started worrying about the implications…" He sighed. "It just seemed like laying low while I figured things out was the right choice. Besides, from what I can see, you've been doing okay on your own, you and your friends, without me cocking things up."

"Of course I'm doing okay," I said with a sigh. "That's the thing you never seem to get. I don't need you to save me, Phillip. I can save myself. It's the fact that you don't believe I can—you don't believe in *me*—that seems to be the problem."

He sighed. "That's not true, Stormy."

But it was. Even if he didn't realize it. I stared at him. We were at an impasse, again. His eyes were so beautiful, so sad. I wanted to rush to him, to feel his strong arms around me, hear his heartbeat in my ear. It had only been a week, but it had felt like a lifetime since I'd touched him. But I made myself stay put. His betrayal was unforgivable. I needed time to process. "I'd better get back," I said. "See about Benny. I'm sure he's itching to get back on the road. After all, we have a bunch of missing people to find."

Part of me secretly hoped Phillip would ask me to stay behind with him. That he'd ask me to explain who Elvin was and what he meant to my childhood. Anything to show he cared. But he didn't. Instead, Phillip nodded, his face full of conflicting emotions, but no words of protest. He reached up and pushed a strand of my hair behind my ear and smiled. "I hope you'll be careful, Stormy. I hope you guys find Lee and the rest of them and that you'll be safe."

He stared down at me, and as my eyes rose to meet his, I noted once again just how tall he was, how majestically he carried himself. So graceful for someone so huge and hulking. His eyes bored into mine as though he were trying to read my every thought—and truth be told, sometimes he could—and his full mouth twitched a little. He leaned closer, the smell of his hair familiar and sweet, and I breathed it in, my eyes starting to close in pleasure before I caught myself and stepped back.

"You could come with us," I said, the words tumbling out of my mouth before I could stop them. My cheeks flushed red with embarrassment. Why was I so damned eager, so pitiful? No matter how strong I tried to be, I just couldn't resist Phillip. "I mean, if you wanted to. If you weren't busy or whatever." My face flushed redder. I tried for a joking tone. "Unless you'd rather spend the night alone at my house, sniffing my underwear."

Phillip laughed. "I'd love to—and I mean that." Then his face fell. "But as much as I do want to help, I was actually getting ready to head back to Savannah when you showed up."

He put a hand lightly on my shoulder as we walked back to the trailer, and I tried not to let the gesture raise my hopes too high. "You probably don't believe me, and I don't blame you, but I really did just pop by to check things out and feed your cat. I remember how Sloan neglected him and I just want to… to see to things for you." His face flushed pink. "But I've got to get back into town this evening for a…meeting."

"A meeting? Here in Brunswick? Who with?" I asked, turning to look at him. "About Lee? Or Guthrie and Elvin?"

"No, actually, it's nothing to do with them, or any of this," Phillip answered, looking uncomfortable. "I'm meeting someone downtown. A dinner thing."

"Oh…" I said, trailing off, giving him a moment to fill me in.

"It's not a big deal," Phillip said quickly, his face coloring. "But I can't cancel."

"Are you trying to tell me that you have a date?" How in the hell was that even possible? It had been only *days!* Phillip Deville was drop-dead gorgeous, to be sure, but…

Phillip looked down at his boots. "Not exactly. I mean, sort of." He ran a hand through his dark hair and sighed. "Since we're talking honesty…Stormy, I'm meeting…I'm meeting Barb."

My mouth dropped open. "You're…she's…why is she here?" All my relief from moments before was suddenly gone. He hadn't decided not to reconnect with her, no, not at all. Instead, he'd decided to bring Barb, his ex-wife, here. To *my* turf.

"I told you that she wanted to meet up," Phillip said, his voice irritatingly calm. "Remember? That day of…of the fight? She was pretty eager to make that happen. When I called and told her I wasn't coming back to Boston after all, well, she understandably thought I was trying to dodge her. She was pissed." He ran a hand through his black hair, a nervous affectation I'd come to know well. "You have to understand, Stormy—she's thought all these years that I was dead. For her to find out I'm not...well, I have some explaining to do. She's so confused and upset and she's afraid reporters are going to start coming around—I have an obligation to explain, to help." He shook his head. "Though I have no idea how to even begin, or what to tell her."

"Why is she *here*, though?" I asked, my voice close to tears. "Why would you have her come here? To my home turf, to where we—"

"You assume I had a choice," Phillip said with a dry laugh. "The second she figured out where I was, she bought a plane ticket. Told me she was on her way and that I had some explaining to do when she got here." He smiled at me. "I guess in some respects, the ball and chain still hold." When I didn't laugh, his smile faded. "She was supposed to have gotten in this afternoon. She was going to rest after the flight and then meet me for dinner." He reached out to grab my hand, but I pulled it back. "Stormy, there's nothing there. Not anymore. I just owe her an explanation, is all."

"You don't know that nothing's there," I said desperately, turning away. I couldn't bear to look at him right now. "You haven't seen her yet. You don't know what chemistry is still there. How you're going to feel when you see her."

"Stormy."

"She's your *wife*." I brushed a tear from my cheek, hoping he hadn't seen.

I turned and started walking back towards the trailer. Roberta and Benny were waiting, and I couldn't think of anything more to say. Phillip followed me, and I could feel his unhappiness coming off him in waves as he locked step behind me.

"*Was* my wife. A lifetime ago. Stormy, please, try and understand," Phillip pleaded.

"Whatever," I said in an acid tone, knowing I was being petulant and mean, but unable to stop myself. "I know that." We'd reached the porch stairs. Roberta and Benny were leaning against her SUV, waiting, watching us curiously.

Phillip made his way up the stairs, walking into the foyer, and stopped there, looking back at me with a wounded expression. "I'm sorry about all of this," he said finally, his eyes searching mine, big and sad. "I didn't mean to hurt you."

I gripped the peeling porch railing and took each step slowly, one by one, trying to keep myself from crying and unable to bite off the cruel words as they emerged from my lips. "I get it, Phillip. She's your wife. You have to see her. You owe it to her." His eyes were huge as he stared at me. I put my hand on the door handle. "And hey, if things go well, by all means, feel free to bring her back here. Since I won't be home and you're used to just letting yourself in." With that, I slammed the door with a *thud*, right in Phillip's face.

I bounded down the stairs to Roberta and Benny, who were staring at me in shock.

"Damn…" Roberta said, looking at me with wide eyes.

"Let's get the fuck out of here before I kill somebody," I said, furiously wiping the angry tears from my cheeks. I didn't have to tell either of them twice.

I was back out on Driftwood, by myself for a blessed moment, for the first time in what seemed like years, even though it had only been a few days. It was windy out on the beach, and the salty air was making my skin feel clammy. I wrapped my arms around my torso, feeling as though I'd swallowed an entire bowling ball. It was hard to breathe, the pain in my chest was so great.

Thankfully, Benny and Roberta had indulged me when I'd asked to come here. Being at Driftwood always centered me, helped me to feel at peace, even when my insides were nothing but turmoil. I suspected Benny only jumped at the opportunity so he could scope out Guthrie's place for himself.

Roberta plopped down beside me in the sand and rested her head on my shoulder. Surprised, I looked at her, then relaxed. It felt comfortable, easy, with her, a stark contrast to just a few days before when I'd sat out here with Sloan in almost the exact same spot. Roberta had a warmth and a familiarity about her that was so different from Sloan, whose cynical, matter-of-fact manner could turn cruel on a dime. I barely knew Roberta, but I knew where I stood with her. I knew she had my back, without a doubt. It had taken me 'til my thirties, but I'd finally figured out that friendships should be easy; chasing after people and haggling for their support was no good. I vowed to stop pushing people away who seemed to genuinely like me in favor of chasing after crumbs from those who really didn't.

Roberta turned to me with an empathetic smile. "God, Stormy, I'm sorry," she said, pressing a cold Coca-Cola into my hand. "Got it from the cooler in the car."

"Thanks," I said, popping the tab and taking a long sip. "Benny's been gone a long time."

"I'm sure he's fine. He would have texted if anything was wrong."

"We should probably go check," I insisted. "If he doesn't come back soon."

"I feel like I should clear the air," Roberta said, her dark eyes meeting mine. She dug her feet into the sand up to her ankles, a childlike movement, and I thought about how much of that sand would make its way into her black chucks later.

"About what?"

"Well, about Tess, for starters," she said, her cheeks

reddening a little, a pretty contrast against her olive skin. "And…about the rest of it. The rest of us."

"Oh." As curious as I'd been to find out more, at this point I was wary. With so much else occupying my mind—Lee missing, knowing that Phillip was on his way to a date with his ex-wife, everything I'd learned about Elvin and Guthrie—I wasn't sure I could handle anything else. Especially not when it came to Tess. I'd worked so hard over the past year to get over him, and I'd finally managed it. I wasn't sure I wanted to look backwards. "It really doesn't matter, Burt."

She smiled. "So now you're calling me that, too." She dug her feet further into the sand. "It *does* matter, Stormy. I feel like we're getting to be friends. And we can't be friends without trust. And we can't have trust if you don't know the whole story."

There was that trust thing again. I sighed. "Lay it on me, then."

She took a deep breath. "First thing you have to know, I don't have any feelings for Tess. I never did. I know that'll probably make you angry to hear, considering everything that happened, but it's true. My reasons for dating Tess were purely…pragmatic."

I frowned at her. Tess, who was not exactly a member of Mensa, was not likely to be associated with a word like *pragmatic.* "What do you mean?"

"I know you're going to think this sounds insane, but…I got close to Tess so I could keep an eye on you."

"*What?*" I stared at her.

Noting my expression, Roberta held her hands out to me in a gesture of surrender. "I know it sounds insane, but like…I didn't know any other way to get close to you without telling you everything, and back then, you didn't remember anything about that time…you didn't know about your own powers…

you didn't know *what* you were. And Tess and I go way back, so it was easy to reconnect with him…"

"You seduced my husband to 'keep an eye' on me? Couldn't you have just, like, shown up at the library and befriended me?" I asked snottily, my hands clenched at my sides. "Oh, wait, you could have *actually* done that, because you *actually* did."

Roberta's eyes widened. "I didn't seduce Tess, Stormy. It wasn't like that. Will you just let me explain?"

"I guess." I tried to keep my voice level, to quell the anger in it. It didn't work.

"I know you're not going to believe me," Roberta said, putting a hand on my arm. "But the truth is that Tess and I never slept together. Not once."

"You're right. I don't believe you." I shook my head. "Tess cheated on me, Roberta. A lot. He never would have wasted time hanging around you if he wasn't…" I trailed off, fresh pain filling my heart.

"I know what he's like, believe me," Roberta said. "I won't lie and say I didn't dangle the possibility in front of him. I'm sure he was hoping it would turn into something, but…I promise you, Stormy. I just hung around, led him on a little—" Her face turned suddenly guilty. "And I hooked him up now and again, to keep him around. Keep him interested. So I could spy on you."

"You mean drugs."

"Yes. I'm sorry," she said, her face filling with color. She knew the pain Tess's drug struggles had put me through. How I'd had to bail him out of the police station many times. How it had put a huge strain on our marriage. "I don't mess with that stuff. But…I did put him onto a connection…just somebody I knew." Her eyes shifted downward, ashamed.

"But why?"

"I needed to see what powers you had. What you remembered. I needed to see if things were starting to change." She sighed. "It wasn't my proudest moment."

"I don't get it," I said. "Why not just walk up to my front door and introduce yourself? You had no problems doing that when Lee went missing. Why infiltrate my life? Why meddle in my marriage, screw things up even worse?" I dug my feet into the sand. "Why not just ask Tess for info? He probably would have told you."

"I did, but he only knew so much," she said, looking down. "And I was scared."

I stared ahead towards the sea. None of what she said made any sense, but I wasn't sure I wanted to know. I should have been relieved that she'd never slept with Tess, but honestly, the knowledge didn't do much to assuage my pain. I'd lost him anyway, hadn't I?

"Right as all of this started, Sloan told me that the two of you had shown up at the Curling Dervish," I said, piecing things together. "That you wanted a haircut. Were you just trying to get close to me then?"

"Yeah," Roberta said. "I didn't expect her to throw us out. Sloan's always been a drama queen with divided loyalties. I figured she'd jump at the chance for some secret drama. But she must have been scared that day, because she didn't want us there."

"I feel like the whole world is in on some conspiracy," I said bitterly. "A conspiracy that goes back to my childhood and everyone knows and remembers except for me."

Roberta sighed. "Tess doesn't remember either, Stormy," she said, grabbing a handful of sand and throwing it back down. "Our childhood, I mean. Back when my dad was doing…all the crap he was doing to us…well, he would always wipe you clean afterward. I'm still not really sure why. He always said that it was better for you not to remember, that it made your powers stronger if they came from your own mind, rather than from memories. He didn't want it to be a suggestion, he wanted them to come from a real place." She swallowed. "After everything…went down…well, he wiped you one last time, and he wiped Tess and Sloan, too."

I was still wrapping my head around the fact that I'd known Tess and Sloan when I was a kid. "Why didn't he get you, Nikolai, and Jamie?" I asked.

"He tried. I'd ask you if you remember, but of course you don't. They hid in an abandoned trailer for the entire day that last time, just to get away from him. And me, well, for some reason, he's never been able to wipe me. Which is kinda ironic, me being his flesh and blood."

"Maybe that's why," I suggested, and she nodded.

"That's what I've always thought," Roberta said, playing with the sand. "Thank god for small favors."

"Go back to the beginning," I said, because I still couldn't wrap my mind around all of this—how all these things had happened, and I could just…not remember. It was enough to make me sick. I wrapped my arms around my torso and rocked back and forth in the sand. "Just tell me the rest, and do it quick."

"Okay," Roberta said, putting an arm around me. "Let's see…where did we leave off…when Lydia brought your mom back, right?"

"Yes."

"Well, after that, my dad was obsessed with you. Him and Guthrie both, but my dad was the one who put in all the work. I told you already that Lydia refused to tell him anything about necromancy or how to do any big spells. He eventually gave up trying, but…he knew you possessed the power. He thought he could get to it that way, through you. Being an innocent child, he thought it'd be easy. So he set to work on you, to hypnotize you and try to 'train' you into using your powers. He figured he could tap into you, learn through you."

"Like a magical conduit?" I whispered.

"Sort of. I think he was hoping he could mold you into this powerful little witch baby while learning how to wield your powers at the same time."

"You were always there, Roberta," I said, halfway between an accusation and gratitude, memories trickling back in. "At every 'session,' you were there."

Roberta nodded. "Yes."

"You shot me dirty looks from the doorway," I said, remembering. "And gave me sour Kool-

Aid."

"He hardly ever kept sugar in the house," Roberta answered. "I tried to ration it...I did the best I could. And those weren't dirty looks. They were to wake you up," she explained. "If I saw you drifting off, I'd make funny faces or give you weird looks to perk you up, so you wouldn't fall asleep. It made it harder for him to hypnotize you."

My brow furrowed. "You were *helping* me?"

"As much as I was able to. Daddy was always hovering around, and if he caught me lingering too much, he'd shove me outside. I tried to stay invisible." She took a deep breath. "I think Daddy worked out some kind of arrangement with your dad—he'd pay him in pills or beer to let you come over for sessions. He even sat in once or twice, but he didn't really believe in magic. He was bored."

As if I didn't already feel enough bitterness and resentment towards my father. "But my dad saw it for himself," I said in disbelief. "He saw Lydia and me bringing Mama back."

"He convinced himself—with my dad's help, probably— that your mom had just been unconscious and that you guys shook her awake. He remembered what he wanted to remember," Roberta said. "So you were coming over for sessions a few times a week, for a good two or three months, and Daddy was getting nowhere. He couldn't get you to harness your powers or use them when you were under. He began to think that you didn't have any powers after all." She sighed. "Then he saw you with Nikolai."

"Nikolai?"

Roberta nodded. "Nik always has had a soft spot for you."

Nikolai, who I only *remembered* meeting a few days before, flashed in my mind. His white-blond hair, his piercing blue eyes. He'd barely said a word to me, but hadn't I felt a strange sensation as he'd stared at me at the bonfire? The way he'd been watching me, almost as though he was trying to talk to me without speaking. How he'd pulled me aside and given me an elaborate knife out of the blue. How he'd blessed it for me. What Roberta was saying tracked. There was something between Nikolai and me, even if I no longer knew him from Adam.

"He'd throw a baseball with you after dinner sometimes. I remember watching you guys from my window, throwing that ball back and forth until it got dark." Roberta smiled at the memory. "Well, I guess one night, my dad just happened to catch a glimpse of you guys, too. And he saw that golden light, the same golden light he'd seen the day your mom came back. He saw it in your hands, in your arms, as you threw the ball at Nikolai. 'Look, Roberta, do you see the light?' he asked me. I wish I'd said 'no.'" Her face was full of guilt.

She went on. "After that, Daddy got the idea that when you were around people you loved, that was when your magic was strongest, when you were able to use it. So he started bringing other people into the sessions. He started with Nikolai—he took special care with him—and eventually some of the other kids in the neighborhood, to see which ones brought out the strongest surge of magic."

"Jamie?" I asked, and she nodded. "And Tess and Sloan?"

"Them, too," Roberta agreed. "And me."

"What happened?" I asked, afraid to hear the answer.

"He started hypnotizing us all pretty regularly, just to see what would happen when we were with you. Sometimes your magic would surge, and you'd do things when you were unconscious, and other times not. The magic was always strongest with Nikolai, but he got some results out of me and Jamie as well." She smiled. "You must have liked us."

"This is…this is fucked," I said in a whisper.

"You don't know the half of it," Roberta agreed. "Daddy also brought Lee into a couple of sessions too, when he and his parents visited. When you guys were under, your magic was off the charts. I saw literal sparks coming from your hands." She looked at me with bright eyes. "You and Lee have a strong connection; always have."

"That explains…some things," I said. "And Benny? Was he part of this, too?"

Roberta shook her head. "Benny isn't one of us," she said with a laugh. "Or at least, he wasn't back then. I'll let him tell you that story."

"Okay, so…you, Jamie, Nikolai, Lee…and even Sloan and Tess…were all part of this weird magic experiment that your whack-a-doodle dad was doing to try and tap into my powers, all when we were little," I said, keenly aware of how batty this all sounded. "So how long did this carry on?"

"Well, like I said, he was seeing you multiple times per week for a while there, for at least a couple of years," Roberta answered. "We were pretty little then, maybe seven or eight? Daddy probably would have continued on with it, but Nikolai…" She frowned.

"Nikolai what?" I asked.

"Nikolai hated the sessions. He hated my father. He told his mom what was going on and she freaked," Roberta said. "One thing I forgot to mention, Stormy, is that when Daddy was doing these experiments to tap into your powers…well, he didn't realize he was doing it, but…we think he imparted some of *your* powers into all of us. We began to see things, to notice we could do things that weren't quite normal."

"Like reading people's thoughts?" I asked.

"That's the main one," Roberta replied. "And other things. Like knowing stuff is going to happen before it does, being able to ward off sickness; things like that." She smiled. "We all got together and talked about it, and most of us were thrilled at our newfound quirks. All of us but Nikolai. He was freaked out. He didn't like being able to read thoughts, and he worried the power Daddy took from you to give to us would hurt you, somehow." She sighed. "He went to his mom and told her that Daddy was making us do weird things in the trailer. You can imagine how that went."

"Pitchforks, I imagine," I said. I wished to hell I could remember *any* of this.

"You will," Roberta said, then laughed. "Sorry, I forgot I promised not to do that. But yeah, you're right. Nikolai's mom all but ran me and Daddy out of the trailer park on a rail. He had just enough time to pack up our stuff and get us out before they had the law out there. And…" She lowered her voice to a whisper, even though it was just us on the beach. "He had just enough time to put you under one more time, and…well, once he got what he wanted…to wipe you clean. For good."

"The dream," I said, as things clicked into place. That had been what I remembered—Nikolai and Jamie's sad faces, Elvin tipping my chin up, his wild, cold eyes meeting mine, the sensation of falling, like water swirling down a drain…he had been wiping my memory of every single 'session,' every interaction I'd ever had with him. "Wait, what do you mean, 'what he wanted'?"

"That last time…apparently…you wrote a spell."

I looked at her in shock. "*What?*"

She nodded, her face grim. "He'd been trying to get you to do it for months, and that day, you finally did. You recited some words, and he wrote them down. He was so excited; I'd never seen him so elated." She frowned at the memory. "You were so woozy when you woke up, I gave you two glasses of Kool-Aid that day."

"This spell," I said, an ominous feeling working its way through my extremities. "What was it about?"

Roberta looked me straight in the eye. "Don't you know?"

"No."

"Yes, you do," she insisted. "Think. What spells have you conducted recently?"

"*No*," I said, my body going cold.

Roberta's voice was gentle but insistent. "It was very lyrical; it kinda flowed like water. Even as a kid, I thought it was beautiful."

"'*With salt in air and water in veins?*'" I recited, my arms erupted in goosebumps, my blood like ice.

Roberta nodded slowly. "Yes…yes, that's the one." She gave me a grim smile. "The necromancy spell."

"That's the spell I used to bring Phillip back," I said, suddenly feeling short of breath. "But Roberta, I pulled that spell from the liner notes of a Bloomer Demons album, like *years* later. After Phillip died. I didn't write that; it's impossible."

"You didn't?"

"No," I rushed to explain. "I couldn't have. Phillip put that spell in the liner notes of one of his albums a good two years before he died. There's no way I could have written it, especially not when I was just a little kid!"

"You wrote it," Roberta insisted. "That's why it worked when you recited it, Stormy…because you're the one who originally came up with it."

"That doesn't make sense," I argued. "And if it was true, why would Guthrie have given it to Phillip of all people?"

"Because he was an asshole," Roberta said simply. "He did shit like that."

"No," I moaned, putting my head in my hands. "No, no, no *no, no, no.*"

"I'm sorry, Stormy," Roberta said, her face grave. "This thing, it goes so much deeper than you can imagine. They've been planning it since you were a child. You wrote that spell to bring Phillip back before he ever even died."

"I think I'm going to be sick."

"Go ahead and puke in the sand," Roberta said, her hand warm on my back. "The water will wash it away."

"Talk to me," I said, my breath feeling short in my chest. I gasped for air. "I think I'm having a panic attack. Just talk to me and help me calm down."

Roberta nodded and continued patting my back. "Um... well, where was I? I went to live with my uncle after we left the trailer park, after all the um, unpleasantness..." she said. "I still saw Daddy sometimes, but only sporadically, and honestly, I was so much happier. And everybody else scattered ...Nikolai's mom packed him up and moved him out almost immediately, and a year or so later, Jamie and his family left. Sloan and Tess and eventually you and Laureen—after the divorce—left, too."

"And I never saw any of you again," I whispered, tears in my eyes, "until now."

"Not true," Roberta said, giving my shoulders a squeeze. "I saw you. You just didn't know it was me."

"You did?"

Roberta held my hand tightly. "I told you that my uncle died a few years after I went to live with him. After that, I ended up going back home to my dad—there was nowhere else for me to go. He'd moved to Jekyll by then, to live near Guthrie and Lydia. He was like a parasite, always trying to leech off other people's power, and he never could stay in one place for long." She sniffed. "He didn't have any real magic of his own, so that's what he had to do, like a gnat buzzing around a sweat sock." I had to smile at the image, though I still felt like I might yack at any moment.

"One weekend, I was at the beach, just hanging—I think I had just turned eighteen, so you would have been a little younger—and I saw a girl who looked familiar," Roberta said, her eyes closed. "It was Sloan, throwing a football around with a group of guys. One of them was Tess. I went over to say hello and she was kind of cold to me—no, I'm sugarcoating it —she was rude as hell." She opened her eyes and looked at me. "I should mention—back when Daddy was hypnotizing us, trying to match your powers with our energy or whatever… well, Sloan and Tess were the *only* two that didn't 'take.' He never could get any kind of reading when they were around. And neither of them ever gained any powers from you like the rest of us did."

"That's weird," I said, interested. "I wonder why that is."

"I'm not sure," Roberta said. "But Sloan has always disliked me, and vice versa. I figured that was the reason why. She was super rude that day, and I went to leave—I didn't need that shit from her—when I noticed you, sitting and reading a rock magazine in a beach chair. Your entire face was stuck in that magazine, so I wouldn't have even recognized you, but… it's like I *felt* you."

My face felt like it was buzzing. I looked at her strangely. "This is weird, Roberta, because…I remember that day. I remember going to Driftwood with Tess and Sloan a lot in high school, and I remember laying there one afternoon reading while they threw a football." She nodded. "But…Roberta, I don't remember meeting you at all."

"Doesn't surprise me," she said. "Anyway, I started to go over and say hi, but Sloan stopped me. She was laughing, saying that you wouldn't be interested in hanging out because you were busy crying about some stupid rock star you were obsessed with who had just died. She said it was all you cared about these days." She shook her head. "The way she was mocking you was so mean, and Tess was laughing like he was at a comedy show. I started to tell her off, to tell both of them off, but I kept looking over at you with your head in that magazine. You'd grown up, of course, but to me, you still looked like that scared, stubborn little girl. I wanted to talk to you so bad, but I didn't. You already looked so sad; the last thing I wanted to do was make it worse. And I knew you wouldn't remember me."

"I thought they were my friends," I said helplessly, feeling near to tears. "Sloan and Tess."

"I know," Roberta said, her voice kind. "And I'm sure they were, as much as they were able to be. We all went through some weird stuff together."

"And that was the last time you saw us?" I asked. "Until you started dating Tess?"

She nodded. "I kept tabs here and there, but I was always too afraid to come close." She dug at the sand with her hand. "I couldn't let it go. I had to know if you were okay. And what... what would happen when you finally did that fucking spell." She shook her head sadly. "We always knew you'd do it some- day. After all, you wrote it." She looked at me, her eyes wet. "Now that I know what I know...about you and Phillip...now I understand."

"Well, this is just a fucking mess," I said through my tears, trying for a laugh.

She gave me a bone-crushing hug. "Isn't it though?" Her sweater was scratchy against my skin. "But I have to say, selfish as it sounds, I'm really fucking glad you're sharing this fucked up experience with me, Stormy. It's nice to not be totally alone in the fucked-up-ness." Despite myself, I began to giggle.

Roberta's phone began to ring. "Who the fuck is *calling* me?" she asked irritably, digging her phone out from her cardigan pocket. "Everybody knows to text me…wait, that's Benny." She put the phone up to her ear. "Hey, Ben. What's up —" Her face paled. "Oh, *fuck!*" Roberta scrambled to her feet, hurrying to pull on her shoes. "Come on, Stormy, we've got to go! Benny just found Lee! Stormy come on, he *found him!*"

It was all too much. Sitting there in the sand at Driftwood Beach, my happy place, I fainted for the second time in a week.

Fourteen

I felt like a voyeur, but I couldn't turn away from the scene in front of me.

Lee's face was streaked with dirt and there was a trickle of blood coming from his nose. His cheeks were flushed and red. His chest heaved. He could barely seem to catch his breath, but the look on his face, even under the blood and dirt, said it all.

His pale blue eyes hadn't left Benny's face from the moment we'd stepped into the room.

Benny's own face, usually so imposing and intimidating, was full of tender concern. I'd noticed he'd taken out his striking, dual-color contacts before we'd left the car. His soft brown eyes were fixed on Lee, as if taking stock of his every freckle. "Are you okay?" he asked in a low tone I'd never heard him use before.

"Yeah, man," Lee said, his voice wavering a little, but he took Benny's extended arm and rose to his feet. "I'm okay. Now."

"I've been looking for you across the entire goddamn state," Benny said, his eyes still not leaving Lee's face. "I thought they'd fucking killed you this time, man. I really did."

"I've been here I don't know how many times," Roberta said, her voice full of tears. "And not just me. Others have come looking for you, too. How did we not find you?"

It was a good thing that Benny had decided to poke around Guthrie's while Roberta and I had been on the beach. He'd broken into the house and found nothing, the same as the rest of us, but hadn't been willing to let things go. He'd ransacked the house, looking for any clue or hint that might tell him where Lee was. Just as he'd been about to give up, he'd tripped over a runner carpet in the hallway and had been shocked to find a latch in the floor. He'd managed to pry it up, opening a small, creaking door that led to a cellar that none of the rest of us had found. There, amidst the cobwebs and mouse droppings, in a corner of the mildewed cellar, he'd found Lee, his voice hoarse from yelling for help that hadn't come.

"You can't have been here the whole time," I said, my heart beating fast. It was so good to see Lee. All this time I'd been worried, but I hadn't realized just *how* worried. A part of me had feared he was truly dead.

Lee tore his eyes away from Benny and looked at us. His face was so pale. "Just a couple of days," he croaked, his voice tender and hoarse.

"Where were you before now?" Roberta asked.

Lee grimaced and started to speak. Benny stopped him, his voice sounding choked. "We can ask him all of this later, when we've got him home. When he's safe. Right now, we need to get him out of here."

Feeling a pang of guilt, I nodded. Benny was right; Lee's safety was more important than peppering him with questions. "I'll go get the car from the street, pull it into the driveway so he doesn't have to walk as far," Roberta said, her gaze lingering on Lee, seemingly reluctant to let him out of her sight. Finally, she exited the cellar, painstakingly making her way up the rickety little steps, and we heard the front door shut upstairs.

"Can you walk well enough to get up those stairs?" I asked Lee. "Or will we need to hoist you up?" Neither man answered me; they were too busy looking at each other. Realization began to dawn on me, and I fell back, giving them a moment.

Benny was still clutching Lee's arm, and I realized that Benny was crying. He made a sound in his throat and pulled Lee close to him in a clumsy half-hug, his huge arms dwarfing him. His cheeks were wet as he spoke into Lee's shoulder. "I thought you were a goner, man."

"Not just yet," Lee said, pressing his face into Benny's chest. He was a good deal shorter than Benny, and it occurred to me as I watched them embrace, Lee using his free arm to pull Benny to him into a real hug, watching Benny's arms engulfing him, squeezing him tight, just how well the two of them fit together. Like they were made for each other. "I'm so glad you're here."

"I'm just glad you're okay," Benny said, tears in his voice. He held Lee tight. "When they told me you were missing, I...I thought..." He took a shaking breath. "They've taken so much already; I couldn't bear the thought of them taking you..."

Lee moved his head from Benny's chest to face him, raising his eyes to his. With his free hand, he brushed the tears from Benny's cheek. Benny swallowed and smiled a slow, shy smile.

"I thought I might never see you again," he continued in his tear-soaked voice. "And I gotta tell you, Lee, I couldn't stand it. I thought I was gonna lose my mind."

Lee's face reddened and he smiled, too. "Are you saying you love me, Wolf?"

"Yes, you motherfucker. I'm saying I love you." Benny leaned down and kissed Lee softly on the lips, his black hair falling down over Lee's face, mingling with his own blond hair. Dark and light. I couldn't help but watch them; they looked so beautiful. Suddenly everything made sense.

I had the sensation of many puzzle pieces being pushed into place, the cogs of a clock clicking together to make perfect time. Nobody had thought to tell me about this—not explicitly, anyway, though the signs had been there—but watching Benny and Lee embrace, I was far from surprised. This just felt *right* to me. I smiled, a feeling of warmth flooding through my body.

Just a few days prior, Lee had sat outside on the stoop of this very house and told me that he loved someone. Now I knew just who that someone was. And I whole-heartedly approved.

After a moment, Lee pulled away and brushed Benny's hair back from his face, tucking it behind his ear. His fingers grazed the tattoo just below his earlobe. "I love you too. Man."

Benny's grin was wide and sweet as he chuckled and ruffled Lee's light hair.

I looked down at my feet, letting them have a moment. My heart swelled with love for them. Then I cleared my throat and they both looked over at me, surprised, like they had completely forgotten I existed.

"If you two hunks are done making out," I said with a grin, "Roberta's waiting outside with the car. Let's get out of this shithole."

Fifteen

As Roberta's SUV pulled back into the dirt track that made up the Wolfden's parking lot and driveway, I felt my heart surge. The place had already begun to feel like home. I found myself genuinely elated to be back, to see Jamie, Nikolai, and the others, to stand in front of the bonfire, letting it warm my blood and my heart.

But first, we had to attend to Lee. The entire drive back, I'd sat in the backseat, watching as he and Benny held hands in the front, smiling at the way Benny's thumb had stroked Lee's pale hand, as if he was afraid to stop touching him.

Lee had said to me, "What makes you think I haven't been in love?" and I'd vainly thought he was talking about me.

Now, watching the two of them, it was abundantly obvious that Lee Courtenay had never loved anyone like he loved Benny.

I turned to Roberta—beside me in the back—with a smile, and she gave me a genuine grin in return. It wasn't over yet, but there was at least this brief respite from the horribleness. We had Lee back, and he was safe. I hoped Jamie would offer us one of his fiery homebrew shots; I was actually in the mood for a celebratory drink.

Benny stopped the SUV and Roberta and I clambered out, opening Lee's door and offering him our arms. "Hey, I'm not an invalid," Lee protested with a small chuckle. "I can walk, you guys. Seriously, I'm fine."

We both stepped back, giving him space. But I noticed with a smile that when Benny came around and offered Lee his arm, Lee took it readily. As the two of them walked towards Jamie and Nikolai's trailer, Lee's head came to rest on Benny's large, muscular arm.

"Why didn't you tell me they were together?" I asked Roberta in a quiet voice as we followed them.

"Because they aren't," Roberta said, then added, "Well, they weren't. Right before all of this happened, they had a huge fight. Broke up for good. They've been on-again, off-again for years, but this time, it seemed final. Lee left the Wolfden and Benny told him to never come back. I thought that was the end of it." She shrugged. "I guess when he disappeared Benny let all of that go."

"I'm glad," I said.

She nodded. "Me, too. But what went down between them…they'll have to talk about it eventually. It's not the kind of thing you can just brush over and move on from."

I found that curious, but I didn't press further. We were on the stoop at Jamie and Nikolai's and could already hear the excited whooping and hollering as everyone realized Lee had been rescued. It was time to celebrate, however briefly.

Outside by the bonfire, the stereo was blaring The Doors' *People Are Strange,* and I couldn't help but sway along, dazzled by the appropriateness of the tune. The folks gathered around were all indeed very strange, and I had come to love them in such a short time.

The celebration at Lee's return had been a big one. There wasn't a single sober person in the place, including old man Tyson and Clara herself, who had downed six or seven shots before finally declaring that she "had a buzz going." If she was upset to see the way Benny and Lee were holding onto each other, stealing kisses in between swigs of beer, she wasn't letting on.

I was developing major respect for the purple-haired ring-side girl. She was tough as nails, just as Roberta had said. She might be dealing with her own private heartbreak, but she put on an outward face of strength and resolve that I admired. I'd have to take some lessons from her.

As if on cue, my phone vibrated in my jacket pocket. I knew without looking that it was Phillip. I could feel him, yes, but also, who else would be texting me? Everybody else was here.

I ignored it, swaying along to Jim Morrison's smoky vocals, determined not to give Phillip any more power over me. I was still fuming at the way he'd lectured me on trust and honesty and then turned around and kept such huge secrets from me. Then there was the small matter of his ex-wife flying to Georgia for a visit. It was going to be a long time before I stopped being angry about that. Besides, thanks to Jamie, I had a glass of home brew in one hand and a beer in the other.

I knew I needed to let Phillip know that we'd found Lee, but for the moment, I didn't care. He could wait. He'd certainly made *me* wait when I'd frantically asked him where he was, hadn't he? Besides, he'd never liked Lee. Let him wait.

My heart hurt, but a newfound feeling had made its way to

the forefront of my consciousness, one that I welcomed. Deep down, I still wanted Phillip as much as ever, even if I did hate him in the moment. I wanted him and I always would, but now I knew…I didn't *need* him. I didn't need anybody. I could handle myself, take care of myself. I would be just fine, one way or another. I had a strength, a power, in my blood, to say nothing of my own steel courage, intellect, and goodness. It was time I leaned into that, into my own self-confidence, to become the woman I was meant to be.

Roberta's eyes found mine over the bonfire and she raised her own beer in a toast. I raised mine back and she smiled curiously, but her eyes asked me a question. *Are you okay?* I wasn't sure if I was hearing her inside my own head or just reading her thoughts—who knew anymore? I was still reeling from everything I'd learned—but I nodded, and she stared at me for a moment, her gaze piercing me, then she finally turned away to talk to Jamie.

After *People are Strange,* a familiar razors-edge bass line began, and I stared at the little black stereo, which someone had propped up on a cinderblock, as if I could will it to stop playing. It was the Bloomer Demons. I now had no doubt that one of the chuckleheads standing around the bonfire had been peering into my head and had started up that song as a joke, a challenge. Well, that was just fine. I raised my hand in a silent gesture of *cheers* and threw back my glass, the fiery liquid going down my throat in a gulp. Cheers rang around the fire, and I grinned.

My phone began to vibrate again. Apparently, I wasn't going to be able to avoid Phillip Deville tonight, no matter how I tried. I pulled the phone from my pocket and stepped away from the bonfire, taking a long, deep swig of my beer. Jamie's front stoop was now dark and deserted since everyone was outside, so I walked over and perched on his steps, happy to be shrouded in darkness for a minute, and read the text messages.

I wanted to check in, was all the first one said.

I scoffed. "Check in," I mumbled, my voice a little slurred. "The bare minimum."

The second text was somewhat more substantial. *I know you're angry at me about everything…especially about Barb. I'm sorry. I haven't handled things well. I'd like to talk about it some more, if you're okay with that.*

My heart pounded. After days of avoiding me and being cagey and weird, now Phillip wanted to talk. Why the sudden change of heart? As recently as yesterday, I would have jumped at the chance, but now…I wasn't so sure I wanted to see him.

Maybe it was time to cut him loose for real. After all, he was back with Barb now.

Barb, I thought to myself meanly, biting the inside of my lip. *Barb, Barb, Barb.* The worst wannabe groupie name ever, the name of a *literal* doll, the most eighties shit ever, and she got to be married to the love of my life. Inherit his fortune. Call the shots at his "estate." And now, on top of it all, she got to be with him again. Phillip had run to her as fast as his legs could carry him the moment she called. Leaving me like some Podunk chump. And now he wanted to 'talk about it.' Well, what good would that do?

Thanks to Roberta, I now knew the truth—it had been me all along. I had written the spell. I had put all of this into motion years ago, before I'd even known about my own power, and I'd unwittingly ensnared Phillip in a trap he'd had no control over. He may have innocently taken that spell from Guthrie, totally unaware of how it had begun, and thrown it into the liner notes as a joke, but his responsibility in all of this was zero. It was all my fault, and it was time to cut him loose from the trap he'd unwittingly stepped into. The fact that I was so angry with him made it a little easier.

It was still going to be hard as hell, though.

I fumbled with the phone, my inebriation making it hard for me to tap out a response without dropping the damn thing under the porch. Finally, I managed to tap out what I wanted to say, hitting 'send' before I had a chance to second-guess myself.

We don't need to talk about anything, Phillip. It took me a while, but I'm finally at a place where I understand all of this, sort of. I don't think we should see each other anymore. The way we met was a manipulation and we just cause each other pain. If you have a chance for happiness with Barb, you should take it. Get back to your life, the life you had before it was stolen from you.

After the text showed as sent, I felt tears rushing down my cheeks. I wiped them away and typed one final message.

Oh, and we found Lee. He's safe. So there's no need to worry about me. Goodbye, Phillip.

I was still dabbing at my eyes, trying to stop the flood of tears that were falling and compose myself enough to head back to the party when someone ran up the walk and thundered up the stairs like a shot, almost knocking me over. He stopped at the door, his shoulders heaving up and down with exertion, his freckled face bright red under the porch light.

I scrambled up from the steps, still wiping at my face. "Lee, are you okay?" I asked, looking at him, trying to determine if he was upset, scared, or both.

Before he could answer, Roberta and Benny had run up behind him, followed by Jamie and Nikolai. Benny's face was a thundercloud of anger, and Roberta looked worried. "What's going on?" I asked, looking back and forth at all of them. I looked at Lee. "What's happened?"

Lee's face was flushed and red as he answered me. "They all knew," he seethed, his eyes flashing as he stared Roberta down, then shifted his furious gaze to Benny, who was staring levelly back at him. "All of you. You knew about all this, for *years,* and nobody thought to tell me?"

"Lee…" Roberta's shoulders slumped. "I wanted to tell you, but…"

"You knew what your trash heap of a father was getting up to, that my dad was involved, and you never thought it…I don't know…prudent…to fill me in?" He whirled towards me. "When did you find out?" His eyes blazed and I shrunk back instinctively.

"Find out what?" I tittered, confused.

"That Elvin and Guthrie were running experiments on us when we were kids," Lee spat. "And that they basically pulled a spell out of your head—a spell which is responsible for every single fucking thing we've had to deal with the past few weeks." His lips were curled in a sneer that froze my blood. Even at his worst, I'd never seen Lee so angry.

"I only just found out myself," I said, throwing my hands up in mock surrender. "Over the past few days. You mean you *didn't know?"* I found that shocking.

"No, I didn't know." Lee seethed. "I grew up with my parents doing all sorts of weird, sometimes evil shit, but I didn't know that they were messing around with *children.* More specifically, *us. Me."*

"I promise. I didn't know until the other day." I assured him, looking into his pale eyes, hoping he could see the sincerity. "I was as clueless as you. More so, actually. I didn't even know about Elvin—I didn't remember him—until a few days ago. You told Phillip about him and his involvement before I ever even found out."

Lee's eyes worked me over. He seemed to believe me, thank goodness. Whatever injuries he'd come to the Wolfden with, they were all but forgotten. He looked angry enough to take down a bear. Which, looking at Benny's huge shoulders, heaving with barely-pent-up anger, it might just come to.

"I'm sorry about that," he said softly, so that only I could hear. Then he turned to Roberta, and thundered, "Why did you keep this a secret all these years, Roberta? Why?" His face was bright red.

Roberta's own face was full of heat now. "Ever since we were kids, Lee, you've been trying to clean up your parents' messes. It was always this or that. I wanted to tell you, but I figured it was…one less thing that you had to carry."

"That 'one thing' is a pretty big fucking thing, Roberta!"

"I know!" She was shouting right back. "Do you think it's been easy for me, Lee? To keep that secret all these years, to know that my dad was running experiments on all the kids in our trailer park? Using me to help him with his 'work,' while he bribed everybody's parents with weed and pills? Let's face it—our childhoods weren't like other people's! It was hard enough reckoning with it myself, much less talking about it with someone else." Her eyes were bright with angry tears. "We never even got to be kids! And ever since Aunt Lydia brought you back, you've been working for Guthrie, doing his dirty work…To be honest, I didn't know if I could even *trust* you! For all I knew, you'd run back to him with everything I told you. I couldn't take the risk!"

"I'm not just anyone, Roberta, I'm your cousin!" Lee shouted. "If you had confided in me, I might have been able to help!"

"Everybody who tries to help me ends up getting hurt!" Roberta shouted. "Look at my fucking brother, Lee! He went to jail because of me!"

My eyes widened. Roberta had told me where her brother was, but she'd been so tight-lipped about it. Had she actually been involved?

Neither of them noticed my shock. They were too busy shouting each other down. Lee continued in an angry voice. "I'm sorry about what happened with Jorge, but I am not him, Roberta! You could have trusted me, relied on me! To do something about it! To fix things before any of this had a chance to happen. Maybe we could have even stopped her before she—" He gestured at me, his face a picture of disgust, but stopped short of finishing his sentence.

"Before I did the stupid spell and ruined everything for everybody," I said in a low voice, looking Lee in the eye. "Go ahead. You might as well just say it."

"I was going to say, 'before she put herself in danger,'" Lee said, his voice a little calmer. The color was coming back into his face. "They've been after you—Guthrie and Elvin—since you were a kid, Stormy. They've been trying to like...tinker with you or something, make you into this...this..."

"Custom-made witch," Roberta offered, but he ignored her, still angry.

"And Roberta has known about it the whole time. The rest of them, too. Yet they kept you and me in the dark. If I had known about it, maybe I could have put a stop to it. I could have warned you. Something. Anything. And you could be living a normal life right now."

Roberta snorted. "Lee, if there's one thing I know for certain, it's that none of us who grew up in that trailer park ever had a chance at *normal*." She waved a fist in the air. "And the fact that we *didn't* tell the two of you is probably *why* you're both still alive right now."

"Did Elvin wipe Lee, too?" I asked, still trying to piece it all together. "Is that why he didn't know?"

"Yes," Roberta said bitterly. "They've wiped him so many times over the years, he can barely keep his own age straight."

"He's good at keeping plenty of other things straight." Benny's voice was ice-cold in the night air, and I turned to look at him. His face was full of anger, his lips stretched tight as though he were trying to keep from speaking, but couldn't hold it in any longer. "Isn't that so, Lee?"

"Don't start, Ben. That has nothing to do with this," Lee said furiously, but Benny cut him off.

"I think it does, man," Benny retorted, his voice full of icy coldness. "You stand here and accuse us of keeping things from you, not trusting you, and yet you're such a coward, you couldn't even tell your own parents that you were in love with a man. You've had years to do it, but you've always been too scared of your daddy dearest." He spat on the ground. "If you couldn't even do that, how could the rest of us trust that you'd stand up to him when it comes to the bigger stuff? You've always known what Guthrie was—you always knew he was working with Elvin, even if you didn't know the dirty details. Yet you continued to do his bidding—and your mother's—for years without losing a single minute of sleep over it. You've always put them first, so tell me. Why should we trust you with our secrets?"

"Benny, that's not quite fair…" Roberta began, but he continued.

"When I told you to get the hell out of this place and never come back, I meant it," Benny said. "You're in no condition to leave right now—you need to rest after your ordeal. And maybe it'll do you some good to lay there and think about the ways you've enabled Guthrie and your mom over the years, how much of this is *your* fault for not standing up to them when you could have." His eyes were blazing fire. "Tomorrow we'll go and get your mother and Renee, because I promised you I'd help you rescue them."

"And then?" Lee asked, his light-blue eyes locked on Benny's, which were staring back at him with cold fury.

"Then? Then I don't give a fuck," Benny said. "Go wherever you want and do whatever you want, as long as it's far, far away from me."

"Benny, can't we all just…" Jamie said, but Lee had already stalked into the trailer and slammed the screen door behind him, seemingly in perfect agreement with Benny's terms.

Sixteen

The room was cold, yet somehow musty and hot at the same time. Typical South Georgia, but still, I was uncomfortable. I shifted, wincing when the bed creaked, hoping Lee wouldn't wake up. God knew he needed his rest. I pulled the thin, threadbare sheet over my legs, hoping for protection against the year-round Georgia mosquitos more than from any real sense of cold. I hesitated, then leaned backwards into Lee's back, wanting to feel the warmth of another human being next to me. He'd understand better than anyone, wouldn't he?

After the explosion of anger outside on the porch, Jamie had offered up his bedroom to Lee and me, taking the couch for himself. Roberta was God knows where—at Benny's, I assumed, in his camper van by the trees—or maybe bunking down at Clara's. I realized that I'd only ever been inside Jamie and Nikolai's trailer, despite having been here for a few days. It was fine with me; this place almost felt more like home now than my own place. There was a warmth and safety here that put me at ease, even when I was in turmoil. *They* felt like home, even though I barely knew them.

I smiled as Lee's weight shifted behind me, and he rolled

over towards me, becoming the big spoon, and wrapped a thin, muscular arm around my waist. "Cold?" His voice was low behind me. I momentarily froze, wondering if I should break away from this unexpected intimacy, but then I thought, *why?* It wasn't as though either of us were attached to anyone. A wave of fresh pain washed over me, remembering the text I'd sent Phillip. I'd turned my phone off afterward, not wanting to hover over it, waiting for notifications.

"No, just…" I searched for the word and found it wouldn't come. How to explain the utter heartbreak, terror, trauma, discomfort and anger I felt all at once? There was no way to explain.

Thankfully, I didn't need to. "I know," Lee said. "Me, too."

"I feel like…like…" I settled closer into him, taking comfort from his warmth, his beating heart against my back. "Like my life is irretrievably changed. There's no going back now. And I'm not sure I'd want to if I could, but…this new thing…it's so big, bigger than me, than all of us. I don't know how I can stand against it, how to cope with it." I sighed. "The power inside me, and…the power outside of me, too. The truth of my childhood, my entire life, Phillip. All of it. You know?"

"Story of my life," Lee murmured sleepily against my shoulder. "I know exactly how you feel. Hey, Stormy?"

"Yeah?"

"You don't…" Now he was the one faltering for words. "What Benny said out there…about me…it's true. I never came out to my folks. I hope you don't think less of me."

"Of course not," I said sympathetically. "I can only imagine how hard it was to have a regular conversation with your parents, as awful as they were, much less about something like that. I don't judge you."

"I wouldn't want you to think less of me because I'm…" His voice was low and quiet in the dark room.

"Whatever you're about to say, don't," I said, turning to

face Lee in the darkness. I could barely make out the shape of his nose, the smattering of freckles there. "I would never judge you. Why would I?"

"I just…" Lee was so close to me that his breath tickled my face. "Like, logically, I know there's nothing wrong with me—well, not in that regard, anyway—but it's like…the way I grew up…Guthrie…and even my mother, well, they made it pretty clear that they…" His voice broke a little, and I ached for him. "They didn't see being bi—or queer, or whatever you want to call it—as something to celebrate." He sighed. "I spent most of my life trying to deny that part of myself because I was so afraid of them, and the more I denied it, the harder it became. I'm not ashamed of who I am." Lee's voice took on new strength and resolve as he spoke. "But you, Stormy…I guess… I respect you so much, and I want you to like me, is that stupid? I want you to like me and care about me the way I— the way I care about you." His hand hovered just at my waist, as though he was afraid to touch me.

"I do care," I said vehemently, pressing my own hand over his, pushing it to rest on my waist. I put my other arm around his neck, pulling him close. "If I'm judging you, it's because of all the shit you put me through, Lee Courtenay. For working with your father to hurt me and the people I love. Not least the small matter of, um, *kidnapping me*." He tensed and I laughed, wrapping him in a hug. "And breaking into my house and letting someone steal my cat, only to put him back…you've done a lot of crazy, stupid shit."

"I'm sorry about your cat," he said. "I never would have hurt him. I had to find a quick way to get your attention, to get you to follow me. It was the best thing I could think of at the time."

"Why were you there in the first place?" I asked. It was the one bit of information he hadn't yet divulged.

"He took me there," Lee answered. "Elvin. He planned to

take you the way he did my mom. But while we were waiting at your place, Renee called Elvin. She knew about Dad's death, and she was demanding to know what happened. She was insisting they meet to talk. She'd already talked to my mom and said she was on her way back to Georgia." I looked at him, surprised. We'd all been assuming that Lydia had been taken from her home, but she'd come of her own volition? That took some strength and gumption, sick as she was. Elvin decided to split from your house, fast. You rolled up right as we were leaving, so we dashed into your barn to wait. I grabbed your cat on my way out and dropped him with my hat in the woods. I was lucky he didn't notice." He smiled in the darkness. "You came so close to catching us, you have no idea." I felt him shudder. "I'm glad you didn't."

"So is that why Elvin took Renee? Because she confronted him about Guthrie?"

"He didn't take her; not exactly. Renee is no dummy, but she's too trusting when it comes to my dad. She waited until my mom had arrived in town, and they both showed up to meet Elvin. You can guess the rest—Elvin obviously wasn't going to just let them go home." He gave me a strange grin. "Especially not with you making friends at the Wolfden and Phillip Deville skulking around Savannah, digging up bones or whatever the hell he was doing."

"Oh yeah," I replied with a sigh. "That."

"Trouble in paradise?" Lee asked, looking at me curiously in the darkness. I didn't know how to immediately answer. I swallowed at the boulder in my throat. "I'm sorry," Lee replied. "I have no right to even ask. Benny really is right. I'm as much at fault as anyone, and I've got no business questioning anyone else's motivations. If I'd just stood up to my dad all the countless times when I had a chance, we'd all be a lot happier." His voice sounded desolate. "I've lost Benny for good, and I deserve it. I was more worried about what my bigoted parents would think than the person who loved me." His voice was quiet and sad in the dark. "It makes me feel better, though, to know that *you* don't judge me. You're a good friend."

"I guarantee you, Lee, I would never, ever judge you for who you love. And I'd never think you any less of a man, or a person, or whatever else, just because of who you are inside." I smiled in the darkness. "Or outside, for that matter."

"For real?" His voice sounded almost boyish. "I don't deserve you. Especially after the guilt I gave you over Phillip."

"For real," I said, pressing a gentle kiss to his cheek. "You will always be my friend, despite everything. I'm sorry your parents made you feel like you couldn't be yourself."

"Guthrie was always good at that," Lee said quietly. "No surprises there. It was my mom that…that hurt."

"Lydia loves you."

"Yes," Lee said. "But it could be selfish sometimes. It wasn't enough. It isn't enough." He coughed. "She should have protected me…from him."

"I know."

Lee's breath was ragged in the dark room, and my heart went out to him. I pressed another gentle kiss on his cheek, then another, not realizing I'd caught the corner of his mouth until I felt his lips beneath my own, kissing me back. I tensed momentarily, aware that this was a point of no return, not sure if I should give into it. His lips were rough and chapped, and he tasted salty, like sweat and tears. His hand on my waist circled around, clasping my lower back, pulling me closer. The kiss deepened and I didn't stop it.

His mouth opened and I could taste him, the sweet, tangy taste of orange juice, his mouth soft against mine, somehow both timid and passionate at the same time. My head filled with thoughts of Phillip, and I marveled how this could feel so good, so right, while my heart was full of someone else. But

Phillip was off on Tybee, no doubt re-connecting with Barb, the one he was probably meant to be with. He wanted shut of me, he'd made that clear time and again—first directly, then later with his silence, his distance. He didn't want me. After my last, final text to him earlier that evening, he'd never written back. It was over. And I was here, with Lee, his warm, familiar body a comfort, his mouth so soft and sweet against my own, his passion and his need evident as he pressed his taut body against mine.

Was he thinking of Benny? Maybe, probably. Who cared? All that mattered was the now, the right now, the feel of our arms around each other; two souls in pain, loving people who didn't want us anymore, offering each other a momentary respite from our torment, relief in the physicality of our bodies, and our hearts that were so much alike.

And the truth was, this was a long time coming. Since the moment I'd stared him down in the foyer of that cheap motel in Boston, I'd known there was something between us. Even if I'd denied it to everyone, including myself, it was there. Now I knew this was a chemistry that had begun years ago, in a dingy trailer neither of us remembered.

I ran my hands under his shirt, feeling the sweaty sheen of his skin; it really was hot in the room beneath the thin sheets. Mosquitoes forgotten, I threw the sheet on the floor and yanked off Lee's shirt, enjoying the growl that came out of him as my hands connected with his naked chest. The moonlight played on his half-naked body, and I memorized the way his body looked, the way a beam of light landed on his pale skin, illuminating it. I could see bruises on his neck and arms from when he'd been held captive. How could his own uncle, his own flesh and blood, do such a thing? I touched one tenderly, and he winced a little. I moved my hands over his shoulders— I'd seen him shirtless in the daylight, and I knew he had freckles there, too, all across his chest and back, and imagined them like constellations in a night sky, running my fingers over the smoothness there, as he pulled me down to him again, his mouth devouring mine, full of urgency and need, and sadness, too.

It seemed like time was both speeding up and standing still. I could feel nothing but Lee's lips on mine, but inside my head, the thoughts were careening around in a jumble, making me feel slightly dizzy. I kissed Lee harder, trying to silence them, to bring on some blessed quiet. Lee's skin was warm and soft beneath my hands.

Then in an instant, Lee pulled away and looked at me, panting, his breath heavy on my face. I looked at him in the darkness, surprised. In the dim room, I saw him smile, but it was a sad smile. I could feel his feathery lashes tickle my forehead as he placed a gentle kiss on my nose, his breath still shuddery as he pulled back, untangling himself from me. We sat on the bed side by side, only our shoulders touching.

"We can't, Stormy," Lee said, his voice so quiet it was almost a whisper. "We just can't."

"I know," I said, my voice mirroring his.

Lee put an arm around me and pulled me close to him, leaning down to place another kiss on my temple as I rested my head on his shoulder.

"It would have been great...if we had..." he said, a dry laugh escaping his lips.

"Totally," I agreed, still leaning into his shoulder, wiping a wayward tear from my cheek. "Totally great."

Lee lay back down on the bed and rolled over to face the wall. Silently, I settled back into his sweaty skin, putting my arm over his waist, my turn to be the big spoon. I nudged at his shoulder with my chin and he chuckled, then pressed his weight against me. *Tomorrow,* was the unspoken word between us, the understanding. Tomorrow we would talk. Tonight— confused, a little let-down, and a lot broken-hearted, yet comforted by the knowledge that we both felt the same way—we would finally get some sleep.

Something about the way Lee stood in the doorway of Jamie's room, holding out a white ceramic cup steaming with fresh coffee, reminded me so much of Phillip that it took me a moment to catch my breath. "Good morning," he said, his eyes working over me, crinkling with bemusement. His foul mood from the night before was gone.

I knew I looked like a total mess. After our weird, passionate—and very brief—encounter, I'd gone straight to sleep, for once feeling safe and secure, despite the awkward, faint sense of rejection I'd also felt. I hadn't bothered to take my hair out of its braid, put my shirt on, brush my teeth, or wash my face. The result was just *me*, clutching a half-zq3`transparent white sheet to my naked chest, my hair half out of its braid, sticking up in tangles all over my head, my eye makeup caked around my eyes like a deranged raccoon. To say nothing of the hideous taste in my mouth.

I reached for the cup wordlessly, and Lee walked over to the bed, chuckling as he handed it to me.

I took a long sip, savoring it, even though it tasted pretty bad—it had to be instant since I knew Jamie's coffeemaker was on the fritz. I wasn't complaining, though, considering I'd just been bouncing checks at Walmart a few days ago. I sat there, letting the steam from the cup invade my senses before finally saying, "Thank you."

"No problem," Lee said, sitting down beside me. He gave my leg a friendly pat. "I figured after last night you might be in need of some high octane."

"Congratulating yourself on your restraint, are you?" I said in a dry voice, taking another long sip. It burned my tongue, but I paid it no attention and kept guzzling.

Lee's cheeks colored; I'd never get tired of the way they looked, rosy and pink beneath the freckles. He really was adorable. "I wasn't referring to *that,* Stormy. Your mind is in the gutter. I was talking about before that. Rescuing me, the party, the fight…"

"Oh," I said, not quite ready to think about that yet. I needed more coffee first. "Well. Yeah. It all made for an interesting evening."

"Are you okay?" Lee asked quietly, his eyes searching my face. "You put on a brave front, but I could tell you were upset last night. And I think it was about more than just the shit with me and Benny. What's going on?"

"I'm okay," I assured him softly, still clutching the cup in my hands, letting it warm me.

"Spill it," Lee said firmly.

"There isn't much to spill," I admitted, taking another sip of sludge. "Phillip and I broke up. I mean, he broke up with me a few days ago, but…I guess I put the final nail in the coffin last night. It's over. For good."

"Damn, Stormy, I'm sorry," Lee said. "I guess that explains why you…well, never mind. Look, it's his loss. I mean that. You're a fucking catch, and if that dead dumbass doesn't realize it—"

"Aren't you also a dead dumbass?" I asked, laughing.

"*Touché*," Lee said, taking a sip of his own coffee, a twinkle in his eyes. "And if you can believe it, I'm an even bigger dead dumbass than Phillip Deville."

"One day I'd like to get that story from you," I said, nursing my cup. "About how you were brought back."

"Okay," he agreed. "One day."

"Did you know your mother brought my mother back when I was just a kid?" I asked. "Did Roberta tell you?"

"Yes," Lee said softly. "That's pretty crazy, huh?"

"Yes," I parroted. I nudged him. "Are *you* okay?"

Lee sighed. "As much as I can be, I guess." He shook his head. "What you said last night about it all being too much… that's how I feel, too. Mom's always telling me I'm her strong man, that I can handle anything, that she never has to worry about me because I'm bulletproof. Well, I can tell you Stormy, I don't feel that way. All I feel is scared. And manipulated. And damn tired. I just wish life would be normal for like, five minutes, you know?"

"I feel exactly the same way," I said, leaning into his sturdy frame. I noticed his coffee was gone, so I offered him the rest of my cup.

"No, thanks," he said, waving it away with a smile. "I already had two cups before you woke up. Another one and I'll have heartburn all day."

"You're too young for heartburn."

"And you're too old to be wearing Strawberry Shortcake panties," Lee said with a grin. "And yet I saw them on you last night."

"Peeping Tom!" I slapped him on the arm, and he laughed. Then his face turned serious.

"I guess at some point we do need to talk about what happened…between us, I mean…" His face colored more. "Or rather, what *almost* happened."

"Yeah," I agreed, staring into my cup. "We probably should."

Silence fell for a few moments, and I tittered, feeling impossibly awkward. I wanted to reach out and hug him, to tell him that whatever happened, we were okay. But I couldn't seem to get my mouth to work.

After a pause, Lee said in a very soft voice, "I don't want you to think I stopped because I didn't want you." His blush deepened. "I did want you. I do still. But I stopped because we're both in love with other people and we would have regretted it later."

I started to protest, but he stopped me with a tender look.

"I know you love Phillip. Breakup or not, you're very much in love with him; I can see that from ten paces away," he said, giving my arm a squeeze. "I won't lie, there's a big part of me that's jealous, that always has been jealous. From the second I laid eyes on you—hell, maybe even before, when I first heard about you and found out what you were—I've had a crush on you. I guess you knew that." I nodded. "But you love someone else and that's okay. I'm in love with someone else, too."

"So, you still love Benny?" I asked. "Despite everything?"

He stared down at his lap. "Of course I do. I always will. I've fucked it up six ways from Sunday so many times that I'll be lucky if he ever nods in my direction again." He looked up at me sheepishly, his cheeks even redder. "But yes, I do. As much as I like you—and believe me, I really do like you, Stormy—I can't shake what I feel for Benny. It's like something bigger than me."

"I get it," I said with a smile.

"I know."

We smiled at each other silently.

"Well," I said finally, draining the dregs of my cup, "it looks like we're on the same page, or at an impasse, one or the other. All I really care about, though, is that you and I are okay. That no matter what, we'll stay friends. We can't let this get in the way of that. Not after all we've been through…all we share."

"I agree," Lee said, putting an arm around my shoulders. I leaned into him, nuzzling my head against his arm.

"In another life, we might have been a great match," I said, sighing contentedly.

"We definitely would've been," Lee agreed. "And if you

don't mind, I might allow myself to think about that from time to time."

"It's a free country," I said, and he laughed.

"Too bad we're both in love with tall, black-haired dickheads who have more muscles than they have sense," Lee said, and I collapsed into laughter.

"Hey, we could always try swinging," I joked, elbowing Lee in the side. "Or a good, old-fashioned four-way. Or better yet, go full-tilt polyamory."

"I'd have a heart attack in five minutes flat," Lee said with a laugh, his eyes sparkling, "trying to contend with the three of *you.*"

I grinned, but then turned serious. "I do love you, you know," I said, placing a gentle kiss on Lee's cheek. "It might not be the way I love Phillip, but it's something. Something that's just ours."

Lee turned his face to mine and kissed me right back. "I love you, too," he said, his hair tickling my face. "My friend."

And that was that.

Benny was tinkering on Jamie's motorcycle, his black hair pulled back in a weird half-mohawk/half-ponytail, which looked strange and seemed to stand up on his head since his hair was so short. A vape pen hung loosely from his mouth, and he had his black shirt unbuttoned almost down to his belly button, a patch of black hair visible on his chest. His arms were sweaty, and his face was scrunched up in concentration as he took a wrench to the bike. I had no idea what on earth he was doing—I didn't know bikes at all—but I had to begrudgingly admit to myself that he looked pretty sexy, all sweaty and covered in grease like that. Benny was a bit terrifying to me, but I could see what Lee saw in him. He caught me looking at him and gave me a sly smile.

"Working on the bike settles my nerves," he said to me as I walked past him to grab a Coke from the cooler. It seemed that nobody around the Wolfden bothered to use their own refrigerators. Everything was in coolers, and they all shared and shared alike.

"You ought to give up that nasty vaping," I said, shooting him a grin so he'd know I wasn't truly chastising him. "They aren't good for you."

"Nothing is," he said with a grin of his own, then snapped his dirty towel in my direction. "I quit smoking cigarettes a while ago; this is the next step. I plan to get them all down eventually."

"Glad to hear it."

"Lee okay?"

I smiled. "He's okay."

Benny went back to working on the bike with a grunt, and I smiled into my Coke, feeling smug. Benny and Lee were both bullheaded and stubborn, and they might both talk a big game, but the love they had for each other was something special. I had no doubt that if they'd come off their high horses a little bit, they'd be able to work it out. I hoped, for Lee's sake, that they would sooner rather than later.

You could do the same, you know. With Phillip.

The thought appeared fully formed in my head—was someone talking to me telepathically, or was I just going nuts? I shook my head and took another sip of Coke, wondering if I'd ever become accustomed to this newfound magical weirdness.

I supposed I'd have to go home soon. After lunch, Roberta, Benny, Lee and I—if they could hold off on killing each other —were supposed to start searching for Lydia and Renee. Lee had no idea where they'd been taken after he'd been dumped at

Guthrie's, but he had a few ideas. Once we'd found them, my part would be over. I'd have to go back to the library—if I still had a job there; I'd called in sick so many times, Jean probably thought I was on a drug bender—and back to my boring, lonely life. The thought was an ache in my chest. The truth was, I didn't want to leave here. I didn't want my old life anymore; the thought of going back to it filled me with dread.

Something about the Wolfden's way of communal living, the way everyone helped each other out, banded together, acted as almost one collective mind—a chosen family—appealed to me. I felt safe and understood. I could see why Lee and Roberta felt at home here, why they'd come here in a time of danger. There was strength in numbers, and even more strength among this group. I had no doubt that each and every one of them could—and would—kill to keep their chosen family safe.

I shuddered at the sudden thought. I hoped it wouldn't come to that. Not again, anyway.

"Oh, don't study on that, darlin'," a voice said behind me in a slow, sleepy drawl. "Ain't no sense in it."

"Jesus, Jamie, you scared me!"

"I reckon we're all a little jumpy after yesterday," he said, cuffing me on the arm, his boyish face erupting into a smile. "You okay?"

"Yeah, I am," I said, forcing a smile in return. "Considering."

"That's all we can do, just put one foot in front of the other," he said in his deeply Southern accent, giving me another bright smile. I grinned back at him, a genuine one this time, unable to resist his charms. It was amazing to me that Jamie didn't have a bevy of hot ladies hanging all over him; he was irresistibly handsome, a little bit dangerous, and full of a boyish exuberance that was undeniably attractive.

"Ain't you a librarian?" Jamie asked me, still smiling. I

noticed how sharp his incisors were, how wolflike his smile could be when he really put it on. "Didn't nobody ever tell you not to judge a book by its cover?"

I looked at him sharply. "Did you just…"

"Guard your thoughts here, darlin'," he said with a playful look. "At least the ones you want to keep secret. All of us got some kind of inkling of this or that. Being around each other makes it stronger, too. And you bein' here makes us all more powerful." He lowered his voice and came a little closer. "We're a family and I trust every single one of these folks with my life, but…not everybody needs to know everything."

"Gotcha," I said, feeling uneasy. From over by the bike, Benny watched us.

Jamie smiled again. "And thanks for the compliment, darlin'. You're pretty cute yourself."

"Hey now, I—"

Jamie's laughter was like music as he walked away, leaving me to stare after him as he sauntered off, crooning the unmistakable words to *Here I Go Again* by 80s hair metal staple Whitesnake in a whiskey-soaked voice that had a lot of laughter in it. I couldn't help but notice how nice Jamie's ass looked, even clad in dingy cargo jeans, and I bit the thought off quickly, heeding his advice. Evidently in addition to making people clairvoyant, being at the Wolfden also made you really horny. Even though neither of them were in my vicinity, I swore I could hear both Jamie and Benny chuckling as I fled, embarrassed, towards the back of the trailer park, clutching my Coke in my sweaty hand. Fuckers.

"So." Roberta was all business as she sat down on the tattered couch with a pen and pad of paper. "Let's make a list of places to look for Lydia and Renee." She turned to Lee. "No idea where they were taken after Guthrie's?"

Lee shook his head. "Nope," he said. "After Elvin figured out I was double-crossing him, he dumped me at Dad's, tied me up in the cellar, and took off. I have no idea where he intended to go after that."

"Can you retrace where all you guys went?" Nikolai asked, tapping on his phone. I assumed he was taking notes.

"Only from when he showed up at my dad's," Lee answered. "He already had Mom by then, and I have no idea how he got her. He confessed that he'd taken Dad's body and that he and Mom had cleaned up the scene—he made her help —and that he'd tried to force her to bring Dad back. She tried, but she was too weak—her powers aren't what they used to be since she got sick, and she couldn't get the spell to work. So they'd wrapped him in a tarp and dumped him." He grimaced. "His own fucking brother. Just dumped Daddy in the swamp like he meant nothing." He bit his lip. "He wouldn't tell me exactly where…just that it was in some swamp. He said he did it for me, so I wouldn't get in trouble. I went with him will-ingly because I didn't like the alternative." He paused, then went on. "Next, we went to Stormy's…he planned to snatch her, too, but then Renee called and when he found out that she'd been with Phillip, he got spooked and we left. We hid in the barn until Stormy cleared out. I took the cat and left a clue for Stormy to come here. After that, we met Renee. Elvin coerced her into going with us, and then we headed to this… this weird place in the woods." Lee frowned. "He hypnotized me a few times, I think, so I wouldn't remember the details. All I remember is a lot of pine trees and hearing voices that didn't belong to anyone in the family. Someone else was there, too, but I never saw them."

"Then what?" Jamie asked.

"At some point, I think Elvin decided I was more of a

liability than a help," Lee answered. "He told me he was going to let me go. We drove back to my dad's. And then he went nuts. He tied me up in the cellar, he punched me in the face, bent my arm back and almost broke it, and threatened me that he'd come back and finish the job if I squealed on him. It was at least two days, maybe more that I was down there. Then you guys found me." He sighed. "That's all I know."

"I bet he's at that compound Lee is describing," I said. "It kind of sounds like that's his home base. And I'm willing to bet anything there's a swamp or a marsh of some kind on the property. It's probably the same area he dumped Guthrie, which means it's nearby."

Roberta's face had gone a little white. I remembered that look; it was the same look I'd seen before, when we'd been driving down the road, passing by the land she'd said was her uncle's, where she'd grown up.

"You know where it is, don't you?" I asked her, and she nodded almost imperceptibly, her lips devoid of color.

"Hey, guys?" We all jumped as Clara poked her head into the living room. "Sorry to interrupt, but someone is here. He says he needs to see Stormy, and that it's urgent."

I tensed, and both Lee and Nikolai both immediately got up as if to defend me. "Who is it?" I asked, more than a little fearful.

"Says his name's Phillip," Clara said, giving me a wink. "And holy shit, girl, he is *fine as hell.* If you don't want him, can I have him?"

Seventeen

Lee insisted on accompanying me outside to see Phillip, just in case, even though I'd assured him I would be fine. As we walked outside, I was surprised to see Nikolai flanking me, too. I looked up into his bright blue eyes with a grateful smile, and he put a warm hand on my shoulder.

"You okay?" he asked in a low voice, and I nodded. It was the first time he'd spoken to me in a while—he didn't seem to say much—but I couldn't shake the sense that I'd felt his presence all along, his protective aura one that I'd come to know as intimately as my own.

As we approached the driveway where Phillip stood, leaned up against a car I didn't recognize, I felt my heart start to thud. The sun was shining down on him, illuminating the slick black leather of his coat, the shiny ink-black of his hair, and his wild green eyes. He stared at me as though he'd never seen me before; his eyes locked on me, a ghost of a smile on his full lips as I approached.

When I was finally standing in front of him, I was surprised that he said nothing, only turned to Lee with his usual sardonic expression.

"Your face looks like a slapped arse," Phillip said somewhat crossly to Lee, and I snorted with laughter. "But I'm glad you're alive." Lee's face turned momentarily red, then he squared his shoulders, his head held high, and stalked back to the trailer. I noticed Nikolai smirk before turning and following him.

"Who's the other guy?" Phillip asked curiously, watching him go.

"That's Nikolai," I said. "He doesn't say much, but he's a good dude."

Phillip digested this, then nodded, turning to me, a bemused, self-satisfied smile on his lips. But there was a nervousness underneath that he couldn't hide from me.

"Let's go inside to talk," I said. "Here, little pitchers have big ears, and even the ones without ears can still hear."

"I have no idea what gobbledygook you just said," Phillip responded.

I grabbed his arm and pulled him towards Jamie's trailer and into Jamie's bedroom, which I knew would be vacated just for this purpose. Reading each other's minds did have some perks, after all. Once we were safely shut in the room, I sat on the bed and looked at Phillip expectantly.

"Where did you learn that particular turn of phrase?" I asked, stalling. "'Your face looks like a slapped arse'?"

"My grandmother was from the UK," Phillip said offhandedly, running a hand over the selection of leather jackets in Jamie's closet. I marveled at just how many he had, since they all looked exactly the same. "She used to say that a lot."

"You never told me that," I mused, watching him. Phillip was fidgeting, and it put a strange feeling in my belly. It was very rare that I'd seen Phillip nervous. "You've never told me much about your family."

I did know bits and pieces, mainly from reading articles that had been written about him posthumously, and the odd interview that the remaining bandmates, Barb, and extended family had given, though there hadn't been many. I knew that Phillip was the oldest of four, with one brother and two sisters. I knew that both of his parents were dead, and that one of his sisters had gone through a round of chemo after a breast cancer diagnosis, but I didn't know much beyond that. I wondered if Phillip had gone to the trouble of finding out the whereabouts of his family yet, if he knew how they were all faring. He'd found the time—in less than a week—to reconnect with Barb, so I could only assume he must have with his family as well, or at least intended to.

"Never had time," Phillip said absently, still rifling through the jackets. "You and I have always been too busy dodging bullets and warlocks to fool much with idle chit-chat." I blanched and he looked at me with a smile. "I'm not saying it's your fault. And I don't know anything about your family, either. Unless you count Tess."

"We do not count Tess," I said firmly, and we both laughed. It did little to break up the tension in the room. Silence fell, and I stared at him awkwardly, waiting for him to say something, to explain why he had come.

Phillip apparently sensed my feelings and thankfully saved me from having to start. "Stormy," he began, coming over to the bed and sitting down, a lot further away from me than I would've liked. "What are we going to do about this mess?"

"Which mess?" I asked, managing a smile. "There are so many."

"All of them," he said with a wry grin. "After all, they're intertwined." Then his face turned dark. "Us. That mess. You and me."

"I mean…I thought it was over and done with," I said, and he looked stricken. "Didn't you get my text?"

"I got it. I wish I hadn't." Phillip took my hands in his and gave them a squeeze. As always, his skin felt so warm, so alive. My nerves erupted with shocks as he touched me. "As soon as I read it, I knew I had to come here and make things right, to beg you to…" He trailed off, then started again. "I know I was the one to pitch the idea that we take some time apart, but…Stormy, it was a mistake. I didn't mean it. I was just upset. When you texted me that it was over, it broke my heart. I've never been so upset—in either life." He looked at me, his eyes unusually bright. "I can't stand the thought of losing you."

Whatever I'd been expecting him to say, it wasn't *that*. My heart started to pound, hard.

"You're right about us causing each other pain," Phillip continued. "But I really believe we can both put a stop to that…if we just…I don't know, instead of walling ourselves in with our worries and fears, if we just talk about them. Be honest with each other. Face all of our problems together." His face was hopeful as his green eyes stared into mine. "I think we can try again and really be happy." He swallowed. "But if you mean what you said…and you really do want to move on…well, I understand. I won't stand in your way."

"Are you serious?" I asked.

"Yes," Phillip said, his eyes wet. "I'm serious. I love you, Stormy. I want to be with you. But if that isn't what you want, then I respect that and I'll leave."

"Phillip…" There was so much to say, and I had no idea where to begin. "Phillip, you don't know the half of what… what I've found out. If you knew just how much we'd been manipulated, used—treated like puppets—I don't know if you'd feel the same way about all this, about me."

"Tell me all of it, then," Phillip said. "I promise you it won't make a damn bit of difference. I love you."

"Also…" I said, shutting my eyes. I didn't want to tell him, but I had to. "You should know…I…I…kissed someone. While we were apart."

"Lee," Phillip said without missing a beat, and my heart skipped. *Shit.*

I had no idea how to explain. What had happened between Lee and me almost seemed like something from a past life, even though it had only been a day. As far away as it felt, I could still remember every detail—how Lee's hands had felt on my skin, the way his mouth tasted, the soft tickle of his feathery, light blond hair. How we'd almost…Up until the minute Lee had said, "We can't," I'd been fully ready to lose myself to him.

How could I explain to Phillip what I myself didn't quite understand?

"There's nothing between us," I said fiercely, sure of that much at least. "Nothing at all. I swear. But if you're standing here saying you want me, you have to know."

"I knew he had a thing for you from the beginning," Phillip said quietly. "I just didn't realize that you had a thing for him, too."

"I didn't," I protested. "I don't."

"Come on, Stormy," he said, not unkindly.

I cut him off. "No. You don't get to do that, Phillip. I was attracted to Lee briefly, mainly because of the connection between us. I scratched an itch, but that's all. We just kissed. And I only did it because…because…"

"Because of Barb," Phillip said softly. "Revenge?"

"No, not revenge," I said, hurt. "Lee does mean more to me than *that.*"

"He's in love with you."

"No." I shook my head. "Lee loves somebody else."

Phillip's eyes met mine, wild and clear, almost sparkling. The room was cold; I inwardly cursed Nikolai for being stingy with the thermostat and crossed my arms over my chest, shivering. I wanted to reach out and put my hands on Phillip, who no doubt would be as hot as a furnace. I wanted to touch him, to reassure him and be reassured, my body seeking that familiarity with his that couldn't be denied. But I couldn't do it. Not until I knew the deal. After all, he'd gone back to Barb before I'd ever considered sharing my bed with Lee.

"Who does he love, then?" Phillip asked.

I shook my head. "That's not my story to tell."

"Then answer this: Who do *you* love?" Phillip asked, his eyes peering into my soul. "I've already told you who *I* love."

I shook my head again. "And yet, you were with *her*."

Phillip seemed to have no rebuttal. He looked down at his hands, his large, familiar, warm hands. I wanted to reach out and grab those hands, cover them with kisses, tell him it was all fine, that we could put it past us. That I did love him, of course I did. Instead, I just stared at his hands, which were tightly clenched in his lap.

"I don't know what I think anymore," I said, my eyes welling up with tears. "All I know is that a couple of days ago, you went back to Barb and she's your *wife* and that's a bond you can't just break, and everything that happened with Lee… even though we're not in love, it was just a comfort thing…a one-night deal…and even though I can't bear the thought of being without you, so much has happened that I don't know if we can ever get back to where we were!"

Phillip kissed me.

He pulled me close, taking me by surprise, rendering me silent, as he pressed his warm, soft lips to mine. His kiss was tender and full of love, almost reverent. I tensed at first, afraid, not wanting to believe it was really happening. I'd been missing him for so long—for years, it seemed like. Those weeks had felt like forever. He tasted just the same, and smelled just the same, and as he wrapped his arms around me, I sunk into him, letting my arms go around his hard torso, my fingers trailing up his back, and sighed into him as his kiss turned from tender and sweet to hurried and full of pent-up passion.

"Promise me," Phillip said, breaking away momentarily, out of breath. "Promise me the thing with Lee was just the once, and that you don't love him."

"I don't," I said, my lips still barely touching his. "He's in love with someone else. And so am I." His arms were cradling me, warm and firm. "I love you, Phillip. It's always you, always. It was just a fling, because I was brokenhearted and lonely, because I missed you so much. And I swear, it'll never, ever happen again…"

Phillip silenced me, pressing his mouth to mine more fervently this time, a little rough. I leaned into him, breathing him in, letting him mold me against him. I never wanted to let him go. I pulled away and looked at him.

"And Barb?"

Phillip stared down at me, a little out of breath, his green eyes flashing. "I dropped Barb off at the airport this morning. She's headed back home to her kids and her life." He ran a finger over my lips, making me shiver. "I loved her once, but that was a lifetime ago. A literal lifetime. Nothing at all happened between us, other than a much-needed conversation." I smiled under his touch. "I love *you*, Stormy."

I pulled his face close to mine, placing a gentle kiss on his lips, letting my cheeks graze his, and rested my forehead against his face, feeling the gentle tickle of his eyelashes. "I love you," I said again, in a fierce whisper, my heart in my throat. "Can we stop with these shenanigans and just be together?"

"Yes," he said without hesitation, running a hand up my neck, past my ear and into my hair. "Yes. That's what I want, too. You and me, together. Always. A team."

"A team."

Our mouths met again, and he pushed me back on the bed,

his weight heavy and solid on top of me, holding himself up by his elbows as his shaggy hair cascaded over his ears. It was already beginning to grow out, and I hoped he'd let it grow long, the way I knew and loved it. He placed a gentle kiss on my collarbone, one on my neck, one on my jawline, and I moaned in pleasure. His free hand trailed up my stomach and to my shoulder, where he squeezed me with urgency, letting me know how much he wanted me. And I wanted him too, so bad I could taste it.

It occurred to me that Jamie could pop in on us at any moment. He might not take kindly to us sexing it up in his room. Then again, it was Jamie. He was so laid-back and easy-going, he probably wouldn't care. Hell, he'd likely offer to bring us refreshments.

"Planning a threesome, are you?" Phillip smiled his wolf-like grin, placing another kiss behind my ear, my skin erupting in goosebumps.

"Get out of my head," I said, and he laughed.

"I missed you saying that," Phillip said with a smile. "I missed a lot of things."

"So did I."

Phillip's hand trailed back down, lingering momentarily on my chest, my stomach, and finally landing on my pants, fiddling with the button. I placed a hand over his, moaning against his mouth, and moved to help him, suddenly not caring who might walk in, my need for Phillip overriding any sense of decorum. So I was a shitty houseguest.

My button popped open, and Phillip moved his hand inside of my shirt, warm and delicious as he caressed my skin. I couldn't wait any longer. I reached down and fumbled with his belt, and he put a hand over mine, helping me to undo his fly, his mouth never leaving mine.

Then he was inside me and I couldn't feel—or think of—anything else but the way Phillip felt moving against me, his skin warm and electric, his black hair falling over his eyes like ink-stained raindrops, his eyes two green jewels. As he moved against me, he kissed me, his mouth wet and delicious, a moan escaping his throat as we moved together in time, erupting with pleasure as one, the way we were always meant to be.

Phillip lay back against the cushions, his black hair soaked with sweat. "You wore me out, woman," he said, panting a little and grinning.

"Are you complaining?"

"Never." He reached out and gave me a gentle slap on the backside. "Come back. I'm not done with you yet."

"I can't," I said with a smile. "Sad though it makes me, I can't stay in here with you all afternoon."

"Why not?" he asked. "Sick of me already?"

"Never." I mirrored his words back to him, meeting his dark eyes, still barely believing he was really here. "I need to check in with everybody. We were going to head out this afternoon, try to find Lydia and Renee. I think Roberta has a pretty good idea where they are. They're going to need my help."

"I'll come, too," Phillip said, and my heart soared. "I'd like to help."

"Thank you," I said sincerely, leaning over to kiss him softly on the lips. "I'm so glad you're here." As his mouth met mine, a surge of heat went through me again and I bit his lower lip, sucking on it gently, my arms going around his neck. Maybe if we were fast…

There was a loud, heavy knock on the door. Phillip groaned audibly.

"Yeah?" I called out, my voice a croak. I cleared my throat and tried again. "What's up?"

"Stormy, come quick." Lee's voice sounded from the other side of the door. "Hurry. It's Benny."

"What about Benny?" I asked, Phillip and I both sitting up, our faces flushed. I fiddled with my pants, buttoning them back up quickly and sliding my phone into my back pocket as Phillip threw on his black t-shirt.

"You'd better just come see. And hurry. Please. Stormy, we need you."

Eighteen

Benny's body was lying on the porch swing, which was wildly swinging back and forth under the weight of his bulky frame. His head was propped up at a weird angle, his chin touching his chest, his large legs hanging off the side, and the rest of his body seemingly crammed into the swing like an afterthought. The rusted chains were squeaking loudly as he swung there, unmoving. Beneath his swinging body, sticky, red blood was collecting on the flaking porch, and I could see it dripping from underneath Benny's ripped leather jacket in a steady pattern. The sound of the squeaking swing and the dripping blood were the only sounds on the porch; everything else was eerily silent. I gingerly stepped forward, trying to inch past the small group of people who had crowded around him. *Drip, drip, drip.* It reminded me, oddly, of my own front porch with its rapidly deteriorating red paint.

"What's happened?" Phillip demanded, extending his arm to gently move aside the people gathered around—Clara, Jamie, Roberta, Nikolai—so I could pass. Given the small finger of dread that was unfurling in my belly, and the strange, buzzing feeling beginning in my arms and hands, I knew exactly why Lee had said I was needed.

"Benny's been shot!" Roberta moaned. She was crouched down beside him, just off to the side of the swing, her face ashen and her cheeks wet with tears.

"Goddammit," I said angrily, surveying the scene. "Can any of us just have one single moment of peace?"

"Please, Stormy," Lee pleaded from somewhere behind me.

Benny was going to die.

I didn't need to look him over further to confirm it. I didn't need to see the blood, assess his injuries, or smell the fear and the panic in the air—the cold winter morning was slick and damp with it—or to read the faces of the people who knew and loved Benny best. I knew because I could *feel* it. Benny was going to die.

They all looked at me, their voices growing hushed, as I stepped forward.

"Who did this?" I asked, but nobody answered. It had gone quiet as a tomb on the porch. "Who shot you?" I asked Benny, leaning down to him, putting a hand on the swing to stop it from moving. Blood splattered on my shoe, but I ignored it.

"I...didn't see..." Benny gasped, clenching one arm tightly against his chest. His hands were white with the effort, dark red blood seeping through his fingers.

"You were shot in the chest?" I asked, but he didn't respond, only continued to gasp.

Lee was suddenly by my side, and I could feel his panic and his fury. "They got him twice—once in the arm and once in the chest." His face was grave. "They peeled in, rolled down the window, and called out to him, you know, like a friend would—and the second Benny turned around, they shot him and lit the fuck out of here." His lips were pressed tightly together. "Nobody saw it. He was the only one out here.

Whoever it was knew he'd be alone, working on the bike. I heard it from inside and I ran out, but by the time I got to the porch, they were gone."

"And you didn't see anything? What the car looked like, or…"

"Not even the bumper," Lee said angrily. He looked down at Benny, tears pooling in his eyes. "This is bad, isn't it?" I put a hand on Lee's knee to try and comfort him. He put his own hand over mine and gave it a squeeze.

"I assume somebody already called an ambulance?" I turned on one knee and looked around. Nobody said a word; everyone was looking down at their feet as though they'd all forgotten how to speak or even think on their own. Phillip locked eyes with me, and we exchanged a silent word. "What the fuck you guys, did somebody call a fucking ambulance?" I fumbled in my pocket for my phone, but my hand was trembling too much. "Phillip, will you call?" He nodded.

"No." Benny's voice was barely a whisper. "No. Don't."

"We didn't call because he doesn't want us to," Lee said to me softly, reaching out a hand to touch Benny. When he pulled his hand back, I saw that his fingers were streaked with blood. "We can't get the authorities involved."

"But Lee, we have to!"

"Would you guys mind giving us some space?" Lee asked, his voice coming out firm, but somehow apologetic. I expected arguments, but everyone, even Clara, even *Phillip*, went inside without so much as a word of protest. I stared at Lee, oddly impressed. Only Roberta hung back, but Lee didn't seem to mind her being there.

"We can't call anyone," Lee said again, looking deep into my eyes. "It's too much of a risk."

Calling the police will open up questions that can't be answered, his eyes seemed to say. *Would open up the Wolfden to scrutiny, to danger. Benny would rather die—literally—than do that to us.*

"I get it," I said, leaning closer to inspect Benny's wound, which he was doing his best to cover with his tense hand. "I understand why we can't call the cops, but Lee…if we don't get him medical care, he's going to die. Do you understand?"

"Yes," Lee said, his face even more pale now. His blood-soaked hand caressed Benny's arm. "That's why I need *you.*"

"You can't possibly expect me to just sit here and let Benny bleed out," I said in a shaking voice.

"We have no other choice," Lee said, his own voice trembling.

"You want to casually hang out here while Benny bleeds to death on the front porch and then you expect me to just wave my hands and *poof,* bring him back to life."

"You've done it before," Lee pleaded, still caressing Benny's arm. "I wouldn't ask if I didn't think you could do it."

The screen door opened and Phillip came back out, his face angry. "Of course she can do it," he spat. "But you have no idea what you're asking of her. How many times will she have to do this because of you all? When does she get to be finished?"

"She brought *you* back, didn't she?" Lee retorted. "Twice. I don't see you complaining."

Phillip had complained plenty, but now wasn't the moment for petty arguments. I held up a hand to silence both of them. "Lee…this just doesn't seem like the right course of action. And I don't have his consent to…to…"

"Benny, baby," Lee said, leaning towards him and crooning in his ear. At his words, Benny turned his pale face to Lee's, and I could see his eyes were glistening—whether they were tears of pain, sadness, or shock, I didn't know. Hearing Lee call him *baby* made my heart ache. "Do you want Stormy to bring you back, if you…when you…"

Benny's mouth formed an *O*, but no words came out. He craned his neck further towards Lee, but he couldn't seem to make any sounds. The blood was still steadily dripping onto the porch, and Benny began to wheeze. A sob escaped my throat.

Phillip crouched down next to me, his strong, warm hand a silent presence on my back. *You don't have to do this,* he seemed to say. *This choice is yours.*

I know, I answered back, unsure if I was really speaking to Phillip or just talking to myself. It didn't matter. All I knew was that I had to know if Benny really wanted this before I could go further. I had learned my lesson on that score, and I'd learned it good. I turned to Phillip with a sad smile. He smiled back at me, his face also full of sadness, and reached up to wipe a tear from my cheek.

Roberta was in the corner, her hand holding the swing in place, silently crying, tears streaming down her face and wetting the collar of her shirt. She'd been through so much the past few days, and my heart went out to her. It was crazy to think that just a couple of weeks before I'd hated her guts and blamed her for most of my problems. Now, all the drama meant less than nothing. She was my sister now.

"Benny, baby…" Lee repeated, his hand clutching Benny tightly. His face was full of desperate love. "Stormy needs your consent before she can…if she's going to bring you back. Tell us what you want. Please. Please."

Benny was still silent, save for the wheezing, which was growing louder, and turning into a rattle. I wondered if he'd been shot in a lung.

"Even just a nod…" Roberta said through her tears, her voice shaky and desolate. My heart clenched.

"Come on, man," Phillip chimed in, to my surprise. His hand was tense on my back. "Let her know. You can't go out like this."

I looked at him gratefully. He mouthed the words, *I love you,* and I mouthed them back. He'd never meant so much to me as he did in that moment.

"Benny?" Lee's voice was now a wail. All I could hear was the gritty, terrible sound of Benny's wheezing and the steady *drip, drip, drip.* I hadn't even agreed to do this, but now all I could think about was how awful it would be if Benny died right in front of us without giving me his consent. I couldn't bear the thought. But without it…I just couldn't do it. "Don't leave like this. Not before I have a chance to make things right. Benny. Please." Lee's frantic expression finally collapsed and gave way to tears. "I love you. Don't leave me." He pressed his face into Benny's jacket, ignoring the blood that smeared across his cheek, his shoulders shaking. Roberta gave another choked sob and ran into the trailer, the screen door slamming behind her.

For a moment, everything was deadly quiet, save for the wheezing and the dripping. We were all silently crying, silently praying or bargaining with the gods. And then, suddenly, the wheezing stopped. My head whipped up and I stared at Benny, unable to make out the rise and fall of his bloody chest or any sign of movement at all.

Lee's shoulders shook harder, and he grasped at Benny, holding him tight.

Then Benny abruptly took a great wrenching breath, rattling and broken, and with a great effort, managed to croak out, "Bring…me back."

Benny took one more ragged, painful breath, and when he exhaled, a stream of blood poured from his mouth, down his chin, and onto his ruined leather jacket. It happened so quickly and violently that I imagined I could almost *see* Benny's soul, the energy that had once comprised such a large, strong, hulk of a man, gather up and fly out of his body and into the cold, damp air. Maybe he hadn't left us yet…if only I could get to him, to feel for a pulse, to check for the slightest breath.

But I let Lee hold him for a minute, let him cry. I knew what he was feeling. Even with Benny having given his last-minute consent, if he was truly gone, it wasn't a tried-and-true fix—there were variables, things that could go wrong. I knew that instinctively, even if I was a "green" witch. And even if I brought him back, the memory and the trauma of his death would always be with us. That was a pain that was very real. Lee needed to sit with it for a moment, acclimate to everything that had happened.

"Lee…" I said quietly, putting my hand on his quaking shoulder. "I'm going to give you a few minutes. Come get me when you're ready." The truth was, *I* needed a few minutes, too. The more I did this, the harder it seemed to become.

Lee's light-blond head gave an almost imperceptible nod; he wasn't really seeing me. I got up from my crouch, reaching for Phillip's arm to steady me, and we walked down the steps towards the back yard. As we walked, I leaned on him for comfort, my teeth chattering. I shoved my hands in my pockets for warmth. I couldn't be trying to practice magic and weave spells with icy-cold hands.

"Are you okay?" Phillip asked softly once we were out of earshot, safely in back of the trailer, just the two of us. He reached out and pulled me into his arms. I rested my head on his soft black t-shirt, breathing in his familiar musk. "You're freezing. It's not even that cold out, but you're like an icicle."

"I'm okay," I said, my voice coming out a little choked. "I'm doing better than Lee is, anyway."

"So Benny's the one," Phillip said, his voice full of wonder. "The one that Lee's in love with."

"Yes."

"I thought you might just be telling me that to make me

feel better," Phillip admitted, stroking my hair. "I really was certain Lee was in love with *you.*"

I pulled back and looked into his deep green eyes. "Nah. And anyway, whatever it was, it's over." I smiled as he pushed my hair back from my face. "Whatever was between us was about the magic, the connection with Guthrie. He wasn't ready to be out yet, and I guess he was trying to forget Benny and be…whatever his parents wanted him to be. I think maybe he thought it'd be easier with me. That's all." I laughed. "He knows better than that now."

"I think it was more than that," Phillip insisted. "You don't give yourself enough credit." He squeezed my shoulders. "But I believe you. I believe he loves Benny. It's pretty clear. And I know you love me. Whatever bond you two have, I know I have nothing to worry about."

"You really don't," I said.

Phillip leaned forward and kissed me gently. "And neither do you."

For a moment, I forgot everything else, relishing the feeling of Phillip's lips on mine. Everything was back where it should be. As long as we were together, everything else would fall back into place. There was nothing we couldn't get through, couldn't fix, if we were together. His arms were strong and warm around me. I vowed, his lips still against mine, that I'd never let him go again.

"Are you ready to do this?" he asked in a soft voice near my ear.

"As ready as I'll ever be, I guess," I said, nuzzling into him for a brief comfort.

Before we broke apart, a shrill scream broke us from our reverie, and we both ran at warp speed around to the front of the house, where chaos had broken out once again.

The scream had come from Roberta, who was bounding down the steps, her tear-streaked face full of terror.

"It's okay," I began, rushing towards her.

"No, Stormy!" Roberta seized me by the shoulder and shook me. "He's gone! Benny is gone!"

"I know," I said. "I'm going to bring him back—"

"No, I mean he's *gone,* Stormy!" She grabbed my arm and pulled me towards the house.

"What? How?" Phillip bounded up the steps to the porch as I stared at her, confused. "He was just there, on the swing, not two minutes ago! I left him with Lee!"

"They took him, Stormy!" Roberta screamed. She shook me again, hard enough to make my teeth rattle, and pointed towards the road. I turned, surprised to see a figure running after a car that was peeling down the road so fast, it'd left tire tracks in the cold asphalt. I realized it was Lee running, chasing after the car, screaming bloody murder. "They just tore into the drive, jumped out, bounded up the steps, and grabbed him before we could stop them! They had guns and…and…" Roberta tried to get her breath, to form words. "They took Benny's body…so we can't…oh god, Stormy, they *took Benny's body!"*

Nineteen

For a moment, all I could do was stare ahead at the dirty, old country road that was badly in need of repaving, the road that seemed to stretch on for miles and miles. Phillip was a silent, infuriated presence behind me. I could hear Roberta wailing, and up ahead was Lee, spent and out of breath, stopped in the middle of the road, crouching on his knees, his face in his hands.

I started to run after him, to comfort him, but something stopped me short.

My fury was palpable. I could be no comfort to him, or anyone else right now.

"Give me your keys," I muttered through clenched teeth, my voice low and full of rage. From the corner of my eye, I saw Nikolai, Jamie, and Clara emerging from the trailer, their faces white.

"What?" Phillip put a hand on my shoulder. "Stormy, maybe we shouldn't—"

"I was talking to Roberta," I said, whipping around and finding her kneeling in the grass, her body convulsing with sobs. "Give me your keys. I'm going after them."

"You'll never catch up," Roberta wailed miserably, but she fished her keys out of her pocket and tossed them to me. I caught them mid-air and began striding towards her SUV, the blood thudding in my ears. I could feel a distinctive hum beginning from deep inside, from my very blood. Whatever magic lived inside me was *mad*.

A furious, accusatory voice said behind me, "How do we know you weren't just stalling so they could take Benny?"

I whirled around to face Clara, her face full of stark fury. "Are you serious?" I asked, incredulous. "You think I had something to do with this?"

"I'm just saying it was sure convenient, you walking around back just long enough for someone to snatch Benny," she retorted, her face red. "After making everybody go inside, leaving him vulnerable."

I looked towards the porch, where Nikolai and Jamie stood, silently observing us. Did they think the same thing? I looked back to Clara, meeting her eyes. "I'm not involved, I swear," I said, shaking. "I would never hurt Benny. Or anyone."

"She's telling the truth," Phillip said, but Clara paid him no attention. Roberta was still crouched on the ground, sobbing, oblivious to us.

"All the trouble started when *you* showed up," she accused. The expression I'd first mistaken for fury was something else: terror. I felt myself soften towards her.

"I promise you, I'm on your side," I assured her.

"Tell me who you are, then," Clara said. "Where you came from and how you came to be at the Wolfden."

"I will," I answered, frantic. "I promise. But it'll have to wait. Because right now, I'm going to go get Benny."

Clara opened her mouth to speak, but the look on my face must have silenced her. She fixed me with one more glare, then turned on her heel and stalked back to the trailer. I sighed with relief; Clara could have easily broken me in half.

I looked back at Phillip, who was watching me, his face grave. "Are you coming or not?" I asked.

He stared at me quizzically for a moment, then his face broke into a grim smile and he jogged to the vehicle, throwing himself into the passenger seat. I flung myself into the car, put the key in the ignition, and backed out of the parking lot, hard enough to squeal the tires. Roberta stared at me as I drove past. I stopped the SUV and gestured for her to get in. She opened the back door and jumped into the car, immediately burying her face in her hands as I pulled out of the drive.

We couldn't let this happen. Not on my watch.

"Are you going to pick him up, too?" Phillip asked in a low voice as we approached Lee, who was still straddling the middle of the road, his shoulders shaking, his pale hair like a damp halo around his head.

"Should I?" I asked him honestly.

"Of course," Phillip said, looking at me with an interesting expression. "If you'd been taken, I sure as hell would want to go."

I nodded and rolled down the window, creeping the SUV to a halt. "Lee," I called out. He didn't look up. "Get in, let's go get Benny back. Hurry."

"It's hopeless," Lee said desperately, but he still scrambled up off the road and hopped in the back of the SUV. I put my foot to the gas and sped forward, grateful for the straight, lonesome stretch of road that hopefully would lead me right to them. Up ahead in the distance, I could see a bloom of red dust.

"Are there many turnoffs they could take?" I asked, looking in the rearview.

Lee looked terrible. His eyes were sunken, his cheeks wet with tears. He was biting at his mouth, hard, the blood pooling on his bottom lip. He shook his head almost imperceptibly. "Maybe one or two cattle roads, but they've got gates. I can only think of one major road in the next three or four miles that they might take, but…"

"We'll decide when we get there, then," I said firmly, stepping harder on the gas. "If we haven't already caught up with them by then."

"They're not going to make it easy," Phillip said, putting his hand on my knee. "If they went to the trouble to shoot the guy, then come back and snatch his body, obviously they don't want him alive. You guys should both…should both come to terms with that."

"I know, but we've got to try," I insisted. Phillip squeezed my knee in response, and I snuck one more glance at Lee in the backseat. His head was pressed up against the glass, his breath fogging up the window. He looked one step away from death himself. I thought back to the story Lydia had told me, about the accident he'd been in, how she had brought him back. I wondered how it felt to be on the other side of that—to lose a loved one and have them snatched away just before getting that chance. As it turned out, I knew, though I didn't remember, and I supposed that was a small favor. How might I react if it were Phillip? I shuddered at the thought.

Glancing from Phillip to Lee and back again, it was odd, thinking about how both of them had once been dead, and now weren't. They were every bit as vital and alive and full of vigor as me or anyone else, and yet…and to think, I'd kissed them both.

"The good thing is…" I said, thinking hard, my hands gripping the wheel. "It doesn't matter how long it takes. I can bring him back regardless. I mean, Phillip was dead for twenty-three years. So even if we don't find him right away, I can still—"

"Do you really think they're just going to let him stick around, waiting to be found?" Lee asked, his voice bitter. "Do you think they'll bury him in a nice cemetery with a lovely granite headstone just ready for us to find him and bring him back? No, of course they won't. They'll…they'll…"

"They'll destroy the body," Phillip finished for him.

"Yes," Lee whispered.

I swallowed. "They aren't going to get that far," I promised him. "We'll find him before they have a chance to hurt a hair on his head."

"They've already done that and then some," Lee said angrily.

"Who's *they*?" I asked, looking at him in the rearview. "Who's helping Elvin, Lee?" There was no doubt in my mind that he was behind this.

"I honestly don't know," he said helplessly. "But whoever it is, I'll rip them limb from limb when I get to them."

"And we'll help you," I said, staring at the road. "I swear to you we will." Phillip squeezed my knee again, and looked at me, his eyes fierce and wild.

Up ahead, I saw something metallic glint, the sun shining bright in my eyes, making it fuzzy, yet unmistakable. It was far, far off in the distance, and I was only able to see it because the road was so straight and flat. A vehicle. I decided to say nothing for now, not wanting to give Lee false hope, but I stepped on the gas, and we surged to 80, the wheels squeaking as we flew down the asphalt. Roberta needed shocks. I made a mental note to tell her later, but for now, I just hoped the little RAV4 held up.

I was so very sick of this. Just…sick to death of it. Sick and tired. And furious. Why couldn't Elvin just leave me the fuck alone? How many people had to suffer or die before he'd stop hunting me? Wanting to tap into my magic, to learn how to wield it, couldn't be enough reason to continue the onslaught that they'd unleashed on me and everybody I cared about. It just couldn't.

I was getting closer and closer to the vehicle ahead of me,

the sunlight glinting on the back bumper. If I could just speed up a little more…the SUV surged to 95.

"Don't wreck the car, Stormy," Phillip said, his voice nervous, but his face was full of excitement. What was it about dudes and fast cars? He shot me a flirty look.

"Not the time, Phillip," I said, but I gave him a wink. We were even closer to the car now. With any luck, I'd be able to catch up to them.

I was maybe twenty yards away. It seemed they were losing speed, slowing down. Impossible, and yet it was true. The car looked like one I recognized; could it be? I surged ahead, faster. Fifteen yards. Now ten. A familiar bumper sticker came into view.

Then suddenly, without warning, my windshield disappeared, bursting into fragments all around us. I slammed on the brakes and instinctively threw my hands in front of my eyes. I felt Phillip's arms clutch at me, pulling me down.

"They shot at us!" I heard Lee scream from the backseat.

"Is everyone okay?" Phillip thundered.

I was shaking like a leaf, but I assessed myself silently, hunching over the broken glass that was all over my lap and the car seat. "I'm okay, I think," I said, my voice shaky. "Burt? Lee?"

"I'm okay, too," Roberta said, her voice small from the backseat. "So is Lee."

I sat up and opened my eyes. There was glass everywhere. They'd shot out our windshield. I looked over at Phillip, who had a cut on his forehead from the glass, but otherwise looked alright. The other car was nowhere to be found, but fresh tire marks on the road suggested they'd turned right and cut into a scraggly, overgrown cow field. The tracks went on for a few yards, then disappeared.

I shook broken glass from my hair. "Roberta, what's the street address where you used to live with your uncle, out in the woods?" I asked, and I saw her look at me in surprise from the rearview mirror. "We're near there, aren't we? Is there any kind of secret road or cattle road or something that leads to it?"

"What does that have to do with…" Lee started, but Roberta cut him off.

"Yes, there is," she said, her voice dull with fear. She rattled off an address, her face still steaked with tears. I noticed there was glass in her hair, and undoubtedly knew there must be some in mine, too.

"Alright," I said, taking a deep breath and turning the wheel abruptly to the left. "I hope your car can take this, Burt. Let's go get our boy back. And if we're lucky, we might just find Lydia and Renee, too."

I parked Burt's SUV beside an old Mustang, jumping out and holding the keys between my knuckles like a weapon. Lee and Phillip flanked me, the three of us running towards the cabin that loomed ahead of us. Roberta was still in the car, texting Nikolai and Jamie to let them know what was going on, though I suspected she needed a few minutes to herself now that she was back here. My instinct—or maybe I'd read her thoughts— told me that she had a lot of memories tied up with this place that she hadn't dealt with. Not to mention the small fact that her father, Elvin, was likely here. How would that reunion go, I wondered.

The cabin was a small, rickety thing that looked like it hadn't been dwelled in or maintained for years. The porch was falling apart, the roof was half caved-in, and the windows were thick with dirty cobwebs.

It hadn't taken us long to find the place once Roberta had told us how to get there. Just a short cattle road behind a couple of marshes, and we'd happened upon the old homestead where Roberta had stayed with her uncle Albert as a pre-teen. Now, it appeared that Elvin had co-opted it for some kind of wayward "home base," a fact that no doubt horrified her. She hadn't said much the whole ride here, and every time I'd glanced back at her in the mirror, she'd been hugging her knees to her chest, rocking back and forth. I felt so bad for my newfound friend; she'd been through so much. And from the sounds of it, had weathered most of it alone.

As for Lee, he had done nothing but stare out the window, tear streaks mingling with his freckles.

"I doubt there's anybody in the house," I said as the three of us rushed towards the cabin. "It doesn't look like anybody has stepped foot into it in years. Roberta said it was condemned by the county."

"Still, we'll check it out," Phillip insisted.

"He brought me out here before," Lee said, stopping short. He looked around. Nothing surrounded us but trees and more trees. "Elvin, I mean. I don't remember everything, but I do remember standing here. And then I was..." His brow furrowed in confusion as he talked to himself. "Then I was underground. Is that right?"

"Are you sure you're not thinking of Guthrie's cellar, where Benny found you?" I asked, and he shook his head.

"No," he said. "It's a similar space, but much bigger, and further underground," he said, rubbing at his eyes absently. "It's like I remember it and don't remember it. How strange is that?"

"If there's anything I've learned in the past few days," I said, stepping forward, continuing towards the cabin, "it's that *strange* is extremely relative." As I said the last word, my foot stepped onto nothing and I felt myself pitch forward into darkness, and then I was falling.

Twenty

I landed with a *thud* onto hard earth with a loud, involuntary "oof." So much for being quiet.

I assessed myself quickly and, realizing I wasn't hurt, stood up, looking around furiously to try and get my bearings. It was black as pitch, the only source of light from a small square above me. A square that Phillip and Lee were staring down at me from. I'd fallen through some kind of trapdoor.

"I can't see a thing," I called up to them.

"Are you okay?" Phillip asked.

"Yeah," I answered, pulling my phone out of my pocket.

"Stay where you are," Phillip advised. "Lee's going back to the car to see if Roberta has some rope or a cable. We'll help you get back up. Don't move until they get back, Stormy. It's not safe."

I flicked on my phone's flashlight app and the small space filled with light. "It's some kind of…jeez, it almost looks like a bunker," I said, taking in the dusty, dirty little space. There was nothing, just dirt walls and floors. Then I saw, off to my right, a small, open door, dim light illuminated from within. "Let me just check." I moved towards the door.

"Stormy, wait for us. Just *wait* a minute."

From a great distance, I heard Lee's voice call out to Phillip, "Dude, Roberta's not in the car! Where did she go?" I felt a chill go up my back.

"Come after me," I called up to Phillip, my nose filling with a familiar scent. It smelled like a certain setting spray, one that I found very familiar. "I can't wait."

"Stormy!"

But I had already entered the room, using my flashlight app as a guide.

I was now in a room smaller than the one before, with more dirt walls and dirt floors, but there was a little table in the back, filled with papers and candles and all sorts of weird things. I stepped forward carefully, unable to fight the curiosity overtaking me.

Then the phone was knocked out of my hand. The flashlight app went out. I heard a door squeak and slam behind me. A deadbolt locking.

And I was trapped in the dark.

"Sloan."

Just the one word, because there was nothing else I could —or wanted to—say. I stood there, for a brief moment forgetting everything else, and just stared at her. I watched her as she moved gracefully in the dark, coming to sit on a stool near a table filled with all sorts of things—candles, oddly shaped stones, bundles of herbs—things that triggered my long-forgotten memories. Though it was dark, I could see Sloan fairly clearly, could see her eyes, her heart. I wasn't surprised—I'd recognized her car back on the road, and again as I'd parked beside it—but I still couldn't help but feel a sense of shock at how far my former best friend had fallen.

Sloan stared back, holding my phone in her hand, her chin raised, a little defiant, a little self-righteous. But beneath her simmering resentment and whatever justifications she felt was something else. Behind her impeccably made-up eyes I could see a wavering, an insecurity…doubt, maybe. Not that I cared, not anymore. Let her live with it.

"You found me," she said with a dry laugh. She reached over to the table and lit a large candle, filling the room with a hazy golden light. "I'm impressed. We took all kinds of precautions to elude you, but I should have known with all of those Wolfden guys on your team you'd find us anyway."

"*I* found you," I said, seething. "Not them."

She looked doubtful, so I added, "I recognized your ugly-ass car from the road. You've had the same bumper stickers since we were in high school."

"You want a cookie or something?" Sloan said with a smirk, hoisting herself off the stool where she was perched and walking closer to me.

"No cookie, thanks. What I want is to knock your teeth down your stupid throat."

Sloan's eyes widened, then she gave another of those dry laughs. She didn't sound well. The bags under her eyes were huge, and her skin was red and irritated around her nose and eyes. From the looks of it, she hadn't been sleeping well, and she'd been majorly stressed out. *Being an evil bitch must be hell on the skin*, I thought to myself, stifling a laugh.

"Well, good luck with that, Stormy," Sloan said with a wry smile, gesturing at the room. "I'm well protected here. You might have your undead army or whatever, but Elvin's armed to the teeth, and nobody is going to let me get hurt."

"Did you do it yourself?" I asked.

"Do what?"

I spoke slowly, as if talking to a child. "Shoot Benny. And then snatch his body."

Sloan smiled benignly. "Now, why would I tell you that?"

I sniffed. "You didn't. For one thing, you're not strong enough—that guy's a tank. Plus, you don't have the guts. Deep down inside, you're a wimp, a coward. You always were. Always letting other people do the dirty work, handle your affairs…you love to join causes, but when it comes to actually putting in the effort, you're more of a sit-on-the-sidelines kind of girl, huh?"

"Insulting me won't change anything," Sloan said mildly, but her lip twitched. I was getting to her.

"It doesn't really matter anyway, does it, Sloan?" I leveled my gaze on her. It felt good, knowing that Lee and Phillip would soon enough be behind me, backing me, even if they were outside the locked door. "Our friendship has been over for a long time. Longer than I ever would have guessed. I think you've been playing the part of the best friend while you've been stabbing me in the back for *years*."

I expected a lackluster argument, or more refusals, but instead she shrugged and said, "Yeah, you're right."

"When?" I demanded. "When did you turn on me?" I had some idea, but I wanted to hear it from her own lips.

Sloan shrugged again. "You still don't get it," she said, inching closer to me. I wondered why she kept up this slow approach; was she planning to try and tackle me or something? My hand closed on the knife in my pocket, the one Nikolai had given me. I'd been so insistent on not taking it—now I was glad he'd made me. I fingered the blade lovingly, furtively, as Sloan spoke. "I never turned on you, exactly. The word 'turn' implies that I was on your side at some point. The truth is, I was never on your side." She smiled a slow, lazy smile. "You're so dumb, Stormy. You really thought I just loved you to death all these years, that I just worshipped the ground you walked on. You were wrong."

Her words stung, even though I'd been prepared for them. I tried not to let it show. "Then why bother to hang around, if you hated me?" I said. "That's kind of sad."

"I never could understand why they were so interested in you," Sloan said absently, with a small shrug. "But they paid well for the information, so…"

"You've been feeding info about me to Guthrie and Elvin all this time?" I asked, even though I already knew the answer. "Informing on me since…we were kids?"

Sloan shrugged. "Since high school, anyway. Before that, they never had much use for me." Her voice was bitter. I remembered back to what Roberta had said. The magic hadn't taken with Sloan and Tess; they'd been the only ones who hadn't received some kind of magical benefit from Elvin's tinkering. Apparently, Sloan had held a grudge.

I felt ill. Sloan had known Guthrie since we were teenagers then, at the very least. Which made their age difference and their weird, dysfunctional relationship even more creepy and predatory than it already was. "Why?" I asked. "Why would you do that?"

"Why not?" she asked with another shrug. "I didn't owe you shit then, and I don't now. We all have to survive."

"I don't believe it's as simple as that," I argued. "You've always had a cruel steak, and you've always been a little cagey. But I *know* you, Sloan. Deep down inside, there's a good person there. You wouldn't have been stabbing me in the back all these years without some reason—other than just petty jealousy or whatever it is. I don't believe it."

"I don't give a shit what you believe," she said with a snort. "You always were a little Girl Scout, and that's been your downfall. Is it so hard to understand that someone just *might not like you?*"

My temper flared. "You know, Sloan, you might think you're coming off all tough, but you just look like a fool. If you're going to play up the evil, then do it *right*. Your babyish shrugs and vague answers don't make you look any tougher; it just makes you look like a minion who doesn't know what's going on. Is that what it is?" I asked. "You're just following orders?"

Sloan pulled something out of her pocket. Of course, her Chapstick. I watched as she glided it on, smacking her lips obnoxiously. She was nervous, then. "I'm not telling you anything because I don't *want* to."

I wasn't going to let her get off so easy. I remembered back to when I'd first decided to try the necromancy spell; Sloan's apparent dismissal and judgmental apathy when I'd told her about the record, how she'd been such a naysayer, insisting she didn't believe, how she'd mocked me, even gaslit me into forcing myself to prove it was real, even when I didn't really believe it myself...It was a brilliant example of reverse psychology. Sloan had all but pushed me into it. "I can't believe it," I said, shaking my head in disgust. "That you could be my best friend all these years, by my side for all of it—you were maid of honor at my wedding! You held me while I cried over my divorce. Bravo," I said, sneering at her. "That was some fine acting."

"Thank you. I did my best," Sloan said with a slick smile. "And yes, in case you were wondering, I turned Tess against you, too," she said in a hot whisper, a smile flooding her cheeks. "It was easy. He's never been very bright."

"There's no way in hell you ended my marriage," I said, and she smiled again.

"Nah, you're right; you two did that. Y'all were so young when you got together. I just gave him a little push once in a while," Sloan confessed. "Tess was so insecure about himself. He always felt bad that he couldn't do magic. We had that in common, he and I—it was something to commiserate about. Add a few comments about how you didn't think he was that smart, how you thought he was a shitty husband…they went a long way."

I wanted to smack the smirk off her face, but I stayed silent as she went on. "I put the idea in his head that you were thinking about cheating on him. Guys like him can't stand the blow to their dignity. I knew it was all but guaranteed that he'd cheat first." She shrugged again, a gesture I was now beginning to understand was from nervousness, but it didn't make me feel any pity for her. "So, when I made my move, he was only too happy to jump in my bed."

Nausea rolled around my belly. I'd wanted to die when things went wrong with Tess. He'd been my everything—god, how I'd loved him—and to find out that he was using again and cheating on me had almost done me in. Sloan had consoled me through all of that; she'd been my rock. And now to find out she'd helped orchestrate it…all while sitting in my house, laughing right along with me as we'd pored though Roberta's Instagram feed, making fun of her appearance…how Sloan had called her "the slut" for months…

"I don't believe you," I said in a hot whisper.

That shrug again. "Believe what you want."

Could this be real? I didn't want to believe it was. However angry I was at Sloan, however done I was with her, I didn't want to face the possibility that she'd been behind it all, using me, manipulating my life, spying on me, delivering my most private information to people that meant me nothing but harm. She had single-handedly tried to ruin me. My own best friend, the person I had trusted most in the world. Hot tears sprang to my eyes, but I blinked them into submission. Not today.

"But *why*?" I implored, levelling my gaze on her. "I understand it's been going on for years, that we…that you were never really my friend…but *why*? It can't just be because you don't have magic. Why did you hate me so much? Why do you still?"

A look of wary regret passed over Sloan's face, but it was gone in a flash. She gave me a smug smile and another one of those maddening shrugs. I vowed to break her damn shoulders if it meant she'd never do that again. She ran her tube of Chapstick over her lips, stalling for time, deliberately baiting me.

"Maybe I was sick of being second fiddle—to you and the others," she said finally, her face clouding over. "You were all so useful to him, and I stuck out like a sore thumb. It wasn't fair, the way he ignored me, the way he was always pulling you into that tiny room, fawning all over you."

"I hated every minute of it," I said. "It traumatized me. Why on earth would you be jealous of that?"

"Because everything he did to you, all the experiments and hypnosis and everything else…no matter what he did, you only became sweeter, kinder. Nicer," Sloan said, looking at me with disgust. "You were always so *good.* I guess it just made me sick."

"Sloan, you could have been good, too," I said, looking at her sadly. "I always thought you were."

Sloan sighed. "I'm bored. Stormy, if you really want to know…the reason I helped Guthrie and Elvin—the reason why I hurt you—is because I *could.*" Then she pounced on me.

TWENTY-ONE

For a moment, all I could hear was a rushing thunder, my limbs moving independently of me as I fought and clawed against my assailant. Only a split second or two passed before I realized that the thunder I was hearing wasn't thunder at all, but rather a loud banging on the door behind us. I could do nothing about that, because directly in front of me, her long, slim arms around my neck, her hands desperately clawing around my throat, was Sloan. Her face was wild and frenzied and murderous, and from her throat came a guttural noise that was almost inhuman.

She was scratching at me like a cat, the long, manicured nail on her right index finger grazing my cheek, drawing blood. It was just the shock to my system that I needed. I reached up and grabbed a fistful of her blonde hair, yanking her head back as she let out a cry of pain. I raised up a knee and kicked my leg out between hers, knocking her off-balance and pulling out a decent chunk of her hair in the process. She yelped again, her hands still trying to close around my throat.

I could feel the magic rising in my hands, thrumming, threatening to burst forth at any moment. A laugh bubbled up to my lips; Sloan was a real fool to jump me. But then, she didn't know the full extent of my power. She hadn't seen what others had. I put my other hand to her face, letting her feel the full impact of the energy that resided there. Her cheek burned red as if I'd slapped her and she yelped again, still trying to claw at me, to draw blood once more. I yanked her head towards mine, kicking my leg out again, knocking her foot askew as she stumbled into me, her head knocking against my shoulder.

"Try to cut me again, and I'll fuck you up," I said hotly in her ear, smiling as Sloan tried to buck out of my grasp. My hand held her hair tight. She couldn't remove herself without losing another chunk of it. I grabbed her shoulder and squeezed, hard, and she gave a cry of pain. "I don't want to hurt you, Sloan, but I can, and I will. Stop trying to fight me and I'll let you go. Keep trying it, and see what happens." I eased up a little on my grip and her eyes met mine, fierce and blue and full of hatred. "The choice is yours."

Sloan's eyes were murderous, but she released her hands from around my neck and dropped her arms to her sides. She gave a curt nod and I let go of her hair, my hand still on her shoulder. She was panting heavily, her cheek red from where I had touched her. What kind of power did I possess that just a simple touch could leave a burn, a brand?

I was pondering that, and not paying full attention, which is why I didn't notice her right arm shoot out again, her perfectly manicured, sharp nails striking me full in the face, opening up the skin and drawing blood. My face burned, and I cried out in pain and anger. Now I had two matching wounds.

"You *bitch!*" With my right hand clutching the open, bleeding, stinging wound in my face, I extended my left hand and without thinking about it, shot a ball of light directly at Sloan. I watched it leave my fingers, extend, thick and golden, and then *wham,* it struck her full in the chest.

Sloan's mouth formed a perfect, shocked "O," right before she clutched at her chest and fell to the ground.

The banging behind me resumed, but I couldn't do anything but just stand there, stunned, staring at the crumpled body of my former best friend. Sloan was completely still, her blonde hair tangled and covering up her face. I watched her for several seconds, but she did not move.

I found my feet and shuffled over to the door, where the banging was threatening to bury the underground shelter in an avalanche. I fumbled with the deadbolts, remembering how Sloan had fiddled with them, and finally was able to wrench them free and open the door. The heavy metal door came open with a loud, slow screech and Phillip and Lee tumbled in, their faces red with exertion and anger.

"Good thing I wasn't waiting for you two to save me," I joked, my voice cracking. "I'd have been a goner for sure. Neither of you strapping young men can open a teeny little door?"

"Are you okay?" Phillip demanded, grabbing me by the shoulders and furiously looking me over. "I heard someone scream."

"That was Sloan," I said, managing a goofy smile, almost feeling a little drunk. I had the sudden craving for a huge glass of Roberta's signature Kool-Aid. "Don't you have any faith in me, Deville?"

"You zapped her pretty good, looks like," Lee said grimly, walking over to Sloan and leaning down. He gave her shoulder a nudge. Sloan's body moved slightly, but she gave no signs of consciousness. He gingerly moved a lock of blonde hair away from her face. Sloan's eyes were closed, and her face was a little gray. Dread filled my belly. Oh, god, had I killed her?

Lee put a finger under Sloan's nose and held it there for a moment, then looked to me with a small nod. "She's breathing," he said, and I gave an audible sigh of relief. "You knocked her out cold, but she's fine, I think."

"Thank god."

"You're hurt." Phillip tilted my chin up, his green eyes blazing with fire. "Your face is bleeding. The right side looks pretty bad."

"She just scratched me with her fingernails," I said, holding a hand up to my stinging cheek. I looked at my own hand in horror as it came away drenched in blood. "Damn. I guess she got me better than I thought."

"I've never seen anybody's fingernails do something like *that,*" Phillip said, touching his hand to my face tenderly. "We need to get that cleaned up and checked out right away."

I pushed his arm away. "No time. We have to get Benny. He's in here somewhere, I know he is."

"Did Sloan give you any idea where he might be?" Lee asked, his face hopeful as he stood up.

I shook my head. "She didn't tell me diddly squat. Which isn't a surprise. She was always cagey on a good day. Now? She'd rather die than tell me anything." I wiped my bloody hand on my jeans, grimacing at the sticky salt smell in the air. She'd really fucked me up. "But I know he's here. It's like I can feel him, you know?"

Lee nodded. "I can, too. By the way, Roberta's fucking disappeared. I don't know where she went." His face was lined with worry. "So, what do we do?"

Phillip was rummaging in the pocket of his dark black jeans. To my surprise, he fished out an old-fashioned embroidered white handkerchief and handed it to me. "Hold that up to your face until I can get you looked at," he said, concern still marking his face.

"Where did this come from?"

"What?" he asked, distracted. "Oh. It was my dad's."

I was touched. "You're just full of surprises, Phil. I don't want to ruin it—it'll stain—"

"Just do it, Stormy," he said, concerned. "We've got to stop the bleeding. And don't ever call me Phil again."

I held the handkerchief to my face, trying for a smile and wincing in pain, then turned back to Lee. "This place is bigger than it looks. I mean, from what I can gather there's only the cabin upstairs, but there's a compound somewhere on this land. I wonder if Roberta knew that. Maybe that's where she went? I bet there are a bunch of other, smaller buildings. Sheds, a barn…there's no telling which one Benny's in, and who has him." I pressed the cloth harder to my face, wincing at how much it still stung. "And how many of them there are."

"I don't care," Lee said furiously, making towards the door. "I'm going to find him. I'll fight off as many people as I have to."

"Wait." I grabbed at Lee's shirt and pulled him back. "You should be prepared…" He looked at me, his icy blue eyes blazing with frustration. "Not only for the possibility that Benny is gone, but…but that your mom…" I didn't have to finish the sentence. From the way his eyes flashed, he knew.

"We'll find them," Lee responded with finality, putting his hands on my shoulders and looking into my eyes. "Then we'll track down Elvin, and I'll kill him myself."

Lee wrenched open the heavy metal door and disappeared into the darkness. Phillip and I had no choice but to follow him.

It seemed like we'd been walking for hours though I knew it had only been about twenty minutes. Phillip, Lee, and I had been carefully traipsing through the woods, trying our best not to crunch leaves or run into any branches, staying as quiet as possible. We assumed that Elvin knew we were here—he had to by this point—but we still wanted the element of surprise if at all possible. We were at a serious disadvantage; none of us knew our way around this land, which was much larger and more overgrown than I had anticipated. And the one person who did—Roberta—had disappeared. God, I hoped she was okay.

It was getting dark now, the sky beginning to turn a shade of slate-gray, and when I looked up past the pine trees, I could make out the first pinprick of a star in the sky. "We need to find him before it's full dark," I said in a whisper, and Phillip found my hand, clutching it tightly.

My foot stuck in mud, and I made a disgusted face. "We're near water," I said, watching the back of Lee's head as he led the way. "I keep stepping in mud."

"Marsh is over to the right," Lee said without turning to look at me. He pushed a branch out of his way and stepped purposely forward, his shoulders tense.

I looked off to the right past the trees, just making out the outline of a marsh in the growing darkness. Reeds stuck up from the murky water, and I could see moss growing on dark rocks, and the faintest hint of movement below the dark depths. There was a smell, too, musty and dank. I shuddered involuntarily; marshes had always made me uneasy. Any matter of thing could be sunk, buried, or hidden there...

Realization dawned on me, and I clamped my hand over my mouth so as not to cry out loud. Phillip squeezed my other hand and mouthed, *"What?"* I shook my head, pointing towards the marsh and gesturing to Lee's tense shoulders. Guthrie. Guthrie's body had been found in that marsh after Elvin had dumped him there. Just a few days ago, Benny had stood at the campfire and told us about it. I felt goosebumps erupt on my arms and legs and tried my best to keep following

Lee, moving forward, without thinking too much about the critters and creatures that had probably fed on Guthrie's body while he'd been submerged in his muddy resting place—Guthrie, whom I had helped kill. How hard it must be for Lee, being here.

Phillip gave my hand another squeeze, but it offered me little comfort. Off in the distance, an owl was hooting, a sound that normally would have made me smile, but out here in the desolate darkness of the woods, near this stinking, terrifying swamp, it sounded sinister and eerie, like a warning. I suddenly wished with all my heart that we were back at the Wolfden, safe in the sparse but warm confines of Jamie and Nikolai's little trailer. Why had I come here?

"To get Benny back," Lee said, his voice tight and full of anger. "We've got to get Benny."

I poked him in the back, feeling just how tense his muscles were. He was really on-edge. "Quit listening to my thoughts, you goon," I said, trying to make my voice light, but it only came out high and strained.

Lee stopped short, giving no sign that he'd heard me. His breath caught in his throat and he turned, pointing at a patch of dirt just ahead of where no trees grew. "Look," he whispered. "You can tell the land was recently disturbed over there."

"Another body?" Phillip asked, his eyes following Lee's line of vision.

"I don't think so," Lee said, his eyes wild and bright. "I remember this now. I think…I think we might've found the demon's lair."

Throwing caution to the wind, I pushed past both Lee and Phillip and made my way over to the disturbed patch of dirt, a mound of rocks and branches on top as if it had been hastily covered, barely noticeable in the dark. I dug my phone from my pocket and turned on the flashlight, peering down at the mound of dirt and sticks, scraping at it with my foot. My shoe hit something solid, and I scraped a little more, unveiling what appeared to be a wooden plank. A trapdoor!

I looked up, meeting Phillip's eyes in the darkness, and nodded. Before he or Lee had a chance to make their way over, I crouched down, grabbed the corner of the wooden door, and pulled it up. Yet another set of stairs. With a deep breath, I made my way down into yet another tunnel of darkness, not bothering to wait. I knew they would follow me.

Twenty-Two

I gaped at the scene in front of me, blinking, disbelieving.

The man who stood before me was one that I had no accessible memory of ever meeting before, but every cell in my body shrunk from him, as though he was the monster of my nightmares. He was part of my muscle memory, it seemed, judging from the visceral reaction I was having—even if my brain did not. He was tall, with dark, black hair pulled back in a low ponytail and wide, almond-shaped brown eyes.

My body gave an involuntary jerk and Phillip grabbed me, held me tight. When I spoke, my voice was a croak. "It's *you.*"

Elvin—"Uncle El"—smiled slowly, a look of genuine pleasure coming over his gaunt face as he regarded me. "Stormy," he said, his voice surprisingly warm amid the cold damp of the bunker and the sinister sense of foreboding that thudded in my heart. "It's so good to see you after all this time. You've grown up to be such a beautiful woman. I never had any doubt that you would."

I watched him warily. Resting on Elvin's long, gaunt face was a pair of clear-framed spectacles that dangled on his nose like an afterthought. He was lanky, wearing a blue-gray madras shirt that hung on his frame, a pair of tattered looking gray slacks, and slip-on buckled sandals on his feet. It was the shoes that finally jogged my brain; I'd seen those sandals shuffling through the dry dirt of the trailer park so many times as a kid, had focused on the shiny silver buckles of those shoes many a time as I'd drifted off into a trance…

He walked over to me with ease, as though Lee and Phillip weren't behind me, as though everything were perfectly normal; me, just a guest in his home, being offered tea and hospitality. As if his own daughter wasn't bound and gagged on the ratty couch, her face streaked with tears, her brown eyes wide with fear. I stared at Burt in horror—how had she gotten here before us? Why had she gone off on her own? My heart lurched, thinking of how much pain and betrayal she must be feeling right now. Her own father, treating her this way…

But my thoughts were interrupted when I noticed another figure, slumped in the corner haphazardly, as though he'd been thrown there like a sack of potatoes. His head was down, his thick arms and legs bound the same way as Burt's, but with twice as much rope. His dark hair fell over his tanned face, his body completely still. Benny. My heart began to pound rapidly as I watched him, desperate for any sign of movement, but I saw none.

I wrenched my eyes away and back to Elvin, the hate in my heart so big, it threatened to jump out of my chest and grab him by the neck, but my limbs suddenly felt as heavy as lead.

Elvin's eyes were large and luminous as he reached out his hands to cradle mine, and they seemed to swallow me as I stared back at him, feeling my heavy limbs start to thrum, my body numb and buzzing, watching as my hands moved independently of me and began to go up in a gesture of surrender. I slow-blinked, the feeling of warmth traveling all though me, like a good, heady, sweet wine. What the hell was happening?

"Stop." Phillip's voice cut into my consciousness, and I felt him wrench me back, hard. His arm tightened around my shoulders, and he put a hand out towards Elvin in warning. "Step back and get away from her."

"Or?"

"Phillip." My voice sounded strange to my own ears. Languid, almost drunk. "It's okay."

"Is it?" Phillip seethed in my ear, his vice-grip tightening. He was beginning to hurt my shoulder. Every part of him was tense; I could feel the tightening of his muscles, the rapid, frantic way he was breathing. Somewhere beneath the languid, drowsy numbness, I was feeling a current of terror snake through my belly. I'd never seen Phillip scared. Nervous, yes. Scared? Never.

He was scared now. Scared enough to damn near break my shoulder. Scared enough he could barely catch his breath.

I reached out and let the man I'd once been forced to call Uncle El clasp my hands in his own. They were warm and sandpapery, and his nails were long and glass-like. Looking at my small hands in his larger ones, I remembered those nails, remembered how they'd dazzled my eyes as they caught the light in the small room in his trailer. How I'd watch them, mesmerized, as he flipped over tarot cards and read me my future. How they'd glinted against the glass as he handed me the lukewarm Kool-Aid. He'd called it "the boost."

The boost. How could I have forgotten it? I remembered now. Remembered how he'd snap those fingers with those glass-like nails, my eyes would open, and Uncle El would bark out, "She's done. She needs the boost. Get the boost, Roberta." And the little dark-eyed girl with the curly dark hair—Burt, *my Burt*—would scuttle into the kitchen and return with a glass of slightly sour Kool-Aid that I'd drink in one long gulp, looking at me with sad, regretful eyes as the man who was cradling my hands in his would hold me fast, his large brown eyes silently working me over.

The boost.

"The boost," I whispered, my voice barely audible in the room. "The boost."

Roberta gave a low moan from the couch, and I felt Phillip's arm tighten around me even harder. If he held onto me any tighter, he really was going to break my bones.

Elvin chuckled, still holding my hands in his. "You're starting to remember. I so hoped you wouldn't."

"Why?" I asked, my head fuzzy. "Why wouldn't you want me to remember?"

But as I asked the question, more came flooding back, and suddenly I knew. I knew why he hadn't wanted me to remember. Why he'd wiped everything from my consciousness.

I remembered it all.

I jerked my hands away from Elvin's, some of the fog dissipating from my mind as I wrenched my eyes free from his stare. The room came into focus again, and I shuddered at what I saw. Roberta, bound and gagged, Benny slumped in the corner, lifeless, and Elvin, standing there with a smile as though butter wouldn't melt in his mouth.

I reached up and placed my hand over Phillip's, the one that was squeezing my shoulder, and tried to silently impart to him, *It's okay. I remember. I know what to do.* Did I feel his hand relax slightly? I gave it another squeeze and took a deep breath. If I was going to get us out of this mess, I was going to have to act—and speak—very carefully.

"I remember it all," I said calmly, meeting Elvin's eyes, steeling myself against his gaze. I would not allow him in this time. "I remember everything you did. Not just to me, but to all of us."

"What do you remember?" Elvin asked casually, brushing at an invisible speck on his gauzy shirt.

"Us kids," I said, searching back through my memory, combing through everything as though it had always been there, catalogued and shelved, just waiting for the right time for me to come collect it. "Me. Lee. Tess, Sloan, Roberta, Jamie, Nikolai...and Benny."

"Benny?" Elvin gestured to the slumped figure in the corner. "You remember Benny?"

"Yes," I answered. "You brought him in later. And that was when things started to unravel, wasn't it? When you brought in Benny, the outsider. You got more than you bargained for with him. That's when things started to go wrong." I remembered the conversation I'd had with Roberta a few days ago, when I'd asked her if Benny was one of us. No, she'd said, he wasn't, he had no magic, *he came later.* That's what she'd said, or something like it. And at the time, something hadn't seemed right to me, but I hadn't recognized what.

I wasn't even sure of what I was remembering; the memories were coming back to me disjointed, disorganized, and muddy. But I knew whatever I was feeling, it was right, and it was true. Glancing over to the pitiful heap in the corner, it was hard to believe that when I'd met Benny just a couple of weeks ago, that I hadn't recognized him immediately. Wiped memory or no, Benny was—and always had been—the kind of person who imprints upon your memory. The kind of person who sticks with you, that you can't let go. Which was exactly why Elvin had wanted him. Why he and Guthrie had gone to so much trouble to secure him.

The same way they had tried to secure me. Tried, and failed.

Or *had* they?

Ever since meeting everyone at the Wolfden, I'd been jealous that my newfound friends all knew things I didn't. Things about each other. Things about *me.* About my family.

They knew things I couldn't remember, had memories I could never share.

As it turned out, I knew something none of them did. Something even Roberta didn't know.

Something about Benny.

My hands were curled by my sides, an almost imperceptible sensation of tingling in my fingers from where Elvin had touched me—or maybe it was the magic—and I clenched them tighter, afraid of what might happen if I gave in to the impulse. If Sloan's pitiful, slack body lying on the floor back in the cellar had shown me anything, it was that I was far stronger than I'd realized.

It wasn't just the power to bring someone back that I possessed. I knew that now. I had many other powers, thanks to Lydia.

The question was: How *much* power did I have, and would I be able to use it to get us out of this mess?

He just moved. The thought came to me completely formed and in someone else's voice. My eyes shifted instinctively to Benny, but he was as still as a corpse. Elvin stared at me oddly; he'd noticed. It didn't matter. If Benny had moved, then he was alive. And we could still save him.

"Why did you take him?" I asked. "Benny?"

Elvin smiled. "He knew too much. And he has contacts within the police department. He wasn't a problem as long as he was away from Lee, but I knew if they started seeing each other again, Benny would develop a conscience and want to turn us in, to protect him. He tried that once before. I couldn't let that happen."

"That's all very interesting, but that's not what I mean," I goaded him. "Why did you take him the first time? When we were just kids? What'd he ever do to deserve it?" I knew the answer, but I wanted to make him say it, say it so that Lee and Roberta could hear. Plus, it behooved me to play dumb.

"You remember now," Elvin said with a smile, not falling for my ploy. "There's no need for me to tell you."

Dammit. I stared at the pitiful bulk in the corner, remembering. Benny was never one of us. He wasn't from the trailer park; he'd grown up in a brick house in Hinesville. He'd just been some slightly older, handsome kid we'd all idolized, gone to see wrestle because he was awe-inspiring and cool. We'd hero-worshipped Benny, loved watching him in the ring, bragging that he was our friend. He'd been so kind to us back then, so sweet to a bunch of poor, pitiful kids who adored him. And he'd paid a very dear price for it. Through us, Elvin had found him. Found him and never let him go.

"You're quite the kidnapper," I said, my voice full of disgust. "Benny, Roberta, Lee, and I assume you've got Lydia and Renee here, too?"

"Of course," Elvin said in a surprised tone, as though it were strange of me to ask. "They're here and they're just fine. My dumb sister and my sweet sister-in-law. I couldn't have done any of this without her. Bless her heart."

Hearing the old Southern colloquialism on Elvin's tongue made me angry. "You think you can just snatch people up and force them to do your bidding. Don't you get tired of using people as pawns? Look at your daughter, what you've done to her! And for what?" I spat. "Everything you've ever tried has been a colossal failure." I sneered. "You're no witch, and you never will be."

Elvin sniffed, affronted. "That's not true! Look at yourself. Look at your powers." He gestured at my hands, which were still clenched by my sides. "You have powers that you yourself don't even know about yet. They laid dormant for years and you had no idea; all of that's *my* doing. Not Lydia's. And in turn, you've imparted some of your powers onto your lover there." He gestured at Phillip, who was still tensed beside me. "Just like you unwittingly did to all those poor, snot-nosed kids back at the trailer park. That's how powerful you are. *I* harnessed it, made you what you are. All I had to do was tinker a little, and look—all of you can hear each other's thoughts, can see the future." He smiled. "Now *that's* power."

"Yeah, power that wasn't yours," I seethed. "It never came from you. You stole it—harnessed it, as you say—from Lydia. You never had any real power yourself. Neither you *or* Guthrie did. All you've ever done is try to emulate, and when that didn't work, outright steal. You may have set all these plans in motion, but none of the magic is actually yours. You can't wield it without us." I sniffed. "Anyway, none of us can see the future, you old windbag."

"You're wrong, Stormy. You see, I'm a shaman," Elvin said. "And shamans are very powerful. We harness the magic and use it for our purposes. Some might say we're the most powerful of all."

"Nobody would say that." I laughed. "Except maybe Jim Morrison, and he was high at the time." I heard Phillip snort with laughter.

"Was there a time he wasn't?" he said in a low voice behind me, and I muffled a guffaw. Phillip Deville was going to get me killed.

"Shut up," Elvin cautioned, his voice taking on a low note of anger. "You don't know what you're dealing with."

"I think I've got a pretty good idea," I said, raising my chin defiantly. "What will you do to me?" I asked, my face a picture of pretty innocence. "Hypnotize me? Make me do a bunch of bad things? Wipe my memory again?"

"I wouldn't bother with any of that," Elvin said, his voice cold. "Not anymore."

A chill went up my back. Something told me he was absolutely serious. Whatever worth I'd once had to Elvin, he was no longer willing to protect his investment. He'd just straight up kill me. Me, Benny, Lee, and Phillip, and whoever else stood in his way. Even his own daughter.

"Fine," I said, preparing for my second negotiation in as many weeks. "Then let's make a deal."

I wasn't sure who looked more shocked, Elvin or Phillip. I reached back and gathered my hair in my hands, pulling it back into a ponytail. I grabbed the elastic I always kept around my wrist and secured it, facing Elvin with a business-like smile. "What are your terms?" I asked him.

"Terms?" Elvin parroted, sneering. "I don't know what you mean."

"I absolutely believe you'll kill me if I get in your way," I said with a Sloan-like shrug. "But I think you'd rather not. Not because you care about me—or anyone—but because it'd be a waste of my magic. That's always been what you were after, right? If I'm dead, my magic's gone. So I feel like you'd rather make a deal than give me the old heave-ho." I looked him square in the eye. "So, what is it that you want from me?"

A look of greed filled Elvin's dark eyes. "What I've wanted all along," he said truthfully. "Access to your powers. They're unique. They fascinate me." He stroked his goatee. "The question is, though—what *you* expect in return. I highly doubt it's something I'm willing to give you."

"The same thing I told the Great Value version of you," I said, and I heard Phillip choke on another laugh behind me. "Guthrie, that is. I want you to leave everyone I care about alone. You get me, you don't have any need to bother Lee, Roberta, Lydia, Phillip, or anyone else, ever again."

Elvin smiled. "And if I agree to this, you'll give me full

access to your powers. You'll let me study you, experiment… hypnotize you."

"Sure, why not," I said, and I smiled myself.

Elvin still looked unsure. I knew not to get too cocky, though. If all the memories rushing back had taught me anything, it was that he could not be trusted. If you gave him an inch, he'd take a mile, and he'd years ago learned how to subdue me with a flick of an eyelid or tilt of the chin.

"Go ahead," I said. "Get pen and paper and write up a contract. I'll sign it."

"Only if you do one more thing," Elvin said, and I looked at him warily. "I want the contract to be a spell. So if you break it, the consequences will be more dire than just my anger. Do you agree?"

I shrugged again. "Suits me fine. Write it up."

"Stormy, no," I heard Phillip whisper desperately behind me, and I tried to quiet him, sending him thoughts of calm. *It's going to be okay. Trust me.*

I could hear his voice in my head. *This is a bad idea.* I silenced the voice and stood there, trying to keep my limbs from shaking, as Elvin walked over to his desk and produced a sheet of paper and a black pen. He wrote quickly in a looping, messy scrawl. The corner of his lip twitched as he wrote. Roberta gave another low moan from the couch. I turned to look at Lee, whose face was scrunched up in anger and sadness.

When he was finished, Elvin came back over to me and produced the paper. I took it from his hand and scanned it, quickly reading over the contents. He'd written out a pretty basic spell, from the looks of it, but it was no joke. It bound me and my powers to him. If I broke the contract in any way—by trying to do him harm or refusing to let him use my powers— vengeance would come to me in the worst form of all—hurting the ones I loved. In return, so long as I upheld the contract, those same friends and family would be free of Elvin and his influence once and for all.

I swallowed hard. I looked at Elvin and nodded slowly. "Okay," I said.

"Stormy…" Phillip's voice sounded far away, even though he was just behind me.

"No funny business this time, Deville," I said with a sad smile. "You see, this is just like before," I explained to Elvin, still holding the paper. "Almost exactly the same. It's weird. I stood in Guthrie's foyer and he wrote out a contract binding my powers to him, in return for him leaving my friends alone. I was going to sign it. I meant it then, and I mean it now. Who I'm signing myself over to—you, Guthrie, the man in the moon—it doesn't matter to me, as long as the people I love are safe."

"I don't care," Elvin said, his smile starting to falter. "You're wasting my time."

"I never got to sign that contract for Guthrie," I said, ignoring him. "Because all hell broke loose, and Guthrie got shot. But you already know that, because you're the one who dragged his body away and cleaned up the bloodstains and dumped him in the marsh." I shook my head. "I can't imagine what type of person feeds their own brother to the gators." I reached out my hand. "Give me the pen."

Elvin handed me the pen, his eyes blazing. He watched me as I pulled off the cap and took a deep breath.

"Do you know what's different? From when I held Guthrie's contract, and holding yours now?" I asked, lifting the paper and looking it over.

"What?" Elvin asked, exasperated, watching the pen and paper as they dangled from my fingers.

"There was a gun then." I said, throwing them to the floor. "But I don't need one today." With one quick movement, I splayed my fingers outward, collecting the ball of bright, golden light that had been pulsing through my arms and hands for the past several minutes, then I shot the light through my fingers towards Elvin.

Elvin's reflexes were quick, and he moved just as the surge of golden light came towards him, but he wasn't fast enough. The powerful orb hit him in the shoulder, knocking him off his feet and to the floor, which he hit with a loud *thud*. Elvin went down considerably harder than Sloan had, and I thought I heard a bone crack. He gave a loud wail of pain.

"Untie Roberta," I called over my shoulder to Phillip. As long as Elvin was alive, I wouldn't be looking away. I had to keep my eyes on him at all times. "Lee, can you lift Benny, do you think?" From somewhere in the room, I heard an unspoken *Yes* in my head.

"You bitch," Elvin spat from the floor. "You'll regret doing that, I swear to Lucifer."

"Lucifer wouldn't have you, *Uncle El*, you ugly piece of shit," I spat right back. "That was for Lee." I gathered up my powers again and splayed my fingers out towards him, this time shooting my light directly into his back. He spasmed and flailed on the floor, crying out in pain.

"That's for Burt."

"Stop," Elvin panted, moving to sit up, holding out a hand in front of him. "Stormy, you don't understand. Please stop, so I can explain."

"Explain?" I began to laugh. I unfurled my hands again, this burst of light catching Elvin directly in the chest. He fell back onto the floor, writhing, tears running down his face.

I could barely hear his whispered voice as he began to plead with me. "Your powers have gotten so strong…just think of what you could do if you had me helping you…it doesn't have to be this way…"

"This one is for Lydia." Another quick flick of my fingers, and Elvin said no more. I looked him over dispassionately. He was breathing, but unconscious. I didn't know how long it would last, but hopefully it would be long enough to get Roberta and Benny to safety, to call the police and get them out here. I only hoped it was *enough* time. If anyone could wake up and evade the police, it was Elvin.

I turned, panting. Phillip was over by the couch, finished with untying Roberta. She was practically falling into his arms, her legs shaking, but her face grateful. "I can't believe you did that," she said, her voice full of awe. "I knew you had powers, but…damn, Stormy."

"Why did you come here alone?" I asked her, pulling her into a clumsy hug. "That was so stupid!"

"I wanted to see him," she said, her voice shaking. "I thought maybe I could…could…talk some sense into him." She collapsed into tears. "I should have known better."

"I'm so sorry, Burt," I said, holding her tight, letting her cry on my shoulder.

Phillip looked at us, his eyes full of sympathy. "You guys, we need to go."

"Phillip's right," I said, pulling away from Roberta and giving her arm a squeeze. "I doubt he'll be down for long. We've got to get out of here, and call the police, right now." Phillip nodded and hoisted one arm under Roberta's other shoulder, lifting her up to help her walk.

As we turned to walk towards the door, I felt a sudden heaviness in my limbs and frowned. My feet seemed to be stuck, as if cemented to the ground. I strained to move my left foot and found I couldn't move it at all. I tried to move my right leg, but it was stuck to the spot. "Oh, fuck," I panted, remembering back to Lydia's house in Boston and how Phillip and I had been bound. "Let me go, let me go." A quick side-long glance at Phillip showed that he was stuck, too, and Roberta, suspended between us, gave a low moan.

"I can't move my legs, Stormy," she said in a hot whisper.

"And you said I didn't have any magic." I turned my torso, only to find myself face to face with Elvin. He was standing on shaky legs and looked very worse for wear, but he was grinning. "You're stuck with me now, Stormy Spooner," he said in a singsong voice, his long, tapered fingers suspended in the air, holding me in place as he moved closer to me. His fingernails shone like glass, and I felt my entire body shudder. I strained at the air, desperate to move my legs and feet, but I could not.

"Let me go, you asshole," I said, and Elvin shook his head, making a clucking sound with his tongue.

"Not until you sign that contract, my love," he said in that same songlike voice, his eyes seeming to dance.

"Go to hell, Uncle El." I reared back my head, cleared my throat, and spat as hard as I could right into his face.

Elvin pressed a hand to his cheek, his eyes wide. Then he began to laugh. His laugh was loud, exuberant. Terrifying. I stared at him with wide eyes as he continued laughing and laughing, until I thought I would go mad from it. I felt dizzy again, that same sensation of swirling down a drain, and all I could hear was his laughter ringing in my ears…

I was going down, and I could feel it. This time, I might not come back up again. All I could hear was the laughter, swirls of it, peals of it…

And then suddenly, abruptly, the laughter stopped.

After a moment, my ears stopped ringing, and I realized I'd been holding my hands over them, my eyes squeezed shut tight. I was breathing heavily, my head still woozy and my stomach rolling with nausea. I felt like I might pass out. All of that was forgotten in an instant, though, when I opened my eyes and saw Benny standing there.

He looked down at me with tender concern, his snake-eye almost seeming to dance. His hands were splayed out in front of him, and he looked from me to Elvin's now-still form and down to his own hands as though he'd never seen them before.

He looked back up at me. "You can move, Stormy. Go ahead, try it. You can walk," he said, his voice sounding faraway and full of wonder.

I took a gingerly step forward and fell into his arms, giving him a bone-crushing hug.

"I really thought you were a goner, Benny and the Jets," I said, and burst into tears. After a moment, I realized it wasn't just us in the embrace—Lee, Phillip, and Roberta had joined too, hugging and crying and snotting all over each other.

"Maybe you should change your wrestling name to The Black Possum, considering how well you play dead," Lee said, his voice cloaked with tears, and Benny kissed him roughly on the mouth in response.

I pulled back from the fray, wiping at my eyes. "We should get out of here," I said, "while we still can. He's bound to wake up anytime, like he did before."

"No," Benny said calmly, looking down at Elvin's crumpled body. "He won't wake up this time, Stormy."

"I don't understand..." I looked down at Elvin, whose body somehow seemed to have lost half its volume. It was as though an old brittle skeleton was dressed in linens, unceremoniously dumped on the floor.

"Elvin is dead," Benny said slowly, as though explaining to a child. "Very, very dead."

Roberta looked at him, her eyes bright. "But how?" she asked, her voice wavering. Whatever he had been, Elvin had also been her father. "What did you do?"

"I guess it's time I tell you all what Stormy already knows," Benny said, locking his arm through Lee's and giving us a sheepish look. "God knows I've kept the secret long enough."

"What is it?" Lee asked, his face darkening with dread.

"You know how Stormy can bring people back?" Benny

asked, in a tone that was a little excited, a little nervous, like someone introducing a lover to his parents.

"Yeah," Lee answered, confused. "What about it?"

"Well," Benny said, "I'm the yin to her yang, so to speak. Stormy can give life…and I can take it away."

The room was silent enough to hear a pin drop. Then Phillip's deep voice sounded in the silence, brooding and annoyed, "Oh, for *fuck's sake.*"

Epilogue

I'd never been more than a handful of miles away from it over the past few weeks, but sitting on Driftwood Beach, listening to Phillip strum an acoustic guitar beside me, I felt a sense of deep relief, of homecoming. My phone buzzed in my pocket with an incoming text message, and I instinctively knew it was my mother, writing me back. My body buzzed with warm, happy feelings. I didn't pick up the phone—right now, I was decompressing, and that meant no technology, no distractions, and Phillip's crooning, low voice in my ear was far too sweet —but I looked forward to talking with her later. I had so much to tell her and so much to find out.

It was hard to imagine. Laureen sober. Texting me, checking in, *caring* about me. She had turned some kind of corner, it seemed. While I was reluctant to trust the feeling fully, after all I'd been through, I had to admit I was excited at the prospect of rebuilding our relationship. Even knowing the hard stuff that would inevitably have to happen—going over the last twenty years, especially the things that had happened with Elvin—was going to be painful, I was weirdly looking forward to that, too.

Most of my memories had come back, but there were still blanks here and there, gaps that needed filling. Things that I couldn't quite understand. There were so many unanswered questions still, about Guthrie and Elvin and how they had come to be so *evil*. No matter how I looked at it, I couldn't understand why the two brothers would wreak havoc just for some dumb magic—not just us children, but the entire community where we'd lived. And for all that, for Guthrie's life to be snuffed out so quickly, so unceremoniously, with his brother's help. What had been the end game? It *couldn't* just have been about the magic. After all, what had the magic given them, really?

From my vantage point, all it had done was take. Taken from all of us, and from them, too. Elvin had taken so much from us, and all we had to show for it was what amounted to a few parlor tricks. The ability to read each other's thoughts was a small price to pay for what he'd taken from us—our childhoods. Oh, sure, apparently Benny and I could give and take life, respectively, but neither one of us *wanted* that power. Or at least I didn't.

Benny was the key. Benny and I needed to sit down and talk things out, figure out how the two of us and our at-odds powers fit into the equation, and what the sum of that equation was supposed to be. If nothing else, so we could ensure we never solved that particular problem, even by accident.

The rest of them were still coming to grips with the truth about Benny—who and what he was. For my part, the memories were still trickling back in, but I was keeping them to myself for now, content to let Benny find a shaky footing back to himself. I knew what it felt like to have someone else in charge of your story, to know things that you had forgotten, and I vowed I wouldn't overstep when it came to Benny. I owed him that much, and more.

Benny and Lee had achieved a tentative sort of peace, though they were dealing with the same sorts of issues Phillip and I had had—neither of them being honest with the other, holding things back, not trusting each other with their true selves. I didn't envy them that battle. Lee had to come to grips with his own awful childhood, and the even more awful past few years when he'd been beholden to every evil, manipulative whim his parents had subjected him to, their homophobic views the least of his worries. And Benny had to contend with a literal lifetime of keeping a huge secret—all the years he'd known his friends from the Wolfden, had confided in them, ran alongside them, protected them—none of them, not even Lee, had ever known he was a powerful witch. He had some trust to make up, and some explanations to give.

After Benny had put Elvin's lights out for good, we'd discovered Lydia and Renee locked in a cold and dirty storage room near the marsh, but no worse for wear from what I could see. Lydia had fallen into Lee's arms, bursting into tears. We had all been shocked to see she had a brand-new oxygen tank —evidently Elvin hadn't been so cruel as to deprive her of that. Renee had sat outside, stunned, rocking back and forth as though she couldn't believe everything that had happened. My heart went out to her. Losing all three of her brothers—even if two out of the three were pure evil—was rough. When her eyes fell on Phillip, her shellshocked face had perked up considerably. "I'm sure glad to see you again, you tall drink of water," she'd said, and I'd laughed so hard at the ludicrousness of it all.

For Lydia's part, she'd asked if she could talk to me and explain. I was reluctant, but she promised she'd tell me every-thing, from that fateful night we'd first met over my mom's lifeless body until the day she'd been kidnapped from her own bed. "I don't have much longer," she'd said, grasping my hand in her own dry, frail one. "And I'd like to make things right. I can start by telling you everything you need to know. No lies, no stories. Just the truth. Will you let me do that, Fee?"

I'd told her I'd think about it. Just as we'd left the compound, once Roberta's childhood home and now the site of horrors we all hoped to forget, I'd squeezed Lydia's arm and told her I'd call her. I'd never forget her relieved smile when I'd said that. I wasn't sure when I'd feel like getting her side of the story, but I knew I wanted to hear it eventually. After all, it was a huge key to my own.

We'd all left in different cars to go our separate ways, leaving Elvin to rot on the floor of his own misery. Whatever happened to him from there—whether discovered by Sloan, who would wake up eventually (I hoped she'd have a monster migraine, at the very least), or some wayward hiker, or eaten by dogs or decomposed among the mold and mildew, was none of our concern. I found I wasn't the least bit worried.

I might be worried tomorrow, but not today.

Today, I intended to do nothing but sit on the beach, letting the sand drift into my shoes, holding Phillip's hand in mine and watching the sunset. Before we left the island, we stopped by Guthrie's house—now Lee's—to pick up the cat. The dirty, mangy old tomcat I'd seen flitting around Guthrie's house hadn't left my mind since the first time I'd seen him. Lee had told me I could have him since neither he nor Renee wanted the responsibility. I'd be taking the half-feral little guy, who I'd already named Nod, back to my place, his new forever home. I hoped he and Blinken would get along.

For now, though, it was time for Phillip and me to be blissfully alone. I rested my head on his shoulder, my hair falling into my eyes, watching as the sun cast beautiful shades of purple and fuchsia and cyan into the sky. It was muggy and clammy out, the air full of its usual humidity; a constant in South Georgia, even in winter. It had gotten on my nerves once, but now I found it a comfort. The elements seemed a new thing to me now, something forever and true. I closed my eyes and enjoyed the humid-but-cool breeze that drifted past my face, breathing it in, pushing my free hand into the soft sand. Water, air, earth…

And fire.

Behind my closed eyes, I had a sudden flash of memory— the lightning that had struck so close to me on the beach that day, just over a year ago, right before things had started to unravel. The man down the beach who had watched me so calmly, not appearing to feel the heavy, pulsing rain as it had coursed over his skin. Guthrie. I saw him in that flash, saw the jagged lightning, so bright and blinding, as it wrenched down from the sky like a pulse from Neptune's own trident.

He'd seemed almost godlike to me then, Guthrie, and yet, he had fallen victim to his own malice so easily—now I knew there were levels of evil that went so far beyond anything he'd ever comprehended. In my mind's eye, I could still see him there, standing on the beach, his posture menacing, his face as dark as the sky.

And then I was somewhere else. Standing on a different stretch of beach, a paler one, with clear, shining blue water, so clear you could see the fish as they grazed and pecked at the seabed. The sky was bright and crisp, almost teal, but off in the distance, a thundercloud loomed; an impending storm. A huge clap of thunder sounded, thudding in my ears, and then a jagged, blinding fork of lightning appeared, jutting down from the sky and hitting a small house off in the distance. As I watched, flames shot from the windows, and within moments, the tiny house was engulfed in flames. Though I did not know recognize the house, or this stretch of beach, my heart was suddenly filled with fear and dread. Goosebumps rose up on my arms, and I began to wail.

My eyes flew open. I was hanging onto Phillip's shoulder for dear life.

"Stormy?" Phillip's voice was alarmed. He put down the guitar. "Are you okay? What just happened?"

"I….I…" I swallowed and pushed my sweaty hair from my eyes. Phillip was peering into my face, searching it. "I'm not sure. It's like I blacked out for a minute. I think I had…I think I had a vision."

"About what?" Phillip asked, his green eyes wide.

"About lightning," I said, puzzled. I stared out at the water, watching the tide as it frothed along the shore, gray and murky. The water in my vision had been so clear, so clean. Not at all like the dark waters of Jekyll Island. I shivered and wrapped my arms around myself. What had Elvin said back at the bunker? Something about seeing the future?

"It's alright," Phillip said, though his voice didn't sound so sure. He rubbed at my shoulders, tying to warm me, pulling me close. "I'm sure it's just…like a flashback or something. You've been through so much lately."

"I'm sure that's all it is," I agreed, settling back into him, knowing that neither of us believed it.

He pulled me in close and wrapped his large arms around me, cradling me to him. He smelled so good, so familiar, his black shirt soft and worn. I wrapped my arms around his torso, loving the feel of him, loving that we were together again at last. I'd missed him so much.

Phillip leaned down and pecked my forehead with his lips. "I love you, Stormy," he said, his voice low. "I know we both wondered if what we felt for each other was just the magic… well, it wasn't. It isn't. When we were apart…all I could think about was you. You're all I want, always. If you'll have me."

"Of course I'll have you," I said, leaning my head up towards his. He kissed me, his lips full of urgent need, long and deep and passionate. As he pressed his lips hard against mine, tasting me, I gave myself back to him fully, loving the feel of his mouth on mine, his stubbly cheek rough against my skin When he pulled away, he was smiling. "You absolute dumbass. Who else on this earth could I possibly want?"

"Well, if you ask me—" Phillip started to quip, his cheeks raising in a familiar grin, but the words died on his lips as he whipped his head around. I turned in the same direction, noticing a man standing a few yards to our left. He was leaning on a huge piece of driftwood, his face halfway hidden, a black puffy jacket obscuring most of his upper body. But one thing was unmistakable: He was holding a camera.

"Who the fuck is that?" Phillip seethed, turning back to me, clearly angry. "He's taking pictures."

I stood, furious, and ran towards the unknown cameraman. He shoved his camera into a knapsack and bolted, his feet kicking up huge clumps of sand as he ran. Without shoes, I was no match for his speed, even though I was running as hard as I could. The man disappeared down a trail and into the woods as I stopped at a wooden walkway, panting and out of breath.

I turned around, breathing heavy, surprised to find Phillip standing beside me. "Damn, you're fast!" I heaved. "I didn't even realize you were behind me. If we weren't barefoot, we would have caught him."

"Who was it?" Phillip repeated, himself panting with exertion. "Who the hell was it?"

I paused, still out of breath. I hadn't gotten a good look at the man's face, but that was no cheap camera he'd been holding. It had had a long lens, the kind designed for taking faraway shots. Invasive shots, like a paparazzi would take. And the camera bag he'd shoved it into hadn't been cheap, either—black leather and very expensive, from the looks of it.

Even without seeing his face, and despite the puffy black jacket and hat he'd tried to disguise himself with, I'd recognized his body language and overall appearance. After all, I'd been a faithful reader of his work since I was a teenager.

I just wished I didn't have to tell Phillip.

"Tell me," Phillip warned.

"Get out of my head," I grumbled, then softened. "He's a writer for GOTHzine," I said with a sigh. "A music journalist; Dylan Quint is his name. I guess the jig is up, Phillip. You've been spotted."

"Fuck." Phillip's face was indescribable.

"Shit, Phillip," I said, reaching out to steady him. "I'm so sorry."

My phone buzzed again in my pocket, and with another deep sigh, I retrieved it from my jacket and peered at the screen. Might as well let the world catch up with us; there was no escaping it now.

I opened the message, my brows immediately furrowing with confusion.

The message was indeed from my mother. But it wasn't a happy "checking in" message as I'd assumed.

Stormy, call me. Right away. Are you okay?

As I clicked out of the message, thinking how strange it was, a new voicemail popped up, also from Mama. I held the phone up to my ear with shaking fingers. As I listened, I felt the blood drain from my face and my legs went weak. Phillip caught me just before I hit the sand.

"Stormy? Stormy, call me as soon as you get this message. I need to know you're okay. I know you wouldn't have any reason to go there, but I just have the worst feeling…oh, Stormy. Your dad's house in Panama City Beach just burned to the ground! The cops called me, of all people…Stormy, they haven't found him yet! Your dad is missing!"

Acknowledgments

As always, my deepest thanks go to Elizabeth Tankard, Dead Rockstar's self-proclaimed biggest fan and the best Phillip Deville stan a girl could ask for, who is also my beta reader extraordinaire, fellow novelist, expert-level music junkie, graphics whiz, and a good friend to boot.

Thanks to Jennifer Babineau, my other faithful test reader and good friend of many years, who is always game to put eyes on something whenever I need it, book-related or otherwise. You're the best.

To Ellen Burke, my "soul twin"; thanks for always being there to listen to me whine, for supporting my work and being my biggest promoter and fangirl, and for all the amazing music you've sent me over the years. Our ongoing conversations often find their way into my work. I quite literally couldn't have done it without you, L N. *"But at the end of the day, we all burn at the stake."*

It's Me Again, Margaret: thanks to Jessica Campbell, aka "Marge," my oldest and dearest, my sister from another mister, the Strawberry Shortcake to my Rainbow Brite, and the strongest woman I've ever known.

My most sincere thanks must go to:

Amanda Wright, Jennia Herold D'Lima (thank you for that perfect line!), Lauren Emily Whalen, Kristin Jacques, Marlena Frank, Tracy Adkins, Flagpole Magazine, UGA Arts, UGA Willson Center, Cate Short, Cydney Flanigan, Amelia Ross, Kelley Lawson, my parents, John and Teresa, grandparents

Clark and Anita, my siblings Chris and Jonathan, and finally, to Blake and Cal: thanks for always supporting my dreams. I couldn't hack this career without y'all believing in my talents.

In loving memory of Nicolae Lisowski and Jesse Campbell, friends who left us far too soon, the memory of whom inspired two very loveable characters at the Wolfden.

And as always, in memory of my personal favorite dead rockstar, Peter Steele.

About the Author

Lillah Lawson is the author of novels Monarchs Under the Sassafras Tree (2019; nominated for Georgia Author of the Year 2020); So Long, Bobby (February 2023); The Dead Rockstar Trilogy ('20-'24); and Tomorrow & Tomorrow with Lauren Emily Whalen (October 2023).

Lillah enjoys writing across genres, specializing in historical fiction, southern gothic, and horror. She also writes a monthly column for her local newspaper. In addition to writing, Lillah works at a non-profit, is a genealogist pursuing her BA in History and English Literature, and proudly serves as secretary on her local library's Board of Trustees. An avid music lover, she's happiest at metal shows. She lives just outside of Athens, Georgia, with her husband, teenager, and two fur friends.

The Hex Next Door by Lou William

What's a little necromancy between family?

For the Crow Witch, Icarus "Rus" Ashthorne, Moondale seemed the perfect hiding place. But like they always say, you can't go home again, and Rus finds out quickly that nothing is how she remembered, while at the same time very little has changed. Then she comes face to face with the only woman she's ever loved, Az Elwood, and... well, things get messier than she thought they ever could.

The Elwoods are a staple of Moondale, respected, feared, powerful, and Azure Elwood was always happy with her place amongst them. Happy to play the part of the good little witch, until Rus Ashthorne. Eleven years ago, Rus got on a bus and left Azure behind, but she's back, with two little girls trailing her like ducklings, and enough unspoken things between them to drown the town.

Now witch hunters are knocking at their proverbial door, the council of magic is being a real pain in the ass, and Rus wonders how much magic it'll take to protect the people she loves from herself and the danger following her.

Available Now

www.ingramcontent.com/pod-product-compliance
Lightning Source LLC
Chambersburg PA
CBHW030118010826
48973CB00002B/316